MW01617376

The Forward Line

K.G. Erin

The Forward Line

K.G. Erin

Print Edition ISBN 978-1-7778805-6-9

E-Book Edition ISBN 978-1-7778805-7-6

First Edition: February 2023

10 9 8 7 6 5 4 3 2 1

This is a work of fiction. Names, characters, places, and incidents either are the product of the author's imagination or are used fictitiously, and any resemblance to actual persons, living or dead, business establishments, events or locales is entirely coincidental.

Cover Design by Rachel Skye Whitehurst

Fictional Floor Plan by Kate S.

Editor Catherine Joseph

To all the girls who had to deal with "Saturday is for the boys", sleeping on a mattress with just a comforter every time you went over, the chewing tobacco and the nasty flows.

I hope this helps you get through those dark memories.

FIRST FLOOR

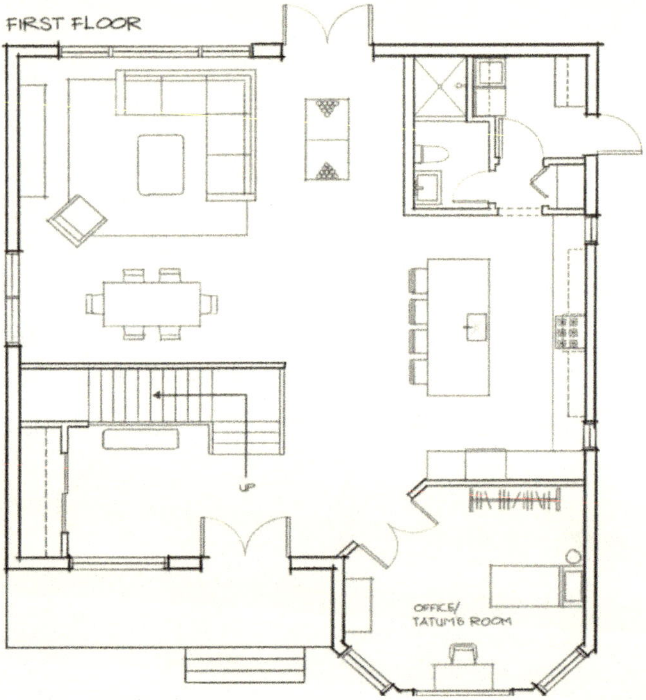

SECOND FLOOR

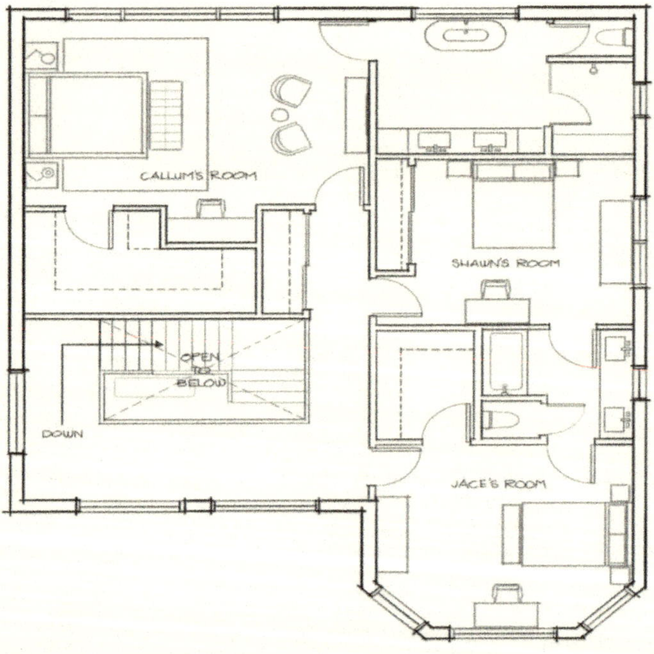

Chapter One

TATUM

"I don't know what to tell you Kelly, it's out of my hands." Coach Miller shrugged as he leaned back against his chair and interlocked his fingers over his bulging beer belly. He didn't seem the least bit phased considering he was our coach, and I narrowed my eyes at him in accusation.

"But we did those fundraisers, we spent all summer raising money to keep our team." Miller blinked at me with a blank stare and I could feel my lower lip begin to tremble.

Great, just great. Of course, the tears were coming.

"You're a solid student and you have a bright future with or without hockey."

"But I have a scholarship *for* hockey, how am I supposed to continue studying here if there's no team to play on?" Sighing, Miller moved forward and grabbed at one of the many brochures that were scattered across his desk.

"Just because North Pacific is cutting the team doesn't mean you don't have options. Arden has a great women's team and nearly all the same classes as you're taking now." He offered while flapping the brochure at me impatiently and I wiped at my damp eyes before taking it from him.

"We made it to finals last year, Arden didn't even make qualifiers Coach." My fingers tightened around the shiny paper while my stomach twisted and I waited for him to say something, anything that could fix this.

"Kel-Tatum," Coach paused, and I knew that if he was switching to my first name, then things really were bad. "I don't have any other options for you. Find a way to make up the finances you need for tuition or transfer. There would be a gap year, but you're a junior and you made captain, that's nearly unheard of. One season of no ice time isn't a big deal."

"I have plans, Coach, you know I want to finish my degree before trying out for the national team. Losing this year would ruin that, all those eyes that have been on me will move on." My vision clouded once more and I rubbed at my eyes in frustration. "And I can't afford school without the scholarship, I'm on my own."

I knew Coach had some idea about my home life and the lack of financial support from my parents, but I was thankful he didn't press the issue. Instead, he sat back once more with a rough sigh and I winced at the pity in his gaze.

"I am sorry, Tatum. If there was something more I could do, I would. But it's not my decision and I am just as upset as you are about this whole mess."

Doubtful. Miller had taken this position when they had replaced him as the men's coach with the new and shiny Jackson Perry, who just happened to have a long career under his belt and quite the reputation for making winners. And now he was nearly put out to pasture, biding his time until it was time to retire.

"Just promise me you'll think about Arden, it's a decent school and with your talent, who knows where that team could go." Stuffing the brochure into the front pocket of my hoodie, I nodded.

That was it then, there was nothing else to say and with one last pathetic sniffle I swung my bag over my shoulder and turned for the door.

"Tatum, I am sorry." Coach called, his voice softer than I had ever heard it and I could feel the wall I had built begin to crack. Swallowing the sob that sat heavily in my throat, I fled from the dingy corner office and ran.

The bright neon lights of the rink were nearly blinding as my feet pounded against the polished floor and I lowered my chin, focusing my eyes on my boots in hopes that no one would notice the tears that had begun to stream. Rounding the last corner I quickened my stride, ready to burst through the back doors that led to the parking lot until I hit a solid wall of muscle. Bouncing off the body, I landed sprawled across the floor and stared at the ceiling in a daze.

"What the fuck man," I could just manage to make out the deep voice over the ringing in my head and I winced at the shadow that crossed my face as they leaned over my form. Deep brown eyes narrowed at me while his curly chestnut hair fell over his forehead and the pit in my stomach sank as he watched me.

Callum O'Neil. Of course, it would be Callum *fucking* O'Neil.

"Cal?" A second voice called and then I was suddenly staring at another face.

Jace Rivers was just as handsome as his friend, with his perfect dark skin, his deep eyes and bright smile and the guy even had dimples, real honest to God dimples. Unlike his counterpart however, Jace had an upstanding reputation, even if he was a little self-involved. He was kind, funny and overall, a solid guy. He had his flock of fans but was not one to relish in the playboy label like his captain.

"Oh shit, you're not a dude." Eying his friend Jace lifted a hand to whack Callum in the shoulder. "Cal, you ran over a lady."

Focusing back on me, Jace shot me a slow, smooth smile as he held out one massive hand in front of him and waited. Heat flooded my cheeks at the gesture though I ignored it and instead pushed myself to my feet before smoothing my palms over my thighs awkwardly.

"Jace Rivers," He introduced himself as if the whole campus didn't know who he was, and I rolled my eyes with a scoff.

"I know who you are." I had meant for the words to come out firm but the lump in my throat was still there and my voice cracked pathetically. Sensing my distress, Jace's dark eyes widened before he shot his friend a quick glance and then he took a step closer.

"Hey, are you crying? Are you hurt?" Lifting my hands in panic, I ran the tips of my fingers over my cheeks only to realize they were still damp. "Cal, how hard did you hit her?"

"She ran into me." Callum drawled as if this entire interaction was boring him to tears. I glared at him sharply.

"Oh, I'm sorry, did *I* hurt *you*?" I snapped sarcastically before wiping at my nose and I watched as heat filled his deep brown eyes. Callum and I had never spent any amount of significant time together, unless the campus parties counted, though I seriously doubt he had ever noticed me, and I held his gaze for a long minute before Jace was clearing his throat.

"Well, if you're sure you're okay we better get going," Jace murmured awkwardly while running his hand over the back of his neck and I sniffed once more before moving aside to let them pass.

Taking the invitation, Jace strode forward while avoiding my eyes but just as he had cleared past me, he turned to his captain who had remained rooted in his place. Callum was still watching me, his face impossible to read even as he tipped his head and then his lips lifted on one side. It couldn't even be considered a grin; it was barely half of a smirk, though the sight of it made me shuffle uncomfortably.

"Yeah, we better get going. Don't want to miss all that time on the ice now that so much has been freed up." I could feel my jaw drop before I could stop it and he chuckled at my expression while lifting a hand to ruffle his perfect curls. "Enjoy your afternoon, Kelly."

Without another word, he tossed me a wink and then sauntered down the hall, pulling his teammate in tow. I, however, remained frozen, standing in place until the heavy door of the men's locker-room slammed shut. The sound broke my trance and I realized not only had the women's team been cut but Callum O'Neil knew and had free reign over the ice, the arena and most definitely the remaining funds for the University's hockey teams.

"He did what?" Chris yelled over the high pitch scream of the kettle, and I rolled my eyes before moving from the couch. Crossing our tiny apartment, I leaned my head against the wall of the kitchen and watched while my brother picked his mug out carefully before pouring his tea.

"He said I could transfer." Sighing I took the offered pug mug from him and blew across the steaming drink.

"Okay, so what does that mean exactly?" Chris's brows pulled in worry, and I felt guilty for overloading him with this when we had meant to be celebrating his engagement to his long-term partner Tommy.

"It means taking a gap year with hockey or figuring out a way to make the money I need for the tuition." Sinking into our worn-down couch, I focused on the steam curling from my ceramic dog shaped mug all while avoiding my brother's gaze.

"I hear feet pictures are all the rage." His face lifted in a grin, and I couldn't help but snort.

"Size eleven feet that have been stuffed into skates for the last decade aren't exactly what I would call ideal for that type of thing."

"Who knows, that might be a niche market." Chris laughed before sinking into the seat next to me. "But seriously Tate, what about-"

My head began to shake before he could finish, and I shuffled away from him. "No."

"Come on Tate, Dad would be thrilled to give you the money if it means you could go pro someday." Even now I could hear the tremor in his voice, and I hated that our father still had that kind of power over my brother's heart.

"I won't ask him for anything Chris."

"Just because I'm his biggest failure doesn't mean you should suffer too." Lifting my feet, I burrowed them under his thighs and then reached for his hand.

"Loving who you choose to love is not a failure and if he can't see that even now, then he's an idiot. Plus, you've been more of a parent than they ever have, and I wouldn't trade any of this for anything." I said as I waved my hand around, gesturing to our tiny run-down apartment.

"Then I guess we figure out a way for you to stay at North Pacific." He offered with a squeeze to my fingers, and I was filled with gratitude as his light grey eyes met my own.

Chris was five years older and had always been my protector growing up, even after I had grown taller than him at age fourteen. He was the best big brother anyone could have ever had and when my parents disowned him after coming out, I was devastated.

Thankfully we found ways to see each other and the moment I turned 18 I moved out of the family home and into the tiny two-bedroom apartment that we now shared. The space was small and overly crowded with Tommy now living with us, but I was happier than I had ever been as a child. My father's constant pressure for me to fill the role he had left for his son and my mother's continuous disdain for my body, and love of hockey had once created open wounds, but those slowly closed over time thanks to Chris, and I knew I owed him everything.

"Enough of that, tell me about the proposal." Setting his mug down, my brother turned to me, and I watched as his face lifted with happiness. North Pacific and hockey could wait, this moment was his and I would be damn sure he knew I was thrilled for him.

Chapter Two

SHAWN

"You're late." Callum scolded as I pressed open the door to the locker room and I rolled my eyes before tossing up a middle finger.

"Get off my ass," I grumbled, pushing my way through the team to get to my locker all while ignoring the two concerned gazes of my best friends. I had been less than my usual self lately and had yet to find the courage to breach the conversation with Jace or Callum.

How do you tell your two best friends that you're nearly failing every class and one more bad mark may cause you to lose everything you've worked so hard on?

"Where were you? I was going to come pick you up like we had decided but you weren't at the house." Jace tugged his jersey over his pads, and I turned my head to my bag while I pretended to rifle through it. I hadn't thought of an excuse on my way over and would die before I told them about the ass chewing I had just received from Professor Peters after my last class.

"I was grabbing a coffee," I offered while stepping out of my shoes but when I glanced up, I knew they had seen right through my feeble attempt at an explanation.

"You don't drink coffee after 8 am." Callum accused, and I absolutely hated how well he knew me.

"Yeah well, I'm trying to get used to these new practice times now that the ice is just ours. How'd that go over by the way? I think I passed a rather pissed off looking Tatum Kelly on my way in." In fact, I knew I had.

Tatum Kelly was hard to miss at her staggering 6'1 height and she had been extremely distracting over the years. We had a class together last semester and if I was honest with myself, I had spent my fair share of time admiring the way the muscles of her back moved and the shine of her light brown hair or how long her legs were. She wasn't what most would deem as hot or pretty, but the features of her face were interestingly mismatched and the way her nose had healed after the last break somehow managed to bring more attention to her full lips and bright grey eyes.

"Was she still crying?" Jace asked with worry, and I turned to him in alarm.

"Crying? Why would she be crying?" Jace's eyes moved to Callum for a quick second, and I watched as our captain avoided my gaze.

"O'Neil, what did you do?" Rolling his eyes, Callum tucked his helmet under his arm before grabbing at his stick and then he turned to me with a shrug.

"She came flying down the hall from Miller's office and ran into me. But honestly, it was barely a tumble to the floor and after her time on the ice I would hope she could handle a little bump. As for the crying, well she was already doing that before our little crash so I'm not to blame for that."

"I think Miller broke the news to her." Jace offered with a wince, and I frowned at the two of them.

"He hadn't told his team yet? The season starts soon, and he's known about this since last year!" Tugging my pads on roughly I looked at my friends in confusion. No wonder her face had been so flushed, though from the distance I couldn't tell if it was from her emotional state or the cold Vancouver winds.

"He waited until the last minute, probably hoping for some miracle." Callum took a step closer and slapped the plastic of my shoulder pads roughly. "Don't worry about it, it's not our fault and we have bigger things to focus on."

"Right." I agreed begrudgingly, though I couldn't shake the sinking feeling in my gut. I felt bad for Kelly and her team. They had worked their asses off the last two seasons and had nearly won the championship last year. They were coming off a high which must have made the news sting all that much more. I honestly didn't understand the cut, we had a number of other teams that had yet to do well and held very little interest for the alumni.

"Seriously Shawn, stop worrying about it, we need you to be on your game." Shrugging out from under Callum's hand I grabbed my helmet.

"Of course, Cap." Following them to the ice, I glanced across the rink at my fellow teammates who moved to their places for the warmup stretch, but before I could make it to my net, I heard Perry call my name from the bench.

Jackson Perry was a big dude, and his face was what you would expect from a lifelong player. His front teeth had been knocked out his first season and replaced with unnaturally white veneers. His mouth had never quite healed right which left him with a permanent scowl, though the grey beard seemed to help with that a bit. Overall, he looked like a super jacked, badass Santa.

A badass Santa who had his terrifying icy blue eyes narrowed in a glare while he lifted a single finger at me. Honestly, his eyes looked like those white runner things from that show with dragons.

"Patrick!" Wincing I hung my head and moved across the ice as he called for me again.

"What is it Coach?" Crossing his arms over his chest, he motioned for me to come closer and when I hesitated, he grabbed at my jersey and pulled me behind the boards.

"Why did I receive an email from Peters today that said the chances of you passing your mid-term were next to none?" Icy blue eyes had zeroed in on my own and I swallowed nervously.

"Coach," But a single finger pointed at me, and my mouth snapped shut.

"I know O'Neil and Rivers have it easy. They don't need a scholarship to be here, they're never worried about grades or money because mommy and daddy will rescue them if they need to. I know how hard you've worked to get to where you are. So don't let that slip through your fingers over a few measly grades. Get a tutor, give up one of your famous parties to study and show us why you deserved this chance over the other thousand kids who tried."

"Yes, sir," I whispered pathetically while dropping my gaze to the ties of my skates.

"Good man." He patted my back sharply. "Go stretch, we're doing two rounds of drills today."

"So, what did Perry want?" Jace asked as he pressed the start engine button of his truck.

"Nothing," I shrugged, focusing my attention on my seatbelt rather than the dark eyes of my best friend.

"C'mon Shawn, don't be like that. We both know he wouldn't have pulled you from warm up if it was nothing."

"He didn't pull me from warm up," I argued, running my fingers over the colourful designs on my forearm. "I was there for the suicides and drills just like everyone else, or are you so self-absorbed you missed me being there?"

"Okay, now I know for sure something is wrong." Lifting my attention to the windshield, I watched as the rain bounced and rolled down the glass. "Seriously man, what's going on with you today?"

"Nothing, it's just been a bad day." My attention slid back to him, and I watched as concern painted its way across Jace's face, and I felt a twinge in my chest. "Honestly, I'm fine."

The muscles of his jaw worked as his teeth clenched and then he exhaled roughly before reaching an arm across my shoulder and tugged me into him. "Okay, but if you need anything, I'm here."

Nodding against his shoulder I pulled away and then gestured to the dash. "Let's get out of here, the keg should be at the house any time now and you know Callum will get all pissy if he's there alone to set up for tonight." Laughing Jace put the truck into drive and then pulled from the lot.

The drive home was quiet, the only noise being the post practice playlist in the background, and I glanced out the window while we drove through the city. The outskirts of Vancouver were just as wet and cold as the rest of the city and it was times like this when I missed the California sunshine. Though that was about all I missed.

"Looks like Callum is in a bitchy mood already." Pulling my attention from the window I glanced through the windshield and smiled. Callum was standing in front of the entry window with his hands on his hips and I could feel his glare from here.

"Why is it he always stands like a middle-aged dad observing his lawn?" Tossing his head back Jace laughed, and then swatted my shoulder.

"Or how he dances like a dad at a Saturday barbeque. Just kind of bobs around while sipping on his vodka soda." Snorting I nodded my head and then pointed as Callum's form moved from the window to the front door. "Okay, we better get in there or we will never hear the end of it."

"About time you two showed up." Callum grumbled and I shot Jace a grin before making my way through the house and dropping my bag into the mudroom while glancing over the red solo cups and half a dozen bags of frozen ice. Callum was the parent of the house, always the organized one, the one who cooked and cleaned though we were also constantly nagged. Thankful we had grown used to it; in fact, it was almost funny at this point. So when he pointed to my hockey bag, I knew what was coming.

"Yes, yes I know. Don't let it sit there." Rolling my eyes, I put the laundry in the washer and made sure the bag was hidden away before our guests arrived.

"Keg is in the back," Callum gestured to the patio and then crossed his arms over his chest. "People will be showing up around eleven."

"In that case, I better get my ass in gear." Jace smiled while he grabbed at one of the bottles of tequila. Opening it, he ignored Callum's dirty look and took a long swig before wiping his mouth with his sleeve. Grabbing at the neck, I plucked the bottle from his hands and pressed the glass to my lips before taking my own mouthful.

"If either of you are planning on getting laid tonight, you best go shower." Jace rolled his eyes, taking the liquor from my grasp before scurrying up the stairs but just as I was about to head to my own bedroom, Callum's arm shot out stopping me from leaving the room.

"You good?" He asked, his brown eyes searching my face with worry.

"Yeah man, all good. Why?"

"Just wondering what Perry wanted." His gaze grew sharper, and I fidgeted under his stare.

"Oh," scrambling I searched for a good excuse. "He wanted to talk about a play."

"A play? He wanted to talk to you about a play?" Fuck, I messed up. There was no way Perry would discuss a play without filling in the team's captain and I could tell Callum wasn't buying it for a second.

"Yeah, honestly O'Neil it was nothing." I shrugged nonchalantly before clearing my throat. "I'm going to go shower before everyone gets here."

Thankfully Callum let it go and I all but ran to my room, ashamed that I not only lied to my best friends but couldn't find the courage to just tell them that I had been struggling.

The music was loud, the drinks were flowing, and the house was packed. It had to be our biggest party to date, and I sank into my chair, pleasantly buzzed off the tequila while I watched a group of girls sway to the music while giggling loudly.

They were hot, fellow juniors if I wasn't mistaken, but nothing that piqued my interest. None of the girls at North Pacific seemed to these days, though my reputation said otherwise. Callum was the man whore of the three of us, Jace was the nice guy, and though I was covered in tattoos and wore the band tees, I was the quiet one.

So when the rumors of my sexual conquests circled through the campus I nearly choked. I had only been with a handful of girls, none of whom were the type to discuss our nights together thankfully. And though the lies irked me, the team couldn't be prouder.

"You alright man?" Jace leaned close to my ear so that he didn't have to try and yell over the music and I nodded before taking another sip out of my cup. "I'm going to switch the shots with some beer, want to come?"

Dipping my chin, I agreed, and we made our way through the crowd until we reached the back door. The rain had stopped but the air was frigid compared to the stifling temperature of the house and I took in a deep breath as I looked around.

Smaller groups had branched out, huddled together in the backyard and I glanced over each of them until I noticed a familiar pair of long, *long* legs and a sandy brown ponytail that curled down a muscular back. Even under her jacket I could tell she was powerfully built, and I felt my mouth go dry as I took her in.

"Man, you are totally staring at that girl." Jace's warm breath fanned across my blonde hair, and I elbowed him sharply in the ribs when I noticed his smug grin. "What? I'm not blaming you, just thought I'd let you know in case you weren't aware."

"Just get your beer, dickhead." Jace shot me one last smile before he moved to the keg, and I glanced at Tatum once more only to realize she wasn't there.

"Bro, don't be an idiot, Stevens!" Callum's worried voice startled me from my search, and I turned to glance back at the house just in time to see O' Neil trying to grab at the sophomore who had decided to climb onto the rickety beer pong table while pouring the contents of two solo cups into his open mouth. "Stevens, get down man!"

The crowd around the table had grown but I could still manage to make out the puddle of beer under the kid's feet and I took two steps forward ready to help Callum. It was too late though, and I watched as the heel of his Nike's slid across the slick tabletop and then he was falling.

Shocked gasps echoed from the crowd, and I ran into the kitchen, pushing the group apart until I managed to get to the table. Stevens was on the floor, his hand grasping at his right ankle while Callum tried to get him to calm down and it took a second for me to realize that his foot should definitely not be facing the way it was.

"Fuck," Jace cursed as he peered over my shoulder. "Perry is going to kill us."

Chapter Three

TATUM

"Kate, I think there are supposed to be pants that go with this shirt." I grumbled while tugging the hem of the so-called dress my best friend had forced me into.

"It's not that short you weirdo." She sighed, glancing at me in the reflection of the vanity as she lined her eyes with the black pencil.

"Not if you're under six feet maybe." Turning in her seat she crossed her arms along the back of the chair and perched her chin on them while watching me change into the jeans and simple tee I had brought with me.

"It was just an option. You constantly complain that you always look like a bum next to me, which I completely disagree with, by the way. I personally love your style but if you want something a bit *more*, the options are there." Turning back around her dark bob swished through the air only to settle perfectly once more and I watched as she added just a touch of blush to her fair coloured skin.

"Are you sure you want to go? Callum O'Neil and his lackeys aren't really our normal scene, and their last party was a disaster." I murmured quietly and Kate's reflection raised a delicate brow while her lips lifted in a smile.

"Are you still mad because that girl puked on your shoes?" My nose immediately scrunched at the memory and Kate giggled at the expression. "Listen, I know you're upset about the team but staying in your room all night while your brother and his fiancé celebrate their engagement won't help you keep your mind off of it. The best thing we can do is go out and maybe socialize a bit, get a little tipsy and then come back here to crash. My mom has already promised a hangover breakfast tomorrow and then I will help you look at jobs, or schools or whatever it is you want to do."

"Fine, but I get chicken nuggets on the way home."

"Done, now come here." Moving to the now vacant chair, I sank onto the seat and managed to shove my knees under the vanity clumsily. Holding a curling iron, Kate sorted through my hair before starting her magic and I managed to sit still long enough for her to curl the thick stands. Adding the finishing touches, we managed to be ready just in time for the Uber's arrival and we headed out.

The older woman was nothing but kind as she carefully drove through the streets and I laid back against the seat, thankful that the pre-drinks had done their job to numb any anxiety I may have had. The warm fuzzy feeling spread pleasantly through me and I smiled at the early 90's music that echoed around me.

"Looks like Vans is having a blast," Kate murmured before passing me her phone to the open text message.

VANESSA VANS: ARE YOU GUYS ON YOUR WAYYYYYY???????

"She's always the first one there and the last to go," I laughed while handing her phone back to her but not before a group selfie came through. Half of the team was already there, and I was glad to see they were all enjoying themselves. It certainly beat the emotional roller coaster I had been on earlier.

"Looks like we're here." Kate lifted her chin towards the window, and I could see the crowd hanging around the front door while the sound of music pounded through the air.

"Thank God their closest neighbours are also students." The entire block was mostly student housing though the buildings were far nicer than I would have ever imagined, and I looked at the two-storey house with longing. The O'Neil family was well off, so much so that they nearly owned this entire block, which was probably why their son always got away with throwing these massive parties.

"Ready?" Kate asked as she tugged on my jacket's sleeve, and I took in a deep breath before sliding my way out of the car. The music was even louder without the shelter of the car, and I noticed that the crowd had ventured into the house rather than hanging out on the lawn.

"Is every student here?" Kate wondered out loud as we zig-zagged through the party goers.

Nodding, I glanced around. Kate was right, it felt like the house was going to burst at the seams as more and more people piled into it. There were other athletes I knew, most of the sororities and frats seemed to be here as well, and then the odd group who I didn't recognize.

"Kelly!" Vanessa Vans called from the kitchen where she was perched on the counter with one arm stretched out towards Callum who was filling her cup with club soda.

Smiling gently at her, I offered a small wave and then glanced towards the brown eyes that had focused on my face. Without the shock of a fall or the stress of learning about the end of my team, I could see the appeal of Callum O' Neil.

He was tall, taller than me and well built. His curls were perfectly formed on his head and his brown eyes were not plain by any means. He was exactly what every girl pictured when she conjured 'tall, dark and handsome' in their minds. And he knew it.

Smirking at me, Callum lifted a hand and gave me a two fingered salute before bending to whisper into Vanessa's ear.

"Do you think he knows she's gay?" Kate whispered after watching the entire interaction and I shrugged.

"I can't see how he wouldn't, he's known her for years." Pushing Callum away with a laugh, Vanessa slid from the counter and made her way to us with open arms.

"I'm so glad you decided to come!" Vanessa tugged me closer, forcing me to bend down to her height and I patted her awkwardly on the back.

"Us too," I offered and then pulled from her grasp. The kitchen had begun to fill with more bodies and the temperature rose to an uncomfortable level. Grabbing my hair, I lifted it into a ponytail and secured it quickly before glancing at my friends.

"It's so hot in here! Want to go out?" I shouted over the bass while pointing to the backyard where most of the men's hockey team had circled around the keg. Both girls nodded and I linked arms with them, pulling both in tow as I made my way through the crowd. They would have a hard time losing sight of me but given the fact that they both barely came to my shoulder, I was certain they would get lost amongst the crowd.

Managing to make it to the yard, I inhaled deeply and glanced around. Most of the other students out here were far quieter, all seeming to seek an escape from the overcrowding of the house, and I pulled my friends to the end of the yard before finding our own space. Once we had settled in a spot, Kate pulled her flask from the pocket of her coat.

"This way we don't have to mix our liquor." She shrugged and twisted open the top before tipping her head back and letting it pour into her open mouth.

"Easy Kate!" Vanessa laughed, watching in wonder as the petite brunette swallowed one last time without so much as a squint. Kate could hold her liquor better than anyone I had met though she usually wasn't one to overindulge and I watched with a frown as she tossed the red head a wink before screwing the lid back on and tucking the flask away.

"Don't look so serious Tatum, I just needed a little extra courage." Lifting her chin, she indicated to space behind me, and I glanced over my shoulder to see Riley Summers and his latest fling. Riley was an all-around star athlete but had settled into the role of starting left winger last year after the previous player had graduated. He and Kate had dated the entirety of their high school years and came to North Pacific together only for their relationship to fall apart last year after Kate's father had passed.

"Are you okay?" I asked while wrapping an arm around Kate's shoulders. She nodded but I could see the tears that were threatening to fall, and I stepped in front of her, shielding her from prying eyes while she wiped at them clumsily. "Do you want to go home?"

She had begun to shake her head but then her lips parted in a gasp, and I turned to watch as Riley dipped his head to kiss the blonde who had been clinging to him. Spinning back around, I watched as Kate's lower lip trembled and I pulled her to my side.

"I lied," she whispered. "Can we go?"

I should have figured Riley would be here given that it was his captain's party but that hadn't even been a thought in my mind and now I wished I had kept us from coming. Kate was very much still in love with Riley, and I knew seeing him must have really hurt her.

"Yeah, let's sneak out the gate and call an Uber out front." After shooting Vanessa an apologetic smile and a promise to catch up with her later, I ushered Kate through the yard.

Sliding my hand across the nightstand, I searched for my phone. The buzzing had interrupted a rather peaceful sleep and I rose on my elbow, tilting the screen towards my face. The brightness of the display was blaring and it took two tries to open my eyes wide enough before the phone would unlock.

VANESSA VANS: HOLY SHIT
VANESSA VANS: HOOLY SHITTTTTT

VANESSA VANS: YOU GUYSSMISSED THE CRAZIEST THING EVERRRRR

VANESSA VANS: SOME DUMBASS BROKE HIS LEG

VANESSA VANS: HE WAS DANCING ON THE TABLE

VANESSA VANS: IT WAS STEVENS!!!!!! HOLY CRAP IT WAS THE STEVENS KIID

Sitting up, I reread the messages twice more before I flicked on the lamp on the nightstand. Kate, who had drunkenly sobbed into her order of fries before finally crashing, rolled onto her back and cracked open an eye at the sudden burst of light.

"Ugh, Tatum, what the hell?" Grabbing at her pillow, she pulled it over her face but I paid her no mind. I was too busy texting Vanessa back.

Stevens had been a newbie to the starting line up this year, young but full of promise and he just happened to play right winger. The same position I had been playing for over a decade.

"Seriously Tatum, can you turn off the light and go back to sleep?" Kate's voice was muffled from under the pillow but when I didn't respond she peeked up at me with curiosity. "What is going on?"

"Stevens broke his leg." When Kate frowned in confusion, I moved my phone, pressing it closer to her face and watched as her eyes scanned across the drunk texts from Vanessa.

"Wow, that sucks," she sighed but then glanced at me for a pause. "Or not? Why are you smiling about some kid breaking a limb."

Snatching the pillow from her hands I laughed and then sank back down into the bed, turning on my side to face her. "Stevens was their starting right winger. They're without a decent player for that position and it's almost the start of the season."

I could tell the moment it dawned on her and Kate smiled brightly at me in realization. "So, there might be an opening for a new player."

Nodding, I wrapped my arm around her and hugged her tightly for a minute before my face nearly split with my smile. "Think I should send Stevens some flowers?"

"So let me be sure I'm understanding what you're asking. You want to join the men's team and take the right winger position?" Coach Perry was far more intimidating than Miller could have ever hoped to be, and I fiddled with my fingers while avoiding his icy blue gaze. Moving my eyes around the office, I glanced to my left only to be met with the hard stare of Callum and I cleared my throat nervously under his scrutiny.

"Stevens is a good player, potentially a great player. But I can promise you, I'm just as decent and I easily have two inches and fifteen pounds on him. So, if you're worried that I can't hold my own, I can assure you I can." Perry leaned back into his chair with a tilted head, and I felt his gaze trace me from head to toe before he turned to Callum.

“Stevens is out for the season O’Neill, who would you send out on the ice to replace him?” Callum’s mouth fell open and I could tell he hadn’t been ready to be put on the spot. “Is she good?”

Turning to the side, I waited for a pause while the muscle in Callum’s jaw twitched and then his brown eyes captured mine. Squaring my shoulders under his attention, I tipped my chin and readied myself for an answer.

“I have no idea Coach; women’s hockey holds no interest for me.” Grinding my teeth together, I narrowed my eyes and watched as his lips lifted into a smirk.

“I can’t blame you for that,” Perry laughed, and I swung my head towards him with a scowl. “Listen Kelly, I’ve heard you can play. Miller has told me as much. But women’s hockey doesn’t have the same rules as the men’s.”

“Oh, how so?” I asked with a raised brow, barely managing to keep my voice pleasant.

“Well, there’s no checking for one.” Perry explained with a roll of his eyes, almost as if that was enough reasoning for him.

“I’m tough, I can handle a few knocks around.” I promised as I crossed my arms in front of me.

“Be that as it may, it’s a men’s league. How would my boys feel having a woman on their team, let alone our opponents.” Perry moved, leaning across his desk and I realized he was waiting for my surrender. He was hoping I would give up and forget this whole thing.

Too bad Jackson Perry had no idea who he was dealing with.

“I think that if your *boys* are that worried about being outshined by me, they should just say so. But I would seriously hope they’re more concerned about doing well this season now that they're down a first string player.” I paused, throwing Callum a glare. “As for the opposing teams, let them try and underestimate me. I’d be more than happy to prove them wrong.”

Coach Perry’s icy blues moved from me to Callum and back again before he ran a hand through his grey beard and then he clapped his hands together roughly. Startling at the noise, I turned to Callum in question, but he paid me no mind and instead waited while his coach rounded the massive wood desk.

“Alright Kelly, come to practice tonight ready to skate your ass off and we will see just how well you could do with my team.” My heart stuttered in my chest while ringing filled my ears and I could scarcely make out the sound of Callum’s protests.

“You hear me, Kelly?” Perry snapped while pointing a finger at me. “I won’t go easy on you. You have the same expectations as the rest of my players and let me be clear, this is not a sure thing. I’ll let you practice with us, but that’s it for now.”

“Yes sir, thank you, sir.” Waving a hand at me in dismissal before he moved towards his chair once more and I took it as a sign to make myself scarce, especially before he could change his mind.

Chapter Four

CALLUM

"You can't be serious Coach." I begged, waiting for him to tell me this was all some horrible joke. But Perry just shot me a glare and then sank into his plush leather chair.

"What are you so worried about O'Neil? So she comes out for a few practices before realizing there's no way she can compete. What's the harm?" I supposed it would be harmless had it been any other player on the women's team. But Tatum Kelly had quite the reputation for her stubbornness and rumor had it that without her scholarship, she was screwed. And that kind of problem was sure to make her desperate enough to try and stick it out.

"The guys just won't be happy about it and there's no way they'll want to scrimmage with her."

"If they have a problem with the decisions I make for my team, they can hand in their jerseys. The same goes for you too." The hardness of Perry's scowl told me just how serious he was being and I ran a frustrated hand through my curls before glancing over my shoulder and out the glass windows behind me.

There was no sign of Kelly in the halls and I couldn't help but wonder how fast she had run, knowing that Perry might change his mind at the drop of a hat. Sighing, I scanned the empty corridor once more, checking that there was no one else out there before turning to my coach.

"So what should our game plan be?" Perry narrowed his eyes at me and swallowed before trying again. "I just mean, how hard should we push it?"

Thick fingers combed through his grey beard while he examined me closely and then he crossed his arms. "We will practice how we always do, just be sure to tell the boys there are no exceptions, we don't pull any punches and we treat each player *equally*."

He had meant for the words to come across as fair, but they sounded anything but. It was an unspoken instruction; Tatum Kelly would not be doted on. If anything, Coach had just painted a target on her back and I felt my stomach twist at the thought.

I didn't like the idea of her skating with us, mostly because I worried that it would somehow give her the opportunity to play a game. That would leave an opening for our opponents and that wasn't a risk I wanted to have in my senior season.

"Alright Coach, I'll let the boys know." I agreed with the tip of my head, though I was silently trying to create a plan that would keep Kelly from doing well all while keeping her fully intact. I knew most of the boys would be careful not to push it too hard, but there were maybe a few fuckers who would find intimidating her funny, and though couldn't stand her or her stuck up attitude, I didn't want anything bad to happen to her.

"Great, now go home and stop worrying about it, O'Neil." Waving me off, Coach turned to his computer, and I sighed before heading to the door, all while hoping this would go over smoothly.

But somehow, I knew I was lying to myself, nothing involving Tatum Kelly would be easy.

"Are you serious?" Jace asked while raising a single brow at me and I nodded with a shrug. "What is with this girl, all of a sudden she's everywhere. I didn't even know who she was until yesterday."

"You didn't know who Tatum Kelly was?" Shawn asked, his hands freezing with the laces in his fingers while his head snapped up. "How?"

Jace narrowed his eyes at our roommate before shaking his head. "Not all of us are obsessed with her like you seem to be."

Shawn's cheeks pinkened and he swallowed twice before glancing at our teammates. Making sure no one was listening; he took a step closer to us with a frown. "I'm not *obsessed* with her. I just happen to be aware of my fellow athletes and I'm not a self-obsessed asshole."

Snorting Jace turned to me with a grin, obviously pleased that he had hit a nerve and I punched his shoulder. I knew the two of them had their own little *thing* happening, but he knew how sensitive Shawn could be and I gave him a warning glare before turning to the blonde.

"Alright, relax Patrick, don't get your panties in a twist." Rolling his eyes, Shawn finished tying his skates and then scowled at us.

"Just don't be dicks to her, she's a great player and she might be an asset to the team if you guys and Perry give her the chance." I could feel my jaw drop before I could stop it and I turned to Jace in bewilderment.

"Man, you can't be serious." Jace was frozen, bent at the waist as his fingers searched blindly for his stick while his dark eyes remained fixated on Shawn. "I know you have the hots for the girl, but you really think she could play with us?"

"She was a vital part in getting her team to finals last year, that's better than we have done in years. So yeah, I do." Snatching his water bottle from the bench, Shawn turned, and I watched as he stormed out of the locker room before sinking onto the hard wood of the bench. When the rest of the team finally made their way to the ice, I grabbed at Jace's shoulder and sighed.

"He's going to be livid if we let anyone go too hard on her and we both know he'll fuck himself over and piss Perry off trying to look out for her. He hasn't been his normal self and I don't want this whole mess to make it worse for him." Jace nodded and then frowned while he searched my face.

"So what do we do Cal?"

"We do our best to stop Kelly from showing off while keeping an eye on her. We'll watch her back and play our cards right. I think the drills alone might do her in and if not then we make sure we keep the puck away from her. She might be good but there's no way she'll keep up to the majority of us."

"And if she does?"

Exhaling, I wiped at my face roughly before turning for the door. "She won't."

I could practically see Kelly's frown from here and I did my best to ignore the urge to glance at her while she moved into position. She had managed her way through the drills surprisingly well and I noticed even Perry had stopped to watch her. The look of bafflement would have been hilarious had the exact same expression not been painted across my face while I had held my breath, waiting for her to call it quits. But that never happened and honestly, I had to admit that she was fast and moved around us with ease. If I hadn't known who she was, I would have guessed she had been on the team for a while.

Jace had also murmured his surprise, his eyes locked on her during the water break, and I nearly smacked the back of his head when I noticed how his gaze moved across her face with piqued interest. I had seen that look before and I did not need both of my roommates itching to get into Tatum Kelly's pants, no matter how often they enjoyed the same women, *together*.

"Told you she was good," Shawn had whispered with a cocky smile, and I waited, nearly groaning when Jace just nodded dumbly before Perry's voice startled them from their observation of the new pain in my ass.

Now Jace was in the goal, safely away from Kelly, which made my life far easier now that I only had to worry about one idiot. Glancing over my shoulder, I checked on the defenseman, making sure that his head was where it should be before I readied myself for the puck drop.

Watching, I felt my blood pound in my ears while the rest of the world faded, and it was as if everything moved into slow motion. The puck dropped, the solid rubber not having the chance to bounce before I was pulling it back towards Stevens and then all of us were moving. We were a well-oiled machine at this point, and I watched as my scrimmage teammates moved forward, pushing until we were nearing the net.

And it was then that I noticed the long-curled ponytail that had escaped from the back of the helmet. I hadn't passed the puck to Stevens; I had given it to Kelly. I had forgotten the sophomore wasn't on the ice. I had forgotten about his injury and had literally handed her the opportunity to shine and could do nothing but follow behind as she dodged my teammates before flicking her wrist, tucking the puck neatly into the corner of the net.

"Well shit," Jace panted from beside me, his eyes locked on Kelly who had continued to skate behind the goal before she noticed no one else had moved.

"What?" Her smooth voice rang out across the silent rink, her grey eyes bouncing from one player to the next and I couldn't help but wonder where the hell she had learned how to perform a wrist shot like that.

Glancing to the bench, I noticed Perry had leaned over the boards, his mouth open while blinking at the net and then he turned to me, his icy blues narrowed while that angered scowl pulled at his mouth. And I knew I was in for it. I had done exactly what he hadn't wanted, I had allowed her to show everyone that she could not only hold her own, but that she could potentially do well.

"O'Neil!" He bellowed, and I turned to Jace for a quick second before begrudgingly making my way to our coach. Grabbing onto the chinstrap of my helmet, he yanked me down, forcing me to bend to his height before lowering his voice. "What the fuck are you doing, boy? Are you trying to make a fool out of all of us?"

"No Coach," I offered, ignoring the way my neck had begun to burn as he held down by the black strap and then I nearly toppled over when he released me harshly before turning to the rest of the team who had yet to move.

"That's enough for today, get the fuck off my ice and be ready for an early morning. I want to see every last one of you here by 5:00 am tomorrow!" Grabbing his clipboard he turned, hitting the wood against the corner of the wall angrily before calling over his shoulder. "Kelly that means you too."

Clenching my teeth together, I inhaled roughly, trying to swallow the anger that bubbled in my gut and then watched as my teammates cautiously crept nearer. This was not how this practice was supposed to go and I shucked off a glove before pulling my mouthguard out before spitting onto the ice.

"Well, that was something," Jace offered, nudging his shoulder into my own with a half-hearted smile. "At least we know we have somethings to work on. Especially Long, he might be second string, but he left that corner totally open for her."

The *her* in question was still in front of the net, her helmet tucked under her arm, and I watched as Shawn nearly had to lift his chin to grin up at her. Her own expression was weary though she offered a shy smile in return, and I could feel my back straighten at the sight of them.

"Patrick, stop dicking around and get changed!" I yelled, ignoring the way Kelly's grey eyes widened.

"Easy Cal," Jace whispered, eyeing the two before focusing back on me. "I get you're a little ticked but it's not fair to be angry at her for taking an opportunity any of us would have. What happened to making sure we don't make Shawn upset?"

"Shawn can stop eye fucking her and worry about his piss poor attitude lately. If he wasn't one of my best friends, I would have knocked some sense into him by now."

Crossing my arms, I waited for the two to finish closing the distance before noticing that Shawn's blue gaze had narrowed at me while Kelly frowned. I had expected her to brag, maybe offer a bitchy remark at just how well she could handle us. But she did neither. Instead, her stare clashed with my own and then her frown deepened.

"Was Perry a complete asshole?" Her voice was heavy with concern that seemed genuine, though I didn't buy it.

"He was pissed that we let you show us up, but I doubt he's seriously worried. He knows tomorrow will kick your ass and you'll give this whole crazy idea up." I could almost see the way her emotions closed off, almost as if she had built a wall inside of herself and

I questioned how long that took her to learn. Or why she was so easily able to do it in the first place.

"Right, well I look forward to proving you wrong, *again*." Pushing passed me, Kelly stomped her way down the hall leaving us alone in silence and I wondered if *I* should be worried.

Chapter Five

TATUM

"Crap. Crap. Crap!" Leaning forward, I rested my forehead against the steering wheel while clenching my eyes closed. This morning had all but gone to shit and I could feel the tears of frustration burn behind my eyelids. Yesterday after practice I had headed home only to find Chris and Tommy carefully going over every cent of their last pay checks. We had been hoping to move into a larger apartment now that there were three of us but the cost in the city was horrendous and I couldn't afford to be farther away from campus or the arena. The worry of that had kept me up for hours while I scoured the internet for a job I could do while still making practice and games but there wasn't anything I could swing.

Then my alarm had been set to evening rather than morning and I would have never woken up in time had it not been for my brother. As always, Chris had set his own alarm to be sure I made it out the door with protein shake in hand and I was reminded just how much my brother cared. And for that reason, I knew I couldn't call him to tell him my car refused to start, again. He would drop everything to come get me, even if it meant being late to his own job and I hated that I was such a burden.

Sitting up, I grabbed at the keys, twisting them once more only to hear the echo of the pouring rain while my car spluttered and then quieted. Of course, today it would be a near torrential downpour and I would be forced to walk to the bus stop two blocks over. Grabbing at my bag, I pulled my hood up and then made a beeline for the sidewalk all while trying to avoid the biggest puddles.

Managing to keep my quick stride, I turned the last corner, peeling my soaked hair from my face as I tried to make out just how far the stop was from me and then I moved. Jumping off the curb, I began to dart across the street only to be blinded by a massive pair of headlights while the horn echoed around us. I was in the wrong but that hadn't stopped me from lifting a hand, ready to flip them off when I heard a voice.

"Kelly?" Squinting in the light, I could just make out the familiar face of Jace Rivers and I groaned, hating that it was him who had found me, scurrying across the road like a drowned rat. "What the hell are you doing in this?" Putting his four ways on, he stepped out of the enormous black truck, and I couldn't help but roll my eyes at his choice of vehicle. How stereotypical.

Coming around the front of the truck, he shot out one hand to grab my bag while the other pressed against my soaked jacket and then he dipped his head low. "Why are you walking in this?"

Shrugging out of his reach, I pointed to the bus stop on the other side of the road with a roll of my eyes. "Going to practice, what else would I be doing?"

Blinking through the rain, I watched as he tilted his head, doing my very best to ignore the way his long black eye lashes were littered with tiny drops of water and then his lips lifted. "Are you staring at me?"

Heat scorched across the skin of my cheeks, and I moved, ready to push my way past him when his hand shot out again.

"Get in my truck, we can take you to practice with us." As if he was summoned, Shawn Patrick opened his door, his blonde head popping out before he waved an arm at me frantically. But I didn't move, not even when another horn blasted from behind Jace's truck.

"Someone is trying to get by your monstrosity," I snapped though he didn't seem to mind and instead his smile grew.

"Well, I'm not leaving until you get in, so they'll just have to learn some patience."

"I'm pretty sure it's illegal to block traffic like that." I argued.

"Good thing we have a large number of supporters in this city and rumor has it I'm a fan favourite." Moving his hand once more, he ushered me forward, but this time I yielded and walked to the rear door on the driver's side.

"Fine, but only because I don't want to be late. I would hate to give O'Neil something to use against me since I out skated his team yesterday." Hauling myself up into the back seat, I nearly hummed at the burst of warm air and was careful not to show the pleasure of being surrounded by the heat of the truck.

"Seat warmer?" Shawn asked, peering at me with a soft grin from his place in the passenger seat and I swallowed before nodding silently while I unzipped my coat. His smile grew and he pressed a button on the centre console before glancing back at me but this time he was frowning. "Your jacket is soaked right through."

Dropping my chin, I lowered my eyes noting that the now exposed material of the t-shirt had in fact darkened and it was then I realized just how wet I was, and I shivered violently. Shawn's face grew concerned and then he was moving, pulling his arms from his hoodie before yanking it over his head and gently placing it on my lap

"Shawn, we are like ten minutes away from the barn." Jace sighed, though I noticed his dark eyes were focused on me in the rear-view mirror.

"She's basically rocking the truck with that shivering and is about to go onto the ice. The least we could do is offer her something to keep her warm in the meantime." Grinning at me, the blonde winked and then turned back around.

Normally I would have put up a fight, especially in front of the roommates of O'Neil. But my skin was cold and clammy and my teeth had begun to chatter, even with the heat of the leather seat below me. Peeling my wet jacket from my skin, I then leant forward and grabbed at the hem of my t-shirt before tugging it over my head. An odd choking noise came from the front seat and I glanced at the two men, noticing the way both faced forward, their spines perfectly straight while I found my way into the hoodie.

"You'd think you would have seen a woman in a sports bra before considering all the action you two see." I murmured, while pulling my wet hair out from the hood of the sweater. The two didn't respond, in fact, Shawn seemed to focus on the street as it passed by and Jace had begun to hum to the radio softly.

"Men." I sighed, forcing myself to ignore the pleased little smile that had found its way onto my face.

"How was practice this morning?" Kate asked before sipping on her coffee and I sank into the hard plastic of my chair while poking at the salad in front of me with my fork.

"Normally I would say great. But it seems like the better I do, the more I piss off Perry and O'Neil." Practice had gone without a hitch, or so I had thought. The suicides were hard, but I loved pushing my body and then the rest of practice seemed flawless. Our team had won the scrimmage, even with Patrick in the goal this time and though I had taken a hit or two, it was nothing that I couldn't handle.

"Ah, well keep at it. They need to get over their fragile egos and see how you could help the team."

"Perry mentioned something about a few of the other girls wondering about joining too. He was nearly fuming when he told me about it." O'Neil on the other hand looked sick at the thought, but I didn't bother mentioning that.

"Well, it looks like you've won over two of the players because they are headed this way." Looking over my shoulder, I watched as Shawn and Jace made their way across the dining hall. Both seemed to have their sights set on our table and I glanced at my friend in question before turning to the pair once they reached us.

"Hey," Jace offered with a grin and then motioned to the two empty chairs. "Can we join?"

I had been too busy trying to figure out their motives to notice Kate's silent nod and when the two men lowered themselves into their seats, I felt my eyes widen in surprise. Jace, who sat next to Kate, lifted one large hand with an introduction and a panty melting smile and then waved to Shawn, as if she wasn't fully aware of who they were.

"Kate Schmidt," she smiled nervously. "And I'm pretty sure everyone knows who you two are. No need for intros."

"Well, I promise we are much nicer than you think," Shawn offered though his eyes darted to me quickly and I blushed at the sudden attention.

"What brings you over here?" I asked, pretending to once again focus on my salad and not on the two star athletes who seemed to always be around these days.

"I was just coming to offer you my number actually," The piece of romaine I had begun to swallow stopped mid-way and I coughed roughly, using my tongue to force it down before I gasped.

"What?!" My eyes were wide as I looked across at Jace, and he laughed quietly for a moment before clearing his throat.

"Relax, no need to die over it." He joked, though I could have sworn I could make out a faint blush under his dark skin. "I just figured you can keep it handy should you need a ride again. Though to be honest, I'm a little confused as to why you were walking in the first place. Especially so far from campus. Have a hot date last night or something?"

"I live out that way," I snapped glaring at him. "And I had some car issues this morning. It won't happen again, so I don't need your number."

"You live all the way over there? Why not move closer to campus? Surely there's student housing or a room you could rent." It was as if the thought that these questions were far too personal didn't even cross his mind and I moved my gaze to Kate for a minute before clearing my throat.

"Listen, I appreciate the ride, but it's none of your business. So thanks again, but I really need to get to class." Collecting my things, I waited for Kate to do the same and then moved from the table. "See you guys at practice."

Linking arms, Kate pulled me towards the door, only glancing back once before she rose on her toes so that she could whisper in my ear. "Well, either they're secretly plotting your demise, or they are hoping to get into your pants with that offer to drive you to practice."

Turning my chin to my shoulder, I watched as Shawn smacked his friend across the back of the head and then forced myself to focus my attention in front of me once more.

"That was so weird right?" Biting her lip in thought, Kate stopped, pulling me back with her and then she turned to face me.

"Weird yes, but if you can get cozy with those two, you might be in for the long run Tatum. O'Neil can't possibly go against his assistant captains *and* roommates. Shawn and Jace might just be the perfect answer for this whole situation."

Jace Rivers and Shawn Patrick were hot, talented and popular but were not the type of friends I had hoped to make in University. Especially considering I was giving my all just to be able to play with their team. Had it not been for me trying to get a place on their roster however, I was sure I would have been open to getting *cozy* with one or the other.

Or both.

But that wasn't an option now. I needed to keep my mind focused and those two were sure to make a mess of me if I allowed them to.

Chapter Six

JACE

"You idiot." Shawn groaned, while covering his face with his hands. "You can't just ask a girl where she lives and why? You are such a creep."

Crossing my arms, I rolled my eyes and turned to the now empty hallway where Kelly had disappeared with her friend. I hadn't meant to come across any certain way, I just wanted to offer her a ride should the need arise but the whole situation got out of hand and now I was sure those two girls were talking shit.

"I was being nice." I argued, sinking lower into my seat while my face burned hotly.

"How do you ever get laid if that's what you think being nice is?" One blue eye peeked out at me from between long pale fingers and I raised a brow before leaning close.

"You've seen exactly how charming I can be, and you have first-hand knowledge of my experiences." The words slipped out before I could stop them, and Shawn gaped at me in shock before glancing around the nearly empty dining hall.

"God Jace, maybe learn to keep that between us. I don't need the whole campus knowing what we do off the ice." Shame burned through me, the feeling sinking heavily into my stomach and for a split second I wondered what would happen if everyone *did* know. Callum had never batted an eye at our little *experiments* and the women who had joined us had seemed *more* than satisfied.

"Relax, no one is around." Clearing my throat, I stood all while ignoring the way my friend studied me closely. Sometimes it felt as if Shawn could see right through me, like those deep blue eyes could find every secret I had kept hidden. Usually, it was unnerving, but I would be lying if I said it wasn't the first thing I found attractive about him.

"Whatever, let's just drop it and get to class before you say some more stupid shit." Shawn's eyes bounced around the empty room nervously and I wiped a hand across my face.

"You have Peters next?" I asked, hoping to change the subject though by the look on his face, it had been the wrong thing to say.

"Yeah, and I swear the guy has it out for me," Shawn grumbled, ducking his head while he moved towards the door.

"Has something happened?" Shawn had never complained about a class before, not even once joining Cal and I in our bitchfests in the previous years. He had always seemed so focused when it came to school and when I noticed his frown deepen, I began to wonder if there was more to it.

"Nah man, he's just being a dick." Picking up his pace, Shawn put more distance between us before waving over his shoulder and I hoped he wouldn't come home from Peters' class in a piss poor mood like he had last time.

"Do you ladies need anything?" I called over the music, watching as the two blondes smiled prettily at me before pointing to their cups and my lips lifted into my well-practiced grin that offered the perfect view of my dimples before nodding.

Another Friday, another party and yet it was the same old crowd. The same girls who used the same lines and all of it was beginning to bore me. Putting on the fake man-whore persona was emotionally draining, and I ducked out of the kitchen before scanning the living room. Shawn had disappeared early in the night, probably hiding somewhere quiet, away from prying eyes and I wished I had gone with him.

Cal on the other hand was front and centre, standing at his full height as he hollered from across the beer pong table. The guy could hold his alcohol like a champ and still be solid the next day and I watched as he tossed the little white ball across the beer-soaked table. As always, it hit its mark and spun around the rim of the red cup before floating across the white foam inside.

"Drink up, bud!" He shouted before raising his arms above his head in celebration and I rolled my eyes before continuing out through the house. There were a few students standing at the front of the lawn quietly talking while passing a joint around the group and there was a couple hidden partly behind a tree obviously in the middle of something. Watching for a quick moment, I made sure they were sober enough to be left alone before I turned back for the house. But just as I reached the door, I noticed a long pair of legs sticking out from around the brick corner.

"Hey, you good?" When no one answered, I moved toward the person only to stop short when a pair of bleary grey eyes peered up at me.

Kelly looked rough, her hair was sticking to her damp face, and I was sure it was vomit that covered the front of her shirt. Beside her sat her friend from the dining hall, her small hands stroking the long strands of sandy brown waves carefully before she turned to me.

"Is she okay? What happened?" Crouching down to their height, I winced at the sickly-sweet smell that wafted off Kelly while checking her over for any other sign of injury.

"She was upset and drank way too much way too fast." Hiccupping, Tatum pulled away from her friend and then pressed her pale cheek clumsily against the brick wall beside her.

"Don't do that Kelly." I warned while moving to put my hand between the delicate flesh of her face and the rough stone. Taking a moment to notice the stark contrast between my dark skin and her pale face, I watched as she leaned into my palm. Resting the weight of her head against my hand, Tatum blinked up at me and then suddenly her eyes were swimming in tears and a rough sob pulled from her.

"Did something happen?" I demanded with a narrow gaze aimed at the other girl.

"Nothing serious, just home stuff." The brunette whispered, while worriedly watching her friend. "It's Kate by the way, in case you can't remember."

"Right sorry," The apology was half hearted as I focused back on Kelly, noticing the way her body seemed to sway and then I huddled closer. "Do you have an Uber coming?"

"Well, that was the plan. But I left my phone in the last one and this drunk put hers down somewhere in your house. It's really been a shit show tonight." Kate frowned as she worried for her friend, and I felt Tatum shiver before she groaned and moved to turn onto her hands and knees.

"Not again." The sob broke off into a heave and I moved to grab her hair while she threw up across grass in front of her.

"Alright, let's get her inside. I can grab a new shirt for her and then we can get you a ride home." Tugging on Kelly's bicep, I pulled her up to her feet and then wrapped her arm around my shoulders before grabbing onto her waist.

"I don't feel good," she whimpered, her head lolling onto my shoulder, and I turned my face away from the acidic smell of her breath before sighing.

"Yeah, I bet you feel like shit." Moving her through the doorway was awkward and clumsy and she had nearly toppled into me twice before we reached the bottom of the stairs.

"Jace?" Callum's voice was loud as he called for me and I glanced over my shoulder to see him begin to weave his way through the crowd.

"It's fine man, I have it sorted." I offered though I noticed a tiny flicker of something pass over his face. Moving his attention, he glanced at Kate with a frown.

"Is she usually like this when she drinks?"

Kate's eyes narrowed at Callum, and then her hands moved to her hips as she stared him down. "Considering this is the first time I have ever seen her truly drunk, obviously not. She had too much and decided it would be an excellent idea to funnel some sort of concoction out back."

"Listen man, we are just getting her a change of clothes and then calling an Uber for them. So as fun as this conversation is, I'd love to get away from the smell of puke a.s.a.p."

Moving to Kelly's other side, Callum bent down and grabbed at her legs before hoisting her up against his chest. Making sure that she was somewhat settled in his grasp, he raised his brows and motioned to the crowded stairs. "What are you waiting for then? Get them out of my way before I trip over them."

Ushering our audience from his path, I carefully led the way up the stairs and to my room before gesturing to my bed. Once I was sure Kelly was sitting securely on the mattress, I pulled an oversized t-shirt and a pair of sweats from my dresser before passing them to Kate.

"These should fit, they are old and I think the shirt has a few holes but it's better than being covered in puke." Taking them carefully, Kate offered a small smile and then I turned for the door ready to follow Callum out.

"Rivers?" It wasn't Kate who had whispered my name but Tatum and I glanced over my shoulder at her. "Thank you, I guess you're not so weird after all."

Nodding my head, I ignored Callum's stare and shut the door behind us.

"Why did she think you were weird? I don't think I've ever heard a girl call you that before." Cal asked while leaning against the wall opposite to me and I huffed quietly before glancing down the now empty hall.

"It's nothing really, don't worry about it." Rubbing at the back of my neck, I pressed into the muscles there while an awkward silence filled the space. Callum had been nothing but livid since the first practice or anytime someone even mentioned Tatum Kelly, so I was sure our little carpool situation and my offer to give her a ride in the future would not go over well now that he had some booze in his system.

Tilting his head, Callum opened his mouth but before he could press any further, the door to his left creaked open and Shawn peered at us through the crack. Puzzled to see us both here rather than downstairs, he swung the wood open the rest of the way and then checked the hallway before his blue eyes met mine.

"What's going on?" He asked in confusion and Callum sighed before waving at my room.

"Kelly threw up all over herself and is now getting changed in River's room before we get them a lift home." Shawn's eyes widened in surprise as he glanced at my closed door and then his attention was on me again.

"She okay?" He frowned tightly in concern, and I nodded gently.

"She's pretty shitfaced and she'll have a nasty hangover tomorrow but otherwise she's alright, I think."

"Well, if you two have this handled, I think I'll go back downstairs. I've had about all the Tatum Kelly I can handle today." Moving past me, I watched as Callum headed down the stairs and sighed in relief now that I wasn't stuck under his constant questioning brown eyes.

"Is someone in there with her?" Shawn asked, drawing my focus back onto him while he stepped into the hallway before closing his door behind him.

"Yeah, her friend Kate." I nodded.

"Bet this isn't how you imagined it would be if Tatum Kelly ever ended up in your room." Lifting my head, I glanced at my friend with surprise before shaking my head.

"Why would you even say that?"

Shawn's mouth moved into a sly smile and then he shrugged. "Because if *I've* thought about it, *you* definitely have."

Rolling my eyes, I didn't bother to deny it and instead moved to my door before rapping my knuckles against the wood. Everything was quiet in there, there were no more sobs or heaving and I hoped the two of them hadn't passed out. Knocking again, I waited for a pause before grabbing for the doorknob but before I could push it open, Kate pulled it back and then glanced up at me nervously.

"I'm so sorry, but she laid down for a second while I rinsed her clothes off in the tub and by the time I came back, she had passed out." Glancing over her head, I looked at my bed and noticed that Kelly had in fact crawled under the worn-down comforter and appeared to be fast asleep.

"I can wake her up." Kate offered nervously but I shook my head before sighing.

"Don't worry about it, it's nearly three already. You two can just stay in there and I'll crash somewhere else."

"You sure?" Kate asked, her eyes moving to Shawn who had crowded in behind me before meeting my own eyes once more.

"Yeah, there's bottled water under the sink in the bathroom and Advil in the top drawer, maybe try and get her to take some before you head to bed though." Nodding her head, Kate stepped back into my room and quietly shut the door.

"I can't wait to see Callum's face in the morning." Shawn laughed and I shoved passed him roughly before barging into his room.

Chapter Seven

TATUM

"Oh God," I groaned as I pressed the heels of my palms against my eyes. My mouth was dry, and I swallowed the bitter taste while I tried to massage the pounding in my head away. Keeping my eyes closed, I sat up and stretched out my legs before daring to squint one eye open.

The room was far bigger than my own with deep blue walls that were nearly covered with jerseys, a few posters of half-naked women and a North Pacific University flag. The bed, though comfortable, was thrown together with mismatching sheets and a worn duvet. Still, I supposed I should have been grateful, most of the beds I had been in previously were lucky to have more than one pillowcase and an extra blanket.

Now if only I knew who this particular room belonged to.

Pulling myself from the bed, I tiptoed across the carpet towards the dresser and then snooped through the items that were piled across the wood. There were half a dozen empty water bottles, the typical shot glasses, and dirty socks. Wrinkling my nose, I pinched at one before tossing it away. There were protein bar wrappers and crumpled up receipts but no obvious indication of whose bed I had spent the night in.

Sighing, my eyes moved to the bedside table where a note with my name had been left.

I'm downstairs starting coffee. Figured you'd need some. Your clothes are in the bathroom (the door is beside the red jersey) and before you panic, I was the one lucky enough to sleep next to your snoring all night.

-Kate

Sighing in relief, I moved to the door, not thinking twice before my fingers curled around the cold handle and then I tugged. A burst of warm steam hit my face, and I blinked at the sudden heat as two heads turned in my direction. Jace was closest to me, his dark skin still damp from the shower and I forced myself not to drop my gaze to the towel that hugged his hips and instead watched as he paused with his toothbrush in his mouth. Shawn was in a similar state, half naked with just a towel though he had been in the process of shaving.

"Hey," Shawn smiled, dropping his razor onto the counter. "How are you feeling this morning?"

"Fine, yeah, way better." I crossed my arms over my chest, very much aware that my favourite dingy white bra – or old faithful as I called it, was piled on top of the rest of my clothes and was sitting just to the right of him. "Do you mind if I-"

I didn't bother finishing and instead pointed to the pile. Both Shawn and Jace followed the direction of my finger and seemed at a loss for words before they panicked. The scene would have been comical had it not been for the fact that in their haste, the clothes tumbled off the counter and as Jace went to catch old faithful, the knot in his towel undid and then I was faced with far more Jace Rivers than I had been prepared for.

"Fuck!' He exclaimed while his massive hands clutched at the white material. Once he was fully covered, he turned with his arm outstretched, and I snatched the bra from his fingers before catching the rest of my clothes that Shawn tossed in my direction.

"I'm just going to go change in-"

"My room," Jace offered though had yet to make eye contact. "That's where you and Kate slept last night."

"Right, I'll be quick. Just maybe knock before you come in." Spinning on my heel, I fled back into Jace's room but not before slamming the bathroom door behind me. Leaning against the wood I caught my breath and then lifted my hand to cover the laugh that had made its way past my lips.

"So ... I think I was just flashed by Jace Rivers," I whispered before lifting the mug to my lips. Kate, who was sitting next to me at the island, had been in the process of swallowing her own coffee. But my poor timing had forced her to choke around the liquid and I watched as she spluttered roughly while I patted her back.

"Okay. One, warning next time before you just spring something like that on me. And two, what do you mean *think*?" Her pretty green eyes were wide as she searched my face, and I blushed before leaning in close.

"He was in the bathroom when I went to grab my clothes and his towel came undone." Kate lifted her brows, and I rolled my eyes. "No, before you ask, I will not tell you anything I saw. But I will need you to be a buffer - use that charm of yours and help make sure things don't get awkward when they come down." As if on cue, I could hear their heavy footfalls shuffling down the stairs and I shot one last glance at my friend before turning towards the stairs.

Considering how hungover I was and looked, I couldn't help but notice that the two were not only remarkably handsome this early in the morning, but neither seemed to be feeling half as bad as I was. Grumbling, I tipped my head back and swallowed down the rest of my coffee before moving to the sink. The house was surprisingly clean seeing as there was a massive party the night before and I glanced at the spotless counters with a frown.

"Dishwasher is on the right side of the island." Shawn offered as he rounded the island and plucked the mug from my hand. "Callum was probably up all night cleaning, he hates clutter."

"Why host parties if he hates the mess?" I wondered out loud, before glancing at Jace, but his dark eyes were bouncing around the kitchen. "You okay, Rivers? You seem a little flustered."

Kate snorted from her place at the island and then offered me a grin. I may not be willing to share any personal details, but I was sure as shit going to tease him. Shawn, who had finished arranging the dishes in their racks, closed the dishwasher with his foot and then glanced at his roommate with a smirk before clearing his throat and then moving his attention to me.

"Do you two want a ride home?" Deep blue eyes moved from my face to my friend's and then back to me and I frowned.

"Oh, that's not necessary, I found my phone we can grab -"

"That would be great," Kate smiled, jumping down from her seat all while ignoring my glare. She was up to something, and I tilted my head in confusion, watching as she pulled on her jacket. "Can you two drop me off first? I have some stuff to do with my family this morning."

Well, that was a lie. Kate was never one to willingly spend time with her younger siblings, especially at this time of the morning but she ignored my questioning stare as she gathered the rest of her things while Jace and Shawn grabbed their coats and shoes.

"What are you up to?" I asked now that our hosts were too distracted to notice my hushed whisper.

"Nothing," she shrugged, but her mouth had lifted into a sly smile. "I just figured we might as well take a free ride home."

"You two coming?" Shawn called from the front door, and I glanced down at Kate.

"Just know you aren't fooling me for a second, you're up to something."

"Whatever you say, Tatum." Grabbing at my hand, she tugged me towards the two men who were waiting in the foyer. "But just know, you will totally be thanking me someday."

"Okay, where to?" Jace asked, his fingers hovering over the screen on the dash as he waited for me to offer my address.

"I can walk." I offered. "It's really not that far from here and you guys have gone out of your way already."

"It's raining and you're hungover, it's no big deal." He was right, it wasn't a big deal and yet I was already embarrassed from the catastrophe that was last night. Kate had not offered any details, but seeing as I had spent the night in Jace River's bed, I was sure they had witnessed my drunken emotional breakdown.

"The corner of Park and Younge." I did my best to ignore Jace's shock as he glanced at me in the rear-view mirror.

Clearing his throat, Shawn glanced at his friend before moving his eyes to me from over his shoulder. "So, uh, did you have fun last night?"

"Are you serious?" My brows lifted and I noticed the way Shawn's mouth turned down and he fidgeted in his seat nervously.

"Sorry, that was a stupid question." Snorting, I nodded my head.

"Yeah, I mean I'm assuming it was pretty obvious I was not having a great night." My swollen face and bloodshot eyes would have been evidence enough, let alone the fact that it must have been really bad if they offered to let us stay the night.

"Did something happen? At the party I mean." Shaking my head, I glanced out the window, breaking eye contact with Shawn before sniffing.

"No nothing like that. Just some home stuff." The truck came to a rolling stop at a set of lights, and I pulled at the zipper of my jacket as the air around me became nearly suffocating.

"Do you want to talk about it?" Those deep blue eyes were on me again, and I sank back into my seat at the open sympathy on Shawn's face.

I didn't want to talk about it, I never did, and I certainly didn't want to divulge anything to the two men in the front seats. They were practically strangers after all and yet, it was as if a dam burst inside and then the words began pouring from me.

"I share an apartment with my older brother and his fiancé, it's far from campus but the only thing we can afford. Or was - my brother was laid off yesterday and it looks like we will have to move in with his fiancé's parents."

"Are they not good people?" Jace's eyes glanced back at me, and I noticed the way his voice had lowered.

"I've never met them but from what I've heard they're great. They must be if they're letting all three of us move in." Glancing at the window, I lifted my finger and traced the rivers of rain that clung to the glass. "But they live almost an hour away and my car is still stuck in the lot, I can't afford to fix it. So, it looks like I'll have to transfer schools anyway. Be sure to tell O'Neil that he won't have to worry about me showing him up anymore."

Jace glanced at me once more before turning his head to Shawn and they seemed to have a silent conversation just before the truck began to move once more.

"What about your parents?" Jace asked, nonchalantly as he turned the corner.

"Not in the picture." My tone was sharp, and I sighed tiredly before wiping at my face. "Sorry, I just, they-"

"Don't worry about it, you don't need to tell us anything else." Turning in his seat, Shawn leaned against the console and searched my face for a long pause. "You know, we have an empty room in the house."

"Shawn," Jace warned, but the blonde ignored him.

"I mean obviously it's not a great solution but maybe it could work for a few days until you -"

"Shawn!" Moving back into his seat, the blonde glared at his friend with a frown.

"It's fine, thank you for the offer but yeah, there's no way that would work." Glancing at the street I noticed we had pulled up to my building and I did my best not to wince at the sight. It was in a sketchy area of town, the building itself was worn down and looked nearly uninhabitable and I could only imagine what Rivers and Patrick were thinking.

"Thanks for the ride," I offered, pulling my seatbelt off but just as I was about to open the door, Jace turned to face me.

"You're welcome," His smile was weak, and I nodded my head while my face flushed. "Listen Kelly, I'm really sorry about your team and everything. It's been great skating with you these past few days, you're crazy talented." Nodding, I pulled on the handle and stepped onto the sidewalk before closing the door carefully, ignoring the way both men watched me through the window.

Reaching the door, I fished my keys out of my jacket pocket and fumbled with the cold metal lock while my eyes burned. Taking a deep breath, I wiped at tears that threatened to fall and tried to slide the silver piece into the lock once more only to turn as Jace called out for me.

"Kelly, wait!" Jace called as he jogged around the front of the truck before closing the distance between us. "Shawn is right, the room is empty and honestly, I know Callum would hate for this to be the way your feud ends. He's really hoping for more of a fight." Sniffing, I ran my nose across my sleeve awkwardly.

"I don't even know you guys, I can't live with you." It wasn't practical and it sure as hell wasn't a smart idea and yet part of me couldn't help but wonder if maybe this was the solution I had been praying for.

"How is it any different than moving into residence freshman year? No one knows their roommates then." Jace pointed out with a grin while shoving his hands into his pockets.

"Well, for one, it's a house with three guys. Two, it's owned by O'Neil and three, I can't afford rent." Running his fingers over his sharp jaw, Jace studied me closely.

"Like you said, O'Neil owns it, or his parents do and none of us pay rent. So that's not something you need to worry about. As far as living with guys, I mean we aren't perfect but O'Neil is anal as fuck so it will be clean. If anything, his nagging might be what scares you off. Otherwise, I can promise you, it's not that bad. You live with a guy now, I'm sure your brother is just as gross."

"Actually, he and his fiancé Tommy are probably the most organized couple I have ever met. I'm the slob of the family so the nagging I am used to."

"Perfect, then you'll fit right in." Pulling a hand from his coat he held it out and I glanced at it nervously before sliding my palm across his. "Welcome, roomie."

Tightening my fingers around his I shook his hand for a minute before stepping away from him. "Only if O'Neil agrees."

"Right, leave that to me, in the meantime let me grab your number and then we can sort out the details." Grabbing at his phone, I typed in my number and then prayed that this wasn't going to be a colossal mistake.

Chapter Eight

CALLUM

"Where have you two been?" I frowned as Jace and Shawn stomped in through the door. The rain had only gotten worse through the morning, and I watched as they stepped out of their soaked boots before tossing their coats on the bannister of the stairs. "That's not where those go you fuckers. You know that."

"Well good morning to you too, sunshine." Shawn rolled his eyes, completely ignoring his coat as he passed the stairs and then moved to the couch with a sigh.

"We were taking Tatum and her friend home," Jace offered, grabbing at the coats before tucking them away in the closet with a knowing smirk and then came to sit next to Shawn.

"Was she okay?" Both of their heads snapped in my direction, moving away from the TV that they had turned on and I rolled my eyes with a scoff when their gazes widened in surprise. "I'm just wondering why she couldn't manage to get home on her own."

"That's the thing." My shoulders stiffened, and I frowned at Shawn as his eyes bounced between Jace and me nervously. "We might have offered her the spare room."

"Spare room?" I asked.

"The office." Jace clarified as my mouth hung open and I stared at them, dumbfounded.

"Our office, you offered Tatum Kelly our office. To do what?!" My voice rose along with my confusion

"To live in." Shawn closed one eye with a wince while he waited for all hell to break loose, and I inhaled roughly.

"You have got to be fucking kidding me." I inhaled again, trying to remind myself that my friends were not the type to take advantage and if they offered Kelly a space to stay in, even after knowing how much I wished she would just get out of my life, then something must have happened.

"Listen man, her place - it's not good. She lives there with her brother but apparently they can't even afford it and now she's looking at transferring schools." Lifting a hand, I pinched the bridge of my nose.

"And why is that a problem? Isn't that the perfect solution? She transfers - can play on a women's team and we don't have to deal with her at practice anymore. I can have the senior year I need to have."

"Well, I mean without her, we would have a second stringer and she's good you can't argue that." Shawn was right but I didn't say anything and instead glared at him. "Listen, it doesn't have to be permanent. Let her stay here until she can figure something else out or until the season is over. With how practices are going, I bet Perry lets her play a few games." There was not a chance in hell Perry would let her play an actual game but I didn't bother saying so and instead moved to the couch, grabbing the forgotten remote from Jace before switching channels.

"Cal, I promise it won't be that bad, Tatum seems nice. She was always super cool in our class last year." Raising a brow, I glanced at Shawn with a lifted brow.

"Right, and your opinion has nothing to do with your obvious thing for her." Shawn's face flushed and I rolled my eyes as Jace snorted in amusement. "What are you snickering at? Don't pretend you haven't been staring at her ass on the ice. Not to mention the sad, pathetic expression on your face when you played hero last night."

Jace's face turned blank and Shawn shot him a look as the two of them pouted silently.

"She can't be one of your *things,* okay? You know I support you no matter who you fuck but Tatum Kelly is off limits. I can't live with her *and* have the three of you hooking up. This is my last year and that drama will sure as shit ruin this season."

"So ... she can move in?" Shawn asked, his face lifting in a half-hearted grin and I fought the urge to smack him upside his head.

"Fine, but I'm serious guys. You are on thin ice." Lifting a hand, Shawn reached out to shake on it and I rolled my eyes at his excitement.

"Good thing we know how to skate." Slapping his hand away, I glared at the pair.

"God you are so lame."

"Hey," Tatum called, making her way off the ice and towards me as I reached the locker room. Practice had gone off without a hitch, though once again Kelly proved just how good she was, and I hated how well she fit in with our team. Perry had even eased up on her, much to my surprise, and I prayed that his scouting would pay off sooner rather than later. We needed a replacement for Stevens before the season really started.

"What do you want Kelly?" Her light grey eyes shifted away from my face as she wrung her hands nervously.

"Shawn said he spoke to you?" Her voice cracked and I watched as her cheeks flushed.

Tatum Kelly was *uncomfortable* and my lips lifted in a smirk. I had never seen her quite like this and I was going to soak up every minute of it. Leaning against the cool cement wall, I crossed my arms over my chest and looked down at her. Shawn was a bit shorter than her, Jace was about the same height, but I had a solid four inches on Kelly, and I waited for her to lift her chin just slightly before I shot her my smoothest smile.

"He talks to me a lot, being my roommate and all." Kelly dropped her eyes to our skates, and I waited for a minute before taking pity on her. "Yes, they talked to me. We took separate cars; they can swing by and grab your stuff if you want."

Her head snapped back up and I rolled my eyes at the surprised expression that filled her face. Glancing over her shoulder, I noticed Shawn hovering and I motioned for him with two fingers before looking back down at Kelly. "Kelly's ready to move in today. Right?"

Turning to the blonde, she nodded her head hesitantly and I watched as Shawn smiled. God, he had it bad.

"Okay, cool. We can grab some stuff today if you want? Your brother was okay with you living with us, right?" Scoffing Kelly crossed her arms and then glared at Shawn.

"I didn't have to ask permission, he trusts my judgement and I promised him that if anything made me feel the least bit uncomfortable, I would kick your asses and *then* call him." Moving her attention between the two of us, she frowned and then tipped her chin to the floor. "I'll meet you here when I'm done changing."

Shawn's blue eyes followed her as she strode down the hallway and I exhaled before slapping at his helmet. "Get your shit together Patrick and remember my one rule."

"God O'Neil you are such a tight ass, get your panties out of that twist." Brushing passed me, he moved into the locker room, and I sighed as Jace approached, obviously watching the entire scene before deciding to make an appearance.

"Ease up Cal, you know it's not that serious," he offered with a shrug, but I shook my head.

"He's been off since the start of the year, the last thing he needs is getting played by Tatum Kelly."

"You think she would do that?" His brows pinched while his dark eyes searched my face.

"I don't know her well enough to say, but I know him. He's soft and if he isn't careful, he will find himself wrapped around some girl's finger. He needs to man up."

"Wow, that was fucking harsh. I wonder what you say about me?" Before I could say anything else, Jace also pushed past me, making sure our shoulders made contact as he entered the locker room and I sighed, wondering if I should have just kept my mouth shut.

Shaking out my damp hair, I hoisted my bag higher up my shoulder and frowned when I noticed that Jace's black truck was still idling in the parking lot. I had lingered in the shower, easily taking twice as long as usual, praying that they would take the subtle hint that I wanted no part of this whole situation, but they had obviously turned a blind eye to it.

"Hey!" Shawn yelled once his window slid down and I glared at him before approaching. "Took you long enough! What were you doing, jacking off?" I could hear Tatum's groan of disgust and I smirked.

"Yup and picturing Jace's mom the whole time."

"What the fuck man!" Rivers growled, moving forward so I could see him past Shawn and I grinned. "You're such a prick, O'Neil."

"Okay children, enough," Shawn sighed with a roll of his eyes and then glanced at the backseat before shaking his head. "Don't worry Kelly, he'll agree to help."

Turning to face me once more, Shawn's eyes studied mine and then he lifted a brow. "Right O'Neil? It can be your way of making it up to Kelly for knocking her over that day, I don't think you've really apologized for that."

"She ran into me, and she's fine." I grumbled under my breath, but Shawn waved it off with a flick of his hand, as if it wasn't an important detail.

"Fine, I'll follow behind with my truck. But this is in no way my idea and I'm already letting her stay with us for the time being so that means I'm just driving from one place to the other. Don't expect me to lift shit all." Grinning triumphantly, Shawn nodded and then closed his window and I glared at the tinted glass for a pause before unlocking my own truck and sliding into it.

While driving through the city the sky began to darken with heavy rain clouds that were typical for Vancouver and the overcast only seemed to enhance the run-down buildings that lined the streets, and it made me frown. This part of town wasn't particularly safe or ideal for a student to live in and I wondered how Kelly had ended up here.

Moving to the side of the road, Jace pulled up to the curb and I slid in behind before ducking to glance at the building we had parked in front of. The bricks looked worn and chipped and there were bars along the windows and door, though the black metal on the entrance had been spray painted a bright blue and I winced when I realized a long dark alley lined the side of the apartment, just a few feet away from the door.

Stepping out of my truck and locking it, I then moved to Kelly's door before pulling it open and I waited for her to step out before ushering her onto the sidewalk that was dimly lit by the streetlight. The fall nights had even less sunlight than normal and I frowned when I realized evening practices would force her to come home long after the sun had set.

"This is it?" I asked, while tipping my head up to glance at the old concrete and she sighed before pulling her jacket tighter around her.

"Yup, home sweet home." Weaving past the three of us, Kelly moved to the door and twisted the key into it, and I flinched at the deep smell of smoke that wafted from the foyer when she opened the door before stepping in behind her.

The walls and carpet of the entry were a dingy yellow and I wondered if they had always been that colour or if they had once been white. After scanning the narrow stairway, I glanced down at Kelly.

"Luckily we live on this floor." She whispered when she noticed where my attention had landed. "The elevator is sketchy, and the stairs can be slippery as hell."

"Well, this will be easy then, I bet we can get you moved out in one trip." Shawn grinned and stepped out of the way as Tatum moved towards the hallway. Closing in behind her, we followed and then she stopped at a door before turning to us.

"Listen, my brother isn't super sold on this whole thing yet, he's really worried I'm making a poor choice by moving in with three guys, so if he comes home early, please,

please be on your best behaviour or whatever. I don't want to cause him any more stress, okay?" All three of us nodded and she sighed before opening the door.

The apartment was nothing like what I was expecting, and I took in the bright atmosphere slowly. Where the walls outside had been grimy and cold, the room we stood in now felt warm and welcoming. There were piles of house plants gathered around the window in the little living room and the tables and shelves had little knickknacks and pictures of Kelly from all ages scattered across them. The kitchen, though tiny, seemed to be well cared for and there was a pleasant smell of something in the air.

"My room is just in here." She pointed to the first door on the left and then pressed the wood open.

Just like the last space, her room was bright, the walls painted in a light green, and I scanned the area carefully. There was a bed pressed against the far side, though it seemed way too small to hold her 6'2 frame and there was an old looking dresser tucked in the corner but other than a photo or two and a couple of books, that was it.

"This is everything?" Jace asked, glancing around the room with concern and Kelly tucked her hair behind her ears before nodding.

"This is it."

"This is everything you own?" Jace questioned again, obviously thinking she had misunderstood what he meant but Kelly just blushed before clearing her throat.

"Yeah, everything I have is right here." The air around us seemed to still in the silence and I shifted uncomfortably before glancing at my friends.

"Well, if this is it, it looks like you guys won't need me after all," I shrugged. Ignoring the way Jace and Shawn glared at me, I grabbed my keys from my pocket. "I'm going to head to Derrick's for a while. See you three at home." Not bothering to wait around for them to call me out for bailing, I moved to the door and hurried out of the apartment before exiting down the hall, all while wondering why I felt a wave of guilt and this desperate need to run.

Chapter Nine

TATUM

"Is he okay?" I asked, still looking towards the door and Shawn sighed before moving to my dresser.

"Just being a douche, don't worry about it, Kelly." He reassured me and then turned to Jace who was still glancing around my room with confusion.

"So, I really just need the clothes from my dresser and my mattress, I guess. It's new but the bed frame isn't and so I can just put it on the floor."

"We are not going to let you sleep on a mattress on the floor Kelly." Shawn argued.

"This is just a 'for-now' type situation, there's no point lugging the frame there since I'll be moving out by the end of the season, if not sooner."

"We can bring this with us or we can get you a new one, either way is fine with me but you are absolutely not sleeping on the floor of the office." Shawn's normally bright blue eyes had hardened, and I could see this was a battle I wouldn't win. Lifting my hands in surrender, I turned for the door

"Fine you guys try and take it apart while I grab some garbage bags for my clothes."

Leaving them to it, I swiftly moved through the small space of the apartment and began searching for the box of black plastic bags when I heard a key slide into the lock and peered my head out of the kitchen as my brother stepped through the entrance.

"Hey!" I greeted warmly but Chris's face didn't lift into a smile, and he instead glanced at my room with concern before taking off his coat.

"Who is parked outside?" He asked and I swallowed nervously.

"That's Jace's truck, he and Shawn are here to help me move." I kept my voice light and nonchalant, but my brother only seemed more worried.

"Already? I thought you were going to take a few more days to think about it."

Sighing, I ran my fingers through my hair. “You said we had to be out of here by the first, that’s coming up fast.”

“I know, but we still have some time to make a plan for you, Tatum.”

“Chris, we’ve been over this so many times. I can’t afford somewhere else on my own; I haven’t found a sublet and probably won’t since the school year has started and moving with you and Tommy won’t work if I plan on staying at North Pacific. Especially since my car was a write off.”

“Tatum -” he started but I shook my head, not wanting to hear it and then grabbed a few bags.

“This is the best solution for right now, can you please just trust me?” Chris searched my face for a second and then his shoulders slumped.

“Fine, but I want to meet them before I agree to anything.” Scoffing, I fisted the plastic in my hands and then rested them on my hips.

“I don’t need you to agree.”

Pinching at the bridge of his nose, he grumbled. “Tatum, just humor me, please.”

“Fine, let me go grab them.” Leaving my brother in the kitchen, I crossed the small space and ducked my head into my room. The two of them were kneeling on the floor, both trying to figure out how to disassemble my bed frame. I cleared my throat.

“Hey, Chris just got home and he would like to meet you,” I informed them and then dropped my voice into a whisper to remind them of my previous warning. “Best behaviour, please.”

Pulling themselves to their feet, Jace smoothed his shirt out and Shawn dusted his hands on his thighs before grinning. “We’ll be so charming he won’t know what hit him.”

Not bothering to acknowledge that, I spun on my heel and led them to the kitchen. “Chris, this is Shawn Patrick and Jace Rivers.”

“Nice to meet you,” Jace smiled, showing off those dimples and then he held out his hand for my brother. Hesitating, Chris glanced at the offered palm and then shook it quickly before doing the same with Shawn.

“I thought there were three of you.” Jace and Shawn looked at each other and I stepped in.

“Callum had something else to do and we don’t really need another set of hands,” I offered and then passed the bags to Jace. “Anyway, we really should get to it.”

"Why don't we pause on the moving and have some coffee or tea first?" Chris suggested, though I knew it wasn't a question and I glared at my brother before opening my mouth to protest but Shawn pressed his palm against my back and grinned. "That would be amazing, thank you so much."

Leading us to the small dinner table, Chris then turned to the kettle and got everything organized and I fell into my seat, watching as the guys followed me. Shawn and Jace seemed at ease as Chris puttered around and I wiped my hands over my thighs nervously while my knee bounced.

"Hey," Shawn said while he grabbed at my knee under the table, his fingers cupping the joint with gentle pressure until it stopped moving and then he smiled. "Relax."

"I won't bother with the whole interrogation tactic," Chis started, though his back was turned to us still. "I'm deciding to trust Tatum on this whole thing."

Spinning on his heel, Chris moved to sit in the empty seat and then smiled at me fondly. "She doesn't need looking after and would kill me if I said otherwise, but I do need some guarantees that she will be safe."

"She will." It was Jace who spoke, and I glanced at him from the corner of my eye. "We can promise you that."

"Good." Chris nodded just before the kettle began to scream and then he stood. "Okay tea or coffee?"

Pulling my hood over my head, I squinted as the cold drizzle soaked through my hood and watched as the guys lifted the metal frame onto the bed of the truck before piling my tarp covered mattress over it. After making sure that it would stay dry under the thick plastic, Shawn jumped down and then glanced at me with a smile and I could have swooned at the way his wet hair draped over his forehead messily, which only seemed to brighten his blue eyes.

"That's everything." His smile only widened and I blinked at him stupidly for a pause, only moving my attention when my brother cleared his throat.

"Are you sure you want to do this?" He asked and I raised a brow.

"A little late to be asking that considering everything is loaded up." Wrapping a slender arm around my shoulders, Chris tugged my forward and I laughed softly when he rose on his toes in order to fit my head under his chin. "You know I've been taller than you since my fifteenth birthday, right?"

"Doesn't matter, I'm still your big brother." He reminded me and I patted his back gently before pulling away. "Promise me you'll call me when you're settled, and you'll text me every day."

"I'm moving like ten minutes away Chris, not moving across the country." I scoffed, but Jace stepped forward to shake my brother's hand.

"I'll make sure she does that." Flashing those dimples, Jace smiled down at Chris and I was shocked to see him return the gesture, sincerely.

"She's a handful you know," he teased, throwing a wink my way.

"Good, we could use that in our house." Jace's dark eyes caught mine and I blushed hotly.

"She also leaves her clothes in the dryer for days, never cleans her hair out of the drain and you'll find these weird little swirls of it all over the shower wall. She sheds more than a dog, I swear." Gasping, I stared at my brother with betrayal.

"They're decent guys, I figured I ought to warn them," Chris shrugged and I noticed the way Shawn seemed to delight at my brother's obvious approval.

"You decided that after like two hours?" I asked, skeptically.

"They had manners, they washed the dishes and made sure to do all the heavy lifting." He smiled but then his eyes darted to the two. "However, you should know that as much as you can be a pain, you're everything to me. So if I hear about them giving you any shit-"

"Okay, okay tough guy," I snorted, before wrapping him in another hug, effectively stopping him from finishing whatever feeble attempt of a threat he was about to use. "Don't worry, okay? I'll text you tonight. Give Tommy my love."

Opening the truck door, Jace held it for me, and I slid into the back seat before pulling my damp hood down and then I glanced out the dark glass, watching as the guys talked to my brother quietly. His face was set in a stern frown but both Patrick and Rivers seemed genuine as they listened to what was probably a ridiculous fatherly speech, especially considering the fact both outweighed Chris by forty pounds. Seeming to agree to his terms, they shook his hand once more and then entered the cab of the truck.

"Ready, Kelly?" Shawn turned to me, and I moved my eyes between him and Jace questioningly.

"What was that about?" I demanded, but they just waved at Chris while the truck pulled into traffic, and I crossed my arms and then glared at the dark gaze in the rear-view mirror. "What did he say?"

"Kelly, it's no big deal, he made sure that we understood how important you are and if anything went wrong, we would have to answer to him."

"I'm sorry, I don't know why he got like that. I'm surprised you were able to keep a straight face." Neither of them said anything for a minute and then Shawn leaned on the middle console and faced me.

"We took his words seriously, not because we're afraid of him or anything but because it's obvious how much he loves you and we both respect him and you. We wanted to reassure him that he had nothing to worry about."

"Oh," I sank back into my seat. "Well thank you, it would have been far harder to do this if he had really fought me on it."

"No worries, Kelly. Now ... I don't know about you guys but I'm starving. Any suggestions?" Jace asked and I chewed at my lower lip thoughtfully for a second.

"I could cook to thank you both for helping me today." I offered.

"Really?" Shawn asked eagerly and I nodded.

"Yeah, we'd have to stop at the store, but I need to shop anyway." Tucking my hair behind my ears I leant forward so that I wasn't quite so far away. "What is the food situation anyway? Do we write our names on our stuff or have our own shelves?"

Snorting Jace shook his head. "No, Kelly. we don't really keep track of that kind of stuff. We shop when we need to, buy what we want and if you finish it, you replace it. That's it."

"What if some of us have a different budget?" I wondered. "I can't afford to be feeding three guys."

"I'll tell you what – buy your stuff and put your name on it and we promise we won't touch it. Right, Patrick?" The blonde nodded his agreement and I sighed in relief.

"Okay now that that's settled, what should we make tonight. Are you guys picky?"

Laughing out loud, Jace shook his head and then caught my eyes in the mirror once more. "Kelly, we are three guys in our young twenties, we eat anything and everything."

"He's right, both of us *love* to eat." Patrick agreed, tossing a wink at me and I flushed at the innuendo, while ignoring the sudden heat in my belly.

The bright florescent lights of the store were harsh as we walked through the aisles, and I watched in amusement as the guys wandered around aimlessly. It was like they had never been grocery shopping before and I smiled as Shawn scanned the produce with a frown.

"Does it always take you guys this long to shop?" I laughed while glancing at my phone.

"What do you mean?" Jace wondered while picking a basket of mushy strawberries and I shook my head. Snatching the plastic from his hands, I lifted a different batch, checking the berries at the bottom before putting it in the cart.

"We dropped my stuff off *and* unpacked it within an hour, no problem. But we got here thirty minutes ago and have barely made it through two aisles." Stuffing his hands into his pocket Jace smiled sheepishly and then glanced at his friend.

"Callum is usually the one to shop." He shrugged and then picked up a bushel of apples. "I don't know if you noticed but he's a little bit of a control freak and he hates that we have to look at everything when we go with him."

"Ah," I nodded." That kind of makes sense, he's one of those people."

"One of what people?" Shawn asked, turning from the lettuce he had been studying.

"There's two types of people in the world: those who hate grocery shopping and those who love it." I explained. "O'Neil seems like the type to be the former but luckily for you, I'm the latter." Grabbing onto the cart, I weaved through the produce and waved the guys along.

The entire run to the store took just over an hour and I watched as both men looped bag after bag over their fingers and arms, determined to make it to the house in one trip rather than two. Noticing three left on the seat, I stepped forward to grab them but stopped when Shawn called out from behind me.

"Don't you dare! Those are mine!" Shimmying forward, he reached to grab the plastic handles and I stood back, watching him struggle before sighing.

"I could just grab them," I offered but he shook his head with narrowed eyes.

"If you do that then Rivers has more than me and he wins."

"Wins what? I didn't realize this was a competition," gaping at me, he stepped back in shock, and I rolled my eyes at his dramatics.

"We are men, that means everything is a competition." He winked and then jogged up the front steps of the house and I shook my head before following along behind them.

Chapter Ten

CALLUM

"That's not how you do it!" Kelly's voice rang out through the house as I closed the front door behind me while listening to her laugh. "Jace, get this kid out of here before he ruins dinner and burns down the house!"

The three of them were piled around the stove, though Jace and Shawn were peering over her shoulder, and I wondered how they had managed to click so easily in such a short time. I had avoided the house all evening, making sure I wouldn't be stuck moving her crap into the office. But now, I could see that had been a mistake, no one was here to keep a careful eye on my two idiot friends.

"What is that smell?" I asked, wrinkling my nose as if the smell of garlic and whatever else was cooking didn't make my mouth water.

"Pasta and garlic bread," Jace smirked, daring me to complain about my favourite meal and I narrowed my eyes at him. Of course, they would try and get her on my good side.

"Yeah, I ate already," I shrugged, ignoring the dirty looks from my friends as I sat on the couch.

"I can save you some for later if you'd like?" Tatum offered, and I glanced at her, watching as her grey eyes hardened like she was waiting for me to push it further.

"Thanks." Was all I could think to say, suddenly at a loss for words and she turned back to the stove, shoving Jace away playfully. The room settled into a comfortable silence, though Jace and Shawn sat at the island rather than on the couch and I cleared my throat at the growing tension.

"The team wants to watch the game here tomorrow," I called, keeping my eyes trained on the tv.

"Whose idea was that?" Shawn asked, though his attention had remained on Kelly.

"Summers, I guess he wants to get away from that blonde. She's a total smoke show but she's obsessed and won't take the hint. He seems to have bad luck with the girls man. His ex sounded like a real piece of work too, totally insane and clingy. It took her months to stop contacting him, he had to ghost her."

"Fuck!" Kelly's voice rang out and I turned, watching as she clutched her hand to her chest. Jace and Shawn stood but seemed unsure on what to do and I rose quickly, crossing the room before grabbing at her wrist.

The flesh of her palm was bright pink, and I pulled at her wrist, steering her towards the sink before turning it on. Testing the water with my own fingers, I adjusted the temperature and then tugged at her gently again before guiding her hand under the stream from the tap.

Hissing at the contact, Kelly tried to pull her wrist away from my fingers, but I moved closer, bringing my other hand to her back. "Relax, let the water cool it down or it's going to hurt like a bitch tomorrow."

Making sure that she had spent enough time under the water, I turned the tap off and then lifted her palm closer to my face. The skin still looked tender, but it wasn't a bad burn and I turned to my friends. "Can you guys grab the first aid kit? There should be some ointment and non-stick bandages."

Jace moved first, striding over to the bathroom and Shawn came to the stove, carefully turning off the burners before shuffling closer.

"You okay, Tatum?" Shawn asked worriedly and she nodded before offering him a small smile.

"It's nothing, I'm just glad dinner is done." Pulling from my grip, she grabbed the first aid kit from Jace and placed it on the island.

"Are you always this clumsy in the kitchen? Should we ban you from it like we did, Shawn?" Jace laughed, watching as she bandaged her palm but she didn't grin back, instead her eyes lifted to meet my own and then she frowned.

"Only when I hear someone speak badly about my best friend."

Confused, my eyes bounced between my friends and then I looked back at Kelly. "What are you talking about?"

"Riley Summers. His ex is Kate, and she wasn't obsessed with him, she didn't become a clinger or whatever you call girls who actually have the maturity to talk about their feelings. She tried to lean on her boyfriend of four years after her dad died. She just needed him there for support and instead he ghosted her. Told her he couldn't handle the pressure and her baggage and then just walked out of her life."

"Shit," Shawn swallowed, and then glanced at me. "We had no idea."

"Yeah, well, I doubt guy talk rarely involves the whole truth. But now that you know I would appreciate you not talking about her like that. As for Summers, the guy is a dick and honestly, he doesn't deserve anyone."

"We don't have to watch the game here? Maybe we could go to Ryan's?" Jace offered but Tatum shook her head.

"No, it's fine. I don't want to be more of a burden and I really don't want the team thinking I'm being a bitch by making you change your plans." Glancing at the forgotten dinner, Tatum moved to the cupboard, grabbing dishes before piling them with pasta and then once they were set on the island, she glanced at us.

"I'm going to head to bed, do you guys mind? Today has been a lot." Jace and Shawn immediately assured her they understood and then she looked around the house awkwardly.

"Thanks for letting me move in, I really do appreciate it and I promise I am doing my best to come up with another plan." She didn't wait for us to respond and instead fled to her room and then the door closed, the sound echoing in the space while we remained frozen.

"Well, one day down and no one killed each other." Shawn whispered and I rolled my eyes. "I think that's a solid start honestly."

Squinting at the bright lights of the kitchen I took in the figure perched on the counter next to the sink and frowned. Kelly had headed to her room hours ago and had not made another appearance all evening, which I had chalked up to her pouting about the whole Summers thing. And while I probably shouldn't have said what I had in front of her, I still thought she took it far too seriously.

Stepping into the kitchen I waited for her to notice me, but she remained silent and watched her spoon stir the contents of her bowl. Moving my attention, I noticed a purple box of cereal beside her and scoffed at the image on the front. Of course, Tatum Kelly would eat that high fibre raisin shit made for seniors.

"God Kelly, what are you eighty?" Jumping at my voice, Kelly tumbled from the counter, and I shot forward, snatching at her arm before her face connected with the floor. Righting herself on her feet, she tore her arm from my grasp and then glanced at the milk that had soaked her shorts and was now dripping down her bare legs.

"What is your problem, O'Neil?" She snapped while grabbing at a handful of paper towels before cleaning up the mess. She put the dishes in the sink before pulling out her earbuds.

"I didn't realize you had those in." I motioned to the black case she had placed on the counter and then moved to the fridge before grabbing a beer.

"Well maybe next time you could give me a little warning before sneaking up on me," she argued but I just shot her a pointed glare.

"Like what, flicker the lights on and off so you know I'm coming? It's not my fault you're so oblivious to your surroundings." Kelly rolled her eyes and then moved to rinse out her dishes before loading them in the dishwasher while I nursed my beer, glancing at the bowl of fresh fruit on the dinner table.

"The guys said you took them shopping; that was brave of you." I commented and watched in annoyance as Kelly's lips curled into a soft smile.

"It was fun." She shrugged. "Though it did take twice as long as it should have."

"Of course, it did - they're easily distracted." I muttered and then lifted my eyes to hers. "That might be something you'll want to be aware of in the future."

"What is that supposed to mean?" She asked while crossing her arms over her chest and I took another sip of my drink while focusing on her grey eyes.

"I'm just warning you that their attention is fleeting. One minute they're focused on something and the next they're moving on." Tipping my head back, I pressed the glass to my lips and finished the bottle before resting it on the island. "Just keep that in mind."

Turning to exit the room I paused and then glanced at her from over my shoulder. "Have a good night, Kelly."

Chapter Eleven

TATUM

The new sounds and echoes of the house were hard to ignore through the night and I groaned, completely exhausted before rolling over, glancing at the grey carpet under my mattress before pulling myself to my feet. Black bags covered the small space of my new room and I glanced at them wearily with a sigh. This was not how I had planned my junior year to go. Opening the plastic, I searched through the mess of clothes until I found the items I needed to make a half decent outfit and then grabbed my toiletry bag before ducking out of the room.

"Hey," Shawn called from the kitchen, easily spotting me given the house's open floor plan and I smiled before offering a small wave.

"I'm just going to go shower, is that okay?"

"Of course, you don't have to ask." He laughed and then turned back to the blender on the counter.

"I thought you were banned from the kitchen?" Shifting, I ignored the coolness of the hardwood floors against my bare feet and glanced at the green smoothie.

"I'm not allowed to use the stove but I bought the blender so they can't stop me from using it." Lifting the lid, he poured some of the green slop into a glass and then crossed the space, holding the smoothie out for me to take. "I figured you might be hungry waking up so late; did you miss your first class?"

Lifting the glass, I sniffed at the liquid in suspicion and then glanced at the blonde doubtfully. "I only have an afternoon lecture today. What about you, why are you here so late?"

Tension clouded Shawn's face and I realized it was an expression I didn't recognize on him. Though he was covered in tattoos and was heavily muscled, he was the easiest going of the group and reminded me of the golden retriever we had growing up.

"I had Peter's class this morning."

"Ah, that explains the frown. I had him last year, he's tough." Shawn nodded with a shrug and then motioned to the glass in my hand. Giving in, I placed the cool rim against my lips and then took the smallest sip possible.

"Oh God!" Wrinkling my nose, I moved the glass away from me and pushed it against Shawn's chest. "Why would you do that to me?"

Moving his fingers to cover my own, Shawn looked down at the smoothie and then plucked the glass from my hands before taking his own sip.

"It's not that bad!" He laughed and I narrowed my eyes at him.

"Why does it taste like you combined cookies and cream powder with celery juice?" A pink blush covered his cheeks and his eyes dropped to the floor.

"You didn't?! How could you think those two would mix?" Taking back the smoothie, I moved to the kitchen, ignoring the way that the hem of my shirt barely covered the tiny sleep shorts I had on and then dumped the rest down the drain.

Spinning back towards Shawn, I noticed his blue eyes had been focused on the flesh of my legs and I swallowed roughly as warmth filled my belly. Shawn was hot on a normal day but that focused look and clenched jaw did all kinds of things to me and I wondered what other expressions I could coax from him if given the chance.

As if he could hear my thoughts, his lips parted and then his eyes were on mine and I could have sworn everything froze. That is until the front door opened as Jace made his way into the house and just like that everything snapped back into focus.

"I'm going to go shower, please don't drink any more of that crap, it might make you sick." Brushing past Jace, I moved through the kitchen and into the bathroom that was tucked behind.

Grasping at the faucet, I turned on the shower before tugging my shirt over my head and then I took a moment to catch my breath. It had been a while since I felt heat like that, especially from just a simple look. Leaning against the door, I closed my eyes and tried to convince myself that the longing I felt was because of the dry spell I was currently in and not because I wanted to fuck Shawn Patrick.

There was absolutely no way I could not sleep with Shawn Patrick, and I certainly could not even *want* to sleep with Shawn Patrick.

"Crap, crap, crap." Thudding the back of my head against the door, I groaned at my stupidity and was about to shimmy out of my shorts when I heard the low mumble of voices.

"What was that?" Jace asked, his voice low but heated and I pressed my ear against the wood carefully before holding my breath.

"I offered her a smoothie, relax Jace."

"I saw the way you were staring at her; you need to learn to be more discreet or Callum is going to kick your ass."

"Callum is not my ruler, and neither are you. Relax, nothing happened and nothing will happen. I heard O'Neil loud and clear."

Moving my face away from the door, I glared at the white painted wood. I knew Callum O'Neil disliked me but that was not the only reason he would have an issue with me hooking up with Shawn and I couldn't disagree with his logic. Sleeping with a teammate who happened to share a living space with me seemed like a horrible idea. Especially considering I was still trying to prove myself on the ice and without them I would have no place to stay. Everything was riding on me keeping the peace and I could not let my horniness ruin that.

Moving my eyes across the steam filled room I glanced at the shining silver shower head that hung on the tiles of the wall and then stepped into the tub. "Well, desperate times I guess."

The house was empty by the time I had stepped back out of the bathroom, and I sighed in relief before hurrying to my room. Kate would be here any minute and I rushed to gather my books and laptop before racing to the door. As always, she was right on time and I locked the front door before hurrying down the steps. Grabbing for the door, I pulled it open and then slid into the passenger seat of her Sedan.

"How was your first night?" Leave it to Kate to be so direct and I rolled my eyes as she began the drive to campus.

"It was fine, I had an early night, only Shawn was home when I got up." Her green eyes narrowed at me worriedly.

"You went to bed early and slept past noon? That's not like you." Patting her shoulder, I smiled.

"I went to bed but it took me ages to fall asleep. Then Shawn tried to poison me with a protein shake."

"Poison you?" Her eyes widened in shock. "I for sure thought he was the one who wanted to sleep with you out of the three of them."

"Kate!" Swatting at her, I frowned. "That is so not going to happen. It can't happen."

"Even though you want to?" One brow lifted as if she was daring me to argue and I sank deeper into my seat with a frown.

"I barely know him and I'm already walking a thin line with Perry. I don't think he'll let me play a single game this year and he will most definitely bench me if he finds out I'm messing around with one of his starters."

"But you want to, you want to mess around with Shawn." Groaning, I tilted my head against the headrest, the same way I had in the bathroom and then glanced at my friend from the corner of my eye.

"Yes, okay? Yes, I do. He's so hot and it's been so long, and I bet he's great in bed. Have you heard anything about him hooking up with anyone?" Kate sank her teeth into her lower lip, and I watched for a minute before my brows pinched. Something was going on inside that head of hers and the longer we sat in silence the more I worried.

"Okay Kate, what is it, what have you heard?"

"Listen, let me be clear. I can't say if anything I heard is actually true, but Vanessa mentioned that Shawn has a little bit of a preference."

"Preference?" I echoed, "I mean don't we all have preferences? Let me guess, he's into role play or has a fascination with road head?"

Shaking her head, Kate sighed. "More like threesomes."

"Ah, how typical," I joked, though I was not at all surprised.

"Threesomes," She hesitated, clearing her throat. "With Rivers."

"As in they happen to sleep with the same woman occasionally? Or are they sharing women often?"

"As in, they not only enjoy sharing their partners, but word is that they also enjoy each other's company during their nights together."

"Oh," was all I could think to say. The University's male athletes hooking up with more than one woman at once was almost a standard and I had heard of a few stories in which there was only one girl and two teammates. But the idea that Rivers and Patrick did this often enough for there to be gossip about it was not what I had been expecting. Though oddly enough I couldn't say I was surprised. The two of them seemed extremely close, and although I hadn't spent much time in their presence, I could see how much they cared for one another.

"So? Thoughts?" Kate wondered.

"Honestly, I would hate for that to spread across campus if it's not true. But more so if it is and they are wanting to keep that aspect of their life private."

"Okay fine, so between you and me, *if* the opportunity presented itself," she grinned and wiggled her brows at me. "Would you?"

"Kate! I am not answering that!"

Laughing, she pulled into the parking lot and then turned off the car.

"Oh - you so would!" Blushing hotly, I refused to meet her eyes and ducked out of the Sedan, all while ignoring the way my skin suddenly felt scorching.

She was right, I *so* would.

Chapter Twelve

JACE

"Don't you have another class today?" I asked, while rinsing out the thick green nastiness from the blender. The smell alone made me gag and I wondered how Shawn had thought it would be a good idea to offer a cup to Tatum Kelly. He honestly had zero game and it was crazy how someone so good looking could be so shitty at picking up girls.

"I'm not going." Shawn snapped, and I watched as he turned on the Xbox with a frown.

"Is that really a smart idea?" Shawn was not one to skip out on his classes and his anger lately had me worried something else was going on.

"Who are you, my father? Callum is enough. I don't need both of you pissing me off with your rules and opinions." Turning off the tap, I wiped my hands across my thighs and then moved to the couch.

"Okay, enough of your crap, Patrick. What is going on with you?" His blue eyes narrowed while he crossed his arms over his chest. But I wasn't backing down. "Talk to me, I'm right here wanting to help you and you can't even tell me what has been up your ass these last few weeks."

He wanted to fight me on it, I could tell but instead he took in a deep breath and then his shoulders crumpled and I shifted closer, bumping my shoulder with his.

"Remember a few practices ago when Perry pulled me aside?"

Nodding, I waited patiently as he rubbed at his face roughly and then he sank into the leather of the couch. "Well, I guess Peters emailed Coach and told him I was on the verge of failing his class. If that happens, I can say goodbye to my scholarship."

"Fuck."

Leaning back, I rested my head against the couch and then turned my chin, watching as Shawn sighed tiredly. "You still have time though, surely we can find a way to scrape by?"

"Perry suggested a tutor." That was the most obvious answer of course, but Shawn and I had completely different majors and I didn't know anyone who had taken a class with Peters though I had heard how tough he was as a prof.

"Okay, well I'm sure there would be a lineup of people wanting to help out Shawn Patrick." I winked with a grin but his frown deepened.

"Tatum said she had taken his class last year."

"That is the worst possible idea you have ever had." I groaned, pressing my fists into my eyes. "You can barely function around her; how will you manage to actually focus on anything other than trying to get her to sleep with you?"

"Us you mean."

My head shot forward, and I turned to face him with a raised brow. "Hold on, I thought you were actually into her."

His face turned pink and he dropped his eyes to his lap shyly. "I am into her, like really into her. I have been since last year. But I didn't plan on hooking up with her on my own, you know that's not what I prefer, and I want *us* Jace, I always do."

"Shawn, if you really like her, I think you should just try and maybe take it one step at a time. She might not even be interested in *that* - in me."

"What if she was though? Would you say no?"

I would absolutely not say no. I knew that the minute he brought it up, and even now I was picturing the three of us. Tatum Kelly was exactly what we preferred. She was strong enough to give Shawn what he needed but seemed like she would be open to my... *authority*. Biting at my bottom lip, I imagined Shawn sprawled across my bed, his blue eyes soft while he begged Kelly so sweetly and I would watch as she made him work for it before making her repeat the same pleas to *me*.

"You would, wouldn't you? You do see how good it could be, don't you?" Pulling at my collar I swallowed roughly.

"Callum would kill us." It was a weak protest but was the only thing that I could come up with. "This is his senior year and he's already livid that she's been practicing with us. He worried this whole thing will fuck up his final season and honestly, I can't believe he let her move in here. We are already pushing our luck, Shawn."

"You don't think he would get over it?"

Blue eyes blinked up at me hopefully, but I couldn't lie.

"Think this through. If we do end up hooking up, would you want it to be a one-time thing?"

Shawn shook his head.

"Exactly, and then what if it ends badly? We would be risking the team, our house and our friendship. Kelly might end up having to transfer schools and our season might not be able to recover. We would fuck ourselves over. Big time."

"Right," Shawn's gaze had dropped to his arms, and I watched as a pointer finger traced some of the colourful designs of his tattoos.

"Let's just focus on finding you some help with your class, keeping the peace here, and getting through the season."

Nodding, Shawn turned to the TV and then tossed me a controller. "Right, you're right."

I was glad he agreed but I couldn't help but feel like this was not the end of this conversation.

"Hey," I said while I turned from the microwave and glanced at Kelly. She dropped her bag on the island and offered a smile before she checked out the frozen dinner that was currently being heated. Rounding the countertop Kelly came to stand next to me with a wrinkled nose and then she rose on her toes, examining the package that was currently spinning on the turntable.

"What is that?"

Rolling my eyes, I leaned away from her and grabbed at the box I had left in the sink.

"Starving Man's roast beef."

Tossing the flimsy cardboard in her direction I stopped the microwave and grabbed at the plastic bowl.

"Is the meat supposed to be grey like that?" She moved a finger to poke at the plastic that covered the meal, and I swatted her hand away.

"Get your own," I grumbled, peeling the clear cover away before swallowing. It didn't smell great, but it was something and today was our only evening without practice. I just wanted to eat and crash without Kelly being in my space.

"Sorry, I just don't think it's a great idea to eat that. I could make you something."

Her grey eyes raised to meet mine and I took in her face. Shawn acted as if she was God's gift to mankind, like she was the hottest thing he had ever seen and to be honest at first, I didn't understand the appeal.

She was taller than most of the team, though was about the same height as me and she had long limbs, but they were thick with muscle. She lacked the curves I usually sought out but there was something about her face. It was what caught my attention most often. She was pale, that is when her cheeks weren't pink and blotchy, and her nose was a little crooked. She had an obvious bump from a previous break, but it only seemed to flatter the rest of her features. Her mouth was full, and I had often wondered what it would look like parted. That is when I wasn't too busy staring at her eyes. The light grey irises were framed by long brown lashes, and I could swear they could make anyone bend to her every demand.

"What?" She asked, her voice filled with confusion, and I realized I had closed the space between us. It would be so easy to dip my chin, to press my mouth to hers while my fingers curled into that thick mass of hair. Would she tip her head back for me? Maybe she'd push against me, using me the way she liked.

Then I'd move my fingers and press my palm under her jaw, wrapping my fingers around her throat carefully. Would she gasp or would she blink up at me before rocking her hips into my own?

"Jace?" She hadn't moved but her tone had lowered, and I inhaled as she tilted her head. One of her hands lifted, sliding up the front of me until it rested against my chest and then her other clutched at my bicep and I couldn't help but flex the muscle under her fingers. "Show off."

My laugh rumbled in my chest, and I watched as her lips lifted in response before she tilted forward and I realized that I was about to kiss Tatum Kelly, Callum and his rules be damned.

"Looks like your food is getting cold," Shawn called softly, but the interruption startled both of us and we jumped apart. The skin of her neck and face had grown pink and blotchy and she focused her attention on her feet while I glanced at my best friend.

"I didn't think you were home," I offered lamely and his blue eyes narrowed at me.

"Clearly."

Lifting his arm, he tossed a box of pizza onto the island and then stuffed his hands into his pockets roughly. "I figured I'd grab us some pizza for dinner before the guys get here, but I can see that you have that handled."

Something in my chest pulled and I glanced at Tatum quickly. I had fucked up, I knew that. I had warned Shawn off Tatum just this morning and now he caught me nearly making out with her in our kitchen. I was a hypocrite and I watched as he turned on his heel before storming up the stairs.

"I should go study," Tatum whispered and then she too ran from the kitchen. Picking my battles, I grabbed two beers from the fridge and then made my way to the stairs. I could hear the music playing in Shawn's room and I winced at the angry beat. This was his pregame playlist which he only listened to when prepping for a game or when he was pissed off and I knew I was in for an ass chewing.

"Shawn?" I called, rapping my knuckles against his door. When he didn't answer I turned the knob and opened the door.

Shawn was laying across his bed, with his knees bent and he didn't bother glancing at me as I closed the distance. Sinking onto the edge of the mattress, I passed him a beer and waited for the sound of the top twisting before I tried apologizing.

"Look man, I messed up." Glancing up at him, I hesitated while he took a long sip and then I tried again. "I won't lie and say it's not what it looked like, because it was. If you hadn't walked in, I am sure I would have kissed her. But I shouldn't have, and I won't try again, I promise."

"Why not?" He asked, his eyes focused on the paper label as his fingers began to peel it.

"Huh?" I frowned.

"Why wouldn't you try again? I mean if she was open to it?"

Moving, I sat beside him and pressed my back against the headboard before taking a long swig. "Because I shouldn't for all the same reasons I gave you, and I really don't want anything to come between us."

"I'd like her to *come* between us." Rolling my eyes at his joke I sipped my beer once more, though my mind was no longer focused. Sitting in silence, we nursed our beers and then Shawn changed the playlist, changing it to a much more relaxed song and I sighed.

"It's going to suck living with her, isn't it?" Shawn laughed quietly and his eyes met mine.

"We are already struggling, and it's been one day, so yeah, it's going to suck." He agreed with a shrug.

"I was worried you'd say that." Leaning forward, Shawn clicked his beer to mine and grinned.

"Here's to suffering together."

The team had shuffled into the house, with beer and food in hand and I sank into the couch before casting a glance at Kelly's room. Her door had been closed all evening but there was a light on and I would occasionally see a shadow move but she had not bothered to come out when the guys showed up.

"So, how's that whole thing going?" Derrick asked, as he nodded his head towards the room I had been staring at and O'Neil scoffed as he grabbed a bottle off the table.

"Can we not talk about that right now?" He asked and I frowned at him but remained quiet.

"She cooks," Shawn answered. "And honestly she's pretty cool."

"I forgot you had a thing for her," Summers laughed with a shake of his head. "You used to stare at her last year in Robert's class. I'm surprised you didn't try anything then, I bet she would have been more than willing."

Shawn's blue eyes narrowed at Summers and then he pressed back into the couch. "Shut up, asshole."

The rest of the guys turned to look at each other and there was a scattering of murmurs, but Summers smirked and then he opened his arms to rest along the back of the sectional, cockily. "Easy Patrick, I'm just saying. Besides it would be easy for you now, close quarters, late nights after practices, I give it a week tops before she's opening her legs for you."

Shawn stood with his fingers clenched into fists and I grabbed at the back of his shirt before pulling him back down. Summers was a prick who fed off people's reactions and Shawn was giving him exactly what he was looking for.

"Relax, Shawn," I whispered once he was seated next to me once more. "Just ignore him."

"Oh c'mon Rivers, you can't tell me I'm wrong. You forget that I've known her longer than you and I can promise that just because she plays like a dude doesn't mean she doesn't want one of us to rise to the challenge and fuck her. And trust me, girls like her are always so grateful for the attention, they're willing to do anything."

Shawn's spine stiffened and I didn't have the will or the want to stop him this time. However, it wasn't Patrick who had moved for Summers, it was Callum. Our captain had risen to his feet, dumping the bowl of chips across the floor in the process and then he wrapped the fabric of Summers's hoodie in his fingers before pulling him from the couch.

"You went too far that time, and I won't just laugh it off." Pulling him to his feet, Callum steered him around the coffee table and then shoved him away. "So - I suggest you shut your mouth before I shut it for you and then get the fuck out of my house."

Smoothing his sweater out, Summers grabbed at his case of beer and stormed out of the door. I glanced at the rest of the guys carefully. They all seemed too nervous to say anything and I looked at O'Neil before saying "Maybe we should call it a night?"

"Yeah." He agreed and the remainder of the team packed up their things before making their escape. Once the main floor was empty, Callum turned to us with a scowl, and I glanced at Shawn uneasily.

"Summers was out of line for those comments but this infatuation you have is not going to make things better." His brown eyes were soft as they watched our friend focus on the floor and he sighed before wiping at his face tiredly. "Let's just go to bed and worry about tomorrow's practice."

Turning from us, Callum began to clean up and Shawn sighed and then moved to the stairs, obviously trying to avoid any more conflict for the night.

"Ease up on him O'Neil, it's not his fault Summers is such a dick."

"He is, but he's not wrong about Kelly and Patrick - he's going to use it to stir the pot. We both know he's not here to play as a team, he wants the spotlight, and he will do whatever he has to in order to move up in Perry's eyes."

O'Neil was right and I nodded begrudgingly.

"Whatever, it doesn't matter tonight, just go check on him." Moving from the living room, I climbed the stairs and then noticed the light was on in my room. Pressing open the door, I watched as Shawn laid back on the bed and then moved to the other side making room for me.

"Summers is such a piece of shit."

"He is." I confirmed. "And if Callum didn't kick him out, I would have kicked his ass. O'Neil is right, he's trying to stir the pot and if we let him, it's only going to fuck us over." Rolling onto my side, I flicked the light off and then exhaled roughly. "Let's just get some sleep, it's been a long day."

"Yeah."

"And Patrick," I murmured.

"Yeah?"

"Stop making those nasty ass smoothies."

A light tapping echoed from the door and I groaned into the pillow before rolling over. Shawn was still fast asleep, his legs tangled with my own and I carefully extracted myself before padding towards the noise. Grabbing at the knob, I smoothed my free hand over my face and then I pulled, ready to face Callum.

Only it wasn't Callum, it was Tatum who stood across from me and her grey eyes widened in shock before peering over my shoulder for a second. Her face pinked and I realized how this must look. I had taken off my shirt sometime throughout the night and swapped my jeans for a pair of grey sweats, that did little to hide my morning wood. Shawn was in a similar state, and I knew she could see his half naked form from over my shoulder.

"Sorry, I wanted to know if I could use your bathroom, the shower isn't working in mine."

Her eyes were bouncing around, not once meeting my own as she shuffled, and I crossed my arms while I watched her in amusement.

"How did you know I would be in here?"

Rolling her eyes, Tatum smoothed her shirt and I allowed myself to drop my eyes. Her long pale legs were bare though her feet were covered in a pair of blue fuzzy slippers, and I smiled before moving my attention. Her shorts were barely visible under the long t-shirt she wore, the hem of them just peeking out slightly when she moved. It was then I noticed that she had not bothered with a bra. Noticing the way her nipples had hardened under the cotton, Tatum moved to cross her arms and her face darkened in embarrassment.

"I knocked on your door first, but no one answered." She grumbled, though her eyes had zeroed in on my chest and I stretch dramatically, smiling when I noticed her little pink tongue dart out to wet her lips.

"Jace?" Lost in my head, I hadn't noticed that Shawn had moved from the bed, and I glanced back at him as he closed the distance. "Oh, hey Tatum."

I hadn't thought Tatum Kelly could blush any harder than she was, but she proved me wrong when her eyes traced Shawn's long lean torso only to pause on the obvious outline of his Prince Albert. He too had stripped down through the night, only sleeping in a pair of thin briefs and I smiled at her deep inhale.

"You okay? You seem a little flushed." Shawn leaned against the doorframe and I glanced at him surprised, not at all prepared for how smooth he was coming across.

"Fine, just need a shower." Tatum offered; her eyes now focused on a spot just over my shoulder.

"Hers isn't working apparently." I nudged my shoulder against Shawn's with a smirk.

"Oh, well by all means then." Moving from the door, Shawn lifted an arm in invitation and laughed as Tatum Kelly roughly pushed past him.

"Of course they'd be all hot and half naked."

The words were barely audible as Kelly scurried to the door and I glanced at Shawn with a grin.

Winking at my roommate, I cupped my hands around my mouth before calling to the bathroom door. "Turn the tap to the left for cold water!"

Chapter Thirteen

TATUM

"In bed *together*, Kate," I whispered, before dropping my head to rest against the cool wood of the table. "In bed, half naked and of course they looked like they could be in GQ or whatever magazine features hot, perfectly sculpted men who are seriously *packing*."

"Packing with a piercing." She reminded me with a wistful sigh and I glared up at her from the corner of my eye. I had texted her as soon as I reached the arena and she had rushed to meet me, too excited to discuss what I had walked in on this morning to wait until after practice.

"This is not what I need right now. I need to focus; show Perry I belong on the ice on Saturday and find a way to get the funding back for the women's team."

"That's a lot of pressure, Tatum," Kate sighed and I shrugged.

"Well, I don't have a choice. I haven't even been able to figure out if I still qualify for my scholarship by playing on the men's team. No one can seem to decide."

Kate studied me with a frown and then nudged me with an elbow.

"I have an idea, how about we go out tonight? We can get a little drunk, dress a little slutty and find a perfect distraction for you. I bet you just need to get laid and then those boys won't even be a blip on your radar."

"How would I do that? I practically live in a frat house now," I grumbled.

"So what? Bring a guy home. Like you said, you basically live in a frat house now. If they bring girls home you can certainly bring a guy home," she suggested.

"They haven't brought anyone home - it's only been like two days."

"Really? No one?" Her brows lifted in surprise

"Again - two days Kate. How often do you think they hook up with people."

"I would think every night considering who they are and all the attention they get."

She had a point and I glanced at my phone before reaching for my bag.

"I have to get to practice." Tossing my bag strap over my shoulder, I stood from the table. "I'll text you after and we can plan Saturday."

"Deal!" She smiled and then I gave her a swift hug before rushing towards the locker room.

Most of the guys had made their way into their locker room but Callum had remained in the hall, his dark eyes focused on me as I approached and I swallowed at the muscle ticking in his jaw. He looked angry, and his expression seemed to be focused solely on me.

"O'Neil," I dipped my head in a greeting as I went to pass, but one hand shot out, his long fingers curling around my bicep, and I glanced down at the contact before raising my eyes to his.

"What are you playing at Kelly?" Callum had moved, stepping into my space and bending until his face was near the side of my own and I inhaled as his voice whispered across the skin of my cheek.

"What do you mean?" I asked, though my own voice was shaky. I cleared my throat before tilting my chin away from him.

"You want to practice with us, be chummy with us, come to our parties? Fine. But don't fuck around with my friends. Leave them alone or you'll find yourself on your ass on the street. I don't care how much pity Perry and my roommates may have for you. This season is my last and I refuse to let some fucking girl ruin it for me or my team."

Ripping my arm out of his grip, I turned before shoving him away roughly. "You must think highly of me if you believe I have enough power to ruin all that for you guys. I really must be a threat, huh?"

His brown eyes narrowed at me and I lifted my face, ready for whatever else he had to say but instead he sighed and his attention drifted to something over my shoulder. Glancing behind me, I noticed Perry had paused in the hallway and he tucked his clipboard under an arm before glaring at us.

"O'Neil, Kelly - go get changed and get on the fucking ice. We don't have all day to wait around for you two!" Frowning at Callum, I stepped away and then jogged down the hall, rushing past the coach all while trying to calm my heart rate.

Callum O'Neil was a dick and whatever gratitude I had for him was gone. I refused to let him get into my head and I promised myself I would prove to him that I deserved to be here.

Tugging at my gloves, I sank into the bench and then undid my helmet. Practice was in full swing and O'Neil had made it his personal goal to ruin any chance I had at getting at the puck. At this rate I would be lucky if Perry let me continue sharing the ice with his team and I grabbed at my water bottle angrily.

"If you're this easy to rile up, you have no place here, Kelly," Perry snapped, though his eyes never moved from the players on the ice, and I shrank back before wiping at my face.

"Sorry sir," I apologized but Perry paid me no mind and carried on shouting at his team as they scrimmaged.

"O'Neil, get over here!" He yelled, and I shuffled down on the bench, ignoring the way Callum glared at me before stepping behind the boards. "Sit your ass down, you look like an idiot out there. I don't know what is going on but you're not helping anyone by showing off."

Callum opened his mouth, ready to rebuttal but wisely shut it when Perry's icy blues locked onto his face with a silent order. Bending in half, Callum sank onto the wood and then tossed his helmet off before shaking out his damp curls. His mouth was shut in a frown though the jaw muscle was twitching, and I wondered if he always grinded his teeth when he was pissed or if I was just that good at irritating him.

Blowing his whistle, Perry ordered the team to stop and cool down and then he turned to face us with a scowl. "O'Neil, I know you're pissed off and Kelly I get that you think you have nothing to lose by doing whatever you can to snatch the puck but we are a team and I will not let two little self-centered fucks ruin everything I have worked for. So - O'Neil, learn to be the captain I expect you to be and Kelly, do better. Be better. Saturday is your one and only chance to show me why I should let you stay, mess that up and you can say goodbye to any chance you have here, and you'll be looking at a gap year at some other school."

Slamming his clipboard down, Coach spun on his heel and strode down the hallway and I remained frozen, feeling like a complete idiot for my behaviour. Perry was right, I had been so focused on showing him what I could do, I forgot that I needed to mesh with his team. That was the only way to earn my spot and I had instead tried to show his players up.

"I guess you got what you wanted." Turning at the sound of his voice, I glanced at O'Neil with a raised brow. "Looks like you'll have some game time Saturday. Lucky for you, Perry doesn't know about this morning."

"What are you talking about?" I snapped, not understanding what I could have possibly done to deserve O'Neil's attitude.

"Do you really think Perry would let you play if he knew you were sleeping with not one but two of his players? He would never take you seriously again, he'd know you're just another glorified puck bunny who happens to be able to skate."

Freezing, my jaw dropped, and I watched as O'Neil's mouth lifted in a smirk before I snapped my mouth closed. "I beg your pardon? I'm not sleeping with anyone."

"Listen, I get that Jace and Shawn probably initiated it, but I expected you of all people to have a little more self-restraint. I mean, is that how you say thank you after I let you move into my house? You just throw yourself at my roommates at the first chance you get?"

"I don't know what you think happened but I can promise you I didn't throw myself at anyone. My shower wouldn't work this morning and I used theirs. That's it, O'Neil. Nothing else happened." Standing, I grabbed at my helmet and tucked it under my arm before pausing to glance at the captain once more. "And don't worry about my lack of gratitude, I'll be out of your house by tomorrow."

"Tequila?!" Kate motions with her hand and I nod my head as I glance around the club. The entire place was packed and I turned to the dance floor, watching as the crowd of bodies moved in sync to the song that was blasting over the speakers.

"Here!" She called, passing me a shot and I grabbed at it before plucking the lemon from her fingers. Licking at my wrist, I let her sprinkle the salt across the damp skin and then I knocked our glasses together.

"Cheers!" Licking at the line of salt before tipping my head back, I swallowed down the burning liquid before biting at the lemon.

"Dance floor?!" She shouted while passing the bartender our empty glasses and I shook my head before slipping onto the empty stool beside me.

"You go!" I motioned for her to go ahead, watching as she eyed Vanessa and the rest of our friends who had already found their place amongst the crowd. Wrapping a slender arm around my waist, Kate gave me a gentle squeeze and then wove her way through the crowd until she reached the girls.

Certain she had made it to our friends I spun on the stool and waved the bartender over before asking for another drink. Practice had drained me and the looming issue of my living situation weighed on my shoulders. I had nearly cancelled on my friends but I knew they would not want to leave me alone tonight and so I decided I'd go out, even if it meant I stuck near the bar and sulked alone.

"Kelly?" A voice shouted and I turned to my left, nearly groaning when Shawn waved at me before making his way over.

The blonde's smile was as bright as ever and I sighed, psyching myself up for this awkward situation before taking a long sip of my vodka soda. I was sure O'Neil had told them about our conversation and I hated that I would have to deal with Patrick's pity tonight after everything. I really didn't need him or Rivers to come play hero again.

"Hey," my eyes remained focused on the mirrored wall that was behind the bar while I chewed on my straw and I watched Shawn's reflection, noticing the way his step faltered before he sank into the stool next to mine and then I gestured to the bar. "Want something?"

I could feel his blue eyes bore into the side of my face but when he didn't answer I turned. "Are you offering to buy me a drink, Kelly?"

His brows rose in amusement, and I sighed before shrugging. "Guess so, what do you want?"

"Can I swap the offer for a dance?" Chewing at my straw, I studied Shawn closely before tipping my head.

"A dance? That sounded very old fashioned," I remarked with a laugh and Shawn grinned while shuffling his stool closer to mine.

"Old fashioned or not, I'd really like for you to agree."

Shawn Patrick was stunning, especially in the low lighting of the club. His blue eyes were striking, his tan skin was bright and golden, and his tattoos seemed to glow. He was what a good-time looked like, and I knew I would be putty in his hands if this scenario was different.

"I wish I could, but I don't need to give O'Neil any more reason to hate me. Especially after today."

"What happened today?"

Frowning, I finished my drink and then cleared my throat. "He didn't tell you?"

"Tell me what, Tatum?"

Sighing, I traced the condensation on my empty glass while my face heated and then I peeked up at Patrick once more.

"He accused me of sleeping with you and Rivers, basically told me that if Perry found out about it, I would be screwed. When I told him nothing happened, that I was just using your shower, he didn't believe me. Glorified puck bunny - that's what he called me. Which is not only humiliating by the way, but it's also so damn misogynistic. The fact that there's even a name like that for women is just so gross."

"He said that?!" Shawn had moved to his feet and my head spun at the sudden movement. "What the fuck is his problem."

"Shawn," I called, watching as his head turned left to right as his eyes searched the club and then they narrowed, and he moved disappearing into the crowd before I could stop him. Slouching in my seat, I traced the damp glass of my empty drink while I decided if I should go after him or not. Choosing to stay out of it, I instead ordered another vodka soda when a hand curled around my shoulder.

"Did your boyfriend leave you all alone?" Tipping my head, I glanced up at the stranger who had crowded into my space, and I frowned when I realized I had no idea who he was. He seemed to be my age and was decently good-looking but was swaying on his feet as he pressed more weight against me and I shuffled under his hand thinking it would make him take a step back. However, it did the opposite, my movement only caused him to lose his balance and he was now nearly curled around me.

"What's your name?" The smell of beer wafted across my face, and I turned my head away from him.

"I'm not interested," I said with a nervous smile, but the man didn't back away and instead his mouth pressed against my ear.

"You don't need to lie," his teeth moved to nip at my lobe, and I recoiled against the bar, trying my best to slide away from him without causing a scene.

"My boyfriend will be back any minute so I -"

His hand moved from my shoulder to my arm, and I winced at the contact as his fingers tightened.

"Don't be such a bitch, I just want to talk to you. You should be flattered I'm paying you any attention at all."

I shivered as his eyes narrowed at me and I turned to the bar in hopes of alerting someone that I needed help. But the people surrounding me either didn't notice or pretended not to. Taking a step away once again, I twisted my head towards the dance floor, and I searched for someone I knew but I couldn't spot the girls or Shawn and I began to panic.

"I really should go find him," my voice broke nervously while I swayed, and the man grinned, pulling me close until my body was against his and then he grinded against my hip.

"Stop being a little cock-tease and come home with me," he whispered while his other hand moved to my waist; I shivered when his fingers skimmed the skin above my jeans.

"How about you let her go."

The relief was instant, and I glanced at Callum as he closed the distance between us. But the stranger wasn't intimidated, his hands tightened against my skin painfully.

Noticing my discomfort, Callum reached past me to grab at the stranger's shirt before tugging him away and then his free fist swung. The contact was sharp, and I watched as the man tumbled to the floor before clutching at his bloodied face and then Callum turned to me, his hands careful as they grabbed at my wrist as he pulled me away.

Before he could get too far however, two security guards swarmed us, suddenly aware of the happenings of the club and I frowned at them while Callum explained. They had been nowhere to be seen when I was being harassed but the minute there's an altercation between two men - they magically appear.

"Just take her home man, we don't need any more bullshit tonight." The shorter of the two snapped and I felt my mouth drop at the implication that I was the issue.

"Come on, Kelly," Callum sighed, ignoring the shouting coming from the man on the floor and I followed behind him dumbly. Moving through the crowd, I struggled to keep my feet straight let alone keep up with O'Neil, and he turned back towards me with a frown.

"Kelly, are you good?" His voice wasn't soft or gentle, but it lacked its usual bite, and I left my lips raise in a grin.

"I think I'm a bit drunk," I giggled. Callum wasn't nearly as amused, and he rolled his eyes before grabbing at my hand.

"Come here." Locking our fingers together, Callum tugged me along and led me to the far corner of the club where Rivers and Patrick were sitting.

"What happened?" Shawn stood as soon as he noticed us and then frowned at me in concern.

"Some asshole was trying to cop a feel, he wouldn't leave Kelly alone. I came over and knocked the fucker out and now security is pissed. They want her out of here and given the fact that she's pretty drunk, I think we all should just head home." Jace studied Callum carefully for a long pause and I shuffled awkwardly while they seemed to have a silent conversation.

"I was with Kate earlier; I should go find her before we leave," I offered, breaking the sudden tension that surrounded us, but Shawn smiled softly before glancing at the dance floor.

"I see her, I'll let her know we are taking you home. That way security doesn't try to throw all of us out." Moving through the crowd, I watched as he tapped my friend on the shoulder and then whispered something in her ear. Her green eyes moved to my face, and she nodded once before tossing me a wink and I blushed hotly at her silent insinuation.

"Come on Kelly, let's go home," Jace suggested while warm fingers tightened around mine and it was then that I noticed Callum hadn't let go of my hand. Blinking down at the contact, Callum frowned and then snatched his hand away as if I had burned him.

"Let's fucking go already," he snapped and spun on his heel before pushing his way to the exit.

"What was that about?" Jace wondered out loud and I couldn't help but think the same thing.

Chapter Fourteen

SHAWN

"Who needs a truck this big, O'Neil? Are you compensating for something?" Tatum grumbled as she crawled her way across the seat.

"Kelly, there is another door on that side, you don't need to crawl all the way over there," Jace laughed, waiting as she slumped against the seat before turning to glare at him.

"Too late now," she whispered and I slid next to her, taking the seat belt from her hands before locking it, making certain she was buckled in. "I think I'm drunk."

"You said that already," Callum reminded her from the front seat and then his eyes shot to mine through the rear-view mirror. "Do not let her throw up back there."

"Hate to ruin your fancy leather seats in your pussy trapping truck?" The cab was silent as we all turned to Kelly in confusion.

"In his what?" I asked, grinning as she wiggled in her seat with a frown, obviously trying to get comfortable.

"I've heard the stories about this truck and the girls that fawn all over it. If those rumors are true, then my barf is the least nasty thing to touch this leather. I just hope you clean up after or I really am going to be sick."

"Kelly, what makes you think it's the truck that gets the girls and not me?" Callum asked, carefully rounding the corner of the parking lot, and I tried to remember if he had ever driven this slowly when I had been shitfaced in the back.

"Because I *know* you, and this is a nice truck. That is...if you're into that sort of stereotype." Tatum grumbled, resting her head against the window and I grinned.

"What stereotype is that?" I asked, while nudging her with my elbow.

"The tall, hot, douchebag hockey player with his fancy black four by four," she sighed with frustration, as if it was the most obvious thing in the world.

"Hear that? You're a stereotype," Jace snickered in the front while slapping Callum's shoulder, but O'Neil shrugged him off and turned up the radio, though I noticed his mouth had lifted in a smirk.

"At least you can throw a good punch," Tatum offered before closing her eyes. "I hope you broke that asshole's nose."

"Me too." Callum murmured, while his eyes darted from the road to the rear-view mirror.

Rubbing at my hair roughly, I glanced at my reflection through the steam and sighed. Today felt like it went on for ages and I was completely exhausted. I had hoped our night out would help with the stress that had been weighing on my shoulders but it ended worse than planned. Poor Kelly had been harassed by some drunk asshole and Callum had decided to play hero. Normally I would have assumed that meant we were all on our way to getting along, especially after the drive home, but he didn't even look in our direction once we pulled into the driveway and stormed to his room the minute we got home. Even now the house was eerily quiet as I made my way to my bed but just as I pulled back the crumpled comforter, Jace wandered in through our shared bathroom.

"Hey," he whispered, leaning against the door frame. "Heading to bed?"

Rolling my eyes, I gestured to the mattress. "Obviously."

"Right."

He laughed awkwardly before crossing his arms and I glanced at him with a raised brow. "I guess I just wanted to check in. I know you were pretty pissed at Cal before all that shit went down at the club."

"If by checking in, you mean you're asking if I'm still mad at him for insulting Tatum and making her feel like she has to leave, then yeah."

"Shawn, it's his house," Jace reminded me unnecessarily and I sank onto my bed

"I know that, but he's punishing her for something we didn't even do," I groaned while rubbing at my face. "She didn't deserve any of that shit."

"No, she didn't but her living here isn't up to us and at the end of the day he looked out for her at the club."

Falling back onto the sheets, I crossed my arms over my eyes and inhaled. "That's another thing I don't get. I mean I'm glad he stepped in but Callum always keeps his shit together and yet he threw a punch over Kelly. If he really hated her like he says he does - why would he do that?"

"Maybe he did it because he knows how much you like her."

"We," I corrected, "How much *we* like her."

"Woah - wait a second, I think she's hot but I'm not an idiot over her like you are."

Laughing I moved my arms and looked at my best friend.

"Stop over exaggerating, I'm not even that bad. I just think she's cool."

"Right, that's it, you just think she's cool." Grabbing at one of my pillows, I whipped it in Jace's direction and then groaned again. I might not admit it out loud, but he was right, I was more than a little into Tatum Kelly, and now she was moving out and chances were, transferring schools. If I didn't figure out something fast, I was totally going to miss my shot and I swallowed at the sudden tightness in my chest.

"Listen, I -" But my confession was interrupted as both Jace and I glanced at the door before looking at each other.

"Shawn?" Tatum's voice rang out through the room and my eyes widened as I slid from the bed and then I was crossing the room. Wrenching the door open, I took in her face and light grey eyes carefully.

"Hey - you okay?" She looked way more sober than she had in the truck and didn't seem upset, but I knew tonight had been shitty for her and I waited as she crossed her arms before blinking up at me in uncertainty.

"Any chance I can use your shower again tonight? I just feel gross after everything that happened tonight, it's like I can't get the feeling of his hands off of me."

I pressed my door open, ready to offer entry when Jace moved from his place before glancing at Tatum. "He really didn't do anything right? Like it wasn't serious?"

"What do you mean? He grabbed my arm, touched my waist and was vulgar to me."

Jace rubbed the back of his neck awkwardly but when he didn't answer, Tatum stepped farther into my room. "I know to you it probably doesn't seem like a big deal, but I was scared. You never know what will happen with men like that when you reject them, so I tried to be polite hoping he'd take the hint. When he didn't, Callum showed up. So yeah, I guess it wasn't serious per se, but I could really use a hot shower."

It was then that I noticed she was trembling, and I shot Jace a concerned look before ushering Tatum to the bathroom door. "Go ahead Kelly, take as long as you'd like."

When the door was firmly shut, I turned on Jace with narrowed eyes. "What the hell was that man?"

"I didn't mean for it to come out that way, I just wanted to be sure she was okay, and I clearly screwed up getting that point across."

"You think? You sounded like a complete asshole."

Jace glanced at the floor guiltily and I turned to my dresser before pulling out a pair of sweats.

"You're right, I totally shouldn't have worded it that way. The whole night just threw me off, and now that Callum has stormed off to his room, I feel like we're all in limbo."

He wasn't wrong, I had expected our roommate to at least offer an olive branch on the way home but when his mood had rapidly changed and he had stormed into his room, I was left wondering where his head was at with Tatum living here.

"Not to mention the fact he was the one who defended her, and did you see him holding her hand? What was that about?" It was hard to miss the way his fingers had curled around hers when they had found us in the back of the room though I had no idea what to think about it.

"I don't know, but we can ask him in the morning. Maybe tonight we should all just go to bed. Hopefully by tomorrow Callum will feel better about Tatum living here for the season and we can just co-exist for more than just a couple days at a time."

Nodding, Jace turned to the door and said goodnight before leaving my room and I pulled on the grey cotton and then did my best to tidy the area before Tatum came out of the bathroom. Once I had shoved most of the clutter into the closet, I made my bed quickly and then perched on the edge of the mattress just in time to hear the water shut off. Opening the door, Tatum stepped out of the room with her hair wrapped in a towel and then she offered me a small smile when smoothing out her pajamas.

"Feel better?" I asked, watching as her grey eyes flickered across my bare torso before she sighed.

"Yeah, much. Thank you."

Nodding I stuffed my hands into my pockets and waited for her to leave, but when she hesitated, I felt my breath stutter.

"Shawn." My name was a whisper and I swallowed roughly before tipping my head in question. "Can I stay with you tonight? I really don't want to be alone."

Alarm bells were going off, shouting at me that it was a stupid, awful, idiotic idea and yet I nodded. Offering her a hand, I pulled her towards the bed and flicked on the nightstand light before closing the bathroom door. Unwrapping her hair, Tatum crawled onto the bed and then sat cross legged as she watched me.

"I just want to be clear that I know this is a bad idea, I know Callum will be mad, but I don't want to be by myself downstairs." Nodding, I sat on the opposite side of the bed but didn't move to pull at the covers. "I also just want to *sleep*, is that okay?"

"Tatum, of course," I reassured her, worried that I had somehow come across the wrong way. "I'll grab my own blanket and we can just crash, okay?"

Agreeing, Tatum tucked herself under the blankets and then watched as I pulled at a knitted blanket that had been shoved under the bed. Settling next to her, I unfolded it across my legs and then I laid down, making sure I kept half a foot of space between us.

"Goodnight," I whispered, moving to flick the light off.

"Night."

Kelly's voice was quiet, and it was the last thing I heard before sleep grabbed a hold of me.

Something was rocking against me, and I groaned before moving my hips forward, letting my cock press into the firm ass that was grinding into it. Blinking my eyes open, I glanced down at the light brown hair that was fanned across my pillow and stilled before pulling myself away in shock. But Tatum only followed me, nudging herself back until we were pressed together once again and then the sweetest moan echoed from her parted mouth.

"Tatum," I warned, though my voice was deep with sleep, and it sounded far more serious than I had meant it to.

Rolling onto her back, her light grey eyes blinked up at me, though they appeared clear, and a pretty pink flush crept up her neck as she gazed at me. Watching me closely, she raised a hand, her long fingers curling up my neck and into my hair before she gave a gentle tug. The sharp sting was a welcome sensation, and my blood pulsed through me before my hips moved on their own accord.

"Hmm, I always wondered," Kelly whispered before tugging once more. This time though with more force and I tipped my chin to the ceiling as I groaned.

Blinking up at the white above me I prayed that I wasn't dreaming before swallowing down another moan. Tatum had swung a leg over my waist while I had been distracted and was now settled on top of me. Tightening her fingers, she guided my face to hers.

"Is this okay?" Her voice was soft and I gaped at her with wide eyes before nodding dumbly and then she shuffled down, pressing her hips into mine. Closing my eyes, I willed myself not to cum in my pants like a fucking idiot and tried to focus on answering her.

"More than okay but is this something you really want to do?" My voice trembled and I so badly wanted to beg for her just to fucking touch me. I wanted to feel her fingers dip under my pants and curl her fist around me.

"I figure I might as well enjoy myself if I'm moving out," she shrugged and then moved forward, letting her hair tickle my chest before her mouth pressed against my throat. Her lips were soft as they traced my skin, mapping out the dove tattoo that covered the left side and then I felt the sharp sting of her teeth.

"Fucking hell Kelly," My hips lifted, pressing right into her covered pussy and I could have sworn I was able to feel the heat of her even through two layers of clothing.

"Easy Shawn," She laughed, "I've barely touched you."

"I know," I whined, struggling to keep still as her tongue chased away any hurt her bite had left.

"Are you really that needy for me already?" She asked as if she was joking but I nodded my head while pinching my eyes shut.

"You have no fucking idea."

Laughing again, Tatum pressed into my dick roughly. "I have some idea."

Untangling her fingers from my hair, she moved her hands across my shoulders and down my torso. The first touch was soft, as her fingertips traced my tattooed skin but the second, she used her nails and I cried out when they scratched along the waistband of my sweats.

"Please Tatum!" The words escaped me before I could stop them and Tatum froze, her grey eyes widening as she blinked down at me.

"Oh -" Breathing heavily, I waited as her teeth sank into her lower lip and then she grinned, her entire face lifting with mischief. "I liked that. Who would have thought I'd find Shawn Patrick begging so hot?"

Shimming down my legs, Tatum slid her hands along the grey fabric again and then her fingers hooked into my pants. This had to be a dream- the best dream I ever had, but definitely a dream.

"You still with me?" She asked, while tucking her long hair behind her ears and I exhaled before dipping my head.

"Hell yeah."

Her smile was blinding, and she pressed a kiss to my stomach while I took in a deep breath, readying myself for what was next.

Chapter Fifteen

TATUM

Having Shawn Patrick between my thighs, half naked and begging felt incredible. His tan skin was flawless in the morning light and I peered up at his stunning blue eyes before running my tongue across the indents of his abs. He had kept his word the night before and had remained on his side of the bed, not once touching me in the dark while I spent hours practically burning with desire, regretting that I had been so adamant that we just sleep. Though now that I had a clear mind, I appreciated that I would be able to memorize every detail in the soft morning light and store it away for another day.

Focusing back on the job at hand, I nipped at the dark ink that curled around his hip bone and smiled as he panted beneath me before repeating the action twice more. "What do you need?"

"You," he moaned. "Just you, Tatum."

"Good answer," I whispered and then pressed my tongue to the skin, watching the way his cock pressed against his sweats. I had always been one to hold my own in the bedroom and I knew I could give just as well as I could take, but hearing Shawn cry out my name brought a new bubbling warmth to my belly. It wasn't something I ever imagined I would enjoy so much and I smiled before I ran the tip of my tongue across the waistband of the grey cotton once more.

"Fuck, Kelly," Shawn sighed, his fingers flexing as he knuckled the sheets under him. "Are you trying to kill me?"

"Not at all, I'm just taking my time."

I grinned before pushing up on my palms and sliding my way forward. Once I was straddling his hips again, I grabbed at his wrists and pulled his fingers from the sheets. "But I want these here."

Moving, I tucked his hands over his head and pressed them down against the pillow before rolling my hips into his. The spark was instantaneous, and I tossed my head back with a sigh and then repeated the movement. It had been a long time since I had taken my time during sex, usually it was a – pull at your clothes, ignore the state of the guy's room, hope they wouldn't fight you on wearing a condom and pray that they could live up to their promises and make you come- type situation. The last time I had spent any time keeping my pants on while I enjoyed a man's company, I had been with my high school boyfriend. And at that time, he had been sure that he could get me off with a round of dry humping before he gave his best three pump performance.

"You're so fucking hot," he groaned, and I glanced down, watching as his eyes traced my body until they met my own.

"You think so?" I teased, pressing into him again while deciding if I should fish for the complements or not. "Tell me how."

Sitting up, Shawn wrapped his arms around my waist, and I shivered as his fingertips moved under the cotton of my shirt. "I don't even know where to start, Kelly."

His fingers moved higher, the pads tracing along the muscles of my shoulders before tickling down my spine. "I spent most of last semester staring at your back, watching as it flexed and moved all while wondering what it would feel like under my hands. I wondered what your skin looks bare, if I could see the shape of the muscles, if the skin would be covered in freckles or smooth."

My eyes widened in surprise at that. I had been expecting compliments on my hair or my eyes, which had always been the go-to for every other guy, especially considering I was barely a B-cup and my ass, though firm, was not much to look at. Most men skirted around the fact that I was strongly built and could most likely keep up with them at the gym.

"And your legs, your fucking legs. They go on for miles and those thighs of yours look like they could crush my head. If I had to pick a way to die, that would be it."

Smiling, I tightened my legs, pressing my inner thighs against his hips teasingly. "I love that you are so damn tall, thinking about how I would have to lift my chin to kiss you makes me hard."

"You like that?" I wondered; my mouth parted in shock.

"Fuck yeah, I like it; I like it a lot. I also like knowing you could pin me down and fuck me silly if you wanted to. Make me take whatever you wanted to give and know I would beg for more."

"Holy crap," I whispered, and Shawn smiled before raising his hips, pressing into me fully again.

Shimming against his headboard, Shawn grabbed at me and tugged me closer before tangling his hands into my hair. There was no force to it and instead he used his nails to scratch at my scalp gently all while smiling up at me. The ministrations were soothing, and I lowered my face, burying my nose into his neck as I relaxed against him.

"If you keep doing that, I'm going to fall asleep and then we won't be able to finish what I started." Shawn hummed under his breath but only pressed me closer while his fingers raked through my hair.

"As much as I want you to finish what you started, I think we would be better off putting a pause on that. I think if that's a line we are going to cross, I need to be open and honest with you."

It felt as if I had been doused with ice water and I pulled away from him in concern, watching as his eyes turned weary while he scanned my face. Removing his hands from my hair, he pressed on my hips carefully, guiding me off of him and then crossed his legs. Everything about his body language was closed off and I readied myself for whatever it was he felt he had to tell me.

"I'm sure you've heard something about my history with women," He started, though his voice was weak, and he cleared his throat before trying again. "My history with women and *Jace.*"

He was right to assume I had heard about it, and I nodded before grabbing at one of his hands. "I won't lie and act surprised, but if this is something you don't feel ready to tell me or don't want to, that's okay. I would never demand that you tell me anything."

"I want to tell you Tatum, I want you to have all the facts before making any kind of decision." Sighing, he moved his attention to our fingers and traced my knuckles with his thumb. "Jace and I have a complicated friendship. He is my best friend and teammate, but he's also more. It's not a lie, the rumour that he and I hook up with women together. Though the amount of said hook ups are greatly exaggerated."

"Are the two of you together?" I asked softly.

"Not really, only when it comes to sex and not every time."

"What does that mean?"

Shawn frowned, and his brows pinched while he cleared his throat.

"I've only had five partners. My high school girlfriend, a guy from freshman year, Jace and two other women. When I was with my ex, it had only been the two of us, same with the guy. Jace was the first person I had ever been with who was into the idea of a threesome. So, the last two women I slept with were with the *both of us*." Pausing, Shawn shot me a sad smile and then grabbed my hand tightly. "Jace introduced me to the idea of multiple partners. He is far more open when it comes to his sexuality, while I struggled for a long time, trying to figure out what I was and what label I wanted."

"You do know you don't need to have that figured out right? You don't need to label yourself as anything." Shawn's eyes widened at my words, and I shuffled closer to him. "I get the whole hockey player thing comes with an image, but it's okay not to fit into a box. I don't think people are supposed to force themselves to be something they're not just because it's ideal."

Exhaling roughly, Shawn rubbed at his eyes. "I never thought you'd see it that way."

"I grew up with a queer brother who tried to lie to himself, and he suffered for years because of it. Watching him all that time made me realize that no one should have to hurt just to be loved by those who should do so unconditionally. So, if you and Jace care for each other in that way, then I support it."

"We do care for each other, but it's not quite like that. I'm doing a crappy job of explaining this." Leaning back, Shawn rested his head against the headboard and then blinked up at the ceiling. "For me, I prefer to share a woman with Jace, it's what I enjoy when it comes to sex, and I have not been with anyone solo since freshman year. Jace, while he likes being with two people, doesn't mind one on one. We don't have any sort of exclusive relationship together because our needs are different."

"Okay, let me get this straight," I started, ignoring the way Shawn lifted a brow at the choice of word. "You and Jace have been involved with each other... physically but are not in a relationship." Glancing at Shawn, I waited until he nodded before continuing. "And you prefer to have him there, involved, when you sleep with someone, but he doesn't care either way?"

"Jace is a solid guy, not nearly the man-whore everyone makes him out to be. He just likes to fuck. Same as any normal twenty-one-year-old. I'm the weird one." Leaning forward, I went to interrupt but Shawn lifted a hand, stopping me. "I need more than just attraction; I need to feel something before I sleep with someone. The last two women Jace and I were with, were friends. We liked each other, they were somewhat aware of our situation and wanted to join. I haven't been with anyone without Jace in a long time but that doesn't mean I couldn't be."

My mind spun at all of the information, not quite able to understand what he was telling me. I knew the rumors of course and had observed how close both men were with each other. But I had thought that maybe they were together and just liked to add a third occasionally. Obviously, I had that wrong, or at least I think I did.

"Okay, so then you want to add Jace to this?" I asked, motioning a hand between us.

"I mean, I don't- maybe?" Shawn shrugged. "I know that I want you, that much is obvious." He laughed, glancing at the tented grey sweatpants, and I blushed. "But I also know I wanted to be honest and maybe gauge how you felt about the idea, because it's something I would be *very* interested in."

"Honestly," I sighed before running my hands through my hair. "I don't care about your sexuality or judge you for it and if I'm being truthful, the idea of the two of you is, well... I'd be lying if I said I hadn't imagined it. But I just don't think any of this is a good idea. Now that I've cleared my head, I've realized how messy this could make things and I think we are better off pretending none of this morning happened."

Shawn's shoulders sagged and he dipped his chin, lowering his eyes to our hands. "Right, of course."

"Shawn, Callum has already accused me of sleeping with you guys and just the idea has caused problems for everyone. I'm still hoping I can find a place to live and not have to transfer schools now that he wants me out of here."

"We won't let him kick you out," Shawn argued, and I smiled at him.

"Then we definitely can't hook up, I doubt O'Neil is really one for second chances." Pulling my hand from his, I slid across the bed and then grabbed at the towel I had left on the floor last night.

"I shouldn't have said anything," he groaned, flopping onto his back before crossing his arms over his eyes.

"No, I'm glad you did. Honestly, I am. And if things were different, I would most certainly be looking to maybe test the waters, with *both* of you, if that's something all of us wanted."

Leaning over, I curled my fingers around his calf and gave a gentle squeeze. "I'm going to go downstairs and pack, I know you think O'Neil will change his mind, but I need to be ready to move. I'll see you down there, okay?"

I didn't wait for his response and instead slipped through the door before running a hand through my hair all while wondering if I had just made a huge mistake. Turning to the stairs, I folded my towel over my arm and then glanced up only to freeze as brown eyes caught mine before narrowing.

"Fuck."

Chapter Sixteen

CALLUM

"I need to give you more credit Kelly, I never would have imagined you could lie to my face so easily." Her grey eyes blinked at me in confusion, and I waited, leaning against the railing on the wall while crossing my arms.

"It's -" she started, her voice breaking but I scoffed.

"Spare me, I know exactly what happened in that room. I'm not a fucking idiot." Moving to climb the last two stairs, I closed the distance between us and then peered down at her pale face.

"I thought we were getting somewhere after last night, I really thought maybe this whole situation could be manageable." Glancing at her toes, Kelly tucked a strand of hair behind her ears. "I was wrong, get your shit and get out."

Nodding silently, Kelly sniffed and wiped at her nose and if I hadn't been so angry by her lying, I may have taken pity on her. But Tatum Kelly turned out to be exactly what I had thought, an opportunist who would be as dishonest as she had to be to get what she wanted.

"Callum," Shawn called, his head poking out of his doorway with a frown as he glanced at Kelly who had slumped into herself awkwardly. "What's going on?"

"Don't play stupid Shawn, I found her creeping out of your room. We both know what happened in there." Shawn's blue eyes glared at me for a pause and then came into the hallway, moving closer until he was able to cup her shoulders and then he glowered at me from behind her back.

"She stayed with me last night because she didn't want to be alone after what happened at the club. I would have thought you'd be a bit more understanding, especially considering you were raised with two sisters." Kelly's face became pink and blotchy, and I glanced down at her. "I think you probably owe her an apology, O'Neil."

Turning her head, she glanced at Shawn with a frown and shook her head. "It's okay Shawn, really it's fine."

"It's not, he has no right to treat you this way and to be honest I'm growing tired of it." He snapped, his fingers flexing on her shoulders. "Apologize to her and get over your stupid fucking rules already or I swear Callum, I'll be moving out too."

He was bluffing, I knew that, but I couldn't help but wonder how serious Shawn was about her if he was willing to threaten something like that. Tilting my head, I studied him silently and then dipped my chin, agreeing to his terms.

"I'm sorry, Kelly. I guess I shouldn't have assumed." Not bothering to wait to hear if she accepted my apology, I brushed past them and moved towards my room only to stop at the door when she called for me.

"O'Neil, I'm not really interested in this power dynamic. I don't want to have to worry about you deciding to kick me out because I do something you don't like. Especially if it's over who I choose to sleep with." Looking over my shoulder, I noticed Kelly had turned to face me with a scowl.

"Which is none of his fucking business anyway." Shawn grumbled under his breath while his eyes narrowed in my direction and the hostility in the normally bright blue irises was startling.

"You're right. It's not fair and I guess it isn't my business unless it affects my friends or team negatively." Squaring my shoulders, I watched the pair for a long minute and then rolled my eyes in exasperation before deciding to call a truce.

"Fine, if you two want my blessing I guess you have it. There - happy?" I asked, directing my attention to Shawn.

The blonde didn't say anything, and his face remained unreadable, but Kelly's scowl deepened. "Fuck off O'Neil, we don't need shit from you, least of all any type of blessing."

Grabbing Shawn's hand, she tugged him to follow and then led him down the stairs, only to shout. "See you at practice, you ass! And don't worry I'll be sure not to negatively affect your team!"

I had a ritual for game days: wake up an hour early, watch last season's highlights and drink a protein shake before showering. I had done it in this order for years, never once changing the pattern but now as I crept down the stairs, I froze when I noticed Kelly sitting at the island.

Her usual jeans and a hoodie had been traded in for what looked to be a pair of black wide leg dress pant-things and a blazer. It reminded me of a suit a lawyer would wear had it not been for the wrinkles in the fabric and the deep green button down that matched our jerseys. Taking a second to watch her, I noticed she had already set aside three cups, each containing what looked to be a protein shake and was now sipping on her coffee.

"You can come downstairs, you know," she whispered, turning on her seat to glance at me and I exhaled roughly before coming down the rest of the stairs and closing the distance between us. "I made you a protein shake."

Grabbing at one of the cups, I lifted it to my nose in suspicion all while holding eye contact with her and she huffed in her seat before rolling her eyes.

"Oh c'mon, I didn't poison it, O'Neil."

Lifting a brow, I took a sip, swishing it around my mouth dramatically before swallowing it down. It was good, better than what I would have made and I took in another mouthful and another, not stopping until I had finished the entire thing.

"I guess we'll know in a few hours, won't we?" Turning away from her piercing eyes, I rinsed the cup and then took in a deep breath. "Practice went well yesterday."

"It did," she hummed, and I realized she wasn't going to make this easy on me.

"I think Perry might let you play if we get desperate enough, but only because it's the exhibition game." Spinning around, I pressed back against the counter but kept my eyes averted from her face.

"Considering I can skate circles around the second stringers, I'm betting I have a better chance than *might.*"

"Not if Perry see's the wrinkles in that suit or whatever it is you're wearing. He takes game days really seriously, and I have had my ass chewed out more times than I can count because my appearance wasn't up to his standards."

"Well, he'll have to deal. I don't have anything else and I don't have any idea how to fix it." Rounding the island, I held out a hand and waited.

"I have a steamer upstairs. Give me your jacket and pants - I'll do it."

Her grey eyes narrowed for a second and then she stood, peeling the black blazer from her arms before her fingers went to the button of her pants. "Wait! God Kelly, I don't need you to strip those off this minute."

But it was too late, she was wiggling them down her pale heavily muscled thighs and then stepping out of them carefully before swinging them over my arm. “You said you wanted my pants, now you have them.”

“I didn’t realize it would be so easy to get you out of them.” The words had slithered out of my mouth before I could think to stop them, and I held my breath while I waited for Kelly’s anger. But it never came, instead she lifted a single brow and then smirked.

“Only if you’re really special, so I guess today is your lucky day, O’Neil.” She teased and I took a step back, not sure what to do in this circumstance. At best we could coexist, but we had never joked with each other and this sudden lightness in the air made me antsy.

“Right, well I’ll go deal with these. Maybe go put some pants on, I don’t need Rivers and Patrick to lose focus.” Sprinting for the stairs, I ignored the sudden tightness of my pants and ran for my room, putting as much distance between Tatum Kelly and I as possible.

The seats were filled though I could barely hear the cheering over my breathing and I watched as the ref approached, puck in hand. We were in the last minutes of the third period, ahead by four and Kelly had been responsible for two of those goals. Tatum Kelly had scored two fucking goals and I couldn’t help but feel resentful.

I knew it was my ego, my own arrogance that kept me from being thankful that she had stepped up, played her heart out, and worked as part of our team. And I knew it was wrong. I should have been grateful; I should have been happy but there was something wrong with me because I only felt jealous.

I was envious of her natural talent. Angered by every pat to her helmet Perry gave her. Resentful of every sweet smile she threw Patrick and Rivers.

I was seething and I was an asshole for it.

“That girl on your team is showing you up, O’Neil. I guess you all get the added benefit of fucking her though. I’d be willing to play like shit too if it meant I had my dick sucked at the snap of my fingers. I bet she’s so grateful for the opportunity, she spends her entire day on her knees.”

I wasn't new to being chirped by my opponents but Davis had a mouth on him, and I glared at his ugly face before tilting my head. "Is that how you show your gratitude Davis? Is that how you know?"

His brown eyes narrowed at me, but I smiled, showing the bright blue of my mouth guard. "As far as Kelly goes, she actually likes cock, not whatever you have tucked away between your legs. I bet she wouldn't even be able to find it."

Glancing at the ref, I changed my weight and lowered myself towards the ice before shooting Rivers a quick nod. Davis was a decent player but he had yet to beat me at a face off and I smiled, watching as the puck dropped before all hell broke loose.

As predicted the puck ended up with me and I passed it back, watching as my team swarmed with practice-like ease while we travelled the length of the rink. Nearly reaching the goal before the whistle was blown and I slowed to a stop, glancing around me in confusion until I saw Jace with his helmet off and fists flying.

"Fucking hell," I swore before speeding towards the pair, immediately noticing it was Davis who was on the receiving end of River's ass kicking. I grabbed at his arms, using my weight to tug him off before he received something worse than a major penalty.

"Say it again, piece of shit!" Jace yelled, pressing against me as he tried to grab a hold of Davis once more. "Say it again I fucking dare you!"

"Jace, stop man you're going to get thrown out of the game," I urged, pulling him farther away from Davis before passing him off to the refs. The two men frowned at me before tugging Rivers to the bench and I winced at Perry's murderous scowl before glancing at the clock.

We had six seconds left, not enough time to do much more but at least it meant we wouldn't be without Jace for any real amount of time. Watching as the rest of us settled, I moved towards the ref who was now palming the puck and glanced at Davis's replacement.

Sharing a look, we made a silent agreement and when the puck dropped, we didn't bother doing anything. Allowing the time to run out, the speakers blared signalling the game was over and I made my way to the bench, watching as Perry turned his icy blue eyes towards Kelly who at least had the decency to look a little ashamed. Afterall, there was no way Jace hadn't started the fight over anyone else.

"Get your shit together, go shake hands like the players I expect you to be and then get your asses in that dressing room," Perry snarled and we all moved from the bench, shuffling across the ice to form the line. Without Davis, most of the guys seemed decent, shaking our hands though some passed over Kelly and I watched as she frowned, biting her lip silently as she finished with the last of our opponents.

"Don't worry about it, Tatum. If they can't lose gracefully, then they don't deserve anything from you," Shawn reassured her and I shot him a warning glare.

"You're going to make it worse for her if Perry hears all that coddling," I snapped, ignoring the sharp gasp that came from Kelly and instead stepped off the ice and strode down the hall.

"What the fuck was that, Rivers?" I could hear Perry from the hall and swallowed nervously before ducking into the dressing room.

"Sorry Coach," Jace whispered, his dark eyes focused on his skates and I noticed the swelling beneath his right eye.

"It was over the girl, wasn't it?" Perry grabbed at his hat and snatched it from his head before throwing it across the room. "Having her on the team isn't worth having my players lose focus. She needs to go before one of you ruins things for us."

Clearing my throat, I waited for Perry to face me and then racked my brain for an excuse. "It wasn't about Kelly, Coach; Davis was running his mouth all game about anything and everything you can think of. If Rivers didn't hit him when he did, I would have."

"That true?" Perry spun, glaring at Jace but my friend was still staring at me, watching me with confusion. When I clenched my jaw and dipped my head, he finally glanced at Perry and nodded.

"Yes sir, it had nothing to do with Kelly, he was just being a dick and I let him get to me. It won't happen again."

"It better not," Perry snapped and then waited for the rest of the team to shuffle into the room.

I sank onto the bench next to Jace and ran my hand through my curls. Shawn had finally stepped through the doorway and his eyes sought mine before he glanced back at Kelly, and I realized they had heard me.

"Thanks man," Jace whispered but my eyes had remained locked on the light grey, though I turned my chin towards my friend.

"Listen, I've decided I can't stop you and Shawn from doing whatever it is that you want to do, and I guess I'm fine with it. But don't ever make me lie for any of you again. Especially about Kelly. Next time I will let him kick her off the team without a second thought." Standing, I moved to the opposite side of the room and watched as Kelly sat next to Jace before offering the spot on the other side of her to Shawn and then my eyes met Perry's, certain he had just noticed them as well.

"O'Neil!" Perry's voice echoed down the hallway, and I tightened the hold on the strap on my shoulder before turning my head towards his office. We had spent an hour stuck in the dressing room while Perry chewed us out and I really did not have the energy to listen to any more. But when his eyes narrowed and he lifted two fingers to beckon me closer, I knew I really didn't have a choice.

"Take a seat," he ordered, pointing to the free chair and I fell into it as he rounded his desk and then he pressed back into his chair. "I'm going to be honest now, you hear me, O'Neil?"

"Yes sir."

"That girl is already causing problems and if I didn't need her, she wouldn't be anywhere near my team. But right now, I don't have much of a choice. We've been scouting some decent players but nothing concrete is in the works just yet. So, in the meantime I need you to keep Patrick and Rivers away from her, you understand me?"

Those ice-cold eyes locked on my face, and I nodded. "Yes, sir."

"The last thing *we* need is to have our players lose their heads on the ice. We were lucky tonight; we only had a few seconds left and it was only the exhibition game. But that shit can't happen again if she keeps playing for us, we can't make it to championships if Rivers fucks up during an actual game all because he can't keep his dick in his pants. This is your last season here O'Neil, it matters, and this will decide what happens in the future. You think you have a chance to go pro if you choke your last year?"

"No, sir."

"Then we have an understanding. I know she's living with you now, and I can't tell you who to let into your house, but I can promise you, that's a bad idea."

"It's not permanent," I shrugged and swallowed at Perry's scowl.

"Good, because her playing with us isn't either and I'd hate for you to lose sight of that. She's a placeholder, nothing more. As soon as I have a player signed, Tatum Kelly is long gone, you understand?"

"Yes, Coach,"

"Good. Now get out of here and go celebrate. I saw more than a dozen girls with your jersey on in the stands, go have fun, don't waste your night." Nodding, I stood from the chair and ducked my head as I strode down the hall all while wondering how the fuck I would keep my friends away from Kelly especially now that they were becoming close.

Chapter Seventeen

TATUM

Walking into the house, I dropped my bag and rolled my neck, before sliding against the door. Kate had been longing to go out, especially when she learned that the rest of the team had plans to meet at one of the less popular bars but I had no desire to go anywhere. I didn't know if it was because of the last experience at the club or my complete lack of energy after tonight's win, but I did know for certain being surrounded by the team did not sound appealing.

Pushing myself away from the door, I tiredly made my way to the kitchen and tugged the fridge open before grabbing at one of the beer bottles that lined the shelves. The house was quiet and I slumped against the island before pressing the cool glass against my lips.

"Is that one of my beers?" A voice called from the stairs, and I jumped, spitting my mouthful across the island before turning to glare at Jace.

But whatever nasty retort I had on my tongue died the second I noticed the bruising around his eye. "Crap, Rivers! You need to put some ice on that."

Coming towards me, Jace grinned, and I nearly sighed at the sight of those dimples before I caught myself. "Shawn and I waited around for you after the game, we were going to give you a lift. How did you get home?"

"Kate. She wanted to go out but I wasn't feeling it."

Tilting my head, I took a step closer and lifted a hand to cup his jaw before turning his face. The swelling wasn't that bad, but it still looked painful and Jace moved my fingers to trace the heated skin. "Did you lie when you told Perry it wasn't about me?"

Stepping even further into my space, Jace lifted a hand to wrap around my wrist and then he pulled me closer, pressing me into the island before reaching around my hip to grab at the forgotten beer I had left on the granite. "Does it matter?"

"It does to me. I don't need you defending my honour or innocence or whatever." I had meant for the words to be sharp, but they came out breathless and I shivered as Jace lowered his face before touching the cold bottle to his injury.

"Your innocence? And here I was hoping you didn't have much of it left to defend." His voice was full of heat while my heart thundered in my chest, and I realized I was close to crossing a line with Jace Rivers in the kitchen of O'Neil's house. For the second time.

"Starting without me?" Glancing over Jace's shoulder, I moved my attention to a shirtless Shawn who had entered the kitchen undetected, and I looked between the two with a frown, wondering how he always seemed to know exactly when to interrupt.

"What is going on? What do you mean starting without you?" Pulling away from me, Jace created a few feet of space between us and then he lifted a hand to Shawn, motioning for him to answer.

"Callum told Jace he's fine with us, *spending time* together, and even if he wasn't, we wouldn't care anymore. He is our best friend, and as much as we respect him, we won't allow him to decide who we spend any time with and we're hoping you feel the same."

"Ah," rolling my eyes, I crossed my arms and then tilted my head. "So, you both are looking for a victory fuck now that you have his blessing."

"Maybe, or maybe we're sick of playing by O'Neil's rules. Aren't you?"

Shawn's blue eyes bore into mine and I shrugged before swiping the beer from Jace's hand and I took a long swig. Both men watched and waited silently and when I was done, I placed the bottle back onto the island and wiped my mouth roughly with the back of my hand.

"Alright then, how do we do this?" I asked with a raised brow, all while ignoring the fluttering in my belly. There was no point denying I wanted what they were offering and now that O'Neil had gotten over himself, I decided to jump at my chance.

"However, you want. First, I'd like to talk about ground rules though," Jace offered, leaning forward until his front half rested on the granite and he looked between his friend and me.

"Well, protection is non-negotiable," I offered, watching as both men nodded. "And I can change my mind at any point in time. Beginning, middle, or end."

"Of course, Tatum, the same goes for us." Shawn said before finally taking a few steps closer. "I don't want any of us to regret this in the morning so if anyone is unsure or needs something to slow down, we say so."

"Is there anything you dislike, Tatum?" This time it was Jace who spoke, and I moved my attention to him. "Anything you don't want to happen?"

"Well, I'll be honest, you weren't wrong when you mentioned my lack of innocence and I'm open to almost anything as long as it is done safely and communicated to me beforehand. But this is my first time with two people so maybe you should explain the mechanics of it. Will you both be with me, or will you be with each other? What is the dynamic here?"

"Would you like us both to fuck you?" Jace asked, his dark eyes heated as they traced the length of my body.

"Yes." It was short but honest. "I would like to have both of you if we are doing this."

"Well okay then." Jace moved, grabbing at my fingers and then we were heading up the stairs.

Stepping into his surprisingly tidy room, Jace flicked the lights on and then I turned to Shawn. The blonde had followed behind us and now his body was close enough I could feel the heat of him through my clothes and I glanced over my shoulder with a soft smile.

"Come here," he whispered and then his fingers were tangling in my hair while his lips pressed to mine. Shawn Patrick knew how to kiss, that much was clear, and I sighed into his mouth as he coaxed my lips open. There was no rushing, no thrusting of his tongue into my mouth and I nearly melted as he sucked my lower lip between his teeth before he pulled back.

Waiting for my eyes to flutter open, he traced my jaw with his thumbs and then after I had held his stare for a pause, he moved forward once again. This time his kiss was less gentle and far more urgent, and he guided me forward, until my knees hit what had to be the bed. Finally pulling away, I glanced at him while I caught my breath and then noticed Jace was watching us with a smile.

"My turn."

Large hands cradled my hips as he tugged me forward and then I tipped my chin, pressing my mouth to his with a whine while fingers traced my spine. Shawn had pressed in behind me and I felt him tug at my shirt, untucking the green material from the waistband of my pants before his fingertips traced the skin of my back.

"Shawn," Jace warned, "You need to learn patience."

Reaching over my shoulder, he cupped the blonde's jaw roughly and gave him a gentle kiss before guiding him to his knees at our feet. Shawn, who had never come across overly submissive, followed Jace's direction and sank into the carpet before resting his hands on his thighs, though his fingers twitched and then curled in on themselves.

"Shawn lives for praise Tatum, be sure to tell him he's a good boy when he earns it."

The breath that escaped through my lips was rough and I blinked down at the bright blue eyes before squirming against Jace. There was no way in hell my panties weren't soaked by now, and I fidgeted once more before lifting a hand. Stroking Shawn's cheek affectionately, I glanced at Jace for reassurance. When he dipped his chin in a nod, I moved my hand to his blonde hair and curled the soft strands through my fingers before tugging on them sharply. When his blue eyes fluttered shut, I pressed my mouth to his for a quick second before pulling back just far enough to whisper my appreciation.

"You're doing so well Shawn; you're being so good." His reaction was instantaneous, and I watched as he trembled with a whimper.

"I think he deserves more than a kiss," Jace chastised with a click of his tongue. "Shawn, are you ready to taste our girl? Will you make her ready for us?"

My breath caught in my chest and my knees wobbled at the words, and though Jace sounded very sure of himself and the situation, he paused, tipping my chin towards him in question. "Would that be okay with you, Tatum? Can Shawn eat you out?"

Sinking my teeth into my lower lip, I nodded but Jace clicked his tongue at me disappointedly. "Words Tatum, I need to hear them before I strip you bare and let Shawn bury his face between your thighs."

"Please," I whispered, while I rocked my hips into Jace's.

"Please? What is it you're begging for?" He was going to make me say the words, he was not going to take any half answers and so I straightened my spine and glared at his handsome face.

"I want you to peel off my clothes, trace every inch of my skin until I am dripping wet and then I want you to part my legs so Shawn can make me cum on his tongue."

"Holy fuck," Shawn whispered, his blue eyes impossibly wide and I smiled down at him before lifting a hand to the buttons of my blouse. When neither man moved to help, I gave up on trying to unfasten it and instead pulled the shirt from over my head.

"You haven't been wearing a bra?" Jace's voice deepened and then his hands moved from my hips and crawled up my torso until they covered both breasts.

"No need." I tried to shrug but the second Jace thumbed my nipples my head lolled against his shoulder and all thoughts left my mind.

"Get her pants off," Rivers ordered while tracing his teeth along my shoulder and I shivered when Shawn's fingers outlined my navel before pulling down my waistband.

Stepping out of the black fabric, I pressed back against Jace, allowing him to hold some of my weight and then I ran my hand through Shawn's hair once more before nodding at his questioning stare. His fingers were far steadier than I had expected, and he carefully peeled my grey cotton panties down my legs, only stopping twice to stroke the skin of my inner thighs on his way down. Once I was left bare, Shawn moved forward, pressing a kiss to my hip and then tipped his head back glancing at Jace.

"Let me open her up," Jace's chest rumbled against my back and then one massive hand was cupping my knee and lifting it, spreading my thighs wide for Shawn. Once I was secure in River's grasp, the blonde tipped forward, bracing his hands on my hips, and then glanced at me, waiting for permission.

"Go ahead Patrick," It wasn't the sexiest thing I could have said but it did the trick and I grunted, tensing when the tip of his tongue circled my clit.

"That was the hottest noise I have ever heard," Jace groaned and had I not been focused on the finger that was now slipping into me I would have swatted him.

"Don't tease me," I sighed, clenching my eyes shut as another finger joined the first and then they curled searching my front wall with precision.

"I'm not Kelly."

Dark hands moved to cup my breasts and then fingers stroked over my nipples softly. I knew I didn't sound like the typical pornstar during sex, mostly because I couldn't bring myself to fake it, nor did I really want to focus my attention on making my voice higher and pleasing when I was in the throes of an orgasm. My ex had often commented on how I made similar sounds at the gym when lifting weights and I had nearly gone a year without getting off because of it.

"Make her do it again, Shawn," Jace ordered, his fingers pinching my nipples sharply at the same moment Patrick had found my g-spot and I trembled, swaying softly before I grunted again. "There it is, now make her come."

Determined to follow orders, Shawn sucked my clit into his mouth, flicking his tongue across the flesh and then pressed his fingers into the front wall. Jace, who had continued to work at my nipples, pressed his mouth to my neck, sucking gently and then I unravelled. The heat that had been simmering in my belly spread through my limbs and I could have sworn my eyes crossed when I finally came.

"Good girl," Jace praised.

Usually, I would have bristled at a phrase like that but now as I slumped against him, I let his words wash over me, realizing they left me wanting.

Chapter Eighteen

TATUM

"Do I get to touch you now?" I asked, still panting while I glanced over my shoulder at Jace. Smiling, he nodded and took a step back once he was sure I was somewhat steady on my feet.

"Tell us what you want, and we'll make it happen Tatum." I had a million things I wanted to do but when I glanced down at Shawn, watching as he shifted uncomfortably on his knees and pulled at the fabric of his pants, I knew my answer.

"I want a taste too."

Blue eyes blinked up at me, their depths filling with heat and then he stood, pulling his pants down quickly. The tattoos didn't stop at his hips like I had assumed. No, the dark ink covered both of his thighs, reaching down to his knees and I wet my lips quickly before glancing at the silver piercing that I knew was there. Shawn was well endowed, not overly long but thick and I ran my tongue across my lower lip again in anticipation.

"Sit on the edge of the bed Patrick, that way she can kneel on the bench and be comfortable." Jace commanded, gesturing to the beige padded bench that sat in front of the footboard.

"And what will you be doing?" I asked with a raised brow, smiling when I noticed he seemed distracted by the skin of my naked torso.

"Hmm," Jace hummed under his breath while one hand moved to the front of his sweats, and he palmed his obvious erection. "I'd like to fuck you from behind while you wrap that pretty mouth around Patrick's cock, if that's alright with you?"

I had begun to nod but when one dark brow lifted, I realized he was waiting for actual words again. "Yeah."

"Yeah?" Shawn asked, his voice light with amusement and I turned to glance at him and nodded enthusiastically.

"Yeah. Scoot up, pretty boy." I winked, watching as a pretty pink flush coloured his cheeks. Dragging himself across the carefully made bed, I took a second to wonder how long Jace had spent preparing his room before following the blonde.

The fabric of the bench was a little coarse though it was padded, and I knelt on it carefully before leaning across Shawn's legs and then I traced one of the tattoos that covered a hip. Taking in a ragged breath, Shawn moved onto his elbows and dipped his chin to his chest as he watched me with interest, and I shot him another wink before moving my fingers to his cock.

It was warm and heavy in my palm, and I curled my fist around him gently before sliding up. His head was deep in colour and the piercing was covered in a drop of precum that had already started leaking from the tip. Moving my thumb, I swirled the wetness around the cool silver and grinned when his thighs twitched as his needy whimper echoed in the nearly silent room.

"What do you need Shawn?" I repeated the words I had asked the last time I had been in bed with him, and his eyes fluttered closed while his chin tipped towards the ceiling.

"Same answer, just you Tatum."

Pleased by his words, I lowered my mouth and licked the length of him slowly before wrapping my lips around the tip. Giving head had always been enjoyable for me, I loved the feeling of power it gave me, and this was no different though the metal was a little distracting.

Setting a smooth rhythm, I widened my jaw and adjusted my head so I would fit more of him into my mouth all while taking care not to let my teeth scrape against him. Once I was confident, I moved my fist in time with my mouth and began to bob along his length, letting the tip of him reach the back of my throat before pulling back.

"Fuck Kelly, you're so good at this," Shawn whined, and I glanced up at him from my place before humming around his cock. My enthusiasm must have been a tipping point for him because the second the sound reached his ears, his hips lifted, and he began to fuck my mouth.

"Don't you dare finish yet Patrick!" Jace snarled while one of his hands circled my hip and the other dipped between my legs, flicking across my clit. "You were rewarded once, now it's Kelly's turn to come for me."

The sound of the condom wrapper was quiet, but I lifted my mouth off of Shawn and glanced over my shoulder, watching as he rolled the latex down his length, immediately noticing he was a bit larger than Shawn, though not as thick and my hips swayed in anticipation. Noticing my gaze, Jace moved a hand to smooth down my spine before wedging it between my thighs, forcing me to widen my stance. Once he was happy with my position, he moved the hand into my hair and directed me back to Shawn's cock.

"I want your mouth on him when I press into you. I want him to feel your gasp, so he knows the exact minute I stretch you open." Following his orders, I lowered my mouth once again, wrapping my lips around Shawn and then Jace was filling me. He didn't take his time, didn't hesitate the way most men did, like they were waiting for some sort of dramatic reaction. No, Jace just moved, gliding into me and then he began to thrust, and I'd be lying if I said it wasn't one of the hottest experiences I had ever had.

"Fuck you take me so well," Jace growled with a snap of his hips, and I shivered before quickening my pace around Shawn. "That's a good girl, swallow down his cock just like that, baby. I'll make you cum all over me."

Desperate for the orgasm that was just out of reach, I pressed back into Jace, letting my ass slap against his thighs before I removed my fist from around Shawn and then I pressed my tongue against my bottom teeth and swallowed him until he was in the back of my throat. Noticing my impatience, Jace crowded in behind me, pressing his chest to my back and then his fingers snaked between my thighs, dipping into the wetness that coated them before moving to circle my clit again.

"You're almost there baby, so close." I couldn't nod, so I grunted in frustration and swung my hips back with more strength. "Stop trying to force it and relax, enjoy the cock in your mouth, feel the way I'm filling your sweet little cunt. Let your body give into it."

Closing my eyes tightly, I inhaled roughly through my nose and did just that. I focused on the heavy feeling of Shawn in my mouth, the way his fingers had tangled with River's as they both guided my head before fixating on the way Jace was thrusting into my pussy all while his other hand softly stroked me.

"That's a good girl, now cum." The pattern changed suddenly, the soft touches became more concentrated, and my toes curled before I lifted my head from Shawn and cried out with my release.

Falling forward, I rested my face on Shawn's hip, watching in a daze as both men wrapped a hand around the blonde's erection and they pumped twice more before his cum was coating his abs. Satisfied that we both had finished, Jace grabbed at my hips tightly, groaning as he gave one last thrust, and I could feel the way he trembled inside me.

My body was shaking, spasming and I closed my eyes while I gasped for air. I had my share of experiences both good and bad but nothing and no one had made me feel like this. I couldn't feel my limbs let alone move and I noticed my cheeks were damp with tears.

"I'm going to clean us up Kelly, is that okay?" Jace whispered while pressing a kiss to my sweaty temple and I nodded before squinting an eye up at Shawn. The blonde was still sprawled on his back, eyes wide as he stared at the ceiling in a daze and the expression made me giggle. Startling at the noise, he glanced down at me and smiled goofily.

"Holy fuck Kelly, you sucked the life out of me." I could feel the burning flush as it crawled up my neck and into my cheeks as his brows rose in surprise. "Seriously? You're still blushing after all that?"

"I think it's charming." Jace chimed in, his hands gentle as he pressed the warm wet cloth between my legs before cleaning me carefully. Once he was satisfied with his work, he wiped down Shawn's stomach taking care to remove every drop of cum before he fell onto the bed next to the blonde.

Making sure that I was able to feel my feet again, I lifted myself from the bench and carefully stood before moving towards the door of the bathroom. "I'm just going to finish cleaning up and stuff and then I'll head downstairs."

Both men sat up with frowns before looking at each other and then Shawn sighed with a roll of his eyes. "Just go pee and get back in here Kelly. We cuddle after sex and this bed is big enough for all of us."

Blushing once more I skipped into the bathroom to use the toilet before washing my hands and then I glanced at my reflection in the mirror. I had a hickey on my shoulder and red marks along my hips that surely matched the shape and size of Jace's fingers. My lips were red and swollen and my mascara had smeared, the black running down my cheeks in thin black lines. I looked thoroughly fucked, they had made a complete mess of me, and I couldn't be more pleased.

"Hurry up, Tatum! Shawn is already fading and he's all pissy that you aren't in here." Jace called, his voice light with laughter and I wiped at my face clumsily, cleaning it quickly and then dashed back into the room.

Both men had moved to either side of the bed and I crawled up the middle before tucking my body under the duvet. Once I was settled on my back, Shawn curled around me, throwing a heavy leg over my own, trapping me against him and then he laid his head against my shoulder. Jace rolled on his side, wrapping a strong arm around both of us before tucking my head under his chin.

"I'm only staying for a bit; I'm absolutely not spending the night in here," I warned and Shawn nestled closer, kissing my collar bone with a grumble.

"Shut up and go to sleep Kelly."

Extracting myself from two men was a struggle and I cursed as I slid from the bed before grabbing at my discarded panties and blouse. Tossing both on, I gathered my pants and then glanced at the sleeping bodies who were sprawled across the mattress. It was still the middle of the night, and I would have stayed cocooned in the warmth of their arms if it hadn't been for my bladder and the persistent voice in my head that reminded me this whole idea was possibly the worst I had ever had.

Sneaking to the door, I shot them one last glance and then tiptoed out of the room. The house was still dark though there was a bit of light coming from the kitchen and I could have sworn we had turned it off before coming upstairs. Carefully making my way to the main floor with a frown, I padded across the hardwood and reached for the light switch along the wall.

"I'd rather you leave that on actually."

Jumping at the stern voice, I spun on my heel and met the brown eyes that were concealed behind the dark curls that had fallen across his forehead. He was pressed into the couch, both arms stretched across the back of it, and it was then that I noticed the blonde head bobbing across his lap.

"What the fuck, O'Neil!?" I shrieked, obviously alerting the woman to my presence and she lifted to face me before wiping at her lips with wide eyes though her body blocked me from seeing any more of Callum.

"Relax Kelly, I'm just celebrating our win and I like to do so with the lights on." The blonde's face flushed, and she glared up at Callum though she didn't rise from her knees and I narrowed my eyes at him.

"You have a bedroom." I reminded him.

"And this is my house," he snapped. "I wouldn't have thought you'd be such a prude. Especially after wetting both my roommates' dicks."

My eyes burned with tears of frustration, and I crossed my arms over my chest. "Fuck you, O'Neil."

"I'll pass. I'm not into sloppy seconds, or would you technically be thirds?" He asked with a smirk, and I felt my lower lip tremble.

"You know what O'Neil, say what you want, but I won't be the one you hurt if you keep this shit up. Your friends are adults, and we can do what we want, and I know for a fact they warned you that you have no say in it." Lowering my arms, I shrugged. "And if you don't stop being such an asshole about all of this, chances are you'll lose more than just this season."

I didn't wait around to hear his retort and instead fled to my room, slamming the door behind me before falling into my bed, all while cursing Callum O'Neil's name.

Chapter Nineteen

JACE

Shawn had rolled through the night, and I glanced over my shoulder as he nestled in close and then he stiffened. Watching his mouth fall into a frown, I smiled and held my breath as his hand searched my torso for the pair of tits that were obviously missing.

"Done copping a feel?" His blue eyes fluttered open to meet mine and then he was lifting himself up, leaning on an elbow before searching the room.

"Kelly in the bathroom?" He asked, his voice hopeful and I groaned, running a hand down my face while I prepared for the pouting I was about to deal with.

"She snuck out around two last night."

Pulling himself up, Shawn sat against the headboard and crossed his arms. "Why would she do that? Do you think she regrets it?"

Grunting, I folded myself in half, stretching my fingers to my toes and then peered at the blonde carefully.

"Shawn, stop reading so much into it, I'm sure she just wanted some space. It's not about you or how she feels." Shawn Patrick may have been tattooed, pierced, and could easily out bench me, but he was soft. He had his baggage, mostly stemming from his absent parents and shitty childhood, but that didn't make him untrusting. It made him long for connection and I knew that he must have seriously felt something for Kelly if he was that eager to be with her. I just hoped I didn't fuck it up for him by joining in.

"I'm going to shower and study. Let me know if you want to hit the gym later," he grumbled, sliding from the bed and I watched him carefully.

"Patrick," I called as he reached the door, "don't shut down man, you haven't even spoken to her yet." Nodding, he entered the bathroom before closing the door softly behind him and then I moved, grabbing at some sweats before heading downstairs.

The kitchen was quiet, and I looked at the beer bottle that was still on the island before glancing at the coffee maker. Tatum always started a pot when she got up and yet it was empty. There was no sign she had been in here at all. Double checking the clock on the microwave, I frowned at the time and then glanced towards her bedroom. There was no noise coming from the room, no sign that she was in there and I would have thought she had left if it wasn't for her black coat and shoes that were tucked neatly by the front door.

Striding to her room, I hesitated outside of it and tipped my head, waiting to see if I could hear anything. But there was silence and I lifted my hand to rap my knuckles against the wood before calling out for her softly.

"Kelly?" Still nothing and I noticed Callum as he slid the back door open before stepping into the house. He looked exhausted, his hair was ruffled like someone had run their hands through it all night and he frowned at me, watching as I knocked again. "Tatum, are you in there?"

"She's probably too embarrassed to come out after I caught her walk of shame last night." Callum laughed dryly and my brows lifted before I tapped the wood once more. "Seriously Rivers, let the girl hide in peace, it's too early to deal with her shit."

"What did you do Cal?" Moving into the kitchen, I watched as my friend grabbed at the bottle of beer before dumping it down the sink but when he didn't answer, I moved in on him, stepping up until we were toe to toe. "O'Neil, what did you do?"

"Back up, Rivers. it's not that serious and I am too hungover to put up with your self-righteous ass right now." He went to move past me, but I shot out an arm, curling my fist around the counter, blocking his way.

"You said you were over this shit Callum, you said that we could do what we wanted, and you didn't care anymore." Taking a step back, Callum crossed his arms and lifted his chin, so he peered down at me.

"I don't care, Rivers. Do what you want, fuck her, put her on her knees. Hell, put them both on their knees, I'm sure Patrick would like th-" My fist made contact before he got to finish and he stumbled away, lifting his hand to his bloodied lip.

"What the fuck is going on with you?!" I snarled, but Callum pulled his fingers away from his face and rubbed them together, watching as the blood smeared between the pads. "Seriously, you have never, not once spoken about Shawn that way. Or me, for that matter. You have never cared about what we do, if anything it was your support that made him more comfortable with himself. Honestly Callum, I don't know what has gotten into you, or why you hate Tatum so much. This person in front of me, I don't know him. And the Callum O'Neil I *do know*, would be ashamed of you."

I could see the minute the words hit their mark and Callum deflated, his shoulders sagging until he was leaning back against the sink, and I took a step back, putting some space between us.

"I'm sorry man, you're right I've been a dick." His brown eyes roamed around the kitchen, though they never met my own and I shook my head with a sigh.

"No, not this time. I won't accept some bullshit blanket apology, O'Neil."

Finally, he looked at me and I held his stare. "There's enough tension in this house. Patrick hasn't been himself lately and won't tell me why, you are on this constant rampage, Tatum is doing anything she can to get by without pissing you off and I'm here trying to keep everything from falling apart."

"I don't know what to tell you." Callum sighed, rubbing at his face tiredly.

"Well, tell me something, because I can't keep going in circles with you."

"It's just everything man, this is my senior year and we lost one of our best players, I'm stuck with fucking Tatum Kelly of all people, and this is not what I pictured."

"Kelly has been saving our asses, she helped us win the last game and we had a bigger crowd than we've had since my freshman year, so what's the problem?" None of this was adding up, none of his reasons explained why he disliked her so much and why he had been such a dick.

"She just annoys the shit out of me, I don't know." Shrugging he stuffed his hands into his pockets, and I rolled my eyes, not believing his sad excuse. "She just, I don't know, okay. It doesn't matter, but I promise I'll knock it off."

"You said that before," I reminded him.

"I know but I mean it, I won't interfere, I'll stop being an ass."

"And you'll apologize to her." Callum narrowed his eyes at me, but I held firm. "You'll apologize to her."

"Fine."

Slapping him on the back I finally smiled and then opened the fridge and grabbed one of the water bottles. "We are going to the gym, come with us. You can spot Shawn and tell him that you won't keep him from spending time with Tatum."

"Is that what we are calling it, spending time?" He lifted his hands, curling his fingers in air quotes and I threw a water at him.

"He likes her Cal, like really likes her." Callum frowned before twisting the lid of the bottle and taking a sip.

"And you? Do you really like her too?" Shrugging, I glanced at my friend cautiously and he groaned. "You barely know her."

"You asked."

Rolling his eyes, Callum grabbed his keys from the counter and moved to the stairs "Great, this is just great."

The smell of something cooking hit me in a wave and I dropped my gym bag before glancing at my friends from over my shoulder. Both Shawn and Callum tried to look past my shoulder, and I pulled them through the door just before slamming it shut behind us. Soft music played from in the kitchen, and I watched as Tatum carefully stirred whatever was in the pan before her eyes met mine.

"Hey," she said - her voice gentle and unsure, and I grinned as I crossed the space.

"Hey yourself." Sitting at the island, I focused on the way her long hair swung as she turned back to the stove and then I cleared my throat. "We uhh – didn't catch you before the gym."

Grey eyes peered at me for a second and I noticed the way her face had filled with pink. "Yeah, I slept in, sorry."

"What are you cooking, Kelly?" An arm slung around my shoulders, and I glanced up at Shawn while he smiled blindingly at Tatum.

"Honey-Garlic chicken stir fry, I hope that's okay?" Both of us nodded and then Shawn sank into the chair beside me.

"Need help?"

Had I not been securely sitting on my chair I would have fallen over in shock, and I turned to Callum, watching while he washed his hands before glancing at the pan.

"Oh," Tatum struggled with her own disbelief and shot me a questioning look before swallowing. "I haven't started the rice or diced the veggies yet."

"Right, I'll get started." His voice wasn't what I would consider warm, but the hostility he usually used was gone and I felt Shawn stiffen beside me as he studied our friend closely.

"Thanks," was all Kelly seemed to be able to say and I cleared my throat before looking at Shawn.

"Why don't we run to the store, grab some beer?" Shawn looked confused and I tried to convey my plan silently, hoping he'd pick up on it somehow. Callum was trying and I knew he would do better doing so without an audience.

"Any way you could grab some white wine for me?" Tatum asked though she was still facing the stove.

"Yeah of course!" Shawn agreed "We will pick up some of that Pineo Grudgeio stuff."

"It's Pinot Grigio, you dumb ass." Callum sighed and Tatum laughed out loud, shocking all of us. The sound wasn't light or girlish. It rumbled out of her in a deep and soothing way, and it reminded me of the sounds she made when I was inside her. The thought alone made me hard.

"Grab two bottles, and some glasses, we don't have any," Callum suggested, his eyes remaining on Tatum, and I cleared my head before raising a brow in his direction.

"What do you know about drinking wine, O'Neil?" Callum lifted a hand and flipped me off before continuing to cut the peppers.

"Some of us have taste and don't only drink beer and cheap liquor, Rivers."

"Your snobbery is showing, asshat." Shawn grumbled, obviously not pleased about being embarrassed in front of the girl he had spent so long wanting and Tatum turned to him, studying his face before leaning over and kissing him softly on the cheek.

"Thank you."

Shawn's eyes were comically wide, and he even lifted a hand, stroking the skin of his cheek, as if it was the first time a girl had touched him and not as though Tatum had wrapped those lips around something else just last night.

"Come on Patrick, let's go." Wrapping his shirt in my fist, I tugged him out of the kitchen while rolling my eyes as he stared after her the entire way.

Chapter Twenty

CALLUM

The sound of oil sizzling was quiet, and I sighed while the tension between Kelly and I grew tenfold after the front door clicked shut. I knew Jace had been right this morning, I owed the girl an apology. Especially if I couldn't offer an explanation, but I hated the idea of asking Kelly for forgiveness. Those sharp grey eyes of hers would see right through my bullshit and I'd have to watch as they filled with judgement.

"Can you pass me the minced garlic please?" Her voice whispered and I glanced at the bowl in front of me before handing it to her. "Thanks."

I grunted in reply, turning my entire focus back on the peppers I had been cutting and tried to ignore the guilt that twisted in my gut. She was obviously trying to get along, the garlic had been within arm's reach, she didn't need me to pass it to her and I sighed.

"Kelly, about last night," placing the knife down, I wiped my palms across my thighs. "I'm sorry for what I said. I did tell the guys I was fine with it and I had no right to speak to you the way I did or have been."

"Then why do you?" I don't know why I expected her to just accept the apology, I should have known it wouldn't be that easy. "What did I do to make you dislike me so much?"

"I could ask you the same question, it's not like you've been sweet any time we've talked."

Scoffing, Kelly turned towards me and pointed the spatula at my face. "We've barely said two words to each other and I would like to remind you that it was you who mocked me when my team was cut."

Blinking at her, I frowned, and she threw her hands up in the air. "You don't even remember? When you ran into me just outside Miller's office? You were a complete ass."

"You're overexaggerating."

"See that's my issue with guys like you! You say things that can hurt people and you don't even remember doing it!" She had taken a step closer, and the spatula was now nearly pressing into my chest. Lifting my chin, I peered down at her and then wrapped my fingers around her wrist before moving her hand away from me.

"You've never met a guy like me, I'm one of a kind." My lips lifted into a smirk, the one that usually had the girls blushing, but Kelly snorted and then snatched her wrist from my hand.

"Seriously O'Neil, what is your issue with me?"

"Your freshman year, at the kegger at Bailey's, do you remember it?" Frowning, she pressed back against the counter and tipped her head before nodding. "Then you remember I had left to grab you a drink while you hung out in the corner with your team. I was nearly at your shoulder with your beer in my hand when I heard them say that my dad must have bought my way onto the team. That my first year had been such a shitshow and they had no idea what Perry was thinking. They couldn't understand how everyone talked about his eye for talent when he scouted me for his team. And then you chimed in, and you told them I was so bad on the ice; it was no wonder my dad never showed up to my games. You told them that if you were him you wouldn't want to be seen at a game either and if he had bought my way onto the team, it was a huge waste of money. I guess you didn't know he had died the year before."

All colour drained from her face and my dry laugh echoed around us. "I suppose you know all about not noticing when you say things that hurt people."

"Callum," She whispered sadly, and I clenched my jaw waiting for her excuse.

"I am so sorry about your father; I didn't know but that doesn't excuse what I said. I just wanted to fit in, I didn't want to seem like the odd man out, so I joined in, and it was at your expense. I'm really sorry, truly I am."

"It's fine," I snapped but Kelly shook her head, placing the spatula down before looking up into my face.

"It's not, and honestly, I'm more ashamed that I don't even remember saying something like that, especially considering I know what it is to not have parents around. Mine haven't passed but they aren't in my life, and I wouldn't wish that on anyone."

Clearing my throat, I glanced at the cutting board and cleared my throat. "You were probably drunk."

"That's not an excuse. I'm really sorry, O'Neil. I hope you can forgive me."

"Yeah, sure whatever." I hadn't raised my eyes, but a pale hand appeared in my line of vision, and I examined it before glancing at Kelly.

"Can we start over?" Understanding what she meant, I grabbed her fingers with my own and gave a firm squeeze.

"Friends?" She asked, her grey eyes hopeful and I snorted before shaking my head.

"Well considering the guys will kick my ass if you move out, how about we start with two people who share the same living space?"

"Those are called roommates," she laughed.

"Yeah, but that sounds too serious, we aren't there yet."

"People who share the same living space it is." Letting go of my hand she turned back to the stove, and I watched her for a second longer, noticing the tiny smile that had spread across her mouth.

Jace and Shawn were anything but quiet when they came through the front door and I frowned, at the sudden interruption. Kelly and I had continued to make dinner in silence, both seeming to enjoy the peaceful feel of the kitchen and I sighed, knowing that was at an end.

"We got the wine!" Shawn called, all but skipping to the table where I had set out the plates and I rolled my eyes at his excitement though I couldn't help but smile.

"And beer, even if it isn't good enough for O'Neil." Walking to the table, Kelly dished out the food onto each plate and then glanced at my friends.

"No one has a problem with the beer Rivers, just sit down and eat." Moving towards Kelly, I grabbed the empty pan from her hand and nodded towards the table.

"Go, I'll clean up." Her grey eyes lacked their usual coolness and I noticed both Jace and Shawn had stilled, taking in our interaction before looking at each other.

"Thanks," she whispered, and then ducked past me before pulling her chair out. The other two followed, Shawn sitting across from her and Jace folded himself into the seat beside hers. The guys didn't bother waiting for me to join before digging in but I noticed Kelly had, and she swatted at them, motioning them to lower their forks.

"But it smells so good," Shawn complained, tightening his hand around the silver and she glared at him, not looking away until he forfeited and lowered it to the table.

Sliding into the chair next to Shaw, I nudged my elbow into his ribs and then grabbed at the wine bottle that sat in the middle of the table. “Have some manners, you didn’t even pour Kelly her wine.”

Snatching her glass, I filled it carefully and then handed it to her before pouring some into my own. Cradling it gently, I lifted it towards the middle of the table and then cleared my throat.

“To people who share the same living space.”

Jace and Shawn looked confused, but Kelly smiled and then clinked her glass with mine.

“To people who share the same living space.”

Weeks had passed since our first dinner together and the time had passed without too many issues. Kelly and I still kept our distance, and I hadn’t caught her coming out of the bedrooms upstairs, but I could see she had only gotten closer to my friends.

Initially I had been only worried about Shawn but after witnessing the way Jace watched her any time she entered a room, I knew that the two of them had stronger feelings than they let on. The whole situation was a fucking mess, but I couldn’t force myself to interfere any more than I already had. I just held onto the fact that eventually she would be replaced, especially now that we had won the last two games.

“Why are we stuck throwing the Halloween party?” Shawn asked, watching his reflection as he finished his set and I placed my water bottle on the floor before lifting my shirt to wipe the sweat out of my eyes.

“We throw it every year.” Jace reminded him but Shawn didn’t look any happier about that fact.

“And every year I complain. The costumes are always uncomfortable and there are way too many drunk fuckers with swords who end up trying to re-enact a show or movie by the end of the night. It’s a disaster. Not to mention the fact that Halloween was almost two weeks ago.”

“Yeah, and we had a game so now it had to wait. Don’t worry Patrick, we can take the swords and any foam weapons at the door.” I offered, winking at Jace with a smile but Shawn groaned.

"I'll put on a mask or a jersey but that's it, that's what I'll agree to." He frowned and then dropped the weights before heading to the locker room. Grinning at Jace I checked my phone and then lifted it showing him a picture of a superhero costume.

"I bet you twenty bucks I can convince him to put this on tonight." Jace grabbed the phone from me and stared at the screen.

"How are you going to manage that? He just told you how much he hates uncomfortable costumes and that looks skin-tight."

"I'll tell him how much girls like Kelly like it." I shrugged and Jace looked back down at the screen.

"Why do I feel like that might work?" Taking the phone back, I stuffed it into my pocket and then collected the rest of my stuff.

"Because he's desperate, she's all but friend-zoned him lately." I laughed, making my way to the locker room while Jace chased after me.

"But do you really think she'll like it?" Rolling my eyes, I pressed open the door and then turned to Jace.

"Man, you used to have way better game, what happened to you?" I asked while clapping Jace on the back and I waited for him to answer, but he didn't say a word, and it was almost as if he was just as puzzled.

Chapter Twenty-One

SHAWN

"Hey," Tatum called, as she bounded towards me, and I offered her a weak smile before glancing down at the textbook in my lap. "Are you studying before the party?"

Lifting the book towards her I shrugged and then dropped it back onto my legs. I had been in a shitty mood for most of the day and the last thing I wanted to do was have a party. Peters' class wasn't getting any easier and I was struggling more than ever, even with the extra time I was taking to go over my notes after each lecture.

"Ah, Peters," she moved, grabbing my backpack from the cushion before settling next to me and then she peered over my shoulder while her eyes scanned across the page. "How was the midterm?"

Sighing, I let my head fall back to rest on the couch and then I squinted up at her. "I barely passed; I think he took pity on me for some reason."

"Peters isn't the type to feel bad for anyone." She smiled and then moved closer. "I can help you if you want? Maybe look over your notes or something?"

"You don't have to do that," I muttered, ignoring the way my face burned in embarrassment. The last person I wanted help from was Tatum, I didn't want her realizing how much I struggled with my classes.

"I know I don't have to; I want to."

Shuffling the loose papers, I watched as she read over them, and I searched for some sign of shock or confusion on her face, but it never came. "I wish I took notes like this, mine are so unorganized, I can barely understand what I wrote half the time."

"Right," I drawled sarcastically before grabbing at the pages and rushing to tuck them into my textbook.

"Woah, wait. Shawn, wait." Her hands grabbed at my fingers, and she pinned them to my legs before moving her face, so she was in my direct line of sight. "What just happened? What's wrong?"

"Nothing."

Her brows furrowed in obvious disbelief, and I cleared my throat awkwardly. "I just don't need you trying to make me feel better, I know I'm stupid." Her mouth parted and she searched my eyes before moving her hands to cup my jaw.

"Shawn," Her voice dropped with concern. "You are not stupid."

"Yeah? Then why have I almost been on academic probation twice. The only reason why my scholarship wasn't canceled this year was because of Perry. He somehow managed to convince them I would get my shit together."

"Shawn, we might not know each other super well, but I know for a fact you spend more time studying and you try harder than anyone else, you deserve your scholarship."

"That's exactly my point, I work my ass off and yet I can barely manage." Her thumb stroked across my jaw, and she tipped my face towards her before lifting her other hand and then she cradled my cheeks between her palms.

"Shawn, people learn differently. Some people don't have to work for anything when it comes to academics and others need extra help. Everyone is different but that doesn't make them stupid. Peters is a hard professor, I struggled with his class too. But now that I've been through it, maybe I can help?"

Lowering my eyes, I studied the stitching of her sweatpants and then swallowed and begrudgingly agreed. "Alright."

Leaning over, she reached for the textbook and flipped through the pages before settling next to me once more. "Okay, so let's go over your notes together and then we can pick up where you left off?"

Her grey eyes were bright as they searched my face. I inhaled sharply and then nodded. Pressing into my shoulder, Tatum then tucked her feet under herself, and I nearly closed my eyes when the sweet scent of her shampoo hit me. Living with her without overstepping had become increasingly challenging and even though I forced myself to keep a distance, I caught myself noticing all the little things I had missed before. Like the way her tongue would peek out between her lips when she was concentrating, or how her nose scrunched when she disagreed with something. Everything she did grabbed my attention and I studied her closely as she examined my notes, and then laughed under my breath when I noticed the tip of pink poke out of her mouth.

"What?" She asked, her grey eyes blinking up at me and I shook my head, unsure how to answer her without coming off too strong.

"Nothing, it's nothing." I assured her and then plucked the notes from her. "So - what do you think? Am I hopeless?"

"Not at all, why would you even say that?" Lowering my eyes, I traced the bright colours of my sleeve, but Tatum snatched at my digits and then tucked her fingers under my chin and lifted my face.

"I've noticed you do that when you're anxious." Her voice was soft and then her fingers picked up where I had left off and I watched as the tattooed flesh rose with goosebumps. "I've also noticed that you really think badly about yourself, almost like you've been told all those horrible things are true."

Moving forward, she cupped my face once more and thumbed my lower lip. "I won't ask you to tell me about it, especially if it hurts you. But I will ask that you give yourself more credit, because I know that those lies that are creeping around in the back of your mind, aren't true. You aren't hopeless Shawn and even though I haven't known you long and I might not know you well, I do see you."

"And what do you see?" My voice was a broken whisper, and I felt my lower lip tremble under the pad of her thumb.

"I see someone who is kind, and warm and despite everything, he hasn't allowed life to make him hard." Smiling, she crept closer and then lowered her voice. "And you are not, in any way, stupid. Do you understand?"

Nodding, I swallowed and then Tatum smiled in response.

"Good," Her fingers moved, stroking up my cheeks until they were threaded in my hair and then she shifted, lifting one leg to cross my lap until she was straddling me. Carefully lowering her weight, she waited a pause and then tightened her fingers until my head lifted towards her. "Now that that's settled, I've been dying to do this."

Lowering her mouth to mine, she brushed our lips together softly once, twice, and then for a third time before finally really kissing me and I nearly sighed. It had been weeks since that night in Jace's room and I had told myself that it would never happen again, no matter how badly I wanted it to. I was sure that whatever she had felt for me then had passed, but now as she rocked her hips into mine, I prayed that was wrong.

"Tatum," I gasped, closing my eyes while her teeth scrapped down my neck, "Fuck Kelly, what are you doing to me?"

I could feel the smile as she hummed against my skin and I lifted myself, pressing into her roughly in response. I was hard - hard and desperate and I whimpered when her fists tugged on my hair.

"I want you Patrick," she whispered roughly, her voice dropping low, and my cock throbbed at the sound. "Can I have you? Will you let me?"

"Yes!" I groaned, tilting my chin to the ceiling while I clenched my jaw. "Please, Kelly."

"Why is it so hot when you beg me like that?" She whispered, almost as if she was talking to herself and I finally lifted my hands, pressing them under her shirt to trace the skin of her back.

"I want this off," I sighed, lifting her shirt past her shoulder blades and then I sat back, glancing at her face for confirmation.

"Tell you what, I'll take this off and you show me how hard you are."

My mouth dropped open in shock and she snickered before stepping away and tugged her shirt over her head. The grey cotton sports bra she wore underneath was nothing special, but it somehow only emphasized the strength of her muscular shoulders and I felt my mouth water as my eyes traced the smooth skin. Then without any other prompting she lowered her sweats, and I took in her long thick thighs before smirking at the matching cotton panties.

"Your turn, pretty boy." The nickname might have been embarrassing had it come from anyone else, but it made my gut swoop, and I felt my dick twitch before I tucked my thumbs under my waistband and pulled. Watching me, Tatum's grey eyes followed the ink on my knees, up my thighs and then she studied the length of my cock while her tongue poked out to wet her bottom lip.

"Listen, now that I know what your mouth can do, I'd usually ask for a repeat performance, but I really don't need the foreplay." She laughed huskily and I itched to wrap my fingers around myself. "What I do need, is for you to be sure this is okay. I know Jace isn't here, and you don't usually fly solo, so if you rather stop or wait, that's fine just tell me."

"Tatum, I can promise you, the only thing I want to stop is your talking. I have a condom in my bag, front pocket." Apparently, that had been all she needed to hear because her shoulders sagged, and she sighed before retrieving the foil packet. Opening it with her teeth she moved towards me, but I lifted my palm, gesturing for her to hand it to me.

"As much as I'd love to watch you put that on me, I am one hundred percent sure that I will cum if you touch me right now."

"That would be a shame, because I'm dying to feel you inside of me." She countered and then tilted her head, her eyes studying my every moment as I rolled the latex down the length of me.

Once the condom was on, Tatum moved, flicking her hair over her shoulder before straddling me once more though her hips hovered above me. Glancing up at her face I waited for her to nod and then I slid my fingers under the damp cotton. She was warm and wet, and I took a second to circle her clit with a fingertip before slipping my attention farther down, and then I pressed two fingers into her.

"Fuck Patrick," she moaned, throwing her head back. "I told you I didn't need foreplay."

"I'm just checking if you're ready for me," I answered, though I didn't remove my hand and instead pulled out just slightly before pressing in once more and she followed the motion, moving her hips to fuck herself on my fingers for a minute before finally stilling.

"Enough," she ordered, and then she moved her hands back into my hair. "I need you in me, pretty boy. Right now."

Pulling my hand from her panties, I peeled them to the side and then waited for her to finally sink down onto me. Getting the head in took a little bit of work, but once it made its way, Tatum moaned and then swirled her hips before pushing down until another inch was swallowed by her pussy.

"You're so thick and that piercing feels so good." It was Kelly who whimpered this time, and I trembled underneath her while I waited for her to finally sink the rest of the way down.

"You okay?" I whispered, my hands lifting to tuck her hair behind her ears and her grey eyes flickered open as her teeth sank into her lower lip.

"Better than okay," She answered before pressing a sweet kiss to my lips while one hand left my hair to clutch at the back of the couch. "I'm going to start moving, alright?"

"Yeah." My throat bobbed, and I grabbed at her hips as she began to rock into me. She was warm and tight, and I had never felt anything better. I couldn't imagine anything better, and I helped her find her rhythm until we were both panting into each other's mouths.

"Fucking hell Kelly, I'm close already." Tilting her head back, Tatum quickened her pace, and I moved a hand to dip into the wetness that coated us. Making sure my fingers were slick, I traced her clit delicately and focused on keeping the same pattern once her pussy began to clutch at me.

"Are you going to make me cum, Shawn?" She asked softly, and I nodded vehemently. "I'm almost there, you're fucking me so well. I'm almost there."

My fingers traced her twice more and then she was tightening around me, and I felt her body shake as her release hit her. Lifting my hips, I fucked my cock into her a few more times and then my own orgasm slammed into me like a freight train.

Falling against me, Tatum huffed into my ear, and I wrapped my arms around her, pressing her into me while I stroked up and down her spine. Her own arms draped across my shoulders, and she turned her face, skimming her lips across my jaw gently.

"Do you think we made a mess?" It wasn't what I had been expecting her to say and I pulled away from her in amusement before glancing down to where we were still joined.

"We'll just flip the cushions if we did. No one needs to know."

"What the hell!" I growled, grabbing at the tight stretchy material as I tried to pull it over my shoulders, but it flung from my hand and snapped against my side painfully. "Come on you piece of shit."

I had been trying to put this stupid thing on for half an hour now and I still couldn't manage to get it past my waist without it crushing my dick painfully and I was sure my ass was chafed raw from the wedgie I was currently sporting. Grabbing at the material once more, I tugged, but it wasn't happening and I peeled it down my legs before tossing it across the room.

"Shawn?" Tatum called, knocking on the door before popping her head in and her face flushed at the sight of me in just my boxers. Smiling at her reaction, I puffed out my chest and flexed my arms before reaching for her. "Where is your costume?"

Ignoring her question, I cupped her face and tilted my chin before pressing a kiss to her mouth. Sighing, Tatum melted into me, and I kissed her once more before stepping away. I hadn't paid attention to her outfit when she had stepped into my room, I had been too excited to see her to even notice but now that she was wrapped in my arms I glanced down and traced the length of her body.

Her calves were enclosed in knee-high leather boots which left her thighs bare though they shimmered, and I moved my fingers to stroke the skin only to realize they were covered by a scratchy translucent material. Moving my hand, I traced the leather that curved over her ass and swallowed when I noticed that the black bodysuit hugged her like a second skin.

"Holy fuck, Kelly." I whispered, stepping away from her so I could really take her in. "I don't know what you're supposed to be, but I vote you wear this all the time."

Wrinkling her nose, she flattened her hands over her torso nervously and then she glanced down at the black material. "I'm some Superhero apparently. But honestly, I don't understand how anyone looks at a costume like this and thinks that it's practical. How on earth would someone wear this and be able to do anything remotely helpful?"

"Shh," I whispered. "You're putting too much thought into it, don't ruin the magic."

Rolling her eyes, Tatum swatted at me, but I caught her hand and pulled until she was pressed against me once more. Lifting my arms, I then wrapped them around her and kissed her throat tenderly before tucking her hair behind her ears.

"God, you're stunning," I whispered, and her mouth lifted in a soft smile before she tangled her hands into my hair.

"You don't need the flattery; you've already gotten into my pants."

It was a joke, I knew that, but I still frowned while I searched her face.

"I hope you know it's not just that for me Tatum, I don't see you as someone I want to fuck." Her smile broadened but it didn't reach her eyes and she pulled out of my grasp.

"Well, I hope that's not true, since I'd really like to do it again." Her tone was light, maybe even playful, or it would have been if it hadn't been for the way her eyes seemed guarded now.

"I meant I don't *only* see you that way." I corrected and she crossed her arms over her chest before glancing at her toes.

"What about Jace?" She whispered and I grinned.

"I can promise you he's in the same boat as I am." Her grey eyes moved to my face in question.

"He said that?"

"He doesn't have to." I reassured her. "I know he would like more than just the occasional hook up, we both would."

Tatum moved to the bed and sank onto the edge before laying her palms on her lap and I watched as she gathered her thoughts before she blinked up at me. "How would that even work?"

"However we want it to." I shrugged and then sat next to her and grabbed at her hand. "Listen, there's no pressure, no rules, it can be whatever we want it to be. I just wanted to be sure you knew how I felt, or rather how *we* felt."

Leaning over, she rested her head against my shoulder and then interlocked our fingers. "This has gotten a lot messier than I planned," she laughed. "The only thing I wanted was to have a chance to see the ice this year."

"You mean you haven't been plotting to seduce us?" I nudged her gently with my shoulder and she laughed again.

"For some reason I think you have that backwards, I was the unsuspecting innocent party in all of this." Turning my head, I pressed a kiss to her hair and then pulled her onto my lap.

"Whatever you say, Kelly." Falling onto the bed, I cupped her ass and lifted my hips into hers. "Now let's forget about the party and focus on you using those powers of yours to suck the life out of me again."

She smiled slyly before running her fingers through my blonde strands. "Are you sure that's a good idea?"

"I think it's the best idea." I promised and then leaned forward to kiss her, but Tatum pulled slightly away and I immediately fell back and moved my hands from her body at her hesitation. "Are you okay?"

"I'm perfect, and would very much like to continue but first, I have to ask," she avoided my gaze, tucking her hair behind her ears and I tucked a finger under her chin, lifting her face until she met my eyes again.

"What is it?" I asked and she chewed on her lower lip nervously before swallowing.

"Should we do this again without Jace? Will he be okay with that?"

Tipping my head back, I laughed quietly, relieved that that was the only thing stopping her and it wasn't something I had done or said. "Kelly, he's going to be fine with it."

"How are you sure?" She asked while her fingers traced the tattoos on my forearms.

"Because we don't keep score, this isn't a transactional situation where we are keeping tabs on who does what." Lifting my hands, I smoothed her hair down her back and then traced the black material of her bodysuit with my fingers.

"Any other questions?" I whispered as my fingers found the zipper of her costume.

"Just one," She grinned before leaning forward until her lips skimmed across mine. "How many times do you think you can make me cum, pretty boy?"

Chapter Twenty-Two

TATUM

Stretching in my bed, I rolled onto my stomach and then smiled at the dull ache between my legs. Shawn and I had spent the entire evening wrapped up in each other, completely skipping out on the party and I could honestly say I had never been fucked so thoroughly. It wasn't until my phone buzzed at four a.m. that I managed to pull myself from his bed to sneak downstairs to my room. The house had been empty at that point, there hadn't been anyone on the main floor and I was glad I wouldn't have to have another awkward interaction with O'Neil, even if we were on better terms.

Grabbing at my phone I checked the time and sighed. It was still early but we were facing Grand Mountain University today and I was sure Jace or Callum would not be feeling their best after last night. I had tried to warn Rivers that having a party the night before game day was a poor idea, but he just waved me off, reassuring me it was tradition, and they would be fine. At least Shawn and I wouldn't be hungover.

Stretching once more, I stood from my bed and grabbed at some leggings and a hoodie before heading to the kitchen. I had thought I would be the only one awake already but was surprised to see O'Neil at the coffee maker and he glanced over his shoulder before grabbing another mug from the cabinet.

"Coffee?" He asked but had already started pouring the coffee and I offered a soft smile as I grabbed the mug from him.

"Thanks."

Blowing across the hot drink, I watched as he sipped on his own and then cleared my throat at the awkward silence.

"Party was fun," I muttered and he narrowed his eyes at me before lifting a brow.

"How would you know that, Kelly? You spent the entire night in Patrick's room." My blush was hot as it crawled across my face, and I glanced around the dimly lit kitchen.

"I, uhh - I didn't think anyone would notice."

Snorting, Callum moved to a stool at the island and then placed his mug to the countertop before crossing his arms. "I'm sure Jace did."

Slumping, I lowered my coffee and stared at the dark liquid while fingering the designs on the ceramic mug.

"Did he say something?" I whispered, worried I had made a mistake last night, but Callum just laughed quietly under his breath and then ran his fingers through his hair.

"He didn't need to; it was written all over his face. But seriously don't worry about it too much, he's not the jealous type."

"Oh, well that's good then." Struggling to stay still under his gaze, I shifted from one foot to the other.

"However," He started, "This whole sneaking out on Shawn every time you hook up is going to hurt him. I'm sure he hasn't said anything yet, because Shawn's not the type to create conflict, but I am. So please, if you're going to keep sleeping with him, the least you could do is stay with him until morning."

Never in a million years did I think Callum O'Neil and I would be having this conversation and I exhaled roughly before glancing up at his face. His normal scowl was missing and if I didn't know any better, I would have sworn I could see some warmth in those captivating brown eyes.

"Right," Glancing at the bread on the counter, I chewed my lower lip in thought and then opened the fridge. "Think he'd forgive me if I brought him breakfast in bed?"

The stool screeched as it slid across the floor and then Callum was moving, rounding the island until he was standing beside me and I glanced up at him, taking in his handsome face as it glowed in the refrigerator light. Ignoring my questioning gaze, he reached for the eggs and then grabbed at some cheese and onions.

"Only if you make his favourite." He explained once he had stepped out of my space and turned to place the items on the counter. "He has simple tastes, a cheese and onion omelette is always his go to."

"Oh, good to know." Standing back, I watched as O'Neil moved around the kitchen with ease before snatching up the onion. "Let me help."

Nodding, he handed me a knife and cutting board and then opened his phone before putting on a quiet soothing playlist. Dicing the onion carefully I tried my best not to gawk at him, but my eyes wouldn't listen, and they eventually circled back to him before I could stop them.

This was not a Callum O'Neil I was familiar with, and I watched for a quick minute, completely fascinated by the change in him and the space around us. The last time we had cooked together, we had been surrounded by an uncomfortable tension. This time however, I found peace in the quiet sounds he made as he whisked the egg and I smiled to myself.

"What?" His voice startled me, and I glanced up at him with wide eyes.

"Huh?"

"What's with the smile?" Blushing again I glanced down at the cutting board and shrugged.

"Oh, nothing. I just like losing myself in the kitchen, I guess. It's relaxing."

"Yeah, I get that," he agreed and then scooped some of the pieces of onion in his hand before turning to the stove.

"Have you always cooked? I mean I know the other two are banned from using the oven and you obviously know your way around a kitchen."

Laughing under his breath, Callum popped two pieces of bread into the toaster and then turned to face me. "I guess, yeah. My dad loved to cook, and he taught me everything I know. It almost makes me feel close to him when I spend time in here." His voice had grown soft, and he moved his gaze to me before clearing his throat. "As for the banning, well when we moved in here Shawn tried to make boxed Mac n' Cheese. I puked for forty-eight hours straight after."

"What? How did he even manage to do that?" I laughed.

"Who knows, but he did, and he hasn't been allowed to cook anything since." Callum rolled his eyes with a grin.

"Probably a wise decision." I smiled before grabbing an empty plate and then I stood next to Callum, holding it out for him to place the omelette on.

"Thanks for this." I motioned to the breakfast with my head, but O'Neil just waved me off.

"Just don't be too loud if he decides to thank you. Knowing about you guys and actually hearing you are two very different things." Ducking my head in embarrassment, I turned to the stairs and sprinted up them.

"I would like us to raise our glasses to these three." Jace lifted his beer towards us with a grin. "To Patrick for not letting a single puck past him! To Kelly for those four assists and to O'Neil for the win over Grand Mountain, I hope those fuckers cry themselves to sleep tonight."

Lifting my glass, I laughed out loud and then tossed the shot back. We had decided to celebrate our win at one of the smaller bars in the next town over and I smiled at my team as they all hollered and cheered before taking their own drink.

Our game had been nothing short of perfect, we had worked together like a well-oiled machine, and I was still buzzing from the victory. It had been so long since I had a high like this and I basked in it while the guys ordered another round.

"Tatum!" A voice called from the door, and I turned to smile at Kate and Vanessa as they approached. Once I knew Summers was going out with his family rather than celebrating with us, I had texted my best friend and invited her. She had been more than eager to join as soon as she clarified her ex would be nowhere to be seen, and I watched as she nearly skipped over towards me in excitement. Moving to greet her, I stood from my chair and wrapped my arms around their shoulders before guiding them to the bar where Jace was waiting with two drinks in his hand.

"Here to celebrate our girl?" He asked, and Kate lifted a brow before glancing at me.

"Our girl? Is that what she is now?" Her voice was teasing but I could hear the interest behind the words and Jace's grin grew double in size before he focused his dark eyes on me.

"I'm certainly working on it, but I think she's still playing a little hard to get. Maybe you two could help convince her for me." My mouth hung open, but Jace just winked before lifting his beer to his mouth.

"I don't think she needs much convincing." Kate giggled before nudging me with her hip and I covered my face with my hands before glancing around the bar.

"That's it, I'm going to dance." I sighed but Jace caught my hand, interlocking our fingers before placing his beer down on the bar.

"Great idea Kelly." Jace agreed and then turned to Shawn who was a few feet away and waved him over. "Our girl wants to dance, Patrick."

"Does she now?" He wondered, his blue eyes filling with heat, and I moved my attention between the two before leaning forward and dropping my voice.

"There are people around you guys." I warned, worried that someone would notice the three of us but the two laughed my concern off.

"Kelly, we are dancing in a bar, that's not weird and no one is going to care, relax." Pulling me towards the dance floor that was partially concealed in the back of the room, Shawn spun around and then drew me in. His face was bright and open and I couldn't help but smile back at him before turning to Jace.

He and I hadn't talked about what Shawn had implied and I wondered what he really meant when he called me their girl. Is that what he wanted? Lifting a hand, I grabbed at his arm and pulled him close, sandwiching myself between the two of them.

"Hi," Rivers whispered softly though the look on his face made my belly flutter and I swallowed before tipping my head.

"So, your girl, huh?" I asked, though I didn't sound nearly as confident as I wanted to.

"Yeah, *our* girl." He nodded, before stepping closer. "That alright with you, Kelly?" I couldn't form the words, so I just nodded dumbly and his smile in response was blinding.

"See, told you." Shawn whispered against my ear, and I turned my head, nearly brushing my nose against his.

"Are you always so proud of yourself when you're right?" I laughed and his blue eyes gleamed with playfulness.

"He's unbearable when he's right." Jace answered. "It's a good thing it rarely happens."

Lost in our own little world I nearly forgot about the rest of the people in the bar, and it wasn't until Kate waved me over that I noticed how the three of us had been swaying together in a gentle rhythm. Stepping out of their embrace I held a hand up to Kate, letting her know I'd be a minute and then I turned to Jace and Shawn.

"I need to spend some time with Kate, I haven't had a chance to really see her, and I invited her out." They both nodded and I inhaled sharply before swallowing. "However, when we get home, I'd very much like to see how you two treat your girl." Not waiting for their response, I turned on my heel and sauntered away, only pausing to toss them a wink over my shoulder.

I had just the slightest buzz going by the time we got home, and I smiled at the pleasant warmth while Jace peeled my coat from the shoulders, only to shiver when his thumb traced a gentle line across the back of my neck. Smoothing my hair down my back, he smiled at me and then looked at Shawn who had bent to his knees to untie my converse.

"Let's get you to bed, Kelly." Shawn smiled, once his job was done and I flushed as I stepped out of my shoes.

"Yes please. Lead the way, pretty boy." Shawn's smile grew and then he was grabbing my hand to lead me to the stairs of the empty house.

Kate and Vanessa had decided to go to one of the parties on campus after a few drinks and Callum hadn't been ready to head home and chose to remain at the bar with the team. Which meant not only did we not have to deal with any complaining on his part, but we had the whole house to ourselves. Following Shawn up the stairs, I glanced back at Jace eagerly and his own eyes locked on mine while they heated with desire.

Once in Jace's room, I ran my fingers through my hair, in an attempt to distract myself from my sudden nervousness and Rivers smiled at me before snatching my wrists. "Easy Tatum, you're going to tug it out if you keep doing that."

Twisting in his grip, I moved to pull my arms from him, but his fingers tightened and then he was lifting my hands above my head while herding me back against a wall. Leaning against the solid surface I widened my stance and then hooked a leg around his hips before grinding against him.

"Are you finally going to show me what being your girl entails, Rivers?" I challenged and he laughed under his breath while bending to grab my other leg and then he wrapped it around him, effectively pinning me to the wall with his hips and hand.

"Tatum, we are going to fuck you senseless." He assured me. "By the time we're done, you won't even remember your own name."

"That's a mighty big promise you're making." I whispered while I rocked into the erection that was now pressing against the zipper of his jeans.

The contact shouldn't have been overwhelming, considering we had layers of clothes between us, but the feel of him against my covered pussy was enough to send sparks through me and I groaned before tilting my head back. Taking the opportunity, Jace ran his teeth down my throat and then sucked the flesh that covered my collarbone.

"Already marking her as ours?" Shawn asked, his blue eyes dark with desire and I watched as his hand travelled south until he was undoing his jeans and palming his dick through his boxers.

Pulling his face from me, Jace took in his handiwork and then lifted his free fingers to trace the damp flesh before moving to cup a breast. Moaning when his fingers found my nipple, I tightened my legs all while continuing to watch Shawn. The blonde had tugged his shirt over his head and now was releasing his cock from the black cotton.

"How do you want it this time?" Jace whispered, as he turned his head to observe his friend and I whimpered as I pictured all the ways tonight could go. I hadn't been with Jace since our first time and as much as I loved the feeling of him filling me, I wanted to know what he tasted like.

"I want you to fuck my mouth until you cum down the back of my throat." I whispered, smiling when his dark eyes fluttered closed. "All while Shawn stretches my pussy open with that thick cock."

"Fuck yeah," Shawn agreed and he turned to the bed but I called him and shook my head.

"No bed, I want it right there on the floor, hot and dirty. I want to have rug burn on my knees for days so I have a reminder of this every time my skin stings." Lowering my feet to the floor, Jace released my hands and took a step back before reaching for his belt, but I swatted his hands away. "Don't, I want to do that."

Certain he was going to leave his pants on, I stripped out of my shirt and jeans before bending over to peel my soaked panties down my legs and I smiled when Shawn groaned at the sight. Swaying my hips for show, I glanced over my shoulder and winked before finally moving my fingers to the cool brass of Jace's belt buckle.

My fingers were surprisingly steady as they undid his belt and I tilted my face, pressing my mouth to Jace's in a slow sweet kiss as I flicked open the button. Humming into my mouth, Jace palmed my hips and then slid his fingers up my ribs before tracing the pads across the soft skin of my breasts.

"Fuck Tatum, you're so soft." He whispered in wonder while dipping his forehead to mine and then his dark eyes flickered to the blonde who had moved in behind me. It was as if I was having deja-vu and a tiny voice in the back of my head wondered if this was their routine, if this is how all the other times they shared a woman played out.

"Our girl is thinking too hard Patrick." Jace murmured and then clicked his tongue in a disapproving manner. "I think she needs something to occupy her mind."

Without a word, Shawn moved his hands to cup my ass and then he gave it a sharp slap and I gasped at the heated sting while my hips rolled. I felt unbearably empty, and I leaned back into his strong chest before spreading my feet. "You heard him pretty boy, I need a distraction."

Pressing a kiss to my temple, Shawn sighed and then moved his hands until they were caressing the skin below my navel. "What do you want, Kelly?"

"I want to cum on your fingers, make it happen pretty boy." I didn't have the patience to sugar coat it and I whimpered when my bluntness was rewarded. Shawn dipped his fingers into me briefly and then moved to circle my clit at a steady tempo.

"When I said on," I gasped, "I meant for them to be in me Patrick." Clitoral stimulation was always appreciated but I preferred to finish with something in me, it never felt nearly as satisfying when I had nothing to tighten around.

"Relax and let him get you off first and then you can have him anyway you want." Jace whispered before capturing my lips with his and I sighed blissfully into his mouth.

Letting Jace distract me with his tongue, I then tilted my hips towards Shawn's fingers and focused on the orgasm that was building. I had to admit that the blonde knew what he was doing, it almost always took me some time to get to the point I was at, especially without having something inside me and I cried out suddenly when the wave finally crashed into me.

Satisfied that I had followed his orders, Jace glanced at his friend and nodded and then Shawn was pulling me to the floor with him. Stretching out onto his back, he reached for a condom and rolled it down before grabbing at my hips. Squeezing the flesh, he turned me so that my back was to him and then circled the base of his cock.

"Ready?" When he nodded with a smirk, I lined us up carefully and eased my way down. Having finished once already, it was easier this time around to fit him into me and I sighed once I bottomed out before glancing at Jace. He had moved and was now standing in front of me, one foot on either side of Shawn's thighs and I looked up at him before widening my jaw and sticking my tongue out.

"That's such a pretty picture, Tatum." He groaned while fisting his cock and I kept eye contact as he directed it onto my tongue before slipping it farther into my mouth. Closing my lips around him, I hummed in pleasure and then began to rock my hips.

Keeping a steady pace was difficult, especially when Shawn began to stroke my clit but I moved my attention on the space next to Jace's hip while I tried to fight off my orgasm, too determined to make one of them cum first. Studying the slightly open door, I picked up my tempo and moaned when a set of hands curled into my hair.

"Good girl Kelly, keep sucking my cock just like that." Looking up at Jace, I flicked my tongue against the underside of him and then went to focus on the door once again. But this time the hall outside wasn't empty, and my eyes lifted, following the long legs up to the muscular torso, and then farther until they met brown.

Callum's jaw was clenched, his gaze steady as he watched me, and I lifted a brow before swallowing Jace farther down and rolling my hips. Both men groaned and cursed, and I did it again, all while staring at O'Neil. Something about him watching made me needy and I lost my rhythm while I chased after my orgasm, suddenly desperate to finish while his eyes were on me.

"She's close, Rivers." Shawn groaned, lifting his hips to pump into me and that piercing pressed into my g-spot. Overwhelmed by the sensation, a high-pitched whine broke from me, and I watched as Callum's eyes flickered shut at the sound and his fingers curled into fists at his side. He looked completely and utterly wrecked and the sight of such an expression on his face was my undoing and had I not had Jace in my mouth, I was sure I would have finished with O'Neil's name on my tongue.

Chapter Twenty-Three

CALLUM

Leaning against the wet shower tiles, I closed my eyes while my fist pumped my cock rapidly. I had been in a constant state of arousal for the last week, unable to focus on anything besides the image of Tatum Kelly on her knees while she was filled with my roommates. It had been the single hottest thing I had ever seen, and I couldn't seem to forget it. In fact, nothing helped me forget it. I had tried everything: porn, my imagination, even my regular friend with benefits had been unable to capture my attention the same way and I was becoming more and more frustrated.

"Fuck!" I growled, clenching my eyes shut while trying to picture whatever I used to use to get off. But it was useless, the only thing I could see were her light grey eyes watching me while she whimpered in pleasure and that was enough. Falling forward, I pressed my cheek against the cool wall and finished down the drain. "Fuck."

Turning off the shower, I snatched my towel from the vanity and quickly dried myself off before stepping into my bedroom. The guys had left for the gym this morning, both of them looking ridiculous as they watched Tatum prepare their pre-workout shakes and then they both kissed her goodbye as if they were all some sort of married throuple and I fled to my room, unwilling to be stuck with her without a buffer. I just knew my dick would be a traitor and have a mind of its own.

"Stupid fucker," I snarled while glaring down at it as I walked into my closet.

Sorting through the clean laundry that had piled up in a basket, I tried to devise a plan for today. I would hide up here, watch some of the game day films, maybe catch up on some tv and avoid Kelly at all costs. Grabbing at a pair of joggers, a tee, and a hoodie, I dressed and then got ready to hide away in my room, only to be interrupted by a knock.

"Yeah?" I called out while searching under my bed for my laptop and I heard the door open softly but whoever it was didn't say anything else and I popped my head to look at the visitor.

“What do you want, Kelly?” I asked roughly, immediately annoyed that the person I had been trying to avoid sought me out and I was ready to tell her to leave me alone when I finally took a good look at her.

She didn’t look anything like the girl who had been bouncing around the kitchen a few hours ago and my eyes scanned her from head to toe, immediately noticing her pale face and dull eyes.

“You okay?” I asked though I knew something was obviously wrong, and I stood from my bed worried that it was because of what had happened the week before. But when she crossed her arms over her lower stomach, I frowned.

“Can I borrow your truck?” Her voice was weak and had I not been paying attention; I would have missed the way she winced and seemed to curl in on herself.

“What’s going on Kelly?” I demanded and then closed the distance between us before lifting a hand to feel her forehead. “You sick?”

Her skin wasn’t warm, but she definitely looked ill, and she sighed before wincing again. “I really need to go to the store.”

“Okay, why?” Her grey eyes narrowed at me in irritation, and I removed my hand before taking a step back. “Listen, you look like shit, so I’m thinking it might be better if I take you to a clinic rather than shopping.”

“I’m not sick O’Neil, I got my period, and I am in desperate need of tampons.” Her cheeks finally looked like they had some colour and I forced myself not to sigh in relief.

“Okay, let’s go.” Waving my hand towards the hallway, I motioned for her to get going but Kelly didn’t move.

“I don’t want you to come with me.” She sounded as if she was trying to reassure me, but I lifted a brow in response.

“You think I’m going to let you drive my truck?” Her scowl was back in full force, and I exhaled roughly before trying again. “Why can’t I come with you?”

“Because it’s weird and embarrassing,” she snapped.

“Embarrassing for who exactly?” I asked.

“I don’t know but it feels weird for *you* to come with me.” Grabbing at her shoulder, I spun her around and gave her a gentle push towards the end of the hallway.

“Kelly, I literally do not give a shit that you have your period and if you wanted to tell me what exactly you needed, I would go buy it for you myself while you waited here.”

She glanced at me from over her shoulder in surprise. "I have two sisters - this isn't something I'm unfamiliar with."

"I'd rather go myself." She grumbled, though the frown had softened.

"Fine, let's go then." Sighing in defeat, Kelly raced down the stairs and pulled on her converse while I grabbed my keys and shoes before ushering her out the door.

The drive to the store was quiet and I glanced at the console before pressing the button to turn on the heated seat for the passenger side. Tatum who had been silent glanced down at the little orange light and then lifted her eyes to my face in question.

"The heat helps with the cramps, right?" I asked and her lips parted before she nodded.

"How old are your sisters?" She asked and I slowed to a stop at the red light before looking at her.

"Katherine is three years older than me; she turned twenty-five last month and Heather is nineteen." Humming, Kelly nodded her head and I focused back on the road before clearing my throat. "What about you, is your brother your only sibling?"

"Yeah."

"He's older?" I asked.

"Yeah, five years older."

"And you two are really close?" Kelly eyed me suspiciously, as if making small talk was all part of some bigger sinister plan I had and I lifted my eyebrows at her, prompting her to answer.

"Very, he practically raised me. He's the absolute best and his fiancé is like a second brother to me." Her tone almost seemed cautious, and I knew she was gauging my reaction.

"You don't need to worry about judgement from me Kelly, I was the best man at Katherine and Rebecca's wedding last year." She looked at me with surprise, and I scoffed in response. "I also happen to live with two bisexual men, surely you didn't think I cared about people's sexuality."

"I did, but obviously I shouldn't have made that assumption. Sorry."

"Don't worry about it." Turning into the parking lot, I parked the truck and then turned to her. "What about your parents? You said they weren't in your life, right?"

Her eyes moved to the windshield, and she chewed at her lower lip before looking at me from the corner of her eye. “We don’t have to do this whole get to know each other thing.

I wanted to say that we probably should given what I had watched last week but since she hadn’t talked about it, I decided to push the thought away. “Nope, not how it works Kelly. I shared, now it’s your turn.”

“Okay, fine, yes they’re not in my life and haven’t been since freshman year,” she grumbled and I tipped my head in question.

“Why?” Her grey eyes no longer looked tired as she glared at me and then she exhaled before slumping into the back of the seat.

“Unlike you, they care about who people choose to love and if it doesn’t align with what they think, they cut you out.”

“I’m guessing they weren’t okay with your brother then.”

“That’s an understatement.” She whispered and then rubbed at her face tiredly. “They treated Chris like he was some sort of monster and not the son they raised. It made me sick to watch and the minute I turned eighteen, I left. I moved here to live with Chris and haven’t spoken to them since.”

“I’m sorry,” I offered, but Kelly shrugged.

“It’s not your fault, you have nothing to be sorry for.”

“I’m not apologizing for them Kelly; I’m saying I’m sorry that you had to go through that.” Turning in her seat, she faced me slowly and I offered her a soft smile. “So now that family history is out of the way, let’s go get you your supplies. You grab the tampons and I’ll get the ice cream and snacks, what flavour should I pick?”

“Oh, no snacks or ice-cream for me.”

“Are you some kind of freak who doesn’t like ice-cream?” I asked skeptically

“I’m living on a budget O’Neil, and I’ve spent my fun money this month on going out to the bar. I don’t have extra to buy that kind of stuff.”

“Relax Kelly, I have it covered, now what flavour am I picking?” Biting at her lower lip, she seemed to think on it and then her eyes turned hopeful

“Cookie dough?”

“Deal.” I nodded before exiting the truck and then I waited for Kelly as she slid from the seat. But when she went to move past me and towards the door, I snatched her elbow and pulled her back.

"What the hell, O'Neil?" She yelped before shoving me away, but I tugged her close again before pulling my hoodie off and then I wrapped it around her, making certain the majority of it would cover her ass while tying the arms around her waist.

"You leaked through," I murmured gently, "and again it doesn't bother me but I'm assuming, given how weird you were about me buying your tampons, it would bother you."

Her face flushed once more, and then she glanced at the black hoodie while tightening it around her. "Crap, I'm so sorry."

Rolling my eyes, I cupped her shoulder and steered her towards the doors of the store before I bent down towards her ear. "Now you're apologizing for something that isn't your fault." I advised her with a chuckle. "Come on Kelly, let's go get your supplies and my snacks."

"Are you using my period as an excuse to pig out?" She pondered out loud and I grinned.

"I'm just a person who shares your living space and is offering you support by joining you on this snack journey."

Kelly was curled on the couch, her knees pressed to her chest, and I frowned when her face twisted into a wince. Her cramps had only continued to get worse on our ride home and I noticed the bowls of snacks remained untouched as she shifted again with a low groan.

"You okay, Kelly?" I called from the kitchen while I grabbed a glass of water.

"Yeah," she confirmed but her voice was weak, and I moved across the space until I was standing in front of her. Pulling at the blanket that was tossed over the arm of the sectional, I shook it out and draped it across her legs before passing her the glass and the two Advil tablets I had gotten from the bathroom.

"Here, these might help." After waiting for her to take them, I rummaged through the drawers of the entertainment center until I found the faded pink square. Plugging it in, I offered her the heating pad, rolling my eyes at her shock. "Just take it Kelly."

Moving it over her abdomen, she sighed and then nestled into the cushions of the couch, and I sat next to where her head rested before flicking the tv on. Scanning through the channels I searched for something of interest but settled for a rerun of one of those girly shows where all the characters happened be hot as fuck and the actors portraying them were easily in their late twenties. Kelly, who had been struggling to get comfortable, froze and then tilted her chin up to look at me.

"This is what we are watching?" Her lips tipped in the corners, and I was relieved to see that her pain was forgotten momentarily, even if it was to tease me.

"I can turn it off and game instead," I threatened with a glare and Kelly shook her head before facing the television once more but I remained watching her. Tatum Kelly was not what I would call hot, but there was something about her that had captivated me two years ago at that party, and the more time I spent around her, the more I realized that feeling really hadn't gone away. Wondering why that was, I searched her face closely. Maybe it was the way her long brown lashes framed her eyes, or how her full lips were naturally a dark pink colour. Completely oblivious to my attention, Kelly watched the TV but when a smile brightened her face, I inhaled sharply and then her grey eyes caught mine.

"You okay, O'Neil?" Her voice was heavy with worry, and I ran my fingers through my hair before clearing my throat.

"Yeah, all good."

Embarrassed that I had been caught, I turned to the screen and watched until the credits rolled across the TV before glancing at her once more.

Her lashes fanned across her cheeks and her mouth had parted as she exhaled softly. Realizing that she was fast asleep, I moved to grab the remote and turned down the volume before reaching for the blanket. Tucking the material around her, I unplugged the heating pad so that she wouldn't overheat and then studied her face once more only to be interrupted by the buzzing of my phone. Pulling it from my pocket, I scanned the screen.

Perry: I need to talk to you. I'm in my office.

Sighing, I shoved my phone back into my hoodie and stood from the couch carefully. Sure, I had managed to leave my spot without waking Kelly, I bent down and tucked a loose strand of hair behind her ear before smoothing the blanket across her once more.

"Sweet dreams, Tatum."

I couldn't decide if I was more annoyed at the fact that I once again found myself stuck in Perry's office or if I was anxious that he had made it seem like it was urgent. And now that I had been waiting for ten minutes, I was leaning towards the latter.

"Sorry, O'Neil," Perry muttered as he burst through the door, and I watched him carefully as he slapped a pile of papers onto his desk.

"No worries Coach, what's up?" Perry glanced at me for a quick second and then he shuffled through the papers. Once he found whatever paper he was looking for, he lifted it towards me, and I plucked it from his fingers wearily.

"That's Mike Huston, a junior at South Valley. He's good, very good and he's looking for a change." Glancing down at the roster picture I frowned as I read his stats.

"For next season? Surely Stevens will be back by then." I asked, not understanding.

"Not for next season, for this one."

"But it's already started, and we have Kelly." Perry's eyes narrowed at me in suspicion, and I handed him back the page.

"Kelly was not a permanent solution, I told you I would be looking to replace her after the exhibition." He was right, he had, and I agreed with that solution assuming it would be done by the first real game, but now that we were a month in and leading the division, I figured he wouldn't bother risking a change.

"I didn't think players could transfer once the season truly started, aren't there rules about that? I thought that's why Kelly didn't really consider it."

"Apparently you two don't bother paying attention to anything. They changed those rules at the end of last year. Any athlete can change schools once without being penalised or losing the opportunity to play. Had I not needed a decent substitute for Stevens, I would have told both her and Miller. But after seeing her skate at practice, I decided to keep that little tidbit of information to myself. No point in risking our team until I had someone secured."

"So, what? Kelly is done?" Something twisted in my gut at the thought, and I clenched my jaw at the sting.

"Not yet, I'm still arranging things with Huston and the school, so we'll have to let Kelly play the next two games."

"And then what? What will she do?" I worried. "Arden is garbage, it would be a waste for her to go play for them."

Perry rested his elbows on his desk while he peered at me and then his lips thinned in a frown. "I'd be a little less worried about Kelly and a lot more focused on your final season, O'Neil. Now get out of my office."

Following his order, I glanced over Huston's photo once more and then stood from my chair, but just as I reached the door, Perry called my name.

"O'Neil, I know I don't need to worry about where your priorities lie, but just in case you felt obligated to let her know, I'm going to advise you that you don't. If she learns that she's going to be replaced and has the option to transfer, she will and then we could be left high and dry if things don't work with this kid. That means your senior season could go down the drain. So - I hope that you will keep that in mind before doing anything stupid."

"I understand, Coach." I whispered.

"Good, I'm glad we are on the same page. Now have a good night, O'Neil."

Chapter Twenty-Four

TATUM

Glancing at the clock I swallowed down the acid that crept up the back of my throat and scanned the back of O'Neil. This was it, our final play before the game was over and we didn't have a hope in hell of winning it. Something had been off with O'Neil and I all day, and now we were paying for it.

Shifting on my skates, I scanned the ice nervously, letting my eyes bounce from player to player until Perry's icy blues caught mine. He had been livid since the first period, his scowl deepening by each passing minute and I knew we were in for it. This game was supposed to be a guaranteed win, we had come into it knowing we had the upper hand and yet that all went to shit.

Moving forward, the ref approached, and I held my breath as the puck dropped. As soon as the rubber bounced, O'Neil rushed forward but he was too slow and the puck was swept out from him only to be passed to our opponents. Giving into the chase, we moved but I could already see the face off had rattled Callum and he seemed turned around as we moved past him.

"O'Neil! What the fuck are you doing?!" Perry's voice somehow carried above the screaming of the crowd, and I bounded around the net, avoiding two players from the other team before closing the distance but just as I reached their center, the buzzer screamed, and I hung my head before sliding to a stop.

"Shit." We hadn't even managed to lead the game once, and the bright red zero was glaring at me from the scoreboard.

"C'mon, Kelly." Jace whispered before nudging me with his elbow and I glanced at him from the corner of my eye. He looked livid and I felt shame creep its way into my belly, knowing that I was partly to blame. I had only received half of the passes directed to me during the game and had overshot both of my attempts on the opposing net. I hadn't skated this poorly in years and I sighed roughly as we formed our line to shake hands.

"Perry is going to be livid," I whispered to Jace, while shaking the last player's hand but he just raised a brow and pursed his lips in answer, and I knew that he was disappointed with how this game went.

"How bad do you think it will be for me?" I wondered, wincing at the shake in my voice and he finally looked at me, those dark eyes softening before his shoulders relaxed.

"It's not going to be good, but we all have bad days, and this wasn't just you. We were all off today." His words did little to comfort me and I winced as Perry stood at the boards, waiting for us to step off the ice. Normally he would have led us to the dressing room, but I guess he wanted to be sure we were all accounted for before tearing us a new one.

Scurrying towards the room, I ignored the way all eyes turned to me as I entered, and I found a spot in the back of the group, hoping it would keep Perry from focusing on me. Following in behind me, Jace pressed himself against my side and then his gloved fingers found mine before they squeezed my hand.

"Just let him say whatever he wants to say and stay quiet."

I wanted to argue, I wanted to tell him that I would be happy to accept my responsibility, but I wasn't a scapegoat. However, the words never came, and I lifted my attention to our coach as he stood at the front of the team.

"I wish I had words to describe how that game made us look. But I don't think pathetic or embarrassing cuts it. So, I'll just say that I expected more from you. Especially you, O'Neil." All heads lifted towards our Captain who was tucked in a corner, and I watched as his brown eyes flickered down to the floor while his jaw clenched. "Get showered and changed, I'll see you on the bus."

Once our coach had left, the team scattered, and I grabbed my bag and ducked out of the room before the guys could start stripping. Finding the women's change room, I pressed open the door and then dropped my stuff before peeling my uniform and pads off. Turning on the shower, I slid under the spray and let the warmth relax my shoulders before I blinked the mist out of my eyes, knowing that it wasn't just the steam but rather tears that had blocked my vision. I felt like such an idiot, so completely humiliated that I had proven them right, I let myself become unfocussed and now I wondered what that would cost me.

Striding up the steps of the bus, I inhaled sharply and then turned down the aisle. The silence was stifling, and I watched my feet while I made my way to the back, not once glancing up until I found an empty seat. Dropping my bag, I fell into it and tucked my earbuds in before pressing play on my phone and then rested my head against the cool glass of the window before closing my eyes.

Perry hadn't looked my way once since he had exited the dressing room and everyone besides Rivers and Patrick, seemed to be following his example. No one had said anything, and I realized that they all decided to place the blame on me. And though I had anticipated this, I was still surprised by how badly it hurt.

Sighing, I clenched my eyes closed and pressed my forehead against the cool glass only to be interrupted by a hand cupping my shoulder. Jumping at the contact, I turned towards the person and blinked up at Jace's concerned face before pulling my ear buds from my ears.

"Can I sit here?" He asked and I glanced around us worriedly before lowering my voice.

"I feel like that might be a bad idea for you."

Rolling his eyes, Jace fell into the seat next to mine and then rested his weight against me.

"First, let me be clear, I do not give a fuck what any of them think. Second, we all failed today, not just you. If our success is solely based on one or two people, then we are a shitty excuse for a team, so stop blaming yourself, okay?" Glancing at my lap, I nodded but Jace wasn't having it and he tucked his fingers under my chin before tipping it up and then raised his brows at me. "Okay?"

"Okay," I agreed weakly and he smiled before shifting his arm and then he used the hand that was still cupping my face to direct my head onto his shoulder. Moving my eyes across the seats that I could see, I made sure no one was watching and then nestled in, pressing into the skin of his neck. "Thank you."

Humming under his breath, Jace pressed a quick kiss to the crown of my head. "No thanks needed."

The bus lurched forward, finally pulling from its place in the parking lot, and I raised my head, scanning the front seats before frowning. "O'Neil and Patrick aren't on here."

"No, his mom and sisters came down for the game, they live about half an hour away and wanted to take them out for dinner. They're staying with his mom for the night." Jace whispered.

The relief was instant, and I slumped against Rivers with a sigh, and he laughed. "Why do you look like I just gave you good news?"

"Because you did, not having to deal with him and his angry face all weekend sounds great."

"Angry face?" He laughed again and I scowled up at him before pointing at my expression.

"This face, this is the face I'm talking about." Jace's dark eyes were bright with amusement, and he smiled, flashing those damn dimples. "Wait, why did Shawn go with them?"

"Oh, we're pretty close to his family and usually crash there when we come here to play."

"So then why didn't you go too?" Jace tilted his head and shrugged.

"I have some studying to do." It was a lie, and not a very good one.

"Jace, c'mon, what's the real reason?" When he didn't answer I elbowed him gently in the ribs. "Fess up."

"I really do have some studying to do and didn't feel like spending the weekend with the guys. But if I'm being honest, part of me didn't want you to be alone and think that we were upset with you."

"Ah," dipping my chin, I glanced at my lap in embarrassment. "You didn't have to come back to keep me company, I'm a big girl, I can deal with a weekend without you three dummies." I reassured him.

"I know that, but I also know sitting at home after a loss can suck and figured we could be bummed out together." Staring into my eyes, Rivers dipped his head closer to mine and I could smell the spice of his cologne as a flush burned its way across my cheeks.

Forcing myself to break eye contact, I swallowed and then glanced at my phone nervously. "Chris and Tommy are actually coming into town, and I suggested they have dinner with Kate and I."

"Oh shit," pulling away, he rubbed the back of his neck awkwardly. "I'm sorry, I shouldn't have assumed you wouldn't have plans."

Shaking my head, I smiled. "Don't worry about it, it's fine."

"Where are you guys going?"

"I don't know yet," I frowned. "We were going to go to Kate's house since it was going to be empty, but she texted me after the game that her mom ended up staying home this weekend."

"Why not invite them over to ours? I'm sure Chris would like to see your home." *Home,* he said it so indifferently, but my stomach flipped at the word. He didn't mean anything by it; I knew that and yet my mind was spinning. "I mean only if you want, and I can make myself scarce or see if one of the guys is free."

"I can't ask you to do that." I murmured, still trying to get my mind to focus and then I blinked up at him. "You should have dinner with us."

"Really?" Jace's face brightened, and I smiled back in response.

"Yeah, of course. But you have to be the buffer between me and the three of them. I somehow always get ganged up on, especially if we end up playing a game of some sort. The last time we played Monopoly someone nearly cried." Jace blinked at me in shock, and I scrunched my nose before nodding.

Grinning, Jace lifted a hand towards me, and I slid my own over it. "Alright Kelly you have a deal, it will be us against them."

"Am I doing this right?" Jace asked worriedly and I turned from the stove to look at his pile of diced peppers. The pieces were chunky and mismatching, nowhere near as small as they should be but I smiled and then pressed in beside him.

"They need to be a little smaller," I offered and then laughed as he frowned at the mountain of red and orange. "Go back through what you have and take your time. They don't need to be perfect, just a bit finer."

Jace began sorting through the pieces and I paused to watch him in amusement before the doorbell rang. Wiping my hands on a dish towel I glanced at Rivers. "I'm going to grab that, don't burn down the kitchen."

His eyes shot to mine, and he scowled. "You're going like ten feet to the door and I'm not even close to the stove, have a little faith in me, Kelly."

Winking at him, I sprinted to the front of the house before flinging the door open and then I threw my arms around Chris. Hugging me tightly, he pressed a kiss to my cheek and then pulled back before passing me to Tommy. His fiancé had a few inches on me and could probably bench twice what the guys did, but his face was warm, and kind and I smiled up at him as he embraced me.

"We've missed you, kid." Rolling my eyes at the nickname, I pulled from his arms and glanced over his shoulder towards Kate.

"Sorry about the change of plans." She apologized before wrapping an arm around me, but I waved her off.

"It's totally fine Kate, come on in." Moving out of the way, I ushered them in and watched as their eyes took in the bright clean space.

"I thought you said she lives with three guys." Tommy whispered as he stepped out of his shoes, and I chuckled.

"I do, but it just so happens one of them is a total neat freak and he nags more than this one." I gestured to Chris with my thumb and my brother's mouth dropped open.

"Excuse me, I don't nag." I didn't bother dignifying that with an answer and just shot Tommy a pointed look while Kate giggled.

"Well come on in, dinner will be ready soon."

Leading them into the kitchen, I noticed the way all three seemed to pause when they noticed Jace, who was still hunched over the peppers, and I glanced at Kate. Her green eyes were surprised but she smirked at me slyly and I cleared my throat, startling Rivers.

"Oh, hey!" He stood from his seat and wiped his hands on the towel I had discarded before coming over. Shaking my brother's hand, he offered a beaming smile and then introduced himself to Tommy before greeting Kate. "It's great to have you guys, thanks for coming."

Jace Rivers was flawless with his manners, this was something I had learned very quickly once I spent more and more time with him, and I watched as he seemed to put everyone at ease with just a single grin while offering our guests something to drink and then he led the couple to the table. Letting him play host for a minute, I grabbed the vegetables he had diced and then finished prepping dinner, all while keeping a careful ear out for the quiet conversation coming from the table.

"Want to tell me why Rivers is here tonight but the others aren't?" Kate whispered as she hopped up onto the counter and I plucked the wine glass from her fingers before taking a sip.

"Patrick went with O'Neil to his mom's house for the weekend, usually Jace goes along with them, but he decided to come home instead."

Her green eyes brightened playfully, and she snatched her drink back. "I bet he did."

Frowning, I turned on the sink, making sure the sound of water would drown out our whispers before turning to my friend.

"Well, he's here, so yeah he did." I shook my head in confusion. "Why don't you just say what you mean?"

Kate took a big swallow of wine and then handed me the half empty glass. "I just mean that things seem to be good between you two. Actually, better than good and it's obvious something has happened."

Blushing hotly, I finished the Pinot Grigio and then nodded subtly. "Something did."

"Oh my fuck, really?!" Shushing her immediately I glanced at the table with three men, making sure they weren't paying attention to us before smiling.

"Listen, it's nothing serious, okay? But yes, we have hooked up."

"And when you say *we* you mean...?" Her brows were nearly in her hairline, and I glanced at the guys once more before confirming.

"That the rumors are true about their...*tastes*."

"That's why they were calling you *their* girl! I thought they were just messing around; I didn't know something had happened already. Why didn't you tell me?" There was no hurt in her voice, but I still felt a pang of guilt and I chewed on my lip.

"Honestly, I think it's because I'm still trying to figure out what it means. On the night of the Halloween party Shawn said they want more than the occasional hookup but I'm not sure what that would entail." I shrugged and her face fell in concern.

"Wow, this is so not like you Tatum, you're usually happy to go with the flow." She was right, I was never one to ask the age-old question *what are we* or *what does this mean,* I was always too focused on hockey and school to really worry about it, but this was different.

"Oh shit." She whispered, her green eyes wide and searching as they scanned across my face. "*Oh shit,* you like them."

"Kate." I sighed but she shook her head and crossed her arms.

"You *really* like them."

"It's too soon," I argued half-heartedly.

"Says who?" She reasoned.

"And it's way too messy." Rolling her eyes, Kate leaned back and lifted one shoulder.

"Who cares?"

"It might screw me over; it might ruin everything." Chewing on her cheek, she moved her attention to the others and then her eyes met mine.

"It might," she agreed. "Or it might be exactly what you need right now. But I have to ask, what about O'Neil?"

Flushing, I stared at her, wondering how she seemed to know about that night, wondering if she had heard something about the four of us even though I hadn't told a soul. In fact, I had done everything in my power to forget the way my skin had tingled and burned under his gaze. I had used every ounce of self-control to push that memory to the back of my mind in hopes it would fade, but after the way I spent the entire game hyper focused on his every move, I knew it hadn't worked.

"Is he livid?" Blinking, I focused back on her pretty face in confusion.

"What?"

"O'Neil. Is he pissed that you're hooking up with his friends? How does he feel about it?" Wiping at my face, I moved my eyes to Jace for a quick second.

"I don't know how he feels anymore." And it was true, I didn't know how he felt or where we stood, but I knew I needed to figure it out, and soon.

"It must have been nice to see your brother tonight." Jace murmured as he dried the pot with a towel, and I glanced at the bubbles in the sink before nodding.

"Yeah, I really missed him. They're going to swing by in the morning again before heading home if that's okay?"

"Tatum of course that's okay, they are welcome anytime. Besides, Tommy and Chris are awesome, they even gave me their numbers." He boasted proudly. "And Kate is hilarious. "

"Yeah, she's the best." My mouth lifted in a grin, and I grabbed the salad bowl and shook off the bubbles before passing it to Rivers. "I'm glad she came by tonight; I've missed spending time with her."

"You know she can come by whenever, right? Even if she does spend all her time watching my every move." His tone was light but I still winced and then looked up guiltily.

“I think that’s my fault,” Putting down the bowl, Jace turned to face me and then crossed his arms over his chest.

“Oh?” He asked with lifted brow, and I flushed hotly before clearing my throat.

“I may have told her about the three of us.” The kitchen was silent for a second and then Jace moved forward and grabbed at one of my soap covered hands.

“Did she not take it well?” His voice was filled with worry, and I took a step closer before shaking my head.

“It’s nothing like that, I promise,” I reassured him. “I just told her it was nothing serious between us and then made her drop the subject before she could bombarde me with her questions. So - I think she was hoping she would find some answers if she watched us interacting with one another.”

Jace’s expression flickered for a second and then he grinned softly, though it didn’t seem to reach his eyes. “Think she figured anything out?”

“She probably would have, but then Uno came out and all hell broke loose,” I laughed.

Jace didn’t say anything in response but rather interlocked his fingers with mine and pulled me closer before lifting his free hand to cup my jaw. Stroking my cheek with his thumb and exhaled roughly and I searched his dark eyes.

“What?” I whispered.

“I love that laugh of yours.” My cheeks burned and I wrinkled my nose. “Don’t make that face, it’s true. In fact, I’m a fan of all your little noises.” Jace lowered his face until his temple rested against mine and I shivered when his warm breath ghosted across the flesh of my ear. “Especially that sweet, soft tiny gasp you make when I start to press into you. It’s like you can’t catch your breath when I first stretch you open.”

I inhaled shakily and a laugh rumbled from Jace. “There it is. It sounds just like that.” Tangling his fingers in my hair, Jace then fisted the strands and tugged until my chin was tipped towards his and when his mouth crashed against mine, I was unable to do anything but surrender to him.

Kissing Shawn was like a dance, there was an easy rhythm with give and take. Jace however, kissed like he wanted to consume me, and right now I wanted nothing more than to let him.

Seeming to sense my willingness, he backed me away from the kitchen and guided me towards the living room until the back of my legs made contact with the cushions. Lifting my hands, I let one tangle into the front of his shirt and the other cupped the back of his head, my fingertips skimming across the closely shorn black hair before lowering to cup the back of his strong neck.

"This okay?" He asked with a deep voice, and I smiled softly before leaning back.

"Are you going to ask me that every time?"

"Yes." He answered firmly. "I will always check to make sure you are alright with what we are doing. I want to know you want me."

"That will never be a problem." I admitted with a blush and he smiled, his dimples flashing.

"Good." He tilted his head, moving to kiss me once more, but I untangled my fingers from his cotton shirt and pressed my palm against his chest.

"But are you okay with it just being the two of us?" I knew Shawn said that Jace had been with other people on his own, but I wanted to be sure that I wasn't overstepping.

"More than okay," Jace promised.

It was the answer I had been hoping for, but I still felt apprehension. After all, I wasn't sure I really knew how he saw his relationship with Shawn and what it meant to him.

Falling onto the couch, I smoothed back my hair and then patted the spot to my left and he perched next to me with a questioning glance.

"Shawn and I have talked about the two of you and how this has worked in the past," I paused with a rough inhale. "But I don't want anyone to be hurt and I guess I just want to understand what it is between the two of you. I want to hear it from your perspective too."

Jace rested against the back of the sectional and rubbed a hand over his sharp jaw before answering.

"He and I have shared partners as you know, and we have been *with* each other occasionally during those times. I care about Shawn and he cares about me and I am attracted to him but we have never explored much more than that."

"Would you?" I asked, unable to help myself.

"I don't know," He shrugged. "If it was something we both wanted, yeah I would be open to trying."

"You know I would be okay with you testing it out even with me being in the picture, I wouldn't be upset about that." I promised, and Jace studied my face carefully for a long moment before he lifted a hand to tangle into my hair.

"And what if we just wanted to be more hands on with each other while we were all together." A black brow lifted and I swallowed roughly at the tingling warmth in my belly.

"Oh, I see I have my answer." The hand in my hair curled into a fist and he moved from the couch as he angled my face up while he loomed over me. "Would you like that, Kelly? Would you like to watch me put our pretty boy on his knees and use him for my own pleasure? Would you be a good girl and wait patiently or would I have to restrain you?"

The gasp that escaped my lips was quiet but did not go undetected and Jace grinned, though this expression was a far cry from the gentlemanly smile he had worn during dinner and I rubbed my thighs together at the sight.

"There's that noise again, it's like you can't stop it from coming out." He whispered and then he leaned down to press a quick kiss to my mouth.

My body trembled with want and when he released my hair, my eyes fluttered open. " I can't help it."

"Well, I think we should test that theory." Jace grinned and then his hands were pushing my shoulders back until I was sprawled across the couch. Happy with my position, he sank to his knees in front of me and then I felt his fingers fiddle with the button of my jeans.

"Tonight I'm going to bury my face between these thighs and eat you out while you try to be as quiet as possible."

Lifting onto my elbows, I glanced down the length of my torso and stared dumbly as his hands made quick work of my jeans. Flinging the denim across the room, Jace then smoothed his palms over the muscles of my thighs and I couldn't help but notice the stark contrast between the colours of our skin. Though my little observation was quickly interrupted when he spread my legs and those long fingers traced the soft blue lace edges of my panties.

Dipping under the wet material, Jace took his time touching me, almost as if he was going to draw this out. But when his index finger traced the sensitive flesh of my clit, I fell onto my back and gasped once more.

"I've barely done anything and you've already broken our agreement." He whispered before pressing a kiss to the inside of my left knee. "That's not like you Kelly."

“I don’t think it was necessarily an agreement Rivers.” I panted out before closing my eyes and taking a deep breath.

“Are you saying you’re not up for the challenge?” He asked, gently lifting my hips so he could slide the lace over my ass and down my legs. “Because if you aren’t, we can stop now and just watch a movie.”

There was no way in hell we were stopping now, not when I was so desperate to finish.

“I'll be quiet.” I promised, though I didn’t sound nearly as confident and Jace laughed softly before tracing his tongue over the sensitive flesh of my inner thigh.

“Good girl.” He praised me and I had to sink my teeth into my lower lip to hold back a whimper. “How about I give you some help?”

Not understanding, I raised my head to look down at him in question but he just lifted the blue lace and his dark eyes heated.

“Open that pretty mouth of yours.” He demanded and then he reached forward and gently cupped my jaw. Following his order, my lips parted and then he was pressing the fabric against my tongue with the utmost care. “Now lay back and show me just how good you can be for me.”

Chapter Twenty-Five

SHAWN

"So - are we going to talk about today?" I asked while I peered at Callum from over my drink.

"What do you mean?" He responded, though his eyes never moved from the TV.

"The game, O'Neil. You know what I'm talking about." Callum stretched his neck from side to side and then turned up the volume.

"There's nothing to talk about, we played like shit. It happens." He tried to make his voice sound casual, but I could see the stiffness in his body, and I turned to face him fully.

"Not to you, it doesn't."

O'Neil lifted his eyes to the ceiling and then exhaled roughly. "I don't know what you want me to say Shawn, there's nothing more to it."

Liar, I screamed in my head, he was so full of shit, and he knew it.

"So it doesn't have anything to do with Kelly then?" His jaw clenched and I smiled in victory.

"That's what I thought."

Brown eyes narrowed at me, and I took a minute to study his face and then grabbed the remote before muting the game. "C'mon man, don't pretend like I haven't noticed the way you've been acting around her, something is up, something has changed."

"You're talking out of your ass, Patrick." Callum warned but I wasn't having it.

"You might think you have us fooled, but I know you Cal, and I know when something is up."

O'Neil lifted his drink and tossed it back, wincing when he swallowed and then looked at me. "It's nothing alright?" He started. "I'm just done being a dick."

The laugh burst from my lips before I could stop it and I nearly flinched at the glare O'Neil sent my way. "Sorry man, it's just- I'm not buying it. Try again."

Callum exhaled roughly and then ran his fingers through his curls, a habit he had when he was nervous. "Fine, you guys were right, she's not that bad. Happy?"

"And that observation is what made you play so shitty today?" Callum nodded hesitantly, and I hummed before nodding my head. "So - it has nothing to do with the fact that you watched her cum all over my cock while she sucked off Rivers."

The silence was heavy, and I smiled smugly before grabbing at the chips on the table and then tossed a handful in my mouth. Callum O'Neil was a lot of things, but he had never been one to show interest in what we did behind closed doors. That is until it happened to be with Tatum Kelly, and I had sat on the little bit of information, waiting until the right time to bring it up.

That night he had been totally focused on her, completely enthralled in the way she moved between us, that he hadn't even noticed me, and I was shocked at their obvious connection. I could feel the way the tension burned between him and Kelly as she reached her orgasm and I had wondered how long it would take for him to acknowledge it. Thinking I would just wait him out, I didn't mention it, but he had been off and now after watching him struggle today, I knew I had to say something.

"Fuck man, I'm sorry," he whispered while hanging his head and I frowned in confusion.

"Why?"

"Because I had no right to intrude on that, it was wrong of me."

Normally I might have agreed but nothing about it felt wrong and I was pretty sure Tatum hadn't had an issue with it. The only person I wasn't certain about, was Jace. Though I doubted he would have minded if Callum joined as long as we were all on board.

"I don't know what to call it, but wrong doesn't seem like the right word." I shrugged and he eyed me carefully. "I'm not sure how to explain it, but it didn't feel *bad*."

"So what, you liked me watching?" He snapped sarcastically, obviously goading me, but I just rubbed my jaw.

"Yeah, maybe. Is that a problem? Do you think I'm wrong for being intrigued by the idea?" I waited for Callum's expression to soften before continuing. "Did it make you feel that way that night?"

Callum shook his head and then whispered hoarsely "No, no it didn't."

"Okay, so maybe now that it's out in the open, we can figure out why it's rattled you so much. I mean you have nothing to feel ashamed about." His brown eyes flashed with something, and my brows pinched in confusion.

"I'm serious, I mean we should all probably talk about it, but now you know you don't have to feel guilty, right?"

"Yeah right," he agreed but his voice was solemn, almost as if there was more to it.

"Is there something else, Cal? Is there something I should know?"

"No, of course not." Grabbing the remote, he unmuted the TV.

"Because if you're worried about your feelings for her, you don't have to be. If anyone gets it, it's me." Callum turned to me in surprise, but I just smiled smugly. "Oh c'mon, you didn't think you were being subtle did you?"

"There are no feelings," he snapped and my grin grew double in size.

"Why is it such a big deal O'Neil? You like her, big whoop, so do we."

"I don't like her. God Patrick, not everything is like a romance movie or whatever. I saw her fuck you guys and thought it was hot, like any guy would."

"Do you know something about romance movies?" I lifted a brow and then dodge the pillow he threw my way. "Hey! There's a better way to deal with your emotions, violence is never the answer." Another pillow was tossed at my face, but I grabbed it from the air before fluffing it. "Don't start ruining your mom's nice decorative pillows, she'll be pissed."

"Why don't you shut up before it's my fist then?" Leaning on the cushion I had just arranged I glanced at my friend carefully.

"Fine, but I'm just saying if you do ever want to talk about Kelly or whatever, I'm here."

"I don't," he responded but I tried again.

"Okay, but *if* you do, I will listen with no judgement, okay?"

Moving his attention to me, he searched my face and then his shoulders slumped. "Okay."

There were quiet voices coming from the kitchen while a sweet aroma filled the house and I turned to Callum in question before shuffling through the door. I had texted Jace letting him know we were on our way home, and he had responded but didn't mention anyone else was here and I shrugged from my coat, brushing the light November snow off of the material before hanging it.

"Hello?" I called and Jace moved, walking backwards until he was in my line of sight and my eyes widened as I took in the frilly white and red apron that was wrapped around his torso.

"Hey!" He smiled though it looked more like a grimace and then he moved his eyes towards the kitchen. "We are just baking Christmas cookies."

"Christmas cookies?" I asked in confusion. "The first isn't until next week."

"Chris and Tatum have decided it's time because it's snowing today, and Tommy and I have been roped into helping." A massive man moved in behind Jace with a kind smile.

"Hey," he offered, lifting a hand in greeting only to wince as the material of his apron stretched tightly across his body and then he dropped his arm and pressed it to his side. "I'm Tommy, Chris's fiancé. I'd come shake your hand but I'm pretty sure I'll rip this thing in two if I move much more."

"You better not!" Chris warned from the kitchen and O'Neil and I moved to the island just in time to watch as Tatum's brother pointed a spatula at his fiancé in warning. "It took me ages this morning to find matching aprons that would fit all of us."

Grey eyes similar to Tatum's caught mine and he frowned. "I should have got you guys some, I'm sorry."

Laughing I shook my head and then slid onto a stool. "Oh please, don't worry about it. I'm just happy I got to see Jace in one. How did you manage to convince him to wear it?"

Rivers glared at me while Chris handed him a big metal bowl and spoon and he began stirring the mix before glancing at Tatum's brother. "The Kelly's are scary when it comes to Christmas, they take it very seriously."

"Oh, come on you big baby," Tatum laughed as she emerged from her room, her hands pulling her long hair into a ponytail. "You were happy to put it on when we promised to make you an extra batch of chocolate chunk." She looked much brighter than she had yesterday after the game, and I felt my lips lift at the difference. "How was your mom's, O'Neil?"

Callum was silently hovering in the back awkwardly, though I could have sworn his eyes hadn't lifted from Tatum's form since she came out of her room. Jace also seemed to notice this as well and he shot me a look before lifting his brows at our captain.

"It was fine," he grumbled while falling into the empty stool beside mine and Tatum hesitated for a second, frowning at his disgruntled tone before moving in beside her brother. Chris also glowered at Callum and then cleared his throat.

"I don't think we've met." He moved until he was standing in front of O'Neil. "I'm Chris."

Callum stood, taking the offered hand in his and I watched in amusement as Chris tipped his head while he sized him up. Kelly's brother may have been smaller, but his scowl was intense, and O'Neil flinched back from the glare the older man shot him.

"Callum," he offered nervously and then his brown eyes glanced at me, obviously pleading for help. This was new territory for O'Neil, Tatum had truly been the first person not to fall for his shit and it was apparent that it was a trait that ran in the family. "I - ah- didn't have a chance to meet you when Kelly moved out, but she speaks very highly of you."

"Really? Because I don't think she's ever really mentioned you." The room grew tense, and I noticed Tatum had begun to fiddle with the ties of her apron before clearing her throat.

"I'm sure I have; you probably just don't remember." It had meant to be reassuring but the way she stumbled over the words made it clear that it was a lie.

"I've heard all about Jace and Shawn." Chris tilted his head, as if he was trying to think back on it and I perked up at my name before smiling slyly at Tatum.

"You telling your brother about me, Kelly?" Rolling her eyes she huffed, but I didn't miss the way she ducked her head, or the fact she didn't deny it.

"She has a lot to say about you both," Chris confirmed and then turned his gaze back to Callum. "But you've never come up. Why is that?"

"Chris," Tatum warned before nudging him softly with her elbow. "It's really not that serious, there's no reason for it."

Callum scanned her face for a second, obviously shocked that she hadn't told him about his treatment of her when she had first moved in, and I didn't blame him for his surprise. He had been a total ass to her and surely if she had told her brother about us in some capacity, O'Neil would have come up as well.

"You don't have to lie for me, Kelly," Callum whispered, and her eyes widened as he turned his attention back to her brother. "She obviously has more integrity than I do if she hasn't told you what a dick I've been to her. I was an asshole and I don't deserve her defending me, that's for sure."

"Callum," Tatum tried but O'Neil shook his head, his focus never leaving Chris.

"She told me that you practically raised her, and I just hope you know how proud you should be. Because honestly," he paused, and his eyes fell to the floor. "She's pretty great."

No one moved, not even her brothers and Tatum's mouth hung as she stared at O'Neil. Things had changed between the two of them, that was obvious, but I never expected that. I never thought he'd say anything so nice, even if it was true.

"Well okay then." Chris nodded before grabbing the forgotten bowl in Jace's hand and began to stir the dough once more.

"Okay?" Tatum repeated. "That's it? You're done with this whole overprotective big brother crap?"

"First, it wasn't crap," Chris sighed as he rolled his eyes. "And second, he obviously knows he was wrong and that you deserved better."

"You got all that from a little speech?" Jace asked, his face filled with amusement, and he ignored O'Neil's scoff.

"I know bullshit when I hear it, and what he just said," Chris lifted his chin in Callum's direction, "he meant. I can see that. So now that the unpleasant conversation is over, how about you four run to the store to grab some more eggs and flour."

"You're serious, that was it?" Jace asked again, and I couldn't help but feel just as confused by the sudden change in Chris's opinion.

"What more do you want?" Chris asked with a smile. "I could try and take him out back, but I doubt that will go over well for me."

"I'm pretty sure you threatened us physically when we helped her move out." I grumbled, annoyed by the blatant favouritism he was showing to Callum.

"I did, and I would have found a way to make that happen." He agreed. "But in this case, I don't have to. Tatum has you now and I am pretty certain that if he really hurt my sister, you two would have taken care of it. Right?"

I couldn't do anything but nod and Chris grinned knowingly before tossing a towel over his shoulder. "See, I have nothing to be worried about then. She's in good hands."

He smiled at his sister with a wink, and I watched as her face flushed and her eyes widened.

"You said you needed more flour?" Jace's voice broke the awkward silence and Tatum grinned at him gratefully and then began to untie her apron.

"Right, flour- we should go grab that." Apparently desperate to escape her brother's knowing gaze, she yanked the red and white material over her head and then tossed it on the island before dashing to the door. "C'mon guys, let's go!"

Taking the excuse to escape, we followed behind her and I pulled her coat from her closet. Helping Tatum into it, I moved out of the way as Jace pulled a wool hat over her head and Callum draped a matching scarf around her shoulders. I hadn't thought anything of it but when I noticed that Tommy and Chris had watched us closely, I blushed and then pulled my own coat on.

"We need eggs too, but no rush." Chris offered casually, though his gaze was intense, and I zipped up my jacket before glancing at my friends. All three of us were frozen, and Tatum just blinked at us in confusion before turning to her brother.

"We won't be long," she assured him but he waved it off.

"Take your time, I bet they already have the Christmas stuff up in the stores and I know how much you like to look at it. In fact, I bet these three have to drag you away." He laughed and I lifted a brow at Tatum.

"You really love Christmas that much?" She shrugged, her hand lifting to fiddle with the scarf in embarrassment.

"She's a fiend for it, I'm surprised she hasn't already convinced you three to cover this house in decorations." Glancing at the open space of the main floor, I tried to think back on the previous years.

"I don't think we've ever even had a tree to be honest." Tatum's gasp was sharp, and I took a step back in surprise.

"What do you mean you don't put a tree up!?" She demanded and Chris snickered before nudging Tommy with his hip.

"They're in for it now." Tatum glared at her brother for a second and then crossed her arms before focusing back on the three of us.

"Relax Kelly, we'll get you your tree." It was Callum who reassured her and then he brushed past to open the door. Holding it open, he motioned for her to go ahead and then followed behind.

"Good luck!" Chris called as we exited the house and I turned on the porch and watched as Callum opened the passenger door for Tatum. When she hesitated, he offered her a small smile and my mouth hung open in surprise.

"Well, that's new." Jace whispered from beside me and I nodded. "I had expected him to still be pissed about the game. What in the hell did you say to him yesterday?"

"Nothing really. I mean he admitted he thought she was hot but denied having any sort of feelings." Laughing under his breath Jace shook his head.

"Callum telling you anything is him admitting there are feelings." Patting my back, Jace jogged down the front steps, and I followed while wondering if he was right.

"Have you ever seen anyone so happy being in a department store?" O'Neil whispered as Tatum stared up at the fake pre-lit trees that lined the aisles, and I tiled my head, watching as her fingers grazed the plastic pine needles.

"Maybe a five-year-old, but I never expected Kelly to be like this." I laughed as she moved on to the next one, though it apparently didn't meet her expectations because she wrinkled her nose and didn't bother touching its branches. Glancing between the two trees, Jace frowned and then lifted a hand to trace the first one, as if he could figure out why Tatum preferred it over the other. But he seemed stumped and then turned to us with a shrug before following Kelly once more.

We had been in the store for nearly an hour, unable to do anything but trail behind Tatum as she moved from lane to lane, and I would have thought it would grow tiresome, but I couldn't help but enjoy Kelly's happiness, though I wasn't sure how O'Neil felt about it.

"Think we should try and direct her back to the food section?" I asked under my breath.

"No, let her do her thing. We have nowhere else to be." O'Neil shrugged and I stopped following the pair ahead of us before turning to Callum.

"Are you okay?" Frowning, Callum stuffed his hands in his pockets and pulled his attention from Tatum to glance at me.

"Yeah, why?"

"You hate this shit. You won't let us shop with you because we take too long but Tatum can wander around here for ages?" Rolling his eyes, Callum sighed.

"I know what you're doing Patrick. You're trying to make this a thing, but it isn't. I just don't want to deal with Kelly's pouting and her brother getting pissy because we rushed her." *Lie.* Callum O'Neil was a liar.

"Right, because you let that kind of thing bother you," I laughed.

"Whatever," Callum snapped and then stopped in front of the tree Tatum had been eyeing. Lifting the tag, he read the paper and then grabbed one of the boxes that were piled beside it. Hoisting it over his shoulder, he pointed to the packages of gold and red ornaments across the aisle. "Grab one of those."

"This is all so we won't have to deal with her pouting, right?" I joked as I moved to grab a package while ignoring Callum while he flipped me off.

"Shut up and let's go before those two get lost." Snorting, I lifted a brow at my friend and then fell in step beside him as we caught up with the pair.

Finding the two in a refrigerated section, I noticed Kelly had a pack of flour under her arm and was currently grabbing a carton of eggs and I wondered how Rivers had managed to rein her in. I figured we would be here for another hour before we managed to grab the stuff we came for and I clapped Jace on the back.

"We thought we lost you two." His eyes moved from the massive box sitting on O'Neil's shoulder to the plastic container in my hand and he lifted a brow in question, but I shook my head and tilted it towards Callum.

"His idea." At my answer, Tatum spun on her heel, and I watched as her gaze bounced between O'Neil and I before she smiled brilliantly.

"Is that a tree?" Her voice was filled with excitement, and she bounded over to Callum, searching the box until she found the picture on the side. "Callum, this is the most expensive one!"

Stepping back, he shooed her hand away from the box. "It's the *best* one and don't worry about the price, I have it covered." Tatum chewed on her lower lip worriedly, almost as if she was deciding if she should fight him on it, but Callum just sighed before cupping her shoulder. "Seriously Kelly, don't worry about it. Let's just get it home before my arm falls off."

Nodding, Tatum turned towards the cashiers at the front of the store, but Jace and I hung back for a pause, both of us watching as she seemed to vibrate with excitement while O'Neil just shook his head, though I could have sworn that soft smile was painted across his face again.

"Oh yeah, I was right, there are definitely feelings," Jace whispered and I turned to him in concern.

"Does that change anything for you?" I asked.

"No." Jace shrugged. "Does it change things for you?"

"No," I answered honestly. "But I'm worried it might for Kelly. I don't think she realizes how much we like her, I'm pretty sure she's assuming it's just a hook-up situation."

"But it's not, it's more than that, right?" Swallowing, I nodded and Jace exhaled roughly. "Yeah, I feel the same."

"So what do we do?" I wondered out loud and Jace rubbed at his jaw.

"I think it's time we're honest and lay it all out for her. Let her make an informed decision and go from there." Nodding, I agreed but couldn't ignore the twisting in my gut.

"Where does that leave Callum?"

"I think it's time we ask him to be honest too."

Chapter Twenty-Six

TATUM

I held the door as Callum and Jace carried in our purchases and then smiled at Shawn excitedly before stepping into the house behind them. The smell of cookies was still wafting in the air, and I could hear the soft sound of Christmas music echoing from the kitchen. Bounding into the room behind the guys, I grinned at my brother and then snatched a cookie from the plate on the island.

"I see Callum followed through on his promise of getting you a tree," he laughed and I bit into the cookie while nodding. "Well in that case, we better get out of your hair."

Setting the box down in the corner of the living room, Callum turned to us. "Don't feel like you two need to leave," he assured my brother. "We grabbed more flour and eggs and would be happy to have you for as long as you'd like."

Glancing at the massive pile of cookies on the counter pointedly my brother shook his head. "I think we are all cookied out for the day, but we appreciate the offer."

My eyes narrowed at the two men in suspicion and pointed to the bag we had left on the island. "Why did we go buy more supplies if you planned on leaving?"

Turning to Tommy, I watched as Chris struggled to come up with an excuse and I crossed my arms while I waited. "There are three guys in this house, I highly doubt those cookies will last the week and I know how much you like to bake when it gets cold."

"Right, of course," I agreed begrudgingly. "Well, we are going to put the tree up, why not help us?"

"We really should get going. We both have work tomorrow and the weather is supposed to be pretty crappy tonight," Tommy shrugged and I sighed before nodding.

Moving from the kitchen, Chris and Tommy approached the guys and thanked them for their hospitality and dinner even though Patrick and O'Neil hadn't been here last night, and I watched as the two hugged my roommates goodbye. It probably should have been a little awkward considering they really didn't know the trio, but it felt completely natural, and I couldn't help but wonder why that was.

"Walk us to the door Tate?" Tommy asked and I dipped my head before following. They stepped into their shoes and tugged on their coats and then glanced at the boys, making sure they were distracted before pulling me in close.

"What? What's wrong?" I whispered glancing between the two worriedly, but Chris just hugged me close and pressed a kiss to my hair before lowering his voice.

"They're good for you." Pulling away from him, I blinked in confusion and watched as Tommy nodded his agreement.

"Good for me? You mean as roommates?" I asked, not understanding. But Chris shook his head and grabbed at my hand before squeezing my fingers gently.

"I won't ask for details, I don't need them, and I don't want them," He laughed under his breath. "But I do need you to be honest. You care about *all* of them, correct?"

"I mean, yeah we're room-" But I stopped when Chris gave me a pointed glare.

"You know that's not what I was alluding to."

"There's three of them." I didn't know what I meant by that, but I couldn't think of anything else to say.

"I'm aware," Chris laughed. "And all three of those boys look at you like you hung the moon."

Blushing hotly, I glanced at my feet and shook my head. "They don't, and Callum doesn't-" I started but Chris squeezed my hand again, interrupting me.

"He does, they *all* do."

"Even if that was true, isn't it wrong?" Tipping his head, Chris searched my face, but it was Tommy who spoke this time.

"If you all feel the same way and are honest with each other, there couldn't be anything wrong with it. No one gets to decide how these things work but the people involved."

Swallowing roughly, I chewed at my lip before tucking a strand of hair behind my ear. "What if we hurt each other?"

"Oh, Tatum," Chris sighed before wrapping an arm around my shoulders. "I won't lie and say I think it will be easy given how many of you are involved, but hurt and heartbreak can happen with any relationship."

"So - what are you saying?" I whispered.

"I'm saying that I support you in anything in life, as long as it makes you happy. Even if it's not necessarily conventional." Wrapping my arms around them, I held them tightly and then stepped back before smoothing my hair.

"Thank you," I murmured and then cleared my throat. "Love you guys, drive safe."

Smiling at me they both nodded, and I waited until the door clicked shut behind them before gathering my courage and turning to the guys who were still in the living room.

"This part is obviously the top," Callum argued as he held up a mass of green and the other two paused, Jace glancing up from the instructions while Shawn narrowed his eyes at the brunette.

"How do you know?" Patrick challenged and I snorted before taking the white sheet out of Jace's hand.

"Guys, there's three pieces and only one of them has a tip that doesn't attach to something else." Shaking my head, I put the middle and bottom part together and then stepped back for Callum, letting him place the top of the tree on the rest.

Certain all three parts were secure, I knelt in front of the tree and began spreading out the branches before glancing over my shoulder. "Have you never done this before?"

The guys just looked at each other in confusion and then Callum shrugged. "My mom always did ours."

Jace nodded in agreement, and I rolled my eyes before glancing at Shawn. But the blonde almost seemed sad, and I shuffled back from the tree before ducking my head as I attempted to catch his attention.

"My foster parents never really cared all that much about the holidays."

I tried not to let my shock show and cleared my throat before reaching for his hand. I knew Shawn did not have the same kind of upbringing as the other two, but I had no idea he had been in the foster care system. He rarely spoke about his home back in California and it had taken ages to get him to open up about his struggles with school let alone anything else, so I never pushed for any other details.

Interlocking our fingers, I smiled up at him and then tugged until he knelt next to me. "We have to spread the branches out so that it looks real, kind of like fluffing it up," I explained and then turned to the other two. "You guys take the top, we'll do the bottom and then we can start on the ornaments."

Moving in close, Jace and Callum set to work, and I began to hum along with the Christmas carols that were still playing from the kitchen. Once the tree was shaped the way we wanted, I stood and opened the large plastic tub of decorations and then passed the guys a handful each.

"So Kelly, are you going to tell us why you love Christmas so much?" Jace asked as he began to hang the red glittered stars amongst the needles

"I don't know," I shrugged. "I guess I just love the nostalgia of it. You know the crafts you would do at school and the assemblies and the excitement. When I was a kid, we would put the tree up together and then watch the classics and bake. It all just felt kind of magical back then," sighing, I leaned back on my heels and scanned the tree before grabbing another handful of ornaments. "Even when things were falling apart between my parents and Chris, we still made sure to follow those traditions, though now I wonder how hard it must have been for him to put on a fake smile and join us as if everything was okay."

"What happened between your family?" Jace asked, though he never looked down at me and my eyes caught Callum's knowing gaze. Stunned by the compassion in those brown eyes, I inhaled sharply before figuring out the fastest way to explain.

"My dad was horrified when Chris came out. It was like he had told him the worst possible news in the world and at first, I thought he would get through the initial shock and come around." There was a burning behind my eyes, and I rubbed at my forehead as I continued. "But he never got over it and the harder Chris tried to make him see he was still the son my father raised, the worse it got. After a few years, he finally gave up and moved out, cutting contact with them but they already acted like he was dead, so it didn't even seem to phase them."

"How can someone do that to their child?" Jace asked in bewilderment, and I just shrugged, not knowing how to answer.

"I don't know, and I will never understand." Sniffing, I hung another glass ball and then continued. "I moved out as soon as I could and haven't spoken to them since. And even though I hate them for what they did to my brother, I still miss parts of them. My first Christmas without them was really hard but Chris did everything he could to make it feel special. We made new memories and traditions and always start on the first real day of snow."

"Hence the baking today," Callum murmured and I nodded.

"Well, what's next after the tree?" Shawn asked as he smiled at me.

"Normally? A warm drink and a movie." Throwing an arm around my shoulders, Shawn tugged me to his chest and kissed my forehead before peering up at the other two.

"That sounds perfect to us."

The glow from the TV was startling when my eyes fluttered open, and I squinted at the rolling credits before lifting my head from the solid chest I was laying on. Glancing towards my feet, I noticed that Shawn had curled over my legs and rested his head against the curve of my ass . Jace was behind him though one arm was thrown over the blonde's waist and his hand was cupping one of my calves. Finally realizing that both Jace and Shawn were behind me I turned my attention to the body I was sprawled across, and my eyes clashed with warm brown.

"Oh shit." The words were hushed but I still winced and glanced at the other two. Certain they were still asleep; I began to try and lift off of O'Neil, but his arms tightened around my waist.

"Relax Kelly," he whispered and it was then I realized that one of his hands was tucked under the back of my shirt and I shivered as his fingers softly stroked across the skin. "Lay back down."

Guiding my head with his free palm, he waited until I relaxed against him and then began to massage my scalp with his fingers. He was warm and solid beneath me, and I shifted until my ear was pressed against his chest and I listened as his heartbeat quickened.

"You okay?" I whispered and his brown eyes scanned across my face while he offered me a soft smile.

"Yeah." His voice was gentle, but I couldn't help but feel like I was missing something.

"You sure?" His chin dipped and his smile remained, but I noticed there was a change in the expression, an unreadable look in his gaze, and I tilted my head in question. "What is it?"

Callum's grin faded into a frown, and I held my breath, waiting for him to answer, but he never did. Instead, he tightened his hold on me and then turned his head towards the TV with newfound interest.

"How about another movie?" Untangling his fingers from my hair, he started another Christmas classic and then began his ministrations once more and my eyes fluttered closed.

"You know you could tell me what's bothering you right?" I asked drowsily.

"I don't think I can Tatum, not now."

Had I not been on the cusp of unconsciousness I would have pointed out that this was the first time he had ever called me by my given name. Maybe that would have been a warning sign that whatever was bothering him, was serious. But I was too far gone to ask any more questions, and rather than responding, I fell into a dreamless sleep.

Chapter Twenty-Seven

SHAWN

Lifting myself up, I rubbed at my eyes and then moved my attention across the space in front of me. The kitchen and living room were bright with the morning sun filtering in through the windows and I raised my arms above my head, ready to stretch when a hand swung and smacked me in the gut sharply. Turning towards Jace, I narrowed my eyes, ready to ream him out but he lifted a finger to his lips before gesturing to the end of the sectional where my head had been.

Moving my attention, my mouth fell open and I took a long pause to study the two other people who were fast asleep on the couch. Callum was on his back with Tatum covering his entire torso and her head was buried under his chin, her face pressing against his neck. Both of his arms were curled around her, and I noticed that his hands had snaked under her shirt, his fingers pressing into the soft smooth skin above the waist of her pants.

"Holy fuck," I whispered and Jace nodded, his face holding as much shock as I felt. *"Holy fuck."*

"Shut up Patrick, you'll wake them," Jace snapped and then he carefully pulled himself from the couch before turning towards me.

"What do you think this means?" I asked, following him into the kitchen, watching as he carefully started the coffee machine before slowly sliding two mugs off the shelf.

"I have no idea," Jace answered honestly while his eyes moved back to the couple. "But I think it's a good thing."

"It feels like a good thing," I agreed. "But why do you think it hasn't ever happened before with O'Neil?"

"What do you mean?" Jace frowned.

"If he was open to this sort of thing with us, I would think it would have happened already." Jace ran his fingers across his jaw and then he exhaled roughly.

"Shawn, this doesn't mean he is." It was me who frowned this time and I moved to brace myself on the island as my stomach twisted.

"Well so now what?" I asked. "He comes into it, and she has to choose?"

"I don't know," Jace shrugged. "I do think you and I are way too ahead of ourselves. We haven't even told her what we are wanting."

"Right, which is?" I prompted, waiting for him to go first.

"I would like to be with her, for both of us to be with her, officially. Callum too if he wants, though I'm not sure he is as interested in that."

"But if he is?"

"Then we find a way to make it work," Jace shrugged. "But first we owe it to Tatum to tell her what we want and see where her head is at." Nodding I sipped my coffee and then glanced at the pair once more. They remained in the same position, but I could see that Tatum had begun to shift restlessly and I moved to grab another mug of coffee for her before approaching the couch.

"Shawn, I didn't mean now!" Jace hissed at me, but I flipped him off and then knelt next to the sectional.

"Kelly?" I whispered and her light grey eyes fluttered open before they caught mine. "Hey, sleeping beauty."

Her nose wrinkled at the nickname and then she lifted her face from the crook of Callum's neck before glancing down at him in surprise. "Did we stay on the couch all night?" She asked quietly and I nodded my head before moving back so she could pull herself from O'Neil and stand.

"Coffee?" I waited for her to take the mug from me and then rose to my feet. "Did you sleep okay?"

The small talk was awkward, but I didn't know what else to do and she lifted a brow before shrugging. "Yeah, a little stiff though."

The elephant in the room was still snoring gently and I ushered her to the kitchen before glancing at Jace. "We were going to go for a run and wanted to know if you want to join."

It wasn't a great plan, but a run was the best way to clear my head and I needed that to happen before we even tried to start this conversation.

"Yeah, sounds good," she agreed and then curled her hand around her mug before tucking it into her chest. "I'll just go get changed."

Tossing Jace a small smile, she hurried to her room, and I emptied the rest of my drink in the sink before looking at my friend with a shrug. "Looks like we are going for a run."

"Yeah, thanks for that. I wasn't really planning on freezing my ass off this early in the morning." He groaned but I just rolled my eyes.

"Maybe if this talk goes well, Kelly will help warm us up after."

The air was cold as it blew against my face, and I wiped at my watery eyes before glancing at Jace and Tatum. Both had bundled up for the cold snap that had hit us through the night, but Jace looked far more miserable than Tatum at the sudden change in temperature.

"You alright, Rivers?" Tatum asked while patting his back, obviously noticing his scowl and he rolled his eyes before glaring at me.

"Fine, I just prefer running indoors on an indoor temperature-controlled track that the University supplies us." Laughing under her breath, she patted his back once more and then tossed me a wink.

"It's not so bad, at least it's sunny and look how pretty the snow is!" She gestured to the piles of white powder that clung to the branches of the trees around us, but my eyes were stuck on her. The cold had brought a pretty pink flush to her cheeks and the tip of her nose, and her grey eyes seemed brighter than normal. Lost in my observation I didn't realize I had slowed my pace and Kelly turned to me in worry.

"Shawn?" She asked but I curled my fingers in her coat and pulled.

Stumbling forward, Tatum crashed into me with a gasp, and I took the opportunity to capture her mouth with mine before sliding my tongue past her lips. Swallowing her moan, I wrapped my arms around her tightly and then pulled back and softened my kiss until our lips were just barely brushing.

"Wow," she sighed as she sagged against me, and I smiled before glancing over her shoulder at Jace. Meeting my eyes, he scoffed but then his attention moved, tracing Kelly's form from head to toe and back again before he reached to pull her from me. Grabbing at her hand, he looked towards the empty road, double checking no one was coming before crossing it and I followed behind as he guided us to the narrow path that led to one of the lesser-known trails.

"What are we-" But Jace cut her off, backing her away from the trail and into the thick tree line before pressing her against a trunk roughly.

"Shut up for a second." His voice was rough and deep, and Tatum had just been ready to narrow her eyes at him when he finally grabbed her jaw. Holding it tightly between his fingers, he hesitated for a pause and then finally kissed her.

It was rough, aggressive- obscene even and I swallowed down my moan before stepping closer. Crowding in behind the two, I waited for Jace to pull back and then he turned his head, glancing at me from over his shoulder for a quick second before facing Tatum once more.

"We're doing this all backwards but I don't fucking care. We need to touch you Kelly, is that okay?" Tatum blinked at us as if she was in a daze and then dipped her head once.

"Not good enough," he snapped as his hand cupped her jaw once more. "Give me the words, tell us."

"You want my words Jace?" She snarled at him, her grey eyes burning as they searched his face. "Fine. Touch me." She demanded. "I want you both to stroke my skin, tease me until I'm soaking. And when I'm desperate and needy, when I can't form words anymore, I want you to push two of those thick fingers into me while Shawn rubs my clit. That's how I want you to make me cum. Is that better?"

Dark eyes sought mine and then Jace smiled slyly. "You heard our girl Shawn, let's get to it."

Tipping her head against the bark, Tatum panted as she tried to catch her breath and I smiled into the soft skin of her neck before pressing my lips to the small indents that had been left from my teeth. Pulling from her, I watched as Jace pressed a sweet kiss to her temple and then stepped back before helping her adjust her clothes.

"The second I get feeling back in my legs, it's your turn." She gasped and I lifted a hand to stroke the flushed skin of her face fondly before chuckling.

"I thought I told you we don't keep score." Her eyes fluttered open, and she swallowed twice before pushing away from the tree.

"I know, but what if I want to?" She asked as her eyes traced down my body until they landed on my obvious hard on.

"I know it probably seems like bullshit, but we really suggested we go for a run so we could talk." Jace laughed awkwardly and Tatum moved her attention between the two of us in confusion.

"Is something wrong?"

"No, nothing's wrong Tatum," Jace cooed softly. "We just haven't had a chance to talk about what's going on with us."

"Yeah, we should probably do that huh?" She smoothed her palms over her thighs nervously and then straightened her shoulders. "Think that can wait until we get home though? I'd really love to shower and change first." Shuffling from foot to foot, Tatum winced and then stroked her hands over her thighs again.

"Are you okay Kelly? Did we hurt you?" I stepped forward in concern, but she flushed again and shook her head.

"No of course not, I just-" Clearing her throat her eyes roamed around the space surrounding us and then she dipped her chin in embarrassment. "I made a little bit of a mess, and my panties are kind of uncomfortable."

"Sorry about that," Jace offered though he didn't sound the least bit sorry, and Tatum frowned at him before shuffling on her feet once more.

"I'm sure you are," she snarked sarcastically and we both grinned.

"You didn't seem to mind during." I shrugged. "In fact, I seem to remember you demanding that we tease you until you- and I quote- were soaking."

Taking a step forward she wobbled, her knees nearly giving out and I moved to catch her only to be pushed away. "I've got it, I'm fine."

"Whatever you say Kelly." I laughed and Jace smiled before stepping in beside me as we followed behind our girl.

"I was wrong," He whispered. "I prefer running outdoors after all."

Callum's truck was not in the driveway when we returned home, and I frowned at Jace when we had walked through the door. Now almost an hour later, he was still nowhere to be seen and was not answering our texts.

"Where do you think he went?" I asked quietly while watching Tatum prepare her tea in the kitchen. Jace and I had waited patiently for her to shower and now were perched on the couch as she puttered around the kitchen.

"No idea. Maybe the gym?" Jace suggested, though his eyes didn't leave Kelly and I leaned back into the cushion.

"Maybe it's a good thing he isn't home right now," I shrugged and then sighed before wiping at my eyes tiredly. "Are you ready for this?"

"Stop worrying so much Patrick, it's going to go fine," he said, slapping my thigh. "Now man up, because our girl is coming, and I can't have her worrying about you."

Squeezing into the small space between us, Tatum leaned against the back of the couch and tucked her feet under her before taking in a deep breath. "Okay, let's do this."

Neither of us said anything, and I realized very quickly that we really hadn't prepared ourselves for this. We should have at least made a game plan, figured out who would start and how we would breach the subject. But we did none of those things and I was now looking at the twinkling of the Christmas tree as I fidgeted in the silence.

"Right, okay," Kelly whispered and then she cleared her throat. "I'll start I guess. I know we talked about us being more than the occasional hook up and I'm not clear on what that would mean, but I like you, *both* of you even though I have my reservations."

"And what are those?" Jace asked as he shuffled closer.

"I'm worried about how messy this would be and not just because there's more than two of us but because of Perry, the team, our living situation." She tipped her head until it rested against the back of the couch and blinked at the ceiling. "At the end of the day, if this goes badly, I am the one who will be fucked over and that terrifies me."

"That scares me too," I admitted. "The last thing I would ever want to do is hurt you Tatum, but I also know that we would regret not giving this a shot."

"I feel the same," Jace agreed.

"But what does giving this a shot mean to you?" Tatum asked as she glanced at me from the corner of her eye.

"It means that we care for each other, that we are honest with each other and that this thing between us has the room to become more than wanting to fuck each other's brains out. Though, I hope that feeling stays." Rolling her eyes, Tatum giggled and then closed her eyes.

"Okay, so we are exclusively with each other. Just the *three* of us?" Moving my eyes to Jace, I lifted a brow.

"Would you want it to be four?" He wondered softly. "Because that would be okay with us if you did."

"You wouldn't hate me?" Tatum's voice shook and I wrapped an arm around her shoulders before pulling her against my chest.

"Why would you think that?"

"I feel horrible for even asking, I don't understand how I could want more than what you both are offering." She sighed. "But I know that when it's the four of us it just feels-"

"Right." I finished for her, and she nodded against my shoulder.

"We feel that way too, Tatum." Jace smiled as he smoothed down her long brown hair. "But I'll be honest, we have no idea where O'Neil's head is at."

"I figured," she shrugged and then she turned to face Jace before taking one of his hands in hers. Interlocking their fingers, she offered the other to me and did the same. "But I want you to know that if this is something he doesn't want, it doesn't change things for me. I would still want to try with the both of you."

Happiness bloomed in my chest, and I inhaled sharply at the pleasant warmth before pressing a kiss to her hair. "So - we're doing this?"

Lifting her chin, she brushed her lips across my jaw and then smiled softly. "We're doing this."

"In that case should we celebrate? Maybe pick up where we left off on our run?" Jace lifted a brow.

"I had my turn," Tatum reminded us and then her eyes scanned me from head to toe. "But that doesn't mean I wouldn't mind if you two of you sorted yourselves out. In fact, I seem to remember being very into that idea, didn't I Jace?"

When I realized what she was implying my eyes flew to Jace in question, but his own attention had zeroed in on our girl, and I watched his throat bob as he swallowed.

"You were," he confirmed. "Shawn, what do you think?"

"Fuck yes." I agreed with an enthusiastic nod and then I stood and grabbed at their hands. "Let's go."

I all but dragged them up the stairs and into the Jace's room, too impatient to bother walking down the hall to go to my own.

Shutting the door behind us, I spun to face Tatum and cupped her face in my hands before kissing her. It was rougher than usual, but I was too excited with how well our conversion went to care. Not to mention I was still recovering from the hard on I had in the woods after we had coaxed her to cum twice on our fingers.

"Easy Patrick." Kelly laughed as she pulled away from me and I blushed at my enthusiasm. "I'm not complaining but like I said, I've had my turn."

My mouth opened ready to remind her it wasn't about turns when she shook her head gently.

"I know, I know no score keeping," she rolled her eyes. "But this is something I want to do, or rather see."

"You heard her Patrick," Jace moved in behind me and pressed a kiss to my neck. "Our girl wants to see how pretty you can be for us and I'm dying to show her what you look like choking on my cock."

As always his deep voice forced all of my blood south and my eyes fluttered closed as he roughly sucked on the skin he had been kissing.

"Will you do that for me Shawn?" Tatum asked sweetly and I nodded with a whimper.

Humming under his breath, Jace then nosed my blonde hair while pressing his mouth next to my ear. "Don't worry Patrick, I'm sure Kelly will be dying to touch you after and then you can remind her how good that piercing feels when she clenches around your dick."

Chapter Twenty-Eight

CALLUM

The alarm of my phone chimed from its place on the vanity, and I paused, lifting my razor from my jaw before turning it off. Inhaling roughly, I turned to the mirror and studied my reflection as I tried to prepare myself for the afternoon.

Today we were facing King's University and I wasn't ready. I wasn't ready to go up against our biggest rival, I wasn't ready to hit that ice with all those eyes watching but most of all, I wasn't ready to play this game knowing it could be Tatum's last.

"Fuck." I cursed under my breath as I rubbed at my eyes tiredly and then finished shaving. Wiping off the access foam, I washed my face and then towel dried my hair. All while ignoring the dark circles under my eyes. Grabbing a pair of sweats, I tugged them on before flicking the bathroom light off and then made my way down the stairs.

Wincing at the soft glow of the kitchen lights, I paused at the bottom of the stairs and studied Tatum as she sat perched on her stool at the island. After last weekend, I had avoided the house as much as possible, but now that it was just the two of us here, I took my time to take her in. Seeming to feel my stare, she flicked her light brown hair over her shoulder and then turned to me with a soft smile.

"Hey stranger," she whispered, and I hummed in response before rounding the counter and turning on the coffee machine, and then I glanced at her questioningly.

"Stranger?"

"I haven't seen you around much lately," she shrugged half-heartedly.

"I saw you at practice all week." I argued and she huffed under her breath. "What? You did."

"I mean around here; you've hardly been home, and I can't help but think I've done something to make you want to avoid me." I flinched at the words before I could stop myself and Tatum gasped. "I knew it! I knew something was wrong. What did I do?"

"Get over yourself Kelly, it doesn't have anything to do with you." I snapped and then poured a mug of coffee before sliding it towards her. "I've been busy."

"Busy," she repeated with disbelief. "Busy with what?" Her fingers curled around the ceramic, and then those grey eyes caught mine.

"What's it to you? It's not like I ask you about what you get up to in your free time." It was her turn to flinch, and I felt my chest tighten at the deflated expression on her face and decided to change the subject. "Listen, let's just forget it, it's not important. Are you ready for today?"

Chewing on her lower lip, she nodded though her eyes remained downcast. "Yeah, I think so. I just hope we play well this time; I don't want to disappoint Perry again. I know he's been unhappy with me and I'm a little worried."

The tense pressure that had been hiding under my ribs for the last while pulsed and I inhaled at the sudden wave of shame that crashed into me. I hadn't told anyone about the private conversation Perry and I had prior to our last disaster of a game and now I knew I couldn't. Things had changed with my roommates and Kelly over the week and though they tried to hide it, I knew that they had only continued to grow closer. Which meant if I tried to talk to Jace and Shawn now, they would not only be pissed that I had kept it to myself for so long, but they would be hurt knowing that Tatum's time with us was limited.

And that would be enough to fuck everything up.

Telling them now could potentially throw off our dynamic and considering we had lost the last game because I had been too distracted thinking about Kelly and the new transfer, I knew I shouldn't risk it. One more situation like that and my season could be screwed, my future could be destroyed, and yet everything in my gut screamed at me to warn them. To just sit them down and be honest. To tell them about Perry, about the new player, about how things had begun to change for me- about all of it.

Even if it meant ruining everything I had been working for.

"Callum?" Tatum's voice pulled me from my thoughts, and I lifted my eyes to her. "Are you okay?"

"Fine," I answered curtly before lifting my mug to my mouth.

"Are you sure? Because I'm here if you want to talk." God, how could she be so *good*, when I continued to be nothing but a complete asshole. A lying, cowardly asshole, who knew her dreams were on the line but still couldn't make himself tell her the truth.

"I'm sure Kelly," I sighed. "I'm going to change. Let the guys know I'll meet them at the barn, okay?" Not waiting for her to answer I bounded up the stairs, praying that the guilt would lift as I put more and more distance between us.

The crowd was massive today and I shoved my mouth guard over my teeth before glancing at the time. First period had gone off without a hitch, we played flawlessly and were leading the game with two points though I knew that could change at any point in time. King's was a good team, many of these guys I had known prior to university and I knew with certainty they would not take a loss laying down.

"Hey," Jace called as he skated towards me, and I frowned as his eyes narrowed at our opponents. "Watch out for Scott, he seems to have it out for you today." Glancing over at the defenceman, I noticed his eyes had locked onto mine and I offered him a wink before smiling at Rivers.

"Scott is a little bitch, don't worry about me." I laughed and then patted him on the back as I moved into position.

The face-off went smoothly and, in our favour, and I watched as the puck reached Kelly who then moved it back to me as we glided towards the goal. Holding my breath, I set it up and then took my shot but had misjudged just slightly and the King's goalie dashed in front, forcing the puck to bounce off his pads.

Racing after it once more, I watched as Kelly sped along the boards and then she was manoeuvring between the opposing team with ease. Leading the pack, she dashed across the ice until the puck was on her stick and then glanced at me before passing it back. Knowing I had a pack of players behind me, I pushed myself hard, rounding a corner while the fans slammed their palms on the glass, and I let their excitement and enthusiasm fuel me as I sped past.

Closing in on the net once more, I couldn't help but feel like something was different today. Maybe we would win this. Maybe I had nothing to worry about because surely if Kelly and I continued to play at this calibre Perry would see her worth and keep her on.

Setting myself up again, I made a second attempt at the goal but was not successful and I cursed under my breath before turning to follow the puck. But this time Kelly wasn't near me, and I clenched my jaw before pursuing after the little black piece of rubber once more, now annoyed that she hadn't found a way to break away from our opponents. Moving my attention to Perry I noticed that he was waiting to catch my attention and then motioned for a line change, and I traveled across the ice before sliding behind the boards. Wiping at the sweat on my face, I then took a long drink from my water and glanced at the ice, noticing both Kelly and Rivers had come to join me on the bench.

"You guys got your shit together today!" Perry shouted at us as he patted them both on the back. "Keep it up." Kelly's grey eyes brightened at the praise, but Perry's icy blues met mine and I felt my stomach twist.

"You good?" Jace asked as he leaned into my shoulder, and I nodded while taking another swig from my bottle.

"Glad to hear it but listen," This time he tipped his head towards me, and I ducked in close. "Scott isn't easing up, he's tailing you even when you don't have the puck."

Pulling away from him I frowned and then shifted back so I could see the bench of the other team. The King's players were focused on their teammates but as I scanned their jerseys, I noticed that Scott had twisted and when our eyes contacted, he let his gaze drift to Kelly before smiling at me smugly.

"Fucking dick." I snarled and Jace nodded his head while he gazed up at the scoreboard.

"He's out for blood today O'Neil." Jace warned. "It's like he has something to prove or something and I just know he's going to try and bait you into a fight."

Laughing under my breath I clapped on Rivers on the back. "Don't worry about me, I can handle him."

"Yeah," Jace grumbled. "That's what I'm worried about."

"Alright boys, get back on that ice." Perry shouted after another long moment, and we stood before hoisting ourselves over the boards to join the game once more.

Thankful that the quick break on the bench had renewed my energy, I jumped right back into the action, determined to finish this period with another goal and set sights on the other team. Chasing after them as they drove the puck down the ice, I closed the space between us and then heard Jace.

"That fucking prick." He cursed and I looked over at him watching as he turned and then rushed towards the opposite end of the rink where Scott was chasing down Kelly all while Perry shouted at him to stop. But Jace ignored our coach and followed the pair all while Tatum did everything in her power to get away from the King's player. And even though there were three refs, not one of them paid any attention.

Deciding to help, I crossed the ice and prepared myself to cut them off, but I was too late. The cat and mouse game they had been playing was at its end and Scott was within an arm's reach.

Watching in horror, I gasped as the King's player lifted his stick and then he slammed into Kelly's back, forcing her to collide with the boards sharply and it was like everything happened in slow motion as her face bounced off the glass violently before her knees buckled and then she slid onto the ice in a heap.

Sliding to a stop in shock, Jace's eyes bounced between Scott and Kelly as his fists clenched, and I knew what was about to happen. Shouting his name, I reached out and grabbed at the printed name across his shoulders and then heaved him backwards. "Check on Tatum! I'll handle this."

Whistles were blown, people were shouting but I barely heard anything over the pounding of my heartbeat in my ears and then I moved. Slamming into Scott's side, I pressed him against the boards and then fisted his jersey before swinging.

My knuckles had made contact with his jaw once, and then twice and I had cocked my arm back for a third time when the refs finally grabbed at my arms and tried dragging me off. But I shrugged out of their hold and went after him again, determined to obliterate that smug little smile.

"O'Neil! Enough!" One of the refs shouted in my ear as they pulled me back once more though this time, they were successful and then they escorted me to the bench. Neither man softened their hold, almost as if they knew I would take any opportunity to continue Scott's ass kicking and I let them shove me through the door.

"That's a match penalty, he's done for the game Perry." Those icy blues zeroed in on my face, though I ignored them and shrugged out of my captors' hands before stepping off the ice.

"What the fuck were you thinking O'Neil." Perry snarled as he grabbed at the front of my jersey, but I pulled out of his grip roughly and then flung my helmet from my head.

"You saw what he did! He had it coming." I spat.

"I guess I shouldn't be surprised that one of my players was fucking fighting over that girl again. But I didn't expect it to be you O'Neil, that was a big mistake for you." Unwilling to listen to him any longer I spun on my heel and headed to the dressing room all while my gut twisted, and I wondered if I had just fucked everything up.

Chapter Twenty-Nine

TATUM

Gasping, I struggled to bring air into my lungs while I pulled myself onto my hands and knees though I kept my head bowed as I fought against the sudden dizziness. Blinking at the surface below me I watched as a spatter of blood landed on the space between my gloves and then another drop came and then another and I shakily lifted my glove to my face, wincing when the cool material touched my lip.

"Kelly?" Someone called from my left, but I couldn't seem to find the will to lift my head and I felt my arms shake under my weight. "Kelly, can you hear me?"

Another pair of bare hands were in my line of vision and then they were moving, cupping my chin and forcing me to sit back on my heels as they directed my head back. It wasn't a face I was super familiar with, but I knew she was staff and I winced at the bright red bag that was slung over her shoulder.

"Tatum, are you okay?" Her voice was gentle, but I could see the worry and I moved to nod, only to freeze when pain shot through me. "We're going to get you off the ice, okay? Can you stand with me?"

Letting her link our arms, we slowly stood, and I ignored the clapping from the crowd while she pulled me towards the bench where Perry had been waiting. His scowl was fierce, but he remained silent as we approached and then the medic ushered me through the opening.

"I'm assuming she's also out for the rest of the game." He snapped and the medic nodded silently. "Great, that's just fucking great." Perry was livid, and I lowered my head in shame as I moved past him and continued on towards the woman's dressing room.

Settling on one of the benches, I watched as the medic opened her bag and then she turned to face me. "Can you tell me how you're feeling?"

"Embarrassed." I shrugged and she smiled softly at me and then moved to hold my face.

"I mean physically. Your lip is split but it doesn't look like it will need stitches and your cheek is pretty bruised." Her fingers moved, gentle palpating my skull as she searched for any other bumps and then she sat back. "Are you hurting anywhere else?"

Thinking over her words, I took a second to focus on my body. My face was sore but I didn't feel nauseous or tired, so I probably avoided a concussion and then I ran my tongue over my teeth, double checking that they were all accounted for.

"My ribs." I admitted once I was done with my assessment. "Where they made contact with the ledge of the boards." Nodding she moved to untie my laces and then pulled my skates off before motioning for me to stand. Once certain I was steady on my feet, she pinched the hem of my jersey and then helped me pull it over my head. Next we took off my pads and lifted my undershirt to inspect my body.

"I won't be able to tell if anything is cracked. We better get you in for an x-ray." She murmured and I shook my head.

"I would know if they were, I'm sure they're just bruised." I tried to reassure her, but she just lifted a brow and I sighed in defeat. "Anyway I can shower before we go at least?"

Frowning, she began to shake her head, but I exhaled roughly. "Please? I'm sweaty and feel disgusting. I really don't want anyone touching me when I'm like this."

"Alright, but I will be standing right outside that stall to make sure you're okay." She relented and I agreed before allowing her to lead me to the showers. With her help, I stripped from the rest of my equipment and then ducked under the warm spray with a rough sigh.

"Are you okay, Kelly?" The medic called and I exhaled again.

"Yeah," I called from behind the curtain before clearing my throat nervously. "Can you tell me what happened with Scott? Did he get a penalty?"

"I think he's out for the rest of the game, I can't see him being okay after O'Neil was done with him."

"What?!" I gasped and then moved to stick my head past the curtain.

"He lost it on Scott after he checked you. I'm pretty sure he was thrown out for it." Tears burned behind my eyes, and she took a step forward in concern.

"What is it?"

"I'm so fucked." I admitted with a shaky voice and then clenched my eyes shut.

"This wasn't your fault." She whispered kindly but I wasn't sure anyone else would see it that way, least of all Perry and I pulled the curtain closed once more while I prayed that this wouldn't be the end of my season.

The halls were empty while I made my way back through the arena and I curled an arm around my ribs as I passed through the dimly lit corridor. Both Jace and Shawn had called me as soon as the game was done, frantic to know how I was but I had been able to convince them to head home rather than accompanying me in the waiting room with the promise that I would text them all updates. So once the doctor was sure my ribs were just bruised rather than cracked, I let them know that the medic was driving me back to the arena to grab my bag and I would call them when I was ready to come home. However, O'Neil had apparently stayed behind and promised that he would take me back to the house when I was ready.

However, as I strode across the shiny floor, I realized he was nowhere to be found and I huffed under my breath before turning towards the men's dressing room. There was no noise coming from behind the door and so I pressed a palm against the wood and then opened it just a crack before calling out.

"O'Neil?" Holding my breath, I tipped my head towards the sliver of space and realized I could hear the shower running.

"Callum?" I tried again but when no one answered, I pushed my way past the door. The men's room remained quiet besides the sound of water, and I glanced at the hockey bag that had been left on the bench under O'Neil's hook before taking a seat next to it.

Deciding to just quietly wait for him to finish, I pulled my phone from my pocket and shot off a quick text to the guys, letting them know I would be home soon and then shifted uncomfortably on the solid wooden slab beneath me.

"Fuck Kelly." Snapping my head up in surprise, I gasped as Callum stood in the doorway to the showers. His curls were damp, and he was only wearing a pair of joggers and yet he had never looked better. Moving towards me, he sank to the floor at my feet and then his massive hands were cradling my face as one of his thumbs stroked across the split lip before moving to the bruise forming on my cheek.

"I'm fine," I whispered but his scowl deepened and then he stood.

"Get up." He ordered and I bristled at the tone.

"Excuse me?"

"Get up," he repeated before grabbing at my wrists. Curling those long rough fingers around the joints, he pulled me on to my feet and then slid his hands up my arms and over the limbs until his palms were cupping my shoulders. Tilting my chin, I watched as his eyes roamed across my face before dropping to my neck and then he was taking a step back.

"Show me." It was another demand but this one I didn't understand, and I frowned in confusion.

"Show you what?" But he paid me no mind and lowered his fingers until they were playing with the bottom of my shirt.

Lifting his face, his eyes searched mine and I gasped when the back of his knuckles skimmed the flesh of my stomach as he began to lift the material slowly. Slanting his head, he watched as more and more of my skin was exposed and then his free palm cupped my hip before rising. Fingertips traced a line from the waistband of my sweats, past my navel and then higher, not stopping until they reached the edge of the deep pink that had begun to bloom across my ribs.

"They're not broken." I whispered softly and Callum nodded but didn't stop his exam and I shivered when his thumb stroked the sore flesh.

"Good. That's good." He muttered, almost as if he was talking to himself and then he peeled his hands from my torso before tangling his fingers in my hair. Tightening his grasp, he forced my head back and I blinked up at those warm brown eyes.

"What are you doing Callum?" He was so close; I could smell the scent of his soap and my lashes fluttered when his nose grazed mine softly.

"I don't know. I know I shouldn't, but I don't think I can stop." I was going to ask what he meant, the words were on the tip of my tongue, but I never got the chance. As soon as my lips had parted, he closed the distance, and my mind went blank at the liquid warmth that had flooded my veins.

Unable to stop myself from succumbing from the sudden heat, I leaned against him and whimpered into his mouth. Callum's answering groan rumbled out of him and it was as if it had flipped a switch inside me. Lifting onto my toes, I ignored the sharp pain in my side and coiled my arms around his shoulders before slipping my tongue past his lips. Flicking it over his own, I hummed softly and then his hands were moving from my hair to my hips and then to the drawstring of my pants before pulling his mouth from my own.

"This okay?" His voice was deeper than normal, and I studied his face in a daze as he traced a finger over my lower lip. "Still with me Tatum?"

"Yeah." The words were shaky at best, and he grinned before untying the knot he had been playing with. Once loosened, my pants slid down my thighs and he knelt before me, carefully taking off one shoe, then the other before slipping my feet from the cotton.

Expecting him to rise once more, I shifted back on my heels, but Callum lifted his head, peering up at me with those brown eyes while he ran his hands up the front of my legs and then toyed with the edge of my simple blue cotton panties. Realizing he was waiting for permission, I smoothed back his curls with my hands, twirling the damp strands between my fingers and then gave a gentle tug of encouragement.

And apparently that had been all he needed because the fabric was pulled down my legs and then a thigh was over his shoulder before I could even ready myself. Using one hand to steady me, he lifted the other and took one of my own from his hair before interlocking our fingers and then his eyes held mine as he tipped his chin.

The first swipe of his tongue was earth shattering, and I cried out as the tip of it found my clit with impressive precision. Not giving me a chance to get accustomed to sudden electric feeling, he lapped at me roughly and then brought the hand that had been on my hip into the mix.

There was no easing into anything with Callum O'Neil, he did everything with a goal in mind. So, it should not have been surprising when he slid not one but two fingers into me before running the tips across my front wall and the overwhelming pressure had my legs trembling.

"Callum," I cried out while my hips tried to work with the steady rhythm he had built and I glanced down at his face, watching as he stared up at me before lightly grazing his teeth across my bundle of nerves playfully. Then, as if he could tell how close I was, he doubled down in his efforts and I grunted as those fingers pressed into me at the perfect angle.

"C'mon Kelly." He encouraged me and I whimpered as his breath fanned across my wet flesh. "Take what you need from me. That's it, fuck yourself on my fingers."

Whining, I pinched my eyes shut and tried to focus on the digits filling me. But it was too much and not enough all at the same time and I grunted in frustration as I continued to chase my release. Sensing my annoyance, Callum slowed his pace but put more force behind the motion and then his thumb was taking the place of his tongue while he sucked a bruising kiss into my hip bone.

"So close eh Kelly? You just need a little more." Nodding my head, I tried to widen my stance, opening myself up to him and he chuckled. "No wonder they couldn't resist you. Look how pretty you are when this pussy is filled."

Growing desperate I tilted my hips towards him and then used my hand in his hair to guide his face back to me. Following my direction, he lapped at me carefully, but never once touched me where I needed him to, and I could feel tears of frustration build until they were squeezing past my lashes.

I was *so* close and teetering on that edge was becoming almost painful.

"Please Callum." I begged hoarsely. "Please, please, *please*!"

"Shhh baby, it's okay." He cooed. "Just take a little more for me, just a little bit more." Slowing his pace, I could feel him begin to press a third finger into me carefully and I sobbed at the stretch while he praised me. "That's it baby, you're doing so good."

Apparently, his approval had been what I needed and as his thumb passed over my clit twice and then, I detonated.

Legs buckling, I fell forward but O'Neil stood and crushed me to him. "Easy Tatum, I've got you."

My cheeks were damp from my tears, and I sniffed as I rested my face against his shoulder. Holding me tightly, he stroked his hands down my spine and kissed me softly before taking a step back though one of his hands remained on my lower back, as if he was ready to steady me should I fall over. Sniffing again, I lifted a hand to wipe at my cheeks and I flushed in embarrassment as he bent down to grab at my sweats and underwear.

"I got it." I grumbled as I reached for my clothes, but he shooed my hands away before kneeling once more.

"Kelly, your ribs are going to be black and blue tomorrow and bending is going to hurt." Crossing my legs, I pulled my shirt as far down as I could, and he blinked up at me before his lips lifted in a smirk. "I just went down on you; my fingers are literally still wet with your cum and now you're embarrassed?"

My face heated once more, and I chewed at my lower lip before leaning forward towards him. But the sudden change made my side ache, and I inhaled sharply before standing straight once more. Tracing his fingers over my bare calves, Callum carefully wrapped a hand around one ankle and lifted my foot before placing it through the hole of my underwear and then he did the same with the other leg before hiking the cotton up. Grabbing my pants, he repeated the process and then stood.

"I'm going to finish getting changed and pack my stuff and then we'll go home, okay?" Nodding, I carefully slid onto the bench once more and he pressed a quick kiss to my hair before heading back towards the showers.

Leaning my head against the headrest, I watched as the lights reflected across Cullum's face as we made our way towards home. The truck was warm and soothing, and I pressed back into my seat as O'Neil fiddled with the dash and then a Christmas carol sounded around us. Glancing at the screen, I turned to him in surprise, but he kept his eyes on the windshield and I moved my gaze across his body and down his arms, not stopping until I noticed the gashes and scabs that covered his knuckles.

"Are these from today?" I asked before leaning forward to touch the cuts, but Callum snatched my hand and then wove our fingers together before placing them on my thigh, but I didn't let that deter me. "Callum, what happened after I was checked?"

O'Neil's jaw clenched, and I felt his body tense, but he didn't turn to me when he answered. "He had no fucking right pulling that shit, and he deserved everything he got."

"But you were thrown from the game," I whispered while my thumb stroked across the ruined flesh.

"It was worth it and besides, we still won." He shrugged but something was left unsaid, and I lifted his hand to my lips, pressing a soft kiss to the skin and I heard his swift inhale.

"Perry must have been livid that he lost two players though." I whispered against him, not missing the way his face grew sombre and then he was pulling his hand from mine as he turned into our driveway. "How bad was it?"

"Kelly, don't worry about it." He shrugged as he killed the engine, but I could see whatever had happened had shaken him and I pulled my seatbelt off before reaching over to unbuckle his and then cupped his face. Turning him to face me, I took a second to examine his features while stroking his sharp jaw with my fingers.

"You shouldn't have gotten involved; you should have left it alone." I whispered. "That kind of stuff happens all the time, it's part of the game and I knew what I was getting into."

"Stop justifying it," he snapped. "It was a dirty, cheap shot, and we both know he set his sights on you because he could see that you are ours."

"*Ours*?" I repeated, as my heart thundered, and Callum lifted his hands to the back of my head before pulling me across the console and then he rested his forehead against mine.

"Ours." He confirmed with a rough voice and then I was moving.

Carefully swinging a leg over, I settled on his lap and pressed my mouth to his. Kissing him deeply, I let the burning heat I thought had cooled in the dressing room wash over me once more and then I rolled my hips into his.

"If that's true O'Neil, you better catch up," I whispered. "Because only Rivers and Patrick can lay that claim."

"Is that a challenge, Kelly?" Smiling, I pressed into the hard length of him again before nodding. "What about your ribs?"

Pulling back, I carefully leaned against the steering wheel and raised a brow. "Don't you think you can make me forget about them?"

"I don't want to hurt you." We both knew it was a feeble excuse and I slid my hand down until my fingers were curled around the grey material of his pants.

"Oh please Callum, I can handle you." I promised with a roll of my eyes and O'Neil swallowed and then lifted his hips for me.

His hands were massive and thick, so I wasn't sure what I had been expecting, but the sheer size of him knocked the air from my lungs and I wondered if I had been too cocky. Seeming to realize my sudden nervousness, Callum gripped my ass and tugged me closer with a grin.

"We'll take it slow." He promised and I nodded while both excitement and apprehension twisted in my belly. Lifting onto my knees, we carefully peeled my pants off and then his fingers were dipping into me.

"Fuck, O'Neil." I whispered as he masterfully coaxed my arousal to the surface while chuckling quietly under his breath.

"That's the plan Kelly." Slipping two fingers into me, he worked my clit skillfully and I was panting in desperation, my breath causing the windows to fog as I closed in on my release.

"Not yet, hold on baby." He grunted and his hand slipped from between my thighs and then opened the middle console. Pulling out a condom, he tore the packet with his teeth and rolled the latex down until he was covered. "Ready?"

Nodding, I tucked my hair behind my ears and then braced my hands on his shoulders as he guided me down. Slowly, I sank one inch, then two and gasped as he stretched me. "Fuck."

"Take your time baby, there's no rush." Callum pressed a soft kiss to my temple and then swiped his thumb over me. The added stimulation was welcome and felt my body relax around him as I sank down the rest of the way. “Fuck Tatum, you feel so good.”

Unable to form words, I carefully rocked myself into him and he helped me, guiding my hips into an easy rhythm as we both gasped for air. Warmth seeped into my belly and spread through my veins, and I closed my eyes, tipping my head back as Callum pressed into me, filling me in a way I didn’t know was possible.

“I’m close,” I grunted, and he nodded against my jaw with a groan.

“What do you need, Tatum?” He asked

“Move your thumb a little faster.” Following the instruction, he set to work, and the change was exactly what my body required to finally release the tension. Crying out, I slumped forward as I finally fell over the edge with Callum following just a second after and he curled his arms around me carefully before snickering.

“What’s so funny?” I snapped, feeling embarrassed that he was laughing at me at such a vulnerable time, but his brown eyes were focused over my shoulder, and I turned my head to the bay window of our house only to see both Shawn and Jace giving us a thumbs up.

“Well, guess we’re even now.”

Chapter Thirty

TATUM

Callum held my door open as I slid from the truck and then ushered me towards the house with a steady hand on my lower back. Taking in a deep breath, I glanced at him from over my shoulder and he offered me a small smile though he seemed to be just as nervous as I was.

I knew that the guys said that they were open to the four of us but saying it and actually going forward with it were two different things and a part of me was worried that this might not work the way they thought it would. Taking in a deep breath, I swallowed anxiously and then reached for the knob before pressing open the door.

The house was warm and bright, but both men had moved from the window, and I could hear the low volume of the TV. Sighing in relief that I would have some time to compose myself, my shoulders sagged, and I bent down, ready to untie my shoes when a sharp pain rocked through me. Gasping at the burning ache, I wrapped an arm around my ribs and then Callum was in front of me, his hands urging me to straighten while he called my name worriedly.

“What is it? Is she okay?” Shawn’s panicked voice was closer than I had been expecting and I squinted open an eye at the blonde before shooting him a weak smile.

“Just bent funny.” I groaned but he frowned and then leaned forward to press a kiss to my forehead before fingering my shirt.

“Can I see?” He asked and I rolled my eyes with a scoff.

“What is with you guys and wanting to see my ribs. It’s not like any of you are doctors, I don’t know what good it will do.” I reasoned but still lifted the hem and Shawn gasped at the sight before turning to glare at Callum.

“What the hell were you thinking fucking her in your truck when she looked like this O’Neil?!” Shawn’s voice raised and my brows lifted before I pressed on his chest firmly.

“First, don’t shout at him. Second, it was my idea, not his and I’m allowed to do whatever I want.” Those bright blue eyes finally turned to me, and when his face crumbled with worry, I felt my chest twist with guilt, so I took a breath before reassuring him. “I’m fine Shawn, sore but fine.”

“Then why don’t we get our girl to the couch so she can relax.” Jace suggested as he sauntered towards us, and I shot him a grateful smile.

“That sounds perfect,” I sighed and patted Shawn’s chest twice as I passed the two men and then made my way to the sectional.

Following behind, Jace cupped my elbow and guided me down onto the long section of the couch before draping the blanket across my knees. Satisfied that I was comfortable, he settled in next to me with a groan and then nestled his head onto my shoulder.

“You sure you’re okay?” He double checked and I smiled at him before running a hand down his spine.

“Bruised, battered and a little embarrassed that an entire arena clapped when I got up, but fine.” His eyes scanned my features, and then he pressed a kiss to my collar bone.

“And Callum?” He whispered against my skin, and I peered up at the two men in the kitchen who appeared to be gathering snacks.

“It seems he also likes the word *ours*,” Jace stilled, and he blinked up at me in surprise while I nodded. “Especially when referring to me.”

“*Only* when referring to you Kelly.” Callum declared as he dropped the bowl of popcorn on the table and then he was lifting my legs to slide under them before lowering them back on his lap. Following behind, Shawn ignored the entire empty part of the sectional and grabbed at a cushion before tossing it to the floor in front of me and then sank onto it. Once settled in the corner he pressed his back against the couch and I ran my free hand through his hair gently.

“Did the doctor say when you could get back on the ice?” Shawn asked while tipping his head back into my hand and I scratched my fingers across his scalp

“He suggested I wait for two to three weeks. Luckily, we have winter break, so I’ll only miss a few practices.” I answered but frowned when I felt Callum stiffened beside me and when I glanced at him, I noticed his eyes were glued to the TV.

“What do we have to do in the meantime?” Jace murmured, his warm breath fanning across my chest and I rested my head on his.

"Well, I still have a bunch of presents to wrap and then Chris wants to come by this week apparently he has news and then-" Jace lifted from his place and laughed softly with a shake of his head.

"No Kelly, I meant about your injuries. Should you be on meds? Are there things you can and can't do?"

"Oh," Pausing I thought back to the doctor and tried to remember all the specifics. "I just need to take it easy and if anything feels worse instead of better, I should probably go back."

All three turned to me with narrowed eyes, and I sank back into the couch nervously. "What?"

"No paraphrasing this time. What exactly did the doctor say?" Shawn asked with a scowl, and I rolled my eyes.

"I should probably sleep more upright and icing them will help. He also suggested anti-inflammatories when I need them, but honestly, they look much worse than they feel." Standing from the floor Shawn handed Jace the pillow, who then tucked it under my head carefully while the blonde headed towards my room. "What is he doing?"

"No idea." Callum murmured and the three of us waited for a few minutes until Shawn emerged, tugging my mattress in tow. Pulling it across the hardwood, he paused at the threshold of the room and then dragged the coffee table away before laying it down.

"What was the point of that?" I wondered but he ignored me while he gathered a few pillows and the extra throw and then he smiled brightly at me.

"We won't all fit in your bed, and I don't really feel like fighting over who gets to stay with you through the night. So – this way you can have the couch with one of us and the other two can sleep on this." His face was so open and excited, I didn't have the heart to show anything, but an enthusiastic smile and I laughed as he fell onto the mattress dramatically before shuffling back to his previous position.

"You guys are something else." I chuckled under my breath and Shawn tipped his head back with a shrug.

"Maybe, but we're yours." My chest warmed at his earnest expression, and I glanced at Jace and then Callum, noticing they too peered at me in a similar fashion and then I nodded with a soft grin.

"That sounds good to me."

"That's way too much tape, Patrick." Laughing, I wrapped an arm around my torso to ease the ache and Shawn lifted his head to narrow his blue eyes at me.

"Hey! No laughing and especially *not* at me!" He lifted the pair of scissors to point at me grumpily and I stuck my tongue out at him.

"Maybe she wouldn't if that present didn't look like a kindergartener's art project." Jace offered as he handed me a mug of tea and I smiled gratefully at him before tilting my head for a quick kiss. All three guys had been nothing short of mother hens while I had spent the last few days recuperating and as much as I liked to pretend to be annoyed at all the fussing, something in me basked in the warmth of their affection and constant doting.

Speaking of the fussing, I searched the main floor for the naggy one of the bunch, realizing he hadn't bothered over me all morning, but Callum was nowhere to be seen and I frowned before glancing at my phone to check the time. "Where is O'Neil?"

Jace yawned beside me while his eyes watched Shawn struggle with the wrapping paper and then he lifted a shoulder. "Said he wanted to try and talk to Perry about something before he heads out for the holidays."

"Is everything okay?" I worried but Jace patted my leg before wrapping an arm around my shoulders carefully.

"I'm sure it's nothing, I bet Perry is just restless with the time off and wants to get organized for our return to the season." Jace reassured me and then pressed his lips to my temple. "Now what did Chris say last night when he called you?"

"Oh!" Momentarily forgetting about my ribs, I sat up excitedly and then grunted at the burning ache that echoed through my side.

"Easy Tatum!" Shawn chastised from his place on the floor, but I glowered at him in response before settling once more.

"It's fine, relax." I promised and then turned my attention to Jace. "Anyway, he called me last night to tell me he and Tommy have decided not to wait until the spring and are going to go to City Hall on Christmas Eve to get married. I guess there was a cancellation and Tommy jumped at the opening."

Shawn threw his hands together with an echoing clap and beamed. "That's awesome! They must be pumped!"

"They seem to be! Chris sounded giddy last night on the phone, and they very much want me to be there but have also extended an invitation to you three if you want to come. But no pressure of course, I know you don't know them well and our thing is still so new. But it's not like a formal wedding thing, it's just us. Which maybe that makes it more important and intimate and if so, then don't worry. I wouldn't have any sort of expectations of you guys especially since it's Christmas Eve and I'm sure you have other plans with your family or the O'Neil's but-" Jace's hands clamped over my mouth, and he shook his head in amusement.

"Tatum breathe, you're going a hundred miles a minute." Slipping his palm from my face, he stroked my cheek fondly and offered a soft smile. "We were planning on staying here this year since Callum's sister and mom are heading south and my family are out in Toronto visiting my brother. So of course, we would like to come if you are okay with it."

"I'd love for you three to be there and I'll let Chris know you said yes." Sighing in relief now that that had been decided I sank into the warmth of Rivers while Shawn continued to wrestle with the red paper. "But first, can we please put on a wrapping presents tutorial before he uses the entire roll?"

"Hey," I called from my place on the couch as O'Neil entered the kitchen and he jumped, startled by my voice before peering at me from over his shoulder.

"Hey," he greeted and then ran a hand through his hair while his eyes moved across the room. "Everything was quiet when I got in, I thought you were sleeping."

"No, just reading while the guys are at the gym." Lifting my novel, I wiggled the pages, but Callum only nodded and then turned his back to me. "Is something wrong?"

"No," he answered and though his tone was kind, the one-word response made me worried.

Dropping my book onto my lap, I tucked my hair behind my ears and then watched him as he collected things from the fridge. "You sure? Did something happen with Perry?"

The loaf of bread that had been cradled in his arms fell from his grasp, but he paid it no mind as he stared at me. "Who told you I was seeing Perry?"

"Jace mentioned it this morning before they left, though he didn't say what it was about. Was it serious?"

"Actually, we didn't have a chance to speak. He had already left for the airport when I got there." Callum shrugged, but there was still something off and I tilted my head as I studied him.

"Maybe you can try calling him later," I offered but he shook his head softly.

"It's fine." Bending to pick up the bread, he rolled his shoulders and then glanced at me once he had straightened. "Now how about some French toast?"

Wrinkling my nose, I stuck out my tongue in disgust. "I'll pass, not a fan."

"You don't like French toast?" He scoffed and I held my hands up.

"It's the soggy bread, it's just too mushy for me." Callum crossed his arms over his chest, and I lifted a shoulder helplessly. "I'd take toast and an egg on the side if you're offering though. I could even help!"

Using a hand, I pulled myself up from the couch and moved onto my feet before Callum raced over. Wrapping an arm around my hips he glared down at me in disapproval, but I just tilted my face and pressed a soft kiss to the edge of his jaw before moving from his hold.

"C'mon O'Neil, come show me those kitchen skills of yours," I smiled and held a hand out for him. "While I try to convince you to come to City Hall on Christmas Eve for Chris and Tommy's wedding."

Wrapping his fingers around mine, he followed me to the kitchen and then pulled a stool out for me. "You want me to go to their wedding with you?"

Blushing, I played with a strand of my hair before clearing my throat. "Well, all three of you are invited actually, and Jace and Shawn already said yes."

"I see." Turning on the stove, he grabbed at the frying pan, and I watched as he seemed to gather his thoughts. "Kelly, I don't know if I should go."

"Why not?" I asked, hurt that he didn't seem the least bit interested in the idea.

"I don't think Chris is my biggest fan, they don't like me nearly as much as the other guys and I just feel like I'm not someone they would want there on their day."

"They were very specific when they said all *three* of you, Callum." I paused before taking in a deep breath. "I know that this thing we have isn't something that fits the norm, but if that's what you're worried about, you should know that my brother is aware of my feelings for each of you and wouldn't ever want to exclude anyone. Besides, Chris likes you just fine, if he didn't, I would hear about it, trust me."

"I just don't want you to regret it later, Kelly." My brows furrowed and I chewed at my lower lip.

"First, I thought we were past this last name thing and second, I wouldn't regret it." Sliding from my stool, I rounded the island and then stood toe to toe with him before slowly curling an arm around his shoulders. "I want you there, with me - with *us*."

Rising on my toes, I skimmed my lips across his slowly and Callum tangled his long fingers into my hair before taking control of the kiss. Backing me towards the counter, he bent and then cupped my thighs before carefully hoisting me up so that I was sitting on the granite, and I took the opportunity to wrap my legs around his waist as I slowed the kiss until our mouths were just barely brushing against each other's.

"When you said *ours,* you meant all three of you right?" I asked and when he nodded, I continued. "Well then, that's what I want. It's a package deal now Callum and you are equally a part of that, okay?" He pressed another kiss to my mouth, and I smiled into it before stroking a hand down his back. "Good. Now that that is settled let's not worry about whatever is going on in that head of yours and let's instead focus on feeding me before I waste away."

Chapter Thirty-One

TATUM

"Shit!" I hissed through my teeth as I shook out my fingers and then lifted my thumb to my mouth to suck at the searing heat.

"Honestly Tatum, how do you manage to burn yourself with every curl?" Kate laughed as she snatched the iron from me, and I fell onto the chair she motioned towards with a pout.

"Listen, straight I can do. Ponytails - I'm a pro. That stupid wand thing though is just difficult." Shaking her head, she grabbed a section of hair and twisted it around the hot metal, and I watched her in our reflection. "Thank you for coming over to help."

Her pretty face rose, and her eyes met mine in the glass before she offered me a grin. "Of course, Tatum, you know I'd never say no to you."

Reaching behind me, I wrapped an arm around her waist and squeezed her gently. "You can still come, you know; the boys would love to have you there."

"I really want to, but you know how hard the holidays are for mom." She sighed and I tightened my hold. "Besides, as much as I would love to see the four of you together, I think this sort of stepping stone is better off with as small of an audience as possible I think."

"What are you talking about?"

"You, them and your brothers all interacting now that you are...together." Her brows lifted towards her hairline, and I blushed before ducking my head.

"It's not that big of deal, Chris and Tommy like them and it's Christmas Eve, it would have been impolite to not invite them to come with me since they're staying home."

"Sure, right," she agreed sarcastically and I rolled my eyes.

"Seriously, I don't think it's a huge deal, things aren't that serious yet and I don't know if they ever will be." I shrugged.

"What do you mean?" Kate probed. "I thought you really liked them?"

"Yeah, but I mean realistically how can this really be anything more than what it is right now?" Peering up through my lashes, I watched Kate, hopeful that she would have a solution.

"I don't know Tatum, but in the future, if it's something you want, I'm sure you'll find a way to make it happen." Deflating, I sank into my seat and let my friend resume her work on my hair.

"What are you going to wear?" She asked, changing the subject and I pointed to the one of the only dresses I owned that was hanging on the back of the bathroom door. "Oh, your little black number. Chris might not appreciate the lack of flare, but I bet the guys will enjoy taking that off you later."

Lifting a hand in front of me, I crossed my fingers. "Here's hoping."

"And I'm going to want all of the details," she laughed before nudging me. "Think of it as a Christmas gift."

"Maybe it's time you get laid, so you don't have to live vicariously through me," I suggested.

"Find me a trio of hot athletes who are actually nice and maybe I'd be down."

"Two are nice, Callum is still his moody self." I snickered.

Twirling another strand over the wand, Kate sighed dramatically. "Yeah, but it's all hot and broody, which just makes him even sexier."

"I guess so," I agreed. "But seriously, has no one caught your eye?"

Kate was hard to read on a good day and I was often left wondering what was going on in that pretty head of hers. But watching her now I noticed she shifted from one foot to the other and began to hum under her breath.

"Katelyn Ann Schmidt, what are you hiding?!" Her cheeks flushed and she carefully put the iron down on the vanity and closed the toilet lid before perching on it.

"Okay, so there is someone I'm kind of interested in, but I don't really know how they feel." Lifting a hand, I twirled my wrist, encouraging her to continue. "It's Vanessa."

The room went silent for a long pause while I tried to wrap my head around this piece of new information and Kate rubbed at her temples anxiously. "As in *Vanessa* Vanessa?"

"Yes, Tatum! Who else would I be talking about?" Lifting my hands in surrender I swallowed and then my lips lifted.

"You know, I can totally see it." Green eyes flashed to mine and my smile grew. "Seriously Kate, that's amazing."

"Really?" She asked doubtfully and I leaned over, grabbing at her hands.

"Yeah, I think that you and her would be amazing together!" Her face brightened and she threw an arm around my shoulder.

"I think so too," she sighed. "But we need to save this conversation for another day, you need to be ready in twenty and we haven't even picked out what you're wearing underneath that dress."

Rolling my eyes, I turned to face the mirror once more. "I was thinking something red."

Standing next to my brother, I wiped at my eyes as he repeated his vows and then I thanked whoever was watching over us from above, that he had not only found someone so perfect, but that Tommy loved him so dearly. It was almost as if the adoration and respect between them was palpable in this room, and I sniffed once more while Tommy began his own words of promise.

"Here," Shawn whispered as he stepped in behind me and I pinched the tissue from his hand with a nod of thanks before dabbing at my eyes.

The guys had each taken the time to put on one of their suits for the evening and Jace had even contacted another student who was studying art and photography to come take pictures for my brother. When he had introduced us, I could have sworn the affection I had for him grew twice in size and I was sure I scandalized the front staff with the way I had all but climbed up his body before sliding my tongue into his mouth. Blushing at the memory, I turned my head to glance at the trio, hoping to sneak a quick peek, but their own eyes had already locked on me, and I blushed at their attention before facing the couple once more.

"I now pronounce you husband and husband," the officiant declared and I clapped gleefully as the guys whooped and hollered while my brother kissed his spouse.

Pulling away from each other, the pair thanked the man for taking the time to marry them and then reached for my hands. Drawing me into a firm embrace, Chris kissed my hair and Tommy held us tightly to his chest while a handful of tears ran down my cheeks and then I stepped back.

“I am so happy for you two,” I sobbed messily. “And Tommy, I couldn’t think of someone more deserving or perfect for my brother.” Tommy’s own eyes glistened with tears, and he wrapped his arms around me once again.

“Alright honey,” Chris laughed wetly. “Don’t suffocate your new sister.”

Moving away, I grinned at my brother, and he mimicked the expression before glancing at the guys. “Thank you for coming tonight, I’m sure it’s not how you expected to celebrate Christmas Eve.”

“We are honored to witness your special day,” Jace reassured him and then glanced down the aisle towards the sophomore with the camera. “But I think Kevin wants to grab a few photos of the two of you by the tree in the foyer.”

Shooing them towards the student, I promised we would wait around for them to finish and then I glanced at my boys. The three of them looked incredible in their attire and I sighed dreamily before closing the distance.

Shawn was the first to meet me and he ran his fingers over my wet cheeks before wrapping an arm around my shoulder and then I was surrounded by them. Shawn on my left with his arm remaining around me, Jace on my right with a hold on my waist and Callum angled just in front, one of his hands tangled with my own.

“Thank you for coming,” I whispered shyly.

Brushing a curl out of my face, Callum shrugged. “Someone had to be here to hand you tissues. Who knew Kelly would be such a crier at weddings?”

“Oh, shut it.” I joked before swatting at him and he dodged the blow with a quiet laugh before leaning forward to press a sweet kiss to my cheek.

“Alright you three, enough horsing around.” Not realizing we had an audience, we jumped at the sudden interruption, and I stepped away from them as I glanced at my brother.

“Done already?” I asked while praying my face wasn’t too red.

“Yup we are very efficient models,” he smiled and then glanced at the guys behind me. “However, we are absolutely exhausted from the drive and everything today, so we’re going to head out.”

“You don’t want to do dinner or anything?” I asked in surprise, but Chris just shook his head.

“I think we are going to go to the hotel and just order room service, but we’ll see you in the morning?” Nodding I wrapped my brother in my arms.

"Merry Christmas Eve, Chris," I whispered.

"Merry Christmas Eve, Tatum," he responded and then lowered his voice. "Now go home with your guys and have a good evening."

Taking a step back, he turned to them and embraced each one before moving for Tommy to do the same and then they made their exit and I sighed happily. "This has been one of the best Christmas Eves I have ever had."

"Well, it's not over yet," Jace purred from my side. "What do you say we head home and finish making tonight one of the most memorable of your life."

The line would have been horribly cringy if it hadn't been for the wave of arousal that rocked through me at the suggestion, and I grinned in anticipation. "First one to the truck gets to unwrap me like a present."

It felt like ages since I had been touched, truly touched and I knew the reason had been because the guys were worried about hurting me. But now as I knelt on the mattress in the living room, I prayed that they would forget about my ribs and my bruises and just *fuck me*.

"How is this going to work?" Shawn asked as he shrugged out of his coat, and I watched in interest as he rolled his sleeves to his elbow.

"What do you mean Patrick, surely you know what we're doing here," Callum responded as he loosened his tie, and I rubbed my thighs together impatiently as they each got comfortable.

"It's only ever been three of us at a time, I'm just wondering about the mechanics, O'Neil."

Blowing a curl out of my eyes, I sank onto my heels and crossed my arms over my chest. "Okay one, can we stop talking about us having sex like it's some sort of procedure, it's kind of ruining the mood. And two, I'm right here, so rather than talking about it like I'm not, let me clear some things up right now."

All eyes turned to me, and I shuffled under the attention before exhaling. "As always, I want us to communicate what feels good or if we should slow down or whatever. All those rules still apply now even though there's four of us this time. But with that being said, I've given this a lot of thought and I have my own ideas on how I would like to proceed."

“Oh, and how is that?” Jace asked, his voice finally dropping into that sexy drawl I loved so much and I wet my lips before turning my eyes to Callum.

“I know how much you like to watch, so I thought we could start with that, though maybe you’d be willing to give a little more direction this time.” His brown eyes darkened at the words, and I chewed at my lower lip and then straightened my spine.

“I should also be clear that I plan on having all of you at once. That’s what I want for tonight and I’m hoping you’ll agree.”

“You mean…” Shawn trailed off and I nodded.

“I’m a pretty big fan of anal and although I’ve never had more than one partner at once, I can promise the idea of feeling two of you fill me while my mouth is… occupied is something I have fantasized about often.”

“Holy fucking shit,” Shawn gasped under his breath, and I lifted a brow at him. “I’m sorry but that is so fucking hot.”

Smiling, I lifted my fingers to one strap of my dress and tugged it down my arm before moving on to the other. “I’m glad you agree. So does this mean we can please get started. Because I swear, if someone doesn’t touch me soon, I’ll fuck my own fingers and call it a night.”

“You absolutely will not. You’ll sit there prettily while Rivers and Patrick peel that fucking dress off of you and then you’ll use your manners and ask to cum.”

My mouth dried at O’Neil’s order, and I dipped my head in agreement.

“You heard him, Jace, let’s go.”

Kneeling before me, Shawn wrapped an arm around my waist and tugged me until I was straddling his knees and then kissed me. Preoccupied by his mouth, I hadn’t noticed Rivers had snuck behind me until his teeth were scraping down the skin of my neck and I moaned into Shawn’s kiss.

“Jace, pull down that zipper and then unwrap our girl slowly. I want her aching to feel your skin before we strip her fully.” I felt the metal slowly give away as he did what he was told and then my dress pooled around my waist, leaving my nipples to tighten in the cool air.

“Fucking hell Kelly.” Shawn gasped as he took me in and then he was turning his head, looking for the direction he so desperately craved.

“What do you want Patrick to do, Tatum?” Callum asked and my eyes moved towards him, realizing he had slid onto a stool while he watched.

"I want him to touch me, I want to feel his fingers on my skin."

"Show him." Swallowing roughly, I lifted my hands to my breasts and cupped the soft flesh before thumbing the nipples. "That's such a good girl Kelly. Now give him permission."

"Touch me just like this, pretty boy." Following my lead, he shooed my hands away and then he was tracing the tight buds before clamping them between his thumbs and forefingers. Applying just the right amount of pressure, my back arched and then his mouth was lowering, and he used his teeth on one and then the other until I cried out.

"What do you need Kelly?" Callum called from across the room, and I lifted on my knees, moving my hips against the aching emptiness between my thighs before leaning my head back on Jace's shoulder.

"I need something in me." I sobbed and he grinned.

"You heard her Rivers, give our girl something to ride." Fingers were sliding up my thighs and then dipping under the black fabric before pulling my red panties aside and I whimpered as they swirled around my clit before sinking into me.

"Fuck she's soaked." Jace choked out and O'Neil chuckled in response.

"Lean her back and spread her open, I want Shawn to use his tongue while you fuck her with your fingers." I was nearly limp as they adjusted me just perfectly and I cried out when Shawn lowered his head to me.

The two of them worked in tandem, playing my body like a finely tuned instrument and I shivered in Jace's hold as my release neared. But sensing my desperation, he slowed his pace and I grabbed at Shawn's blonde locks, tugging him tighter to me while I chased Jace's fingers.

"Please, Callum." I begged, knowing the guys wouldn't let me finish until he gave the okay and I turned my head, my eyes wide and pleading as I waited.

"Soon, but first, we need to make sure you're ready for us." Moving to his feet, he walked across the room, and I whimpered, watching as he disappeared up the stairs.

"Soon baby, be patient." Jace cooed against my temple while his fingers continued to thrust into me at that slow, punishing pace.

Taking his time to come back down, Callum finally entered the living room though he hesitated, his head tipping as he watched his friends torture me and then he finally fell to his knees next to Jace. Tapping Shawn, he directed him back a foot and then grabbed Jace's wrist before pulling and I shook my head as the fingers left me.

"Wait, what?"

"Relax, Tatum," He shushed me and then lifted a bottle of lube. "We're going to get these clothes off of you and then Jace is going to make sure you're prepared for him."

Pulling my panties down my legs, he then tugged the dress over my head and then once I was naked, he urged me onto my back before grabbing at his own clothes. One by one they undressed, and I stretched out across the mattress before bending my knees and splaying my legs open.

"We'll take this slow and when you're ready you tell us, okay?" Jace asked and had I not been distracted by the three very prominent erections surrounding me, I would have melted at his concern.

"Please." Was the only thing I could think to say once words came back to me, and he smiled before spreading an ample amount of lube on his fingers. Making sure they were coated, he lowered his hand and traced me carefully before gently pressing a finger in.

The stretch wasn't foreign, but it had been a while and I wiggled just a little before relaxing my body. Happy to continue, I nodded, and he pressed in another beside the first while Shawn lowered his tongue to my clit and then Callum was pressing his own fingers into my pussy.

"Holy fuck," I wailed as my nerves were pushed into overdrive and my body spasmed, then shivered and I wondered why I had never tried something like this before.

"Good?" Callum asked and I grunted in response. "Ready to come for us?"

Lifting my hips, I opened my legs farther in answer and the three set to work. Taking me to the edge in no time, they quickened their pace and then I was falling, my body tightening before turning to putty and I panted as I tried to regain feeling of my limbs.

"Condoms?" I heard Callum ask somewhere from behind me and I blinked up at the ceiling in a daze while they organized themselves.

"You okay, Tatum?" Shawn whispered into my ear and my head lolled to the side before I grinned.

"Better than okay." I promised and then lifted my head as the mattress dipped under the weight of Callum.

"Do you want to keep going?" He asked and I lifted a brow.

"What do you think?" Grinning, he bent forward to kiss me and then lifted my thighs, turning me onto my knees once more before sliding under my body.

"I'm going to start and then once you're ready, Jace will join." He explained. "Then when you're comfortable, Shawn will come in. But Tatum, we need you to speak up if anything feels wrong or off. I've never done anything like this, and three partners is a first for them too."

Glancing behind me, I looked at Jace and reached a hand out for him to take. Once our fingers were interlocked, I reached for Shawn and did the same with him and then inhaled deeply. "I'm ready."

Lifting higher onto my knees, I let Callum line us up and then slowly, I sank down. Gasping for air when I finally bottomed out and Jace pressed a kiss to my shoulder before guiding my hips gradually and when I found my rhythm, I peered back at Rivers.

"Fuck my ass Jace." It may have been crude, or maybe too direct but the words worked, and he was fisting his cock before rolling a condom on and then he was spreading lube over the length of him and around my entrance. Certain I was slick enough, he pressed his head into me and then one inch at a time and I sagged forward, closing my eyes as my body stretched around the both of them.

It was unlike anything I had ever felt before and tears filled my eyes at the pleasure while they picked up a steady pace. Moving together, I followed the push and pull frantically, eager for another release but unwilling to finish without the final party.

Opening my eyes, I peered up into the deep blue irises that were burning with lust and wet my lower lip. Making sure I had his full attention, I tilted my chin and lowered my jaw before sticking out my tongue in invitation.

"Tatum." My name rumbled from him, and I moaned eagerly in reply.

"Take her mouth, Shawn." Callum grunted from beneath me and the blonde tangled my long brown hair in his fist before directing my face towards him.

Happy to finally have all three of them, I swallowed his length down, inhaling through my nose as I relaxed my throat and then I closed my eyes. It was like four bodies became one as we moved together, the ebb and flow growing stronger by every passing minute, and I felt my chest warm at the feeling.

This was what I wanted, what I needed.

"She's close," Jace warned as he panted against my shoulder blade and then he reached a hand around, his thumb strumming my clit softly.

But sensing I needed more, Callum traced his fingers across my breasts and over my collar bones, continuing to move until the digits curled around my neck and then he tightened his grasp, and I wondered if he could feel Shawn as he pressed into the back of my throat.

"Cum for us baby." Callum demanded and I shivered at the tone. "C'mon Kelly, you're almost there."

Pulling my mouth from Shawn, I cried out, my voice hoarse as the noise echoed around us and then I fell over the edge. Following behind me, Shawn finished next, his cum splattering across my chin and chest and then Jace grunted into my back as he trembled. Callum, who was still pumping into me, gripped my hips and when his body began to shake, I lifted a hand, copying his move from earlier and pressed my palm against the tender skin of his throat.

"Cum for us, O'Neil." I demanded and he tossed his head back with a groan, finally finding his release.

Chapter Thirty-Two

JACE

The body under mine was vibrating with quiet whispers and I nuzzled into the soft skin while chasing the deep sleep I had been caught up in just moments before. Last night had been one for the books and even now I felt the exhaustion from my release deep in my bones.

"Merry Christmas, sleepy head," Tatum whispered softly with a press of her lips to my forehead, and I grunted before pressing my nose into her shoulder. "Don't you want to open presents?"

"The only thing I want right now is to go back to sleep," I grumbled and Shawn laughed from somewhere on the couch.

"Then go back to sleep, but at least let Kelly up, she's been patiently waiting for you to wake for like an hour." Lifting my head, I squinted one eye at my friends as they sipped their coffees on the couch and then I gazed down at Tatum, who was still sprawled across the mattress.

"I do really want to get a coffee and then open presents," she shrugged with a soft smile, and I groaned before flopping onto my back, effectively releasing her. Grabbing at her newfound freedom, she staggered onto her feet and raced to the bathroom while I admired her naked ass in the morning light.

"I don't know what kind of magic Christmas has, but she's been practically vibrating with excitement since five this morning." Callum sighed as he rubbed at his face tiredly and I pulled myself up until I was leaning against the couch.

"I guess we didn't tire her out enough last night," I suggested slyly just as Tatum reappeared, though this time she was wearing an oversized t-shirt and a tiny pair of shorts.

"Did you guys move the ibuprofen?" Tatum asked as she grabbed a mug of coffee, and I frowned in concern.

"They're by the fridge, are you okay?" Nodding she opened the bottle and then tossed two into her mouth before chasing them down with a sip of coffee.

Standing from the couch, Shawn approached her and then wrapped an arm around her waist. "Did we hurt you last night?"

"Of course not," she assured him. "My ribs are just a little tender."

Escorting her to the couch, he waited for her to sit and then wrapped a blanket around her shoulders. "You just sit there then, and we'll pass the presents out."

"But I wanted to be Santa this morning." She argued, only to pout when both O'Neil and Patrick shot her a look. "Fine, but if you're going to act like I'm this fragile, I get out of cleaning up too."

"Deal," I agreed and she offered me a pleased smile. "Now let's get this going before Chris and Tommy come by. I have a few, *special* gifts under that tree and I'm not sure I'll ever be able to look them in the eyes if they are here when they are opened."

The arena's air was cold as I stepped onto the ice, and I moved to my spot before sinking to the surface all while thinking about yesterday. Christmas had always just been an okay holiday for me growing up, something that was fun; fine but nothing special. However, after spending the morning with Tatum practically glowing with happiness and then dinner with the guys and her brothers, I knew without a doubt yesterday would be one of the best of my life. It was like everything I had ever wanted was there and for the first time in my life I just felt... *whole*.

Not to mention the evening we had after Chris and Tommy headed home. My God, that girl was something else. Bending one knee, I stretched my other leg out, letting the muscles extend while I pictured the way she had been in a similar position the night before.

"Rivers!" Perry called, breaking me from my reminiscing and I cursed under my breath before rising to my feet.

"What's up, Coach?" His light blue eyes lifted from the phone of his screen and then he stuffed it into his back pocket before crossing his arms with a huff.

"That extra hook and cubby, whose crap is in it?" My brows furrowed in confusion, and I shrugged.

"I think we all have something in there, we just kind of use it as a drop off station."

"Well clear it out after practice, I need it open." Turning on his heel, he shuffled down the bench and picked up his clipboard and then raised his eyes to mine once more. "What are you doing standing there? Get out there and stretch before we start. I have another player injured."

Whatever warmth and contentment that had been surrounding me was now replaced with this cold feeling of dread and I wondered why that was as I glided across the ice. Finding my place again, I continued my stretching, going through the motions carefully and then stood. Readying myself for drills I glanced to my left and noticed O'Neil was approaching me cautiously.

"Everything good?" He asked, his brown eyes worried and I frowned.

"Yeah man, why?" Sighing, his shoulders lowered in relief.

"Just wondering what Perry wanted."

"He wants us to clear out the extra space, didn't say why though." O'Neil paled and I froze, watching as his eyes shot to our coach. "Callum, are you okay?"

Ignoring me, he turned towards the boards and I remained frozen, watching as he crossed the ice before approaching Perry. Our coach, who had been completely occupied with the plays on his clipboard, lowered the wood and then his scowl deepened when he realized Callum was there.

"What is that about?" Shawn asked as he left his net and I turned to him and lifted my hands, not sure what to say. The two men were in a heated discussion but had kept their voices low enough that we weren't able to make anything out from this distance.

"I have no idea, but it doesn't look good." Perry's long finger was stabbing at Callum's chest, and I could see the muscle in his jaw working as he tried to keep his cool.

"What did Perry say to you?"

"He just asked that we clear out the extra cubby," I snapped exasperated, not understanding how such a simple request could cause so much chaos and Shawn's blue eyes moved back to the pair.

"Well, that certainly doesn't look like that's what the issue is." He guessed and I watched as Perry slammed his clipboard across the boards and then Callum was heading toward us, his face furious and I nearly moved out of his line of vision when his face turned to mine.

"Stop standing around gossiping like a bunch of girls and get ready for drills," he snapped at us, and I rubbed at my jaw in irritation.

"I guess the holiday spirit is over."

The dressing room was quiet as we all grabbed the random shit we had piled in the empty space, and I chucked some of the older crap into the garbage before turning to Shawn. The blonde had been anxiously hovering in the back since we had finished practice and I offered him a smile as he fidgeted. Shawn never did well when there was any sort of major conflict between Callum and I, but this somehow seemed worse. This wasn't one of O'Neil's typical pissy moods, our friend was obviously livid about something, but he wouldn't tell us what and being left in the dark irritated me beyond belief.

"Where did he disappear to?" Shawn wondered as he held up a forgotten t-shirt up in front of him and then crumpled the fabric into a ball before tossing it in the black plastic bag.

"I have no idea, it's like he vanished as soon as the whistle blew," I huffed, "but he needs to get over whatever it is, because I thought we were past this shit, things have been so good these past few weeks."

Nodding, Shawn hummed under his breath and then fell onto the bench. "You don't think he's having second thoughts, do you?"

"About what?"

"Kelly."

Scoffing under my breath, I shook my head. "There's no way, have you seen how he is with her? It's like she's the only thing that exists when they're together."

Tilting his head, Shawn studied me closely. "You don't sound the least bit jealous."

"That's because I'm not. How can I be when I feel the exact same way." I smiled and then glanced at him. "Are you? Jealous I mean."

"No, but I sometimes worry that I'm out of my league with three of us in it now." Falling onto the bench next to Shawn, I wrapped an arm around him.

"If you feel that way, you've been focused on the wrong things and haven't been paying attention to our girl at all."

His brows furrowed in confusion, and he looked up at me. "What?"

"Shawn, Tatum is so into you, it's ridiculous," I promised, "you guys click in a way that Callum and I don't and honestly, I'm glad for it. I love seeing you open up to someone like that."

His face brightened and I watched as he grinned to himself. "I haven't told her I passed Peters' class yet, I was going to mention it tonight at dinner."

"What? That's amazing man!" Clapping him on the back in congratulations I smirked. "Guess all that one-on-one attention during those study sessions worked. Tell me - what kind of reward system does she use?"

Shrugging my arm off of his shoulders, he rolled his eyes and then stood. "You're a dick."

There was no heat to his words, and I chuckled. "Seriously, maybe I need to start flunking some classes."

"Whatever man, we both know she'd be too smart to fall for your crap."

Standing, I stretched my arms over my head and then sighed fondly. "Yeah, our girl is pretty brilliant, isn't she?" Nodding Shawn followed and then we grabbed at our bags.

The rest of the team had already left for the night and the hallways were quiet as we made our way out of the arena but when we reached the parking lot, I realized O'Neil's truck was still there and I frowned.

"Here." Passing Shawn the keys, I turned back towards the doors. "I'll be right back; I'm going to go see if I can find him before we head home."

Pressing on the glass, I entered the arena once more and scanned the foyer before heading back down the hall towards the dressing room. Reaching the door, I pushed it open but there was still no sign of him, and I ran a hand over my face.

Deciding to check the ice, I turned on my heel. But the light glowing from Perry's office caught my eye and I watched as Callum stood from his chair before turning to someone who was in the opposite seat. The back of their head wasn't one I recognized and I held my breath as the stranger moved to his feet. He was wearing a deep red jersey, and I recognized the colour immediately, knowing it was one of ours and the white letters across his back were bright in contrast.

HUSTON

Frowning, I studied the scene while Perry motioned between Callum and Huston and then they were shaking hands, the same way I had shaken the previous captain's hand my freshman year, and I knew then that something was wrong.

Chapter Thirty-Three

TATUM

The house was quiet, too quiet and I rubbed my eyes before groaning in boredom. The guys had left early today, wanting to stop to pick up new protein powder before the first practice back and I wished I had gone with them. Even though I hadn't been cleared for the ice, I wanted to show Perry I was still very serious about my position and had planned on just watching today, but the guys had told me there was no point: this afternoon would be all about drills and I was better off taking these last few days to rest.

"They weren't that worried about my rest this morning," I grumbled to myself as I tossed my book onto the coffee table, only to blush at the slight twinge between my thighs and ache on my ass cheeks. Suddenly flustered, I thought back to just two hours ago and knew full well there would be a hand shaped bruise on each globe.

"Focus Kelly," I muttered to myself and then searched for my phone in the creases of the blanket that was draped over my legs. There was no way reading was going to happen so instead I scrolled through my apps and had just decided to play a round of Tetris when my ringtone chimed.

COACH PERRY: Kelly, can you meet me in my office in 20?

Frowning at the screen, I chewed at my lower lip nervously. Perry hadn't bothered to reach out since the game before Christmas, he was upset that I was out for the next few weeks *and* had been the reason for Callum being thrown out and so I had decided to keep my distance, too keen on keeping the peace to even bother contacting him. But maybe this was the olive branch I had been waiting on and I shot a quick text to Kate, seeing if she could give me lift to the arena. Once she confirmed, I replied to Perry.

Of course Coach, I'll be right over!

Throwing myself off the couch, I ran to my room and grabbed an arm full of clothes before rushing up the stairs. Turning on the shower, I quickly got all my things organized and then ducked under the spray. I had never showered so fast in my life and I did my best to ignore the hickeys that littered my body while I quickly scrubbed at my skin before washing my hair. Satisfied I was clean, I dried off, threw my hair up in a ponytail and pulled on my clothes and then the doorbell rang.

"Coming!" I called as I bounded to the door and Kate's eyes were wide as I threw it open.

"Woah easy there," she laughed and I slammed it behind me before throwing an arm over her shoulder.

"Thank you so much for coming to get me." Kate waved me off with a flick of her hand and then she was leading me to her car.

"No worries, Tatum, you know that." Moving into the passenger seat, I buckled myself in and then sighed.

"Did he say what he wanted?" Kate wondered as we made our way toward campus, and I shook my head.

"Of course not, that would be too easy. But he didn't cuss me out so I'm hopeful it's nothing bad." Resting my head against the window, I watched as buildings passed and then my stomach filled with nerves as the arena came into view. Pulling into the lot carefully, Kate brought me right to the front doors and idled.

"Do you want me to wait?" She asked and I shook my head before grinning.

"No, practice will be starting soon, I'll let the guys know I'll stick around for it when they get here."

"Maybe fulfill a locker room fantasy after?" She laughed with a wink and my teeth sank into my lower lip. "Oh my god! Has that already happened?"

"I can't keep Perry waiting," I shrugged and moved to open the door.

"You owe me a girl's night this week and I want all the details, no holding out on me Tatum Kelly." Stepping onto the sidewalk, I ducked so I could see her. "Deal but then I want to hear all about how you got that bruise on your collar bone." Her face pinkened and I laughed before shutting the door firmly.

Perry's office was empty when I entered it and I poked my head out the door, glancing down the hall before crossing my arms and moving back to the empty chairs. Checking my phone, I made sure I wasn't late, and then sighed. The arena was eerily quiet, the halls were empty with no one insight and I wondered what the reason had been to ask me to come down.

Becoming restless, I ran my eyes across the trophies and pictures that lined the shelves behind his chair and then lowered my attention to his desk. The beautiful wood was normally neat, meticulously organized and I scowled at the piles of papers that were strewn across the surface. There were statistics from previous games, what looked to be a handful of printed emails and then a photo of a young blonde man. It was obviously a roster picture, and I tilted my head in an attempt to read the info.

He was a junior with impressive stats and happened to play the same position as I did. My gut churned as his light eyes stared up and me and I lifted a shaking hand, my fingers pinching the corner of the page and then I turned it around. Mike Huston had been playing for South Valley for his entire university career so far but would be an excellent addition to any team, should the opportunity arise. I let go of the page filled with details before setting my sight on the contract that laid next to it.

It was something I recognized given that it was the same as the one I had signed before my freshman year, and I swallowed the bitter acid that had crept up the back of my throat while my eyes traced the bottom. Right there in messy writing was Perry's signature and beside it in a big looping font, sat Mike Huston's, the date clearly stating it had been filled the day before our last game.

"I see you know why you're here." Perry called as he entered the office and I flinched at the coolness in those icy blue eyes.

"I don't understand," I admitted shakily and Perry gestured to the chair I had vacated.

"Take a seat." He ordered and then slid into his own. "You're a smart girl Kelly but I'll explain it to you." Folding his hands on his desk, he leant over them, and I pressed back, trying to create as much distance between us as possible.

"We both know you're a talented player and to be honest, you did far better than I had ever thought you would." Hurt bloomed in my chest and I lowered my eyes to my lap as he continued. "But it wouldn't be truthful to say there haven't been a number of ... *hiccups*. Issues that have become more regular are far more detrimental to my team and I can't have it, Kelly."

My eyes prickled and I took in a shuddering breath. "But what about the rules, switching schools means a gap year for athletic careers."

Perry's mouth tipped in the corners, and he shook his head, almost as if he was pitying me. "Miller really did you a disservice this year when the school cut your team, though considering he's a few crayons short I'm not surprised he wasn't aware of the change in policies.

"Change in policies?" I whispered.

"Last year they decided that any athlete could transfer once during their academic career without any penalty, including having to take a year off, even if it's part way through the sport's season." My heart pounded in my chest and my eyes dropped to Mike Huston's photo.

"I know this probably feels unfair and it's tough to hear, but I have found someone to take Steven's place for the rest of the season." Perry shrugged. "I should thank you for your contribution though, you have been an asset to the team at times."

Inhaling through my nose, I stared down at my hands, wondering why it felt as if they were tingling and when I rubbed my fingers together, I winced at the clammy feel of my skin.

"You can hand in your jersey sometime this week of course, I can't see you wanting to keep it if you're playing for another school." Lifting my chin, I blinked stupidly at the older man.

"Another school?"

"Surely you'll transfer now that you know you can," he assumed. "Any women's team would be lucky to have you and you don't need to worry about being out of shape since you've had quite a bit of ice time. Not to mention the lesser body contact means those ribs of yours can really heal."

His tone reminded me of my father's when he used to talk down to me as a child and I clenched my jaw in rage. This was not what I had been prepared for, this was not what was supposed to happen, and I suddenly realized how stupid I had been.

"Now if that's everything, I have some things to do before practice starts." He lifted his hand towards the door in dismissal and I stood on shaky legs. But when I reached the threshold, he stopped me.

"One last thing Kelly," Those icy eyes only seemed to brighten, and I steeled myself for whatever was coming next. "Try not to be too hard on O'Neil. I'm sure he wanted to tell you, but it was a rock and a hard place you know? He had to put his team first and I'm sure you can appreciate that."

"But Tatum, that doesn't make any sense!" Kate exclaimed, her hand flying out to stop me from shoving the armful of clothes into the black plastic bag and I stepped out of her reach while tears rolled down my cheeks. "There is no way they wouldn't have told you if they knew what Perry was planning."

Using my sleeve, I wiped at my face roughly and then brushed past her to continue packing. "Kate, of course they wouldn't tell me. They needed me to fill the spot until they had someone lined up."

"Tatum," she tried again, her fingers stretching to touch me, but I shrugged away from her.

"Callum knew, and if he knew then there's no way the other two didn't. Which means this whole time they were just -" I sobbed, and then I lowered my head into my hands while I cried.

"What can I do?" She asked softly and then she carefully wrapped one arm and then the other around my waist and I laid my cheek on her head as I fought to catch my breath.

"Can I stay with you for a few days? Just until I sort everything out with admissions and what not." She nodded against me, and I took in a long breath before stepping out of her embrace. "Okay, then let's finish here before the guys get home."

The words felt cowardly and had I been more prideful, I might have been embarrassed. Afterall, normally I wouldn't be one to hide from a fight but this, I wasn't sure I could do. Perry's words had cracked me open, and the betrayal had left me raw and vulnerable and *weak*. So fucking weak.

"Alright," Kate agreed and then she scooped her own armful of clothes before tossing them into a garbage bag.

Luckily, I didn't have much and I surveyed the room, making note of anything that I might have missed before glancing at the mattress that was still laying in the middle of the living room. The sight of the pile of blankets and pillows stabbed at my heart, and I felt a fresh round of tears burn the back of my eyes.

"That won't fit in my car," Kate whispered from beside me and I glanced down at her.

"I'll just grab my duvet and pillows; they can deal with the rest." Straightening my spine, I moved across the main floor but just as I neared the living room, the front door opened, and I turned to face the two people I had been praying I would avoid.

Chapter Thirty-Four

SHAWN

Tatum's eyes were wide but red rimmed and I frowned as I noticed the moisture clinging to her pale cheeks. Taking a step forward, I began to approach her, but her face crumbled before she backed away. Freezing at her retreat, I glanced at Jace from over my shoulder, but he seemed to be just as confused and concerned as he watched her.

"Kelly?" He asked, his tone low and soft, almost like he was talking to a spooked animal, but it did nothing to calm her, and I began to panic as more tears formed in her eyes.

"She's just getting her things and then we are leaving." It was Kate who spoke, and she appeared from Tatum's room with a fierce expression painted across her face.

"Leaving?" Not understanding, I looked back and forth between the two women. "What do you mean?"

Tatum only appeared to be more stricken at my words, though Kate scoffed angrily. "Don't play stupid Patrick, you know exactly what we are talking about."

But I didn't have a fucking clue and I turned to Jace, desperate for help in sorting this out. "Kate, I don't know what you think is going on here, but I can promise you we aren't playing some game-"

"Right, because that wouldn't be something you do, right?" She snapped as she crossed the room until she reached Kelly. "You would never just use someone, would never make them your plaything while you wait for a better solution."

"Okay, now I know for sure I have no idea what you're referring to," I retorted.

Sighing, Tatum curled her hand around Kate's and then lifted her chin while ignoring the tears that had managed to escape her lashes. "Listen, there's no need for any of this. I know about Huston, Perry told me, and I would very much like to leave now before this," she gestured between us. "Gets any more heated.

"Tatum what do you mean? What is Huston?" I threw my hands in the air, but no one answered and then Jace was brushing past me.

"What did Perry tell you?" His voice barely contained his anger, and I nearly flinched at the sudden change in my friend.

"He told me about the adjustment to the regulations for athletes and that Huston was officially part of the team." Lifting a hand, she rubbed at her face roughly. "Congratulations are in order I guess, not only do you have your new player, but you got to have a little fun in the meantime while you waited."

"We didn't know that Perry was replacing you Kelly, I swear." Gasping, my eyes darted from Rivers to Tatum in shock, but she held her stoic expression flawlessly and then shrugged.

"O'Neil did."

No one said anything for a long minute, but I felt my knees wobble while my heartbeat thundered in my ears.

"There's no way," I whispered but Jace just sighed before casting a sad look my way, and then I began to shake my head. "No, there's no way Jace, he would never keep something like that from us. Things are different now. Things are different for us, for him."

"They aren't," Tatum argued and then finally moved as she reached towards the mattress that was still on the hardwood floor. Collecting the soft duvet, she wrapped it around an arm and then grabbed at the two pillows. "I appreciate you allowing me to stay here and for letting me be on your team. It's been enlightening."

Heat prickled behind my eyes and my lower lip trembled. "Don't! Don't do that. Don't act like everything we are, everything we have, has been a lie."

"But it has," she said softly while lifting one shoulder casually and I felt a sob catch in my chest as her grey eyes hardened.

Not knowing what to do, I remained rooted in place, helpless to do anything as she finished collecting her things and Jace seemed to be in the same position. Brushing past us, she entered her room one last time and heaved the black bags over her shoulder before heading for the door.

Realizing this was it, this was my chance, I gave one last ditch effort, hoping the words would be enough to stop her. "But you're our girl."

Lowering her chin, Tatum stared at her shoes for a pause and then slowly her eyes met mine. "Not anymore."

"He's not answering," I growled while pacing the length of the kitchen and Jace slumped in his seat. "Why isn't he answering?!"

"Probably because he knows what's waiting for him if he does." Jace growled and I scanned his face, taking in the anger and hurt, knowing I most definitely looked the same.

"She has to have it wrong though. She doesn't have the whole story, there must be more to it right?" I was grasping at straws, praying that this was all because of some fucked up miscommunication.

"I saw the kid in Perry's office before we left today." My head snapped to Jace's, but his eyes were glued to the granite countertop. "He was in our colours and shaking O'Neil's hand."

Dread churned in my gut "What? You said you couldn't find him."

"I know," he sighed. "I didn't know for sure what I had just witnessed, and I didn't want to make assumptions, but it proves what Kelly is saying is true."

Crossing my arms over my chest, I took in a long shuddering breath, trying to soothe the painful ache under my ribs. It hadn't been more than an hour since Kelly had left and yet I was already missing her.

"I know man." Jace rose, before reaching out to squeeze my shoulder. "I feel the same."

Leaning into him, I wrapped my arms around his back and then pressed my face into his neck, needing the comfort and support that he was offering. Grabbing at the back of my shirt, Jace tugged me closer, holding me for dear life and then the front lock clicked.

Entering the house, Callum looked pale and exhausted, but it did nothing to quell my anger. He had no right to look so distraught; not after hurting Kelly, hurting us.

"Guys -"

But O'Neil didn't have a chance to plead his case before Jace's fist was connecting with his jaw and I watched as he bent in half, cupping his face. "What the fuck, Rivers!"

Lifting a hand, Jace pointed one long finger at Callum's while he practically trembled with rage. "Did you or did you not know about Huston?"

Brown eyes widened for a split second and then he was lowering his gaze to the floor guiltily. "I knew."

All the facts pointed to that, but still his admission rocked me to the core, and I staggered back before catching myself on the counter. Never once had I felt anything but admiration for Callum O'Neil even when he was difficult to get along with because I always knew he was an honest, stand up, take no bullshit kind of person. Or at least I thought he was. But now as I watched him rub at his jaw, I felt nothing but anger.

"I know I should have told you guys."

Scoffing, I shook my head and then ran my fingers through my hair. "You still don't get it. It's not us you should have told."

"I know," he said weakly.

"And actually had the guts to let her believe things changed? You pretended to actually give a shit to what? To fuck her?"

"No!" He denied. "It wasn't like that."

"But that's exactly what it looks like, O'Neil!" Jace shouted and O'Neil lifted his hands to tug at his curls before sinking onto a stool.

"I know," Callum's voice broke. "I know that's how it looks, but it's not what happened. Perry did tell me that he was scouting other players, that Huston might be a good fit, but nothing was concrete."

Blowing out a long breath he lifted his palms to rub at his eyes. "I had thought given how well we played before Christmas, Perry would change his mind but then that whole thing with Scott happened and I screwed whatever chance she had. I tried to talk him down after the game, I begged him to reconsider but he refused."

"That's why you were there when she got back from the hospital," I murmured and Callum nodded.

"He wasn't listening, I couldn't get him to hear me out, so I tried again before he left. I called him over and over and then tried to catch him at his office, but he wasn't there. He wouldn't even answer my calls."

"Why didn't you say something?"

"I wanted to, I wanted to tell Tatum so badly, but it wasn't that easy. I couldn't figure out a way to explain it without hurting her."

"You mean without putting any blame on yourself or risking the team," Jace snapped.

"Yeah, okay? You're right. I didn't want to risk the team; I didn't want us to be stuck in a lurch but mostly I didn't want her to hate me. I didn't want her to leave at all but especially not after I realized how I felt," he paused and then corrected himself. "How

I feel about her. I thought if I just had a little more time, I could figure out a way to make this right, to keep her here, to keep her with us."

"You fucked up, O'Neil," I whispered and he hung his head.

"I know."

"You should have told us, yeah. But you should have at least given her a warning, she should have been the one to decide what happens." I paused, taking in a deep breath. "Not only did you hurt her, but you also took her options away. She could have transferred schools; she could be on another team by now," I explained, swallowing around the tightness in my throat.

"Then we would have lost her," he whispered and I sighed roughly.

"Callum, that's not how you care for someone, you don't force their hand and make them stay. Who wants to be loved like that?" Sniffing, I wiped at my nose and then looked at Jace.

"We know it was a hard position to be in Cal, but I don't understand how you didn't mention a single thing. Especially once things changed between the four of us. You not only hurt Tatum, you hurt me, you hurt Shawn and honestly man, I don't think I can stay here."

"What?" His brown eyes bounced between the two of us.

"I never once thought you had it in you to lie to my face, now that I know you do, I need space," Jace shrugged.

"So... not only do I lose Kelly, I lose both of you too?"

"We all lost her O'Neil but only you are to blame for that, and I need some time to figure out how I feel about it." I knew the words hit their mark when Callum sucked in a sharp breath, and I felt a wave of pity for him.

"I'm sorry," He whispered and I reached out a hand to cup his shoulder.

"We know."

My neck was stiff from sleeping on a couch all night and I rolled my shoulders while I found my place in my net. Glancing across the ice, my eyes moved from player to player, but she wasn't here, and I slumped tiredly. It had been a week since Tatum had moved out and Jace and I had spent the nights at Summers' place, much to my dismay. It had not been ideal, but it was the best we could come up with on such short notice and now I was not only heartbroken about Kelly but, I was also exhausted and sore.

Spinning red lights began to move rapidly across the arena and the sudden change pulled me from my thoughts as the announcer began his spiel. It was the normal one though this time Mike Huston got a special shout out and I rolled my eyes.

The guy was fast, but he didn't know how to play on a team and the last two practices had been disastrous at best. Both he and Callum had it out for each other, Huston because he had something to prove and there was no better way to do so than undermining the captain. Callum however, had looked worse and worse as the days passed and I knew he was taking out his hurt on the new kid. Glancing at him now, I watched as he got into position for the face off and prayed that we would have our shit together for this.

The period began swiftly with the puck being driven back and forth between ends but neither team had an upper hand and I waited, ready for our opponents to close in on me but anytime they got close, our defenseman were ready. Thinking we were finally getting into the swing of things, I worried less about how we were playing and more on my job. That is until Huston slid into the pack and moved to snatch the puck from O'Neil and my mouth dropped open in surprise.

"What the fuck is he doing?" I whispered to myself as my eyes followed the pair and I could just hear Perry's shout as the newbie moved, only to be checked by another player and then they had control of the puck. Setting their sights on me, they rapidly approached and took their shot, aiming for the upper left corner and I shot a hand out - catching the puck in my glove.

The game continued on the same way, we would finally have a lead and Huston would swoop in and fucking ruin it with his cocky little attitude. By the third period, we still had yet to get a point on the board, and I silently begged Perry to make a change, to see that this wasn't working, and we needed Huston and O'Neil to not be on the ice at the same time. As if he read my mind, he swapped Huston out for the second stringer and in minutes we not only gained the upper hand but Callum had managed to score not one, but two goals and I sighed in relief as the final buzzer rang.

Following in the line, we shook the other team's hands, only pausing for a second when McDonald, their goalie, pulled me in close.

"Man, that Huston guy is a total tool," he whispered and I nodded. "What was Perry thinking swapping that girl out for him?" Not knowing how to answer that I just shrugged.

"That's too bad, you guys really had a shot at the Championship, but I don't think you'll make it if he keeps playing like that." Patting McDonald on the back I offered him a grimace of a smile and then moved to the open door in the boards.

The dressing room was tense, and I was not excited for our trip home, knowing that the bus would either be deadly silent, or we would have to listen to Perry's ass chewing for the next hour. Preparing myself for either, I stripped out of my pads and then padded my way to the shower.

"Hey Patrick," Callum called as I moved toward the tap, and I turned to face him.

"Hey."

In all the years we had been friends, it had never been this awkward and rubbed at the back of my neck awkwardly.

"You played well," he muttered and I wanted to wince at the small talk but instead I shot him a weak smile.

"You too," Callum seemed to shrink two sizes as his shoulders caved in and I noticed the dark circles under his eyes.

"Have you heard from her?" It was the first time he had said anything to me about Tatum, though in his defense, he really hadn't had the chance considering how effectively I had been avoiding him. But I shook my head sadly.

"No man, she hasn't answered any of our calls or texts." Callum's lower lip trembled, and he blinked down at the tiled floor.

"You'll let me know if she does?" I didn't have the heart to disagree, so I dipped my chin in agreement. "But you don't think she will."

"No, I don't think she will." I was too hurt to speak anything but the truth, I didn't have the energy or the mind for any more lies.

"I'm sorry, I didn't want it to end this way, I didn't mean to hurt everyone," he whispered and I swallowed roughly.

"We know that and listen - in time we'll be fine." I didn't know if it was true, or why I felt the need to say the words, but they were out there now, and I couldn't stand to see that wounded look on his face any longer.

"Right. In time." He nodded and I wasn't sure if he believed me, but I hoped that it would ease just a little of his pain.

Chapter Thirty-Five

CALLUM

Tearing off my gloves, I rushed toward Huston ready to knock that fucking smirk right off his face, but Jace moved in, wrapping an arm around my waist before hauling me away. Things had gone from bad to worse between us and I was at my boiling point. Huston constantly overstepped, ignored any and all instructions, and had yet to show me he knew what being on a team meant. I was on my last nerve.

"Relax, O'Neil!" Perry shouted from the bench, and I turned to him with a glare before shoving Rivers off of me.

Bending to pick up my stick and glove, I then tugged my helmet from my head and spat on the ice. Flipping Huston off, I skated towards our coach and threw my stick at him. "I'm fucking out of here."

His jaw went slack, and he spluttered in surprise. "What do you mean you're out of here?"

"I'm done, I'm not wasting my time with that little dick." I jabbed a finger towards my new teammate and then stepped off the ice.

"Get back here, O'Neil!" Perry shouted after me, but I didn't falter and continued to make my way towards the dressing room. "O'Neil!"

Spinning on my heel I turned towards my red-faced coach and crossed my arms with a lifted brow. "I won't play with him Coach, I refuse."

"That's not up to you." He growled and I shrugged.

"Fine, then I quit." His icy blue eyes burned with anger, but I didn't back down. "I would rather give up my position than play with that fucking tool."

"I know it's been an adjustment."

Scoffing, I shook my head.

"It's not an adjustment, it's an embarrassment! Everything we have worked for is heading down the drain because of him and I want no part in it."

"What would you have me do, O'Neil?" He asked, but I could have sworn there was a hint of desperation in his voice.

"Get rid of him and bring Kelly back." Pinching his nose in frustration, Perry inhaled before blinking up at me.

"You cannot be serious."

"I am." I insisted.

"That girl caused nothing but problems for all of us. I realize you probably can't see that considering you were thinking with your dick when she was around-"

"Shut up!" I snapped.

Narrowing his eyes, Perry straightened his spine. "What did you just say to me?"

"I said shut up. I wasn't thinking with my dick and she wasn't a problem. Without her we wouldn't be nearly as good as we are and now that she's gone, we are fucked for the rest of the season." My fists clenched and I took one step forward. "You told me she was jeopardizing my future and like an idiot I believed you. But you were wrong. She wasn't ruining anything for me, she was making it better and I was just too blind to see that."

"C'mon, O'Neil." Perry said with a roll of his eyes.

"You c'mon, Perry. Get her back or I'm done."

"Even if I wanted to, I don't even know where she is." The words stabbed at me painfully, and I blinked in confusion.

"What?"

"You thought I would keep tabs on her or something? As far as I know she was looking into transferring, but I don't have a clue as to where or when."

"But you could find out right?" Worry bubbled in my gut, and I swallowed down the acid that had crept up the back of my throat. Obviously, I knew that there was a chance she could transfer schools, but I had somehow convinced myself that she wouldn't. That she was just laying low on campus, and I would eventually see her; that it was just a matter of time.

"O'Neil," Perry groaned but I just shook my head.

"I'm serious Perry, bring her back or I'm out." Not waiting for his response, I ducked into the dressing room and prayed that I hadn't seen the last of Tatum Kelly.

The house was quiet as I grabbed a beer from the fridge and I thought I had almost managed to escape the sinking feeling that had settled in my bones after practice. However, when I nudged the door closed, the shimmering lights of the tree glimmered at me from the corner, and I swallowed at the sight of them. Christmas had come and gone and though the holiday was over, I couldn't bring myself to take down the tree or fix the living room. It was almost as if it was the last reminder I had of Kelly and what she had meant to us for that short time. Now it was just another souvenir of the biggest mistake I had ever made.

Dropping the can of beer into the sink, I braced my hands on the edge and inhaled roughly, surprised by the sudden wave of sadness that rocked through me, and I blinked past the mist that had clouded my vision.

"Fuck," I sniffed and then ran my knuckles over my eyes shakily. I had been like this for days, just seeming to coast through the hours while a dark cloud clung to me and then I would be wrecked with emotion. The last time I had felt this way had been when my dad passed, and I wondered if my body was just remembering that grief now that I was left alone in the house. Or maybe this loss reopened those wounds I had thought healed long ago.

"What the fuck did you do, O'Neil?" I whispered to myself with a sad shake of my head.

"Talking about yourself in the third person, Cal?" Jace laughed gently and I spun to face him, in surprise before running the sleeve of my shirt under my eyes.

"What are you doing here?" I asked wetly and Shawn's blue eyes widened at the crack in my voice.

"We came to check on you," he answered and I crossed my arms, steeling myself for this conversation.

"Why?" Exhaling roughly Jace patted the blonde on the back and then stepped forward.

"Callum, you know why," He murmured. "We are worried after that blow out at the barn."

Stuffing my hands in the pocket of my hoodie, I shifted from one foot to the other and then hung my head. "Perry thinks she might have transferred schools already."

"Yeah, he said that," Shawn said quietly and then cleared his throat. "He also said you told him you'd quit if he didn't bring her back."

"Yeah, I did."

"Huston is kind of a bust, eh?" Jace laughed dryly.

"He's an idiot, but that's not just it." Running a hand through my curls, I finally lifted my eyes to gaze at my friends. "I don't want to play without her."

I watched as their stares filled with sympathy and then Jace smiled sadly. "We know, we feel the same."

"What do we do? How do I fix this?" I asked desperately.

"I'm not sure we can," Shawn answered honestly and that feeling of dread grew heavier.

"So then now what?" I wondered out loud.

"Well, for starters, we were hoping you might be okay with us moving back in." Blinking at Jace in surprise, I fell silent. "Summers really is an ass and I'm not sure I can deal with his shit anymore. And I don't mean his attitude or stupidity, the kid literally has the nastiest shits."

Snorting, I rubbed at my eyes and then stepped forward before throwing an arm around him. "Yeah man, you can come back. You both can, always."

The doorbell was loud as it echoed through the main floor and the guys turned towards the front of the house in surprise and then moved their attention to me. Shrugging, I stood and wrapped the strand of lights around my hand before putting them in their box and then headed to the door. We hadn't been expecting anyone and I frowned as I wrapped my fingers around the knob, ready to tell whoever it was to go away. But when the cold air hit me as the door opened, I felt my heart sink.

"Tommy?" His name came out of me far louder than I had meant it to, and his brows lifted and then he offered me a weak smile.

"Can I come in?"

Realizing I had just been staring at him, I moved aside and gestured for him to follow me in before closing the door softly shut behind him. The guys must have heard his name because they had shuffled towards the foyer and were watching Tommy with hopeful eyes as he peeled his coat off and then pulled off his shoes.

"How are you guys?" He asked and then winced as he scanned our faces. "Yeah, sorry stupid question I guess."

"Is everything okay?" Shawn asked worriedly, his eyes bouncing between the three of us and then his fingers began to run down his forearm.

"Why don't we sit down?" He said, motioning to the table. I led the way and then slid into the chair directly across from him. "I think it's time I get some honest answers."

Guilt slammed into me and I clenched my jaw, waiting for the look of disappointment to come my way. But it never did, Tommy's eyes were nothing but kind, and I lowered my attention to the wood of the table.

"Is she okay?" I asked with a weak voice.

Humming under his breath, Tommy rubbed at his jaw. "It depends on what your definition of 'okay' is, I guess. But physically, yes - she's fine."

"So - what answers do you need from us?" Jace wondered.

"I'm not here looking to place blame; I've already formed my opinion on that." His pointed look was less warm this time and I squirmed under the attention. "But I do want to know five things and I want you to be truthful with your answers."

"Okay," Shawn agreed immediately.

"Did you know that she was going to be replaced?" Jace and Shawn turned towards me, and I inhaled sharply before nodding. "Okay, did you lie to her about it?"

"I didn't lie to her," I argued and Tommy's eyes narrowed into a hard glare.

"Withholding the truth is a lie, Callum. Not telling her is just as bad." He was right of course, and I begrudgingly nodded again.

"Have you done everything in your power to change your coach's mind?" Again, my friends remained silent but I released a harsh breath.

"Yes," I whispered weakly.

"Is his offer to bring her back on the team genuine then? Is he really willing to let her stay at North Pacific and play?"

"What?" Shawn gasped and Tommy nodded.

"Your coach called her today and offered her old spot back. Apparently, the new player is not working out, but I had a feeling there was more to it."

"I threatened to leave the team if he didn't bring her back." Tommy nodded and then curled a fist under his chin.

"I wondered if it was something along those lines given how desperate he was on the phone." The warmth was back in his gaze, and I finally felt that tightness loosen in my chest. "I'm doing what I can to assure her it's a real offer and convince her to take it. Arden isn't nearly good enough for her and her other option is in Ontario, and we don't want her to leave."

"Do you think she'll listen?" There was a nervousness in Shawn's voice and Tommy shook his head.

"I'm not sure, but I think I might have a better chance of convincing her now that I know your coach was serious." Standing from his chair, he rounded the table and then walked toward the closet in the front of the house. Opening the doors, he pulled out his jacket and began rifling through its pockets before producing a white envelope. Slipping his fingers into the opening, he slid a small piece of paper out and then placed it on the table.

Glancing down at it, my breath caught in my throat, and I examined the familiar faces closely. The dim lighting of City Hall made the background look dingy and outdated and the red, faded carpet under our feet was not ideal. However, Tatum made all those little details irrelevant because she was stunning. Pure unaltered happiness glowed across her features, and I noticed how all three of us were completely captivated by her. Jace was on one side, his arm wrapped around her, and Shawn on the other -both gazing longingly at her. I however was just off centered and though I couldn't see my face, I knew this was just a split second before I leaned forward to kiss her cheek.

"Where did you get this?" Jace murmured.

"That Kevin kid took it just before we interrupted you, he sent it with the rest of the photos, and I just thought maybe you'd like a copy of it."

"Thank you," I choked out and Tommy patted my shoulder gently.

"Okay, I think I better head home, the drive is pretty long, and I don't want Chris to worry." Throwing his coat on, he nodded at us and turned for the door when Jace called out for him.

"Wait! You said you wanted to know five things, you only asked us four."

"I didn't need to ask the last one, I had my answer the second I saw your expressions when you looked at that photo."

Glancing at the table once more I inspected the portrait of the four of us again and whispered. "Ask us anyway."

"Do you love her?" None of us had ever voiced the words, but at that moment, I knew how we all felt. I could see the physical proof of it at just an arm's reach away.

"That's what I thought." Tommy nodded with a warm grin and then he walked to the door. Following behind him, we waited as he put on his shoes and then he reached for the brass knob only to pause to look at us once more. "Just so you know, I hope you get the chance to tell her."

Chapter Thirty-Six

TATUM

I told myself I would never come back into this office again, and yet here I was. Lifting my chin, I peered down at Perry's face and his fingers fidgeted on the desk. Pleased to see a crack in his usually hard façade, I smirked.

"Why don't you sit down," he asked, his tone far kinder than I had ever heard it before and I lifted a brow.

"I'll stand thanks." I wasn't sure where this sudden bravery came from. Maybe it was because I had nothing to lose now or maybe it was the fact that my heart had been so crushed, I no longer had any expectations for anyone, at least that way they couldn't let me down. But whatever the reason, I was glad for it. Especially when I noticed Perry shifting uncomfortably in his seat.

"I know things didn't end well between us."

Scoffing, I rolled my eyes. "I think that's an understatement."

Ignoring me, Perry sighed and then braced his elbows on his desk. "But I am hoping that we can move past it, and you will be willing to give me a second chance."

"What happened?" I snapped. "Did Huston not work out for you?"

"I think we both know the answer to that Kelly, I know you were at our last game."

Flushing, I cleared my throat and then tucked a strand of hair behind my ear. He was right, I had gone to the game with Kate and Chris, but I refused to acknowledge it as anything other than morbid curiosity and so I just shrugged nonchalantly.

"Then you know why I've been trying to get into contact with you." He rubbed at his face in frustration. "That and the fact that O'Neil refuses to step back onto that ice without you."

"*What*?" I felt like the air had been knocked out of me and pressed against the door I had been leaning against.

Perry's icy blue eyes studied me carefully. "He didn't tell you?"

He hadn't, but I wouldn't have a way to know because I had blocked their numbers. I had cut all contact with the three of them after moving out and had thought that they were out of my life for good, no matter how much the idea may have hurt.

In fact, I finally gave up on the idea of playing the rest of the season and had begun the process of transferring schools for next semester when Chris had come home and begged me to listen to Perry's dozen voicemails. Something had changed in my brother-in-law, though he refused to tell me what. After his persistent nagging, I called Perry back.

But to know O'Neil had told Perry he refused to skate, that was not something I was prepared for.

"No, I didn't know." I finally answered and Perry's brows lifted to his hairline.

"Well, now you do." Tilting his head, he examined me closely. "Does that sway your decision at all?"

Clenching my jaw, I exhaled roughly. "Callum O'Neil will have no part in the decision I make. No one from your team will."

"Okay, fair enough." He lifted his hands in surrender. "But what can I do to get you on board?"

Never in my life had I thought Jackson Perry would be willing to negotiate my return to his team and part of me was oddly satisfied with the turn of events. However, knowing that this would be the most ideal solution to my problem, I thought long and hard about what I wanted.

"I won't be a scapegoat for the team's fuck ups anymore." Nodding, he waved for me to continue. "I want to see as much ice time as possible, which I'm assuming won't be an issue."

"It won't," Perry assured me.

"And I want a place on your team next year." Rubbing at his eyes, Perry sighed tiredly.

"Steven's will be healed by then Kelly." Crossing my arms, I nodded.

"Maybe, he might be," I agreed. "Or he might not. Who knows if he'll be at the same skill level he was. So, I would ask that you give me the opportunity to go up against him. If he's better than I am, I'll agree to be second string."

"Deal." He stood with a hand out and I looked at the rough flesh of his palm before sliding my own into his grasp. "Welcome back, Kelly."

My stomach twisted and I rolled my shoulders, hoping it would alleviate some of the tension but the longer I avoided the ice, the worse it got, and I shoved my helmet on before stepping out of the women's locker room. Luckily the rest of the team would be on the ice by now and I tucked my stick under my arm while sliding my hands into my gloves and then I strode down the empty hallway.

"You can do this," I whispered to myself as the ice came into view. The guys were in their designated places on the ice, taking their time to stretch and I opened the door and then ducked my head as my blade touched the ice. Keeping my eyes on the laces of my skates, I had no way of knowing if anyone had noticed my entrance but the change in atmosphere as I moved to the far corner told me they had.

Sliding to the cold surface, I began to go through the motions, all while trying to keep my breath even and avoid lifting my eyes. I hadn't seen the guys since the day I had walked out of their house with my things in hand and now I wondered if that had been the right decision. Not because I wanted to face them but because I wasn't sure I could focus when anticipating the inevitable.

"Hey." Wincing, I cursed under my breath and then blinked up at Summers.

"Hey." Lowering himself next to me, he glanced towards the rest of the team and then grinned.

"So, you're back."

Rolling my legs, I swapped legs. "It appears that way."

"Does that mean I have a shot now?" Freezing halfway through my stretch, I glanced at him from the corner of my eye.

"What?"

"Oh c'mon Kelly, you know what I mean." His grin only grew, and I glared.

"I can promise you, I don't."

Laughing under his breath, he lifted a hand and waved at the guys in a teasing manner. "Well, I just figured now that you're done your rounds with O'Neil and his lackeys -"

Unwilling to listen to anymore, I stood and then grabbed at my stick before glowering down at him. "Summers, you literally make my skin crawl and there is nothing in the world that could make me want to even imagine doing anything with you."

His smirk slid from his face and then his eyes hardened. “God you’re a bitch, Kelly.”

Stiffening, I opened my mouth, ready to call him out but Perry’s whistle blew and I glanced at the bench before glancing down at Summers once more. “You remember that when I out skate you today.”

The team huddled around the boards, and I slowed my speed as I approached. Feeling those three sets of eyes on me, I remained in the back of the group as Perry went over the plans for practice and as he droned on, I shifted uncomfortably before turning my head and lifting my gaze.

Immediately my eyes met those deep blue irises and I gasped at the overwhelming sadness that filled them. I had been prepared for anger, maybe disappointment but not that, never that. I reeled back at the hurt I felt at seeing such an expression.

Swallowing roughly, I pulled my attention from Shawn and then moved to the handsome face beside his. Jace was as stunning as always, his dark flawless skin and deep eyes were the same as I remembered, but they also seemed almost lifeless, and I frowned.

“And of course, we can welcome back Kelly.” My name startled me, and I looked at Perry before ducking my head as the team turned to face me. “I know it’s been a rough few weeks with the changes on the team but I’m hoping we can get back into the swing of things and pick up where we left off before the holidays.”

No one said anything and I shifted from foot to foot anxiously. “Now that the cats out of the bag - let’s get to it. I want to see everyone putting in maximum effort today, no excuses, no distractions.”

Thinking he was talking to me, I turned to glare at our coach, but his eyes were stuck on the three men on the other side of the group, and I prayed this practice went off without a hitch.

My hair was soaked with sweat by the time the clock buzzed and I panted as I leaned against the boards before pulling my helmet off. My body was humming with adrenaline, and I sighed happily as the team began to shuffle out of the rink. The drills were killer, harder than I remembered them being even though it had only been a few weeks and my side ached a bit and yet, I was thrilled.

The ice was the place I felt most like myself and I was overjoyed to be back on it, even if it meant dealing with the awkwardness and hurt of seeing the guys.

Passing the boards, I strode across the rubber floor and caught my breath, but just as I turned the corner I ran directly into a mass of muscle and pads. Staggering back at the sudden feeling of déjà vu, I blinked up at the other person.

"Kelly," Callum's voice was full of surprise as he looked down at me and I steadied myself on my feet before taking a step back. "Hey."

The air was tense and I looked everywhere but at the warm brown eyes I had been so fond of. "Hey."

"You uh, skated well today."

My smile was weak, and I dipped my head. "Thanks, you too."

"How have you been?"

Snorting, I raised my chin and finally met his gaze. "Just swell, O'Neil. Everything has just been absolutely perfect." I snarled sarcastically.

Running a hand through his curls, a blush crept across his face, and he sighed roughly, and I watched as his body almost seemed to deflate. "Yeah, I guess I deserved that."

Scoffing, I crossed my arms. "Yeah, I would say so."

"I know it probably won't matter, but I do want you to know how sorry I am. I'm sorry for all of it but mostly for hurting you." His voice broke and he ran a hand across his face roughly. "I can't say I didn't mean to, that would be a lie. I might not have set out to cause you pain, but I knew the way I was treating you and then the whole thing with Huston would hurt, and I didn't stop it from happening."

"Why didn't you tell me? I thought things had changed between us, I thought you guys cared about me."

His eyes widened and he took a step forward with a hand stretched out towards me before he seemed to think better of it and then his arm lowered back to his side. "We do," he promised. "I do."

"Funny way of showing it." I argued.

"I know. I know. I fucked up." He swallowed roughly. "But that's on me, only me. Shawn and Jace knew nothing about Huston, I didn't tell them."

"Right," I muttered in disbelief.

“I didn’t Kelly,” he swore. “They had no idea and I can promise they are just as pissed as you are.”

Shaking my head, I sighed in exhaustion and then glanced down the corridor. “It doesn’t matter O’Neil; it doesn’t matter anymore. I just want to skate; I want to play the rest of the season and do the best I can. That’s what’s important to me now. So ... let’s just forget about all of this and worry about the game on Thursday.”

“But Kelly,” he tried again, and I lifted a hand, stopping him from continuing.

“It’s done now O’Neil, let it go. I have.”

Chapter Thirty-Seven

SHAWN

Having Kelly so close and yet knowing she was no longer wanting anything to do with us was a special kind of torture. I was dying to see her, to hold her, to just witness her smile, to hear that husky laugh of hers and yet I couldn't bring myself to push it. The last thing I wanted was to hurt her further, so I forced myself to keep my distance, telling myself that it was better this way even though it crushed me.

Sighing, I leaned back into my seat and watched as the snow-covered buildings passed by. Today was an away-game and we had somehow managed to convince Perry to let us drive ourselves since it was only a town over and I was glad not to be stuck on that stupid bus with all those knowing looks and that blank expression Tatum had seemingly mastered over the time she had been gone.

"You good, Patrick?" Jace asked from the passenger seat, as if he knew where my mind had gone and I hummed not knowing what else to say and I knew he was feeling the same way. I could see it every time I caught him watching her at practice or when he searched for her around campus. Callum had been the only one to talk to her though it hadn't gone well and that night when got home, he pulled that picture of us from its hiding place and stared at it for ages before tucking it back away and slamming the drawer closed.

"How do you think today will go? Think we'll manage a win?" Jace asked and I watched as Callum sighed roughly.

"I mean I think we have a really good ch -" Lurching forward, I braced myself against the back of Jace's seat as the truck slammed to a stop.

"What the fuck, O'Neil!" I growled before punching him in the shoulder, but he paid me no attention, his eyes were too focused on the windshield.

"Why is she walking in this shit?" He muttered under his breath, and I moved to the left, squinting in hopes I'd be able to make out what he was looking at through the snow.

"What, what is it?" I asked, confused as to what would make Callum stop so suddenly.

"It's Kelly." He whispered and then pulled over to park along the curb.

"There's no way she's going to make it to the arena in time for the bus. Why isn't she there already?" Jace wondered and my eyes roamed the street until they found her. Her bag was slung over her shoulder and her massive puffy jacket was covered in snow. She looked absolutely miserable and I unbuckled my seat belt.

"Stay here," I ordered the guys.

"Patrick, don't." Callum warned but I had already pressed the door open and then shot him a smile over my shoulder.

"I am way more charming than your ugly ass O'Neil and besides it couldn't possibly go worse than your last attempt." Sliding from the warmth of the truck, I stepped into the grey slush and slammed the door behind me before jogging across the road.

Kelly had tugged her hood over her hair and was curling in on herself as she walked against the wind and snow and I felt a pang of worry when I noticed her worn out converse and bare hands. Hurrying my pace, I closed the distance and then called out for her.

"Kelly! Wait up." Her spine straightened at the sound of my voice, and she turned, lifting her hood from her eyes.

"Shawn?" Her eyes widened and I offered her my best smile before closing the distance. "What are you doing here?

"We're heading to the game," I laughed softly as I pointed out the obvious. "What are you doing?"

"Heading to the arena to catch the bus and honestly I'm already late, so if you'll excuse me." She went to move past me, but I caught her arm and halted her in the process.

"Kelly, there's no way you're going to make it in time. Not on foot and not in this weather." Pulling my phone from my pocket I checked the time with a frown. "In fact, I bet it's just about to leave."

"Shit," she hissed under her breath. "Perry is going to lose it."

"Come with us." I suggested eagerly but she chewed on her lower lip. "Kelly, please it's just a ride, nothing more."

"Fine, but it's just a ride." She confirmed and I nodded my head before reaching for her bag. Slipping my fingers under the strap I pulled it off her arm.

"Patrick," she warned but I ignored her and lifted the bag over my own shoulder.

"You'll be lucky not to slip as it is in those shoes, you don't need the extra weight throwing you off." I grinned, praying she would buy it. Rolling her eyes, she brushed past me, but I counted it as a win and followed behind.

I could see Rivers and O'Neil look at each other and I gave them a shrug, hopeful my giddiness wasn't too obvious as Kelly moved to the back door. Throwing it open, she stepped back with a frown, and I rubbed the back of my neck.

"Right sorry, I forgot to tell you it will be a little tight. The snow is too wet to put the bags in the bed, they'll get soaked." Sighing, she moved aside, and I tossed her bag with ours before gesturing for her to slide in.

"Nope. No way - you get the little seat." She argued and I raised a brow. "Patrick, I'm taller than you."

"I weigh more than you." I pointed out and she crossed her arms.

"I have a bigger ass." Biting at my lip, I forced myself not to reply and she growled under her breath before hauling herself into the seat.

"Were you two talking about asses?" Jace asked, and I winked at him before pressing in next to Tatum but didn't say anything and his dark eyes scanned across Tatum's form.

"Hey," he greeted her softly and her shoulders fell slightly.

"Hey Jace." Her grey eyes slid from him to the driver, and she cleared her throat. "Callum."

His brown eyes caught hers in the rear-view mirror and he dipped his chin at her, but he remained silent, which was probably for the best. Buckling myself in, I did my best to create as much space as possible in hopes I wouldn't make this more awkward for her and she gave me a half smile in return.

"Thanks for the ride." Her voice was steady but I noticed the flush that had pinkened her face and O'Neil looked at her once more and then glanced at me with a hopeful look.

"No thanks needed Kelly, anytime."

The atmosphere in the dressing room was full of excitement and smiles and I pulled my shirt over my head before collecting the rest of my things while my body buzzed from today's victory. We had absolutely annihilated our opponents which meant we had made it to the quarter finals, and everyone was ecstatic, including our coach. In fact, we didn't even receive one of his exhausting speeches. It was all "atta boys" and pats on the back and I had even noticed a smile or two tossed Tatum's way.

"I'm going to wait for you guys in the hall." I tossed over my shoulder and Jace rolled his eyes.

"You mean you're going to wait in the hall in hopes you'll see Kelly." There was no point in denying it, so I just shrugged and then grabbed my bag before entering the hallway.

The rest of the team was filtering out, most heading towards the bus though some lingered to chat to friends and families, and I searched the halls for the familiar face, but she was nowhere to be seen. Wandering down the hall, I scanned across the bodies but still no luck and I frowned, wondering where she had gone to.

"She's already on the bus, Patrick," Perry called out and I turned, blushing at the knowing look in his eyes. "She was the first one on."

Glancing at the bus in front of the glass doors, I sighed, wondering if I should even try, if it was worth a shot. But then again if I didn't, would I regret it later? Would I always wonder if that missed opportunity could have changed things?

Deciding I had to try, I moved through the automatic doors, dropped my bag at the side and jogged up the stairs of the bus before making my way down the narrow aisle. Setting my sights on her pale face and then slid into the empty chair next to hers, I held my breath as her eyes blinked up at me.

"Shouldn't you be with the guys?"

Lifting a shoulder, I smiled nervously. "I figured if there's a time to join the team on the bus it's after winning the quarter finals."

Her face relaxed and I watched as that hardness in her eyes softened just a touch. "Yeah, today was pretty awesome, eh?"

"Absolutely, and we wouldn't be here without you." Even though I meant every word, I knew it was too much. She would think I was laying it on too thick, like I was just trying to get in her good books again.

"Right, whatever you say Shawn." Her body had moved closer to the window, and I felt like such an idiot.

“I’m serious, Tatum.” I promised.

“Shawn,” she sighed but I shook my head gently.

“We’re a mess without you, it’s like we fall apart without you holding us together.” Somehow, I knew she understood that I wasn’t just talking about the team, but she remained silent, though that blush deepened.

“Alright Patrick, enough of your praises,” she whispered shyly. “At this rate my head will explode from you feeding my ego.”

Nudging my shoulder against hers, I grinned stupidly and then the words escaped me before I could stop them. “I missed you, Kelly.”

The words hung between us, and the silence grew to an uncomfortable point. But when I opened my mouth, ready to take them back Tatum inhaled softly and then her grey eyes met mine.

“I missed you too.” The words came out of her slowly, almost like she wasn’t sure if she should say them, and it took everything in me not to react.

My heart may have been pounding but there was no way I was going to show it and instead I relaxed into my chair. Watching me closely Kelly did the same and then wet her lips nervously.

“Did you really not know about Huston?” That was not what I had been expecting and I took a second to process her question before I shook my head.

“No, I didn’t. Do you really think I would have kept it from you if I had?” Her fingers fidgeted in her lap and then she focused her on the window.

“Callum did.”

“Callum is an idiot,” I snapped and then pinched the bridge of my nose for a second. “Listen, he messed up Kelly, he made the wrong choice, and he knows it now.”

I felt her stiffen and then she looked at me from the corner of her eye. “He had sex with us knowing Perry was planning on replacing me.”

I didn’t have an excuse or argument for that, and I hung my head. “I know.”

“But Tommy says he tried to fix it.”

“He did.” I confirmed.

“And Perry said he threatened to quit the team if he didn’t bring me back.”

Humming under my breath, I nodded. “He did that too.”

Her face finally turned to me, and I noticed the way her lower lip trembled just slightly. "Why?"

Not willing to divulge too many details, I lowered my face closer to hers and held her eyes with my own, praying she would see the truth there. "You know why."

Chapter Thirty-Eight

CALLUM

Lining up my shot, I flicked my wrist and watched as the puck soared past the goalie's shoulder and then tangled into the back of the net and I could have sworn my heart stopped. This was it, this was the tie breaker, I realized as I soared around the goal posts pumping my fist before a body collided with mine.

Wrapping my arms around her waist, I tugged her to me while laughing into her shoulder and when our eyes met, it was like everything else disappeared. Tightening my hold, I swallowed down the sudden wave of emotion, but I didn't know what to say and when Tatum's eyes turned downcast, I readied myself to let go of her. However, before she could distance herself, Jace sped towards us, curling one arm around my back, crushing Kelly back against me while he lifted the other hand to pat my helmet.

"Holy shit man! We did it!" He cheered and Tatum's deep laugh echoed in my ear, the sound making my heart sing.

However, I wouldn't have long to bask in her presence because within seconds the rest of the team was on us, and I grinned broadly as we celebrated for another minute before settling when Perry began to shout at us to knock it off. As always, he expected us to be calm, cool and collected on the ice, but I could see his happiness from here and I formed the line to shake our opponents' hands before exiting the ice.

Filtering through the narrow door of the dressing room, we gathered around our coach, taking a seat while he waited, and I scanned the group searching for my friends. Jace was huddled just a few feet away, his bright smile nearly blinding under the fluorescent lights, and I returned his grin before moving my attention, searching for Shawn and Kelly. Realizing they weren't close, I stood, lifting my chin to check the back and my chest tightened when I finally scouted the blonde.

Patrick was farthest away, the colour of his damp hair not nearly as shocking when it was slightly darker, and I watched as he ran a hand through it while laughing softly at something Kelly said. Her own face was flushed, though whether it was from the game or from something he said, I wasn't sure; there was an openness to her face I hadn't seen in ages and a pang of envy rocked through me at the sight. I had noticed that the tension had eased between the two of them since our last game, though I only saw glimpses of their interactions during practice. As far as I knew that was the only time they saw each other, and yet I was so fucking jealous.

Of course, I was thrilled for Patrick, I knew how badly he was missing her and seeing that light come back into his blue eyes was great. But I wanted to feel that warmth that only Kelly could bring too.

Noticing where my attention had been focused, Jace turned his head and rose for a second before slumping to face Perry once more. "They have a study date tomorrow."

"A date?" The words choked out of me and Jace shrugged.

"I think it's really just studying, but he is pumped man. He picked out his clothes for it days ago." Swallowing roughly, I grimaced.

"Of course, he is. I bet he hasn't slept either. You know how he gets when he's excited about something, like a kid on Christmas." Jace chuckled dryly and nodded. "But do you think he'll put in a good word for us?"

His dark eyes lifted to mine, and he examined my face closely. "You still want that?"

My mouth parted as I stared at him in shock and then I lowered my eyes to the floor before whispering. "More than anything."

"Me too," he muttered, and I wrapped an arm around his shoulders.

"Alright quiet down guys." Perry clapped his hands as he gathered our attention and I turned to glance at the pair once more before the speech started.

Seeming to feel my gaze, Tatum's grey eyes lifted, and she smiled softly at me before offering a little wave. Grinning back, I copied the motion while my heart pounded in my chest. I knew it wasn't anything to get excited about and yet I couldn't wipe that stupid grin off my face if I tried.

The bar was packed, and I leaned against the counter while I waited for my beer and took in the crowd. The team had decided to go out after our win, all of us were too high on adrenaline from the game to go home and grabbed at the beer the bartender slid my way before taking a long sip.

"Hey," a voice sounded from my left, and I turned, the bottle still pressed to my lips as I gazed at Tatum in surprise.

"Hey," I spluttered awkwardly and then wiped my mouth with the back of my hand before trying again. "Hey."

"Congratulations on the win today, O'Neil." She smiled softly and my breath caught at the sight of it.

"It's our win Tatum," I reminded her with a low voice.

Flushing, she tucked a strand of hair behind her ears and chewed on her lower lip, almost like she was nervous, and I took an uncertain step forward. "Can I buy you a drink?"

Her grey eyes glanced at the bar for a second before she shook her head. "No, I think I'd rather have this talk sober if that's okay."

"Talk?" I repeated worriedly.

"Yeah, I think we need to clear the air, mind stepping outside with me?" Not willing to let this chance pass, I handed my beer to one of the guys, grabbed my coat and then followed Tatum as she led us to the stairs.

Stepping into the cold January air, I tugged the wool of my jacket closed and Tatum turned around the corner of the building, standing just under the glow of the streetlight and I watched as the golden hue bounced off her shining hair, illuminating her in the most incredible way before stepping up beside her.

"As I'm sure you know, I've spoken to Tommy, Perry and Shawn, but I can't help but feel like I am missing something, so I wanted to hear it from you. Again," she spoke quietly, but I could hear the nervousness in her voice, and I moved in closer.

"What do you want to know?" Letting her lead the conversation could be a mistake, it could leave me open to questions I really didn't want to answer but I knew that if I wanted her forgiveness, I had to be honest about everything.

"Why didn't you tell me about Huston?"

"Kelly, I've tried to explain this to you, but you didn't want to hear it."

Her grey eyes narrowed, and she tilted her chin. "Tell me now, try again."

Running my hand through my curls, I glanced at the snow beneath our feet and then inhaled sharply. "At first it was because I let Perry convince me that it would jeopardize the team and the season. I let him persuade me into thinking that if I told you, you would leave, and we would be stuck without a replacement. We both know the second stringers aren't ready, and I didn't want to lose the future I had been working so hard for."

"And then why?" She tilted her head and I blinked at her in confusion. "You said first."

"Then things changed for us, and I worried that if I told you, warned you, you would leave anyway. But that scared me for a different reason." I swallowed. "I still didn't want to risk my future, but it was my future with you I was afraid of losing."

"Callum," she gasped, her grey eyes wide.

"I am sorry. I am so fucking sorry for hurting you. I'm sorry for my words, my actions, my lies. All of it. I am more sorry than you will ever know." My eyes burned and I sniffed before stuffing my hands into the pockets of my coat.

"Why did you tell Perry you wouldn't play without me?" She demanded and I lifted my head, not caring that tears had begun to form in my eyes

"Because I didn't see the point," I whispered honestly. "I didn't want to play if you weren't there with me, with us."

"You should have told me, especially before you decided to sleep with me." Her tone was angrier than it had been, and I flinched at the sound.

"I know."

"That wasn't an okay thing to do O'Neil, it made me feel used and humiliated."

"God, Kelly," I sniffed again before wiping at my face. "I never ever want you to feel that way. I am so sorry."

"I don't know if I'll ever be able to trust you," she whimpered while hugging her middle tightly and my heart cracked at the sound.

"I know."

"I wish you had just told me, I wish you were honest because this hurts," she lifted a hand to motion between us. "Seeing you and the guys and knowing that it wasn't anything more than a good fuck for you, hurts more than anything else."

"Don't say that," I snapped. "It wasn't just sex Kelly, you have to know that."

"How am I supposed to know anything when you weren't honest. If you really cared for me, you wouldn't have lied for so long. I asked you time and time again to tell me what was wrong, but you didn't."

"I was scared!" Tatum stepped away from me and I rolled my shoulders, forcing myself to try and calm down. "I was scared to ruin it, Tatum."

"But you ruined it anyway," she whispered brokenly.

"I know."

Nodding she lifted her arm to rub at her nose and I noticed the moisture that clung to her long lashes. Taking one step forward, I lifted a hand cautiously and when she didn't back away, I curled it around her back and pressed the palm between her shoulder blades. Giving into the pressure, she fell forward and then rested her face against my chest. Nestling her closer, I lowered my cheek to rest on her head. "I'm sorry."

Nodding against my shoulder, Tatum slumped into me. "I know you are."

We stood like that for a long moment, neither of us speaking as the snow fell around us and I tried to force myself to memorize the feel of her in my arms, not knowing if I would ever feel it again.

"I should get inside - I'm sure Kate is looking for me," she whispered and then slowly pulled from my arms, and I reluctantly took a step back, giving her more space.

"Right, of course. I'll see you at practice?" I asked weakly and her eyes caught mine.

"Of course, someone needs to put you in your place," she laughed wetly and I rolled my eyes. "Have a good night. O'Neil."

Exhaling, I gave her a timid smile. "You too, Kelly."

Chapter Thirty-Nine

TATUM

The crowd was massive, and I scanned the stands, searching for my brothers and Kate while the announcer introduced us one by one. Nerves ate away at me while I searched for their familiar faces and just as I was about to run my eyes through the same section of seats for the third time, a hand gripped mine.

"You okay, Kelly?" Jace asked, his own gaze lifting to where I had been searching.

"Nervous," I answered honestly, and he gave my gloved hand a gentle squeeze.

"Me too." Not believing him for a second, I pulled my hand from his and nudged him in the ribs. "Yeah, whatever, Rivers."

Lifting a glove to his chest, he gasped dramatically as if I had shocked him. "What do you mean whatever?!"

"We both know you are as calm and cool as they come," I muttered, flushing when he flashed me those dimples.

"That's not true, I get nervous sometimes," he argued and I lifted a brow.

"Oh yeah? When?" Those dark eyes focused on me for a pause and then he leaned down, his helmet nearly touching mine.

"Around you. You, Tatum Kelly, make me all kinds of nervous." Thrown off by his answer, I was unable to think of a witty retort and then his name was being announced and he turned to the ice before gliding across it while waving to the crowd.

"You'll be next, Kelly!" Perry shouted from at the other end of the bench, and I gave him a subtle nod before taking in a deep breath and then when my name was echoed through the speakers, I stepped onto the ice as the audience cheered.

Even after almost an entire season, I still wasn't used to the amount of fans the men's team had and I waved awkwardly at the people in the stands before glancing at O'Neil and then Rivers and then slid into my place in line. Shuffling on my feet awkwardly, I readied myself for the last player to be announced, knowing that once we were all accounted for, the singing of the national anthem would happen and then the game would start and we would be one step closer to the championship.

Taking in a deep breath, I waited for the final name to be called, and Shawn moved across the ice with ease, his massive pads not hindering his movement one bit and I smiled at him as his eyes caught mine. Sliding to his spot next to me, I glanced down the line and realized I was flocked by O'Neil, Rivers and Patrick and there was something about that little detail that made my heart pound. It was almost as if I was meant to be here, right in the middle of them and I smiled to myself as the lights dimmed.

"We played our hearts out," Callum assured us as he commanded the room with his presence and I watched as those brown eyes roamed across our faces. "We played incredibly but sometimes it doesn't always mean a win and it is what it is. We knew today was going to be tough, we knew that it was going to be one of the hardest games we have ever played, and we should be proud of ourselves for what we accomplished today."

The words were honest and kind, but they did little to ease the disappointment I felt. We had held our own the entire game, keeping up with the other team at every turn, every moment until we hit overtime. It was then that they gained their winning goal and we had lost the chance to compete at the championship finals.

"O'Neil is right," Perry agreed from beside our captain, and I moved my eyes to his face, watching as he scanned the team. "That was one of the best games I've seen played in a long time and I couldn't be prouder to be this team's Coach. You gave your all on that ice tonight and though we didn't make it to finals, you still have every reason to be proud of what you did here. Now get changed and go enjoy your night, celebrate the end of a great season."

Turning for the door, he left the room and I slowly rose, weaving my way through the team before making my own exit. Tucking my helmet and stick under my arm I strode towards the women's locker room, forcing myself to focus on the idea of a warm shower and not worrying about what we could have done differently.

Sighing, I had just rounded the corner when I noticed Perry waiting outside the door and his light blue eyes rose as I approached.

"Hi, Coach." Nodding he straightened, and then stuffed his hands into the pockets of his dress pants, almost as if he was nervous.

"Kelly," he muttered. "I wanted to just talk to you for a minute." Frowning I hesitated, knowing that talks with Perry had never gone over well for me in the past and he seemed to notice my apprehension. "It's nothing bad Kelly, I just, well I supposed I just wanted to say I was sorry for the way I treated you at the beginning of the season and for the Huston shit."

Surprised that he was actually acknowledging any of his wrongdoing, I blinked up at him in disbelief. Perry had bargained for me to get back on the team, agreed to my terms but never, not once had he ever actually apologized, and I wasn't sure how to respond.

"I know that you probably don't believe that I'm being sincere, and I can't say that I blame you, but I just wanted to at least tell you that I was sorry, that I regret behaving that way."

"Are you just saying that just because we did well this season?" I couldn't help but wonder and Perry's brows lifted, like he wasn't sure how to answer.

"No Kelly, of course not." It was a lie but at least he tried, and I nodded my head.

"Well, thank you for the apology." Stepping away from the wall, Perry allowed me to move past and I ducked into the room, happy to be done with that uncomfortable conversation though I doubted it would be the last.

Stripping from my jersey and pads, I turned on the tap and stepped into the shower. The warm water was an instant relief, and I braced my hands against the tile walls as the stream beat against the sore muscles of my back. Normally, I would take this time to relax, forcing myself to forget about all the 'would haves', 'could haves', and 'should haves'. I would force myself to move on from the mistakes of the game but now there was something else that haunted me. Losing the semi-finals meant that our season was done and though that sucked, the idea of not being on the team, not having practices, not seeing *them* is what made my mind race.

I had spent the last little while convincing myself that all I had to do was get through this season and then I could move on. I would forget the feelings and the memories and only see those three as teammates. But this was O'Neil's last season and who knew what would happen next year for Rivers and Patrick. By then, their warm smiles and attempts at small talk might change to quick greetings and nothing more and the very idea chipped away at my heart.

I had tried to tell myself it shouldn't matter if they gave up, that I wanted them to, and yet in this quiet room, all by myself, I could finally admit that wasn't what I desired. And if I was being completely honest, I knew what I wanted, what I needed, was them.

Turning the water off, I wrapped a towel around my body and quickly dried my hair before grabbing my clothes from my bag. Throwing them on, I glanced at the mirror for a second, making sure I didn't look like a complete disaster and then I rushed from the room, hoping I hadn't missed them.

The halls were quiet, and I scanned the brightly lit corridor quickly, but when they were nowhere to be seen, I pulled my phone from my pocket. Tapping in the passcode, I opened my messages and texted both Kate and Chris that I wouldn't be going out for dinner with them, that I had something else I needed to do and then I tucked the phone back into my pocket before jogging to the doors.

Seeing that the big black trucks were still in the lot, I passed through the doors and made my way across the snowy parking lot until I reached them. My heart was pounding, and I shivered in the cold but I was determined to see this through, I was ready to finally be honest and it was my turn to be honest with them.

"Kelly?" Shawn called as the three of them approached. "What are you doing out here?"

Taking in a deep breath, I fidgeted with my coat and then I lifted my eyes, moving them across the trio. "I thought maybe I could come home."

All three of them froze, staring at me like I had three heads and I blushed hotly.

"Home?" Jace asked, his voice filled with hopefulness, and I grinned with a nod.

"Yeah, I want to go home," I repeated. "To *our* home."

The house was warm and bright, exactly as I remembered it and I sighed as we stepped through the door. Following me in, the three guys crowded in behind me and then Callum was peeling my coat from my shoulders while Jace grabbed my bag from my arm. Once free, I stepped out of my shoes and then took Shawn's offered hand, allowing him to pull me farther into the house.

"It's so good to have you back," he whispered and then he froze. "You are back, right? Like really back?"

Lifting a hand to cup his cheek, I stroked a thumb across the sharp edge of his jaw and nodded. "I'm back."

"Thank fuck," Jace sighed, and I glanced over my shoulder at him, and he shrugged. "We missed you."

"I missed you guys too," I responded after a pause but when I noticed that Callum was hovering in the back, almost like he wasn't sure if he belonged, I cleared my throat and waited for those brown eyes to meet mine. "I missed all of you."

His face brightened and I felt my heart stutter at the expression and then I was glancing around the kitchen nervously. Nothing looked different but being here again in this way just made everything feel new somehow. Swallowing nervously, my eyes roamed across the counter tops, and I noticed a small frame placed directly in the middle of the island. They guys had never been the type for centerpieces or décor, so I frowned at the black wood and then took a step closer.

It wasn't a picture I recognized even though I could clearly see myself in the frame and I plucked the wood off of the granite before lifting it closer to my face.

"Tommy gave it to us," Callum whispered from behind me, but I didn't turn to him, I was too enthralled by the image. The three guys were looking nothing short of perfect in their suits, though I couldn't see O'Neil's face and I was right in the middle of the trio, almost seeming to belong there. My eyes were bright, my mouth lifted in what must have been a laugh and it struck me that I had never seen myself look so happy in a photo before.

"You framed it?" I was holding the answer in my hands, my fingers had curled around the smooth wood, but it was all I could think of to say and Jace laughed quietly under his breath.

"Yeah, Shawn picked out the frame." Lowering it back onto the smooth grey surface I turned to them.

"Why?"

Both Shawn and Jace turned to Callum, and he smoothed his curls before lifting his eyes to mine. "Because we always wanted to remember that day and how it felt to be in love with you."

My lower lip trembled, and I crossed my arms, holding myself tightly as I took in a deep breath. "You love me?"

"Absolutely," Shawn sighed, almost as if a weight had been lifted from his shoulders. "We are completely and totally in love with you, Tatum Kelly."

"All of you?" I just had to clarify, I had to know before I risked my heart again.

"Yes Tatum, all of us," tears filled my eyes and I glanced at the photo for a long moment before turning to face my guys.

"I love you too."

Chapter Forty

TATUM

My body ached in all the right places as I winced at the morning light, and I stretched, extending my legs as I lifted my arms above my head and then I glanced to my side. Callum was softly snoring beside me, his face relaxed in sleep, and I lifted a hand to stroke his curls back before I peeked to the other side. Shawn was pressed against me from head to toe, his arm moving to curl around my ribs as I shifted to turn on my side and I leaned down, pressing a kiss to his mouth softly.

"Hmm," he sighed while his blue eyes fluttered open and I nuzzled my nose against his softly.

"Morning," I whispered, and his lips lifted into that goofy smile I liked so much.

"How are you feeling?" He asked quietly while his hand stroked the skin of my naked waist, and I felt a rush of arousal pulse through me at the simple touch.

"Good, really good." Sliding his fingers from my waist, he moved them down until they were cupping my thigh and then he hoisted it to his hip and pulled me until I was straddling him.

"Good enough for another round?" He asked slyly and I sat back, rolling my hips into his before I nodded.

"Perfect." Swinging an arm, Shawn slapped Callum in the chest. "Wake up fucker, our girl needs us."

Groaning, Callum opened his bleary eyes at me, and I smiled from above him, waiting for his brain to piece together what was happening. One second passed, then another and then his eyes widened a fraction. "Where's Rivers?"

"Here," Jace called from the bathroom, and I looked over my shoulder at him. He was still naked, and my eyes traced the long lean lines of his body before I flushed. "Seriously Kelly? You're still blushing?"

"Hey, I like her blush," Shawn protested from below me and then he lifted a hand and stroked the back of his knuckles from my temple to my cheek then to my jaw and down farther until the skin glided over a hardened nipple. "And I love that it goes all the way down."

Squirming at the heat in my belly, I whimpered and then traced my own fingers over Shawn's tattoos. The four of us had spent the night tangled up with each other and though I ached from the strain and exhaustion, I so badly wanted them again.

Sensing my desperation, Shawn lowered his touch until he was tucked between my thighs, and I tossed my head back as the pads of his fingers circled my clit softly. "Condoms Jace, grab them."

There was movement behind me, but I was too focused on the pleasure the friction was creating and then Jace was lifting me farther onto my knees. Blinking down at him I watched as he tore open the foil wrapper with his teeth and then his fingers were slipping into me carefully.

"I'm ready," I promised, shifting my hips away from his touch. "I want your cock pretty boy, not your fingers."

"Fuck, Kelly." He groaned and then he was lining us up before cupping my hips. "Have at it, baby."

Smiling at him, I widened my stance and slowly sank down, gasping as that piercing rubbed against me in just the right way. It always felt so good to have him in me and I panted before falling forward, bracing my palms on his chest.

"I need more." I whispered once I was accustomed to the feeling of him inside me and I felt a hand run down the length of my spine.

"We got you Kelly, but don't rush." Callum's voice was soft as he whispered into my ear and then his hand was stroking down my belly, tracing my navel slowly. "Hand me the lube, Rivers."

Growing impatient, Shawn lifted his hips from the bed and pressed into me with a groan. "I know we aren't rushing her but can you two get organized, I can't hold out all day."

"It's been like three minutes. Surely you can do better than that?" Jace laughed and Shawn's eyes narrowed in a glare.

"Tell me that next time *you're* inside her. I bet you would have blown by now." Rolling my eyes at their bantering, I rolled my hips and Shawn tossed his head back against the pillow. "Fuck."

"That's the plan, Patrick." Callum chuckled and then his lips were peppering kisses across my shoulders and I felt his fingers trace me carefully before he pressed them into me.

"Good, Kelly?" There was a little bit of an ache from last night, but it didn't last long and soon enough I was pressing back into his hand, desperate for him to fill me.

Slipping his fingers from me, Callum moved his palm to rest between my shoulder blades and then he was coaxing me down. Happy with my position, he moved in behind me and then he was pressing in. "Good girl Kelly, let me in."

Relaxing my body, I followed his instructions and he eased into me carefully until I was filled to the brink. The stretch was not as intense as it was last night, but it still knocked the air from my lungs, and I whimpered as they began to pick up a slow pace and I felt Jace wrap his fingers in my hair.

Blinking up at him, I whimpered when he flashed me his dimples. "Just take it Tatum, let them make you feel good." Sinking my teeth into my lower lip, I nodded weakly, and his smile grew. "That's it, just like that."

"You're not joining us?" Callum panted from behind me, my eyes fluttered as he snapped his hips forward.

"This is joining," Jace sighed happily as his thumb ran across my lower lip and I opened my mouth, letting him press the pad onto my tongue. "You should know better than anyone how good watching can be. And besides, she's going to need a shower after all this."

"You have a point." Callum moaned as his pace increased and my teeth clamped around Jace as I frantically tried to wave off my orgasm. I was desperate to make this last as long as possible but when Rivers pulled his hand away from my face and lowered his slicked thumb to my clit, I knew I was a goner.

Stepping closer, Jace continued his ministrations but pressed his forehead to mine and my eyes locked onto his. "Is our girl going to cum for us?"

Nodding, I cried out sharply as Shawn tipped his hips just right and I felt my thighs begin to shake. There was no way I was going to last, not at this rate and I gasped for air as the pleasure reached a boiling point. Fisting my hair, Jace dragged my mouth to his and I whimpered against him as I finally tipped over the edge.

Hanging up the phone, I placed it on the table and then settled once more between Jace and Shawn. We had spent the morning in bed, only crawling our way out when Callum promised us waffles. Once finished we cleaned the kitchen, per O'Neil's request, and then curled up on the couch for the rest of the day. It had been quiet, tranquil and I felt completely at ease until the shrill sound of my phone interrupted us.

Kate had been patient all morning, only sending me three texts asking for details but when they had gone ignored, she brought in the big guns and called my brother. Chris and Tommy had been less worried about the nitty gritty and just wanted to be sure I was safe and happy. It seemed all was forgiven when it concerned the guys, and I was surprised to know that Tommy had bet my brother fifty bucks I would end up back in their house by the end of the season. It seemed my new brother-in-law was more attuned to everyone's feelings than I realized.

"Everything okay?" Callum asked as he folded himself onto the floor in front of me and I ran a hand through his curls.

"All good. The boys want to have dinner with us sometime next week if that's okay?"

"Absolutely," O'Neil agreed, and Shawn nodded.

"Only if you promise not to bring out a board game," Jace laughed. "They're a little too competitive for me and that's saying something considering the whole hockey player thing."

Shaking my head, I leaned over and rested my cheek against his shoulder. "I think it's just because you're a big baby who hates losing."

"Maybe," he agreed. "But now that you love us, I don't have to try so hard to impress them. Which means no more throwing the game on purpose."

"No, if anyone has to lose it's O'Neil," Shawn yawned as he snuggled into my shoulder. "He's still in his ass-kissing stage."

"Don't be jealous that they like me more than you, Patrick," Callum grumbled from the floor and Shawn snorted.

"No one likes you more than me, not even your sisters or mom." Closing my eyes, I listened as the guys bickered back and forth, not once willing to give the other the last word and I smiled to myself softly, wondering how I ended up here, but so thankful I did.

Epilogue

TATUM

"What do you want to do tonight Kelly?" Callum asked as he threw an arm over my shoulder and I wrapped my own around his waist before leaning against him. His schedule had been nothing short of chaotic now that he was on a professional team and trying to find time for him to come back to the house had been nearly impossible. Thankfully though, he had managed to find a few free days and had taken the red eye the night before.

"Honestly? Pizza and a movie sounds great." I suggested while readjusting the strap of my gym bag.

"Seriously? It's Valentine's Day, surely we could do better than that." He grumbled while reaching for the passenger door and I blushed at the sweet gesture.

"You just made me do legs and cardio today, anything more than just hanging out on the couch sounds like too much effort. Besides, I just want to spend the day with my guys, I missed having all three of you with me." I shrugged before tossing my bag into the back and sliding into my seat.

Callum paused with his arm on the open door and then he leant forward and pressed a bruising kiss to my mouth.

"Fine but tomorrow we are doing something special."

"How about you just get us home before the guys decide to try and make dinner for themselves and burn down the house." His brows furrowed as he glanced down at his watch and then he closed my door before jogging around the front of the truck and settling into his own seat.

"You'd think they'd learn how to cook by now," he shook his head with disbelief as he started the engine. "You've been ours for almost a year now."

Warmth bloomed in my chest at the words and I rested my cheek against the headrest as I gazed at O'Neil. Although the beginning of our relationship had been rough, and the past few months without him in the house had been hard, the four of us had grown and I fell more and more in love with the three of them as each day passed.

"I can't believe how fast time has gone." I murmured quietly and his warm brown eyes shot to mine.

"Don't worry Kelly, you're stuck with us for the long haul. That means years and years of putting up with our crap." He talked about the future so nonchalantly that I knew I shouldn't read into it, but the idea of being in their lives, being in love with them for any length of time made my heart ache in the best way.

"Alright O'Neil," I laughed softly. "Let's just focus on the here and now."

"Whatever you say Kelly. Just know I'm being completely serious." Callum grinned and then pulled out of the parking lot.

The drive through the city was quiet and I sank into the leather of my chair as Callum rested one hand on my knee while the other maneuvered the truck with ease and I sighed as we turned onto our street.

"Looks like everything is intact." I whispered with a smile and Callum rolled his eyes as he pulled into the drive and then parked.

"Let's not jinx it Kelly," He argued before exiting the truck.

Pressing open the front door, I took a step into the front of the house and then froze. The room was filled with bright red and pink heart shaped balloons and there was a massive bouquet of roses sitting on the old beer pong table.

"Surprise!" Shawn called as he raced down the stairs and then a loud pop echoed around the room and there was an explosion of tiny pieces of tissue paper and glitter.

"Fuck Patrick," Callum groaned from beside me. "I told you the one without the shiny shit!"

"I know but it looked prettier!" Shawn argued as he crossed his arms, and I glanced over his shoulder towards Jace who was coming from the kitchen.

"I tried to tell him, but he wouldn't listen." He shrugged and Shawn turned towards him with narrowed eyes.

"Why would I listen to you? You wanted to get blue balloons on Valentine's Day. That literally makes zero sense." The blonde grumbled.

Callum shook his head and then pointed a long finger in Jace's direction. "Well Rivers, since you let him buy it, you get to help him clean it up while our girl and I get comfortable on the couch."

"You can't be serious. Do you know how hard it's going to be to get this shit off of the floor?"

"Not my problem," He shrugged and then grabbed my hand before leading me towards the living room.

"And here I thought your nagging and clean freak tendencies would have eased a bit with you on the road so much." I joked as I fell onto the plush cushions of the couch.

"Maybe I just wanted to get you all to myself for a few minutes." He whispered as moved to lean in close, but just as he was about to kiss me, his eyes glanced at the other two and then narrowed.

"Don't use your feet to sweep it into a pile you assholes, it will get all over your socks!"

My kiss was immediately forgotten, and I turned to watch the three of them argue about the best way to clean up glitter all while that subtle warmth I had felt in the truck grew tenfold.

Sensing my gaze on them, Callum turned and then his face softened into a gentle smile.

"Years and years of this Kelly. I hope you're prepared."

One Year Later

JACE

Shawn was nearly vibrating with nerves, and I untangled my hand from Tatum's before reaching across her to squeeze his knee.

"Relax Patrick." I whispered, and his blue eyes searched my face in the dim lighting of the room before he nodded.

Knowing he could use the extra support, Tatum pressed a quick kiss to his jaw and I watched as his thumb skimmed over the three diamonds that sat proudly on her ring finger. This had become his new habit, he no longer traced the tattoos on his arms but rather sought out those sparkling stones that he knew signified Tatum's decision to be with us. Forever.

"He needs to breathe or he'll pass out on his way to the stage." Callum murmured quietly from beside me and I turned to him with a lifted brow.

"Right, cause you were so much better on your draft day."

Callum snorted and then rolled his eyes. "Oh please, I was fine. It was you three who were the issue."

"So, you didn't throw up in the parking lot from nerves?" I whispered. "Not to mention the fact you almost fell on your ass walking up the stairs after they called your name."

"Fair enough." He reluctantly agreed, and Tatum glanced over at the two of us with a frown.

"Not helping you two." She snapped and then she turned back to Shawn.

"What if I end up on a team across the country?" He asked worriedly for what felt like the hundredth time.

"Then we make it work, you know that." I reassured him and Tatum nodded.

"Rivers is right Shawn, we know what all the possibilities are and we are ready for anything." She promised sweetly and he closed his eyes and inhaled deeply before turning to the stage.

The minutes seemed to drag on as the first few teams made their selections and Callum and I discussed each decision quietly as our girl continued to reassure Shawn. And then, just as he was becoming completely restless, a familiar face appeared on the massive screen in front of me and I studied the man at the podium.

"Hello everyone." Ray Koso greeted the crowd and I glanced at Callum, wondering if he knew what players his team had decided on.

As if he could read my mind, he shook his head with a frown. "They don't tell us, those decisions are made higher up and they sure as shit don't give us any idea on who they are interested in."

Sighing, I faced the stage once more and Tatum snatched my hand in hers before giving it a nervous squeeze and then we waited as Koso began to speak once more.

"The Vancouver Howlers are proud to select Shawn Patrick."

The spotlight circled the audience until it found us and yet none of us moved for a moment and then Shawn turned to Kelly in shock.

"Holy shit." He muttered under his breath and Callum snorted.

"Patrick, the camera is on you, you better get your ass up there and shake your bosses' hands." Glancing up at the stage, Shawn stared at the line-up of coaches and executives in bewilderment and then pressed a quick kiss to Tatum's cheek before finally making his way to the stage.

The three of us watched with pride as he made his way through the line and then turned to the crowd as they held his jersey up and I inhaled sharply at his blinding smile.

"I don't think I've ever seen him look so happy." Tatum whispered and I wrapped my arm around her before pressing my lips to her temple.

"He has that exact same expression every time he looks at you, Kelly."

"He's not wrong," Callum agreed. "And just wait until he sees your white dress at our ceremony."

Pulling her close once more, I lowered my lips to her ear. "That smile will put this one he's wearing to shame. But I bet you twenty bucks O'Neil cries."

"If I don't see tears from all three of you, I'm not walking down that aisle." She warned with a soft laugh and my heart skipped at the sound.

"Alright Tatum Kelly, you have yourself a deal."

Acknowledgements

Writing this novel has been nothing short of a wild ride and I am so thankful to have so many people who encouraged me to continue with this fun little story. Without them I know this would have ended up in one of my many 'unfinished' folders and I would have always wondered what would have happened had I completed it.

First, I'd like to thank Rachel. Rach, you have just been the kindest, warmest, and greatest friend over the last year. Thank you for always being there for me when I need you and for reminding me to rest when I need it. You are the big sister I never had, and I would be lost without you.

To my darling Izzy, you are such a light and I am so grateful for our friendship. You always manage to make me laugh and then somehow direct my attention to my "to do list" without me even noticing. You are the optimist to my pessimist, and I am so glad that weird clock app brought us together.

Kate, goodness girl I have a lot to thank you for! Thank you for allowing me to bounce all of these ideas off of you. Thank you for listening to my rambling and thank you for all your darn patience.

And lastly, thank you to the readers for not only taking a chance on this spicy little book, but for taking the time to read it to the very end. I am so grateful for each and every one of you.

P.S. If any of those puck chasing, tobacco chewing, flow loving, 'for the boys' idiots I dated in my youth read this... none of you will measure up to the fictional hockey players I wrote, but you might want to take notes.

Made in United States
North Haven, CT
11 March 2023

33921138R00168